YOU WANT MORE

WITHDRAWN

ALSO BY GEORGE SINGLETON

YOU WANT MORE

SELECTED STORIES

GEORGE SINGLETON

HUB CITY PRESS
SPARTANBURG, SC

Copyright © 2020
George Singleton

All rights reserved. No part of this book may
be reproduced in any form or by any electronic
means, including information storage and
retrieval systems, without permission in writing
from the publisher, except by a reviewer, who
may quote brief passages in a review.

BOOK DESIGN: Meg Reid
FRONT COVER: © Chris Strickland / Alamy
AUTHOR PHOTOGRAPH © Mark Olenki
PROOFREADERS: Kalee Lineberger,
Jacque Lancaster, Kendall Owens

This book is a work of fiction. References
to real people, events, establishments,
organizations, or locales are intended only
to provide a sense of authenticity, and are
used fictitiously. All other characters, and all
incidents and dialogue, are drawn from the
author's imagination and are not to be
construed as real.

Library of Congress
Cataloging-in-Publication Data

Singleton, George, 1958- author.
You want more : selected stories / George Singleton.
Spartanburg, SC : Hub City Press, [2020] |
  "With his signature darkly acerbic and sharp-witted humor,
  George Singleton has built a reputation as one of the most
  astute and wise observers of the South. Now Tom Franklin
  introduces this master of the form with a compilation of
  acclaimed and prize-winning short fiction spanning twenty
  years and eight collections, including stories originally
  published in outlets like the *Atlantic Monthly, Harper's,
  Playboy, the Georgia Review, the Southern Review*, and many
  more. These stories bear the influence of Flannery O'Connor
  and Raymond Carver, at other times Lewis Nordan and
  Donald Barthelme, and touch on the mysteries of childhood,
  the complexities of human relationships, and the absurdity
  of everyday life, with its inexorable defeats and small
  triumphs."—Provided by publisher.
Identifiers:
  LCCN 2020029057
  ISBN 9781938235696 (hardcover)
  ISBN 9781938235702 (ebook)
Classification:
  LCC PS3569.I5747 A6 2020
  DDC 813/.54—dc23
LC record available at https://lccn.loc.gov/2020029057

Hub City Press gratefully acknowledges support from the National Endowment for the Arts,
the Amazon Literary Partnership, South Carolina Arts Commission, and
Chapman Cultural Center in Spartanburg, South Carolina.

Manufactured in the United States of America
First Edition

HUB CITY PRESS
200 Ezell Street
Spartanburg, SC 29306
864.577.9349 | www.hubcity.org

In memory of my father, George (1925-1983), and mother, Bev (1928-2015)—plus their odd assortment of friends, merchant seamen to lawyers—who raised me with outlandish, questionable stories.

TABLE OF CONTENTS

FOREWORD

by Tom Franklin

G EORGE SINGLETON CAN MAKE CAULK FUNNY. A YARD-
stick. Goody's Headache Powders. He can find humor in anything, hex keys, a rock, a rock pit, the metal numbers you put on
your mailbox... And don't even get me started on fishing lures.

In person, George's got these gleaming eyes, and he usually needs
a shave. He has a smoker's scratchy voice and a cartoon ha-ha-ha of a
laugh that he uses a lot. He wears baseball caps. He's a college professor
who plays pranks on his pals. He nabs opossums in his yard at night and
carries them around, for fun, then lets them go. He catches rat snakes
and posts Facebook pictures of himself holding the snake, his forearm
bloody from where it bit him. He's had up to 11 dogs at once, mostly
rescue animals, and lots of cats. He lives with a brilliant visual artist,
Glenda Guion, in a rural, rambling house, and he doesn't care if your
youngest son pees on the fence by his pool.

And also? He's a goddamn mad genius at writing stories. This book,
page by page, is one of the funniest you'll ever read. I kept laughing and
quoting lines to my wife and 14-year-old son, who asked if he could read
the book next. "Absolutely," I said. "And remember when your brother
peed on his fence?"

George's stories are filled with rocky marriages, lovelorn fathers, young boys who do things like screw other young boys in the armpits using Noxema Skin Cream. The stories are filled with dogs, too, dogs being vaccinated, being euthanized, even a dog that heals by licking. You'll also find herein some of the most hilarious character names in literature—Owe Posey, Libby Belcher, Stonewall Harrell, Tapeworm Johnson (a dog)—and even a story where a young teacher is fired when she has her class sing the "Name Game" ("Mendal, Mendal bo bendal banana fanna fo fendal, etc."), not considering that her class "included two Chucks, a boy named Lucky, another named Tucker, and an unfortunate girl—unless later on in life she had gathered work in a Nevada brothel—whose parents tabbed her Bucky."

This all takes place in George's native South Carolina, in the fictional towns of Forty-Five, Calloustown and Gruel, towns populated with broken, confused, abandoned, lonely people who're looking for some connection to somebody else. A few try to escape their surroundings but most fail to achieve what Charles Portis calls "escape velocity." Unlike many other Southern characters, though, these people are often educated—for all the good it does them in Calloustown. It's as if Binx Bolling got misplaced among the Snopses, and was funnier. George's people sometimes teach college, they quote Marx and Kierkegaard, they strive for low-residency graduate degrees (a master's in Southern Studies at the Ole Miss-Taylor campus). They try to apply theories and logic to a place like Gruel, for all the good that does.

You can usually describe the premise of a George Singleton story in one sentence: A man's entire life is colored by his having a single line of dialogue ("This itches, y'all") in a local documentary about head lice. A recent high school graduate is sent to write articles about places not to visit for a travel guide called *Wish You Weren't Here*. A college instructor scams his school by teaching a class called "The Novels of Raymond Carver" (Carver never wrote a novel). So the stories are funny, first, because they're based on funny ideas.

Yet they're hilarious on the micro-level, too. One of my many favorites in here is "Show-and-Tell." A father, abandoned by his wife, tries to re-woo his old high school sweetheart, now his young son's teacher, by making the boy take elaborate (and fake) love memorabilia to show-and-tell each week—for example, a "long-lost love letter from famed lovers Heloise and Peter Abelard." The aforementioned letter is in English, not French, as the nonplussed teacher points out, and "handwritten on lined and hole-punched Blue Horse filler paper." Sentence by sentence, nobody is funnier.

And yet, no matter how absurd these stories can be, no matter how hard you laugh, you can't escape the sadness augered into their architecture. Like his literary uncle, Lewis Nordan, and his literary cousin, Jack Pendarvis, George is brilliant at teetering us on that singing wire between joy and grief.

And speaking of grief, what happens after you've read this whole book, all thirty stories? What happens when withdrawal begins? Not to worry! You can read the rest of George's fiction—a total of almost ninety more short stories in eight collections! Also, you can find his two novels, *Novel: A Novel* and *Workshirts for Madmen* (an excerpt of which, "Director's Cut," appears in this volume).

Yes, George Singleton is a mad genius. Southern Literature's trickster, its rascal, catching its opossums and booby-trapping its woods and towns to find humor in his characters' tragedy and tragedy in their humor, reminding us that laughter might not be able to save us, but, goddamn, it can help.

TOM FRANKLIN
Oxford, February 2020

SELECTED STORIES OF GEORGE SINGLETON

THE HALF-MAMMALS OF DIXIE

I TOOK A FOLDING CHAIR IN THE BACK OF THE RAMADA INN'S Azalea Room without looking for any of my coworkers. I'd parked next to the guest speaker's car, I figured—the vanity tag read MOTIV8R—but restrained myself from slicing the goddamn evolved Lincoln Continental, headlight to atrophied fin, with my own car key. My boss had paid to have his entire six-person southeastern sales force attend, in hopes that we would pick up pointers on how to talk more seafood restaurants into setting up giant aquariums in their dining areas, stocked with everything from horseshoe crabs to sand sharks, cleaned and maintained by trained and licensed aquatic technicians who spent most hours thinking up ways to kill salesmen like me so *they* could travel from Virginia to Mississippi, lolling around places like Whitey's Crab Shack, the Splashing Mermaid, and Grouper Therapy. I sat down and stripped the back of my name tag. I placed it askew over the Salty's Showfish logo on my left breast pocket. Then I looked over at the woman seated next to me, a thirty-year-old wearing a black-and-silver skirt that provided her lap with only a cocktail-napkin-sized piece of cloth. She crossed her right leg over toward me in such a way that created a tunnel to look into. I thought, *This ain't going to be bad at all.*

Then I looked up to see that her face had a giant tic-tac-toe pattern carved into it.

A man from the Jacksonville Chamber of Commerce went to the podium and said, "We want to welcome all of you to this workshop. As you can see from the agenda, after Mooney Gray speaks we'll break for lunch, then reconvene in smaller groups to brainstorm. Also, as you can see in your packet, we have more than thirty businesses represented, and y'all know that it only takes two companies to get a little networking done, so there's no telling what can happen here. Especially—" this guy held up his hand as if holding a champagne glass shaking with plutonium "—once y'all discover the two complimentary drink tickets stapled to the room-service menu."

I didn't notice how everyone in the audience clapped or hooted, really. I focused on the podium but peripherally saw the woman's scars. Her nose was in the center space, her eyes to the top left and right corners. The woman's mouth took up the entire bottom middle space but spilled over to the lower corners of the game.

When I dropped my pen by accident, I pretended it hadn't happened. But the woman bent down, tapped my knee, and said, "Here you go."

"I'm sorry. Thanks. I'm truly sorry," I said.

"My name's Lorene." She swiveled her torso a quarter turn and touched her name tag. I could only look at her face and wonder what had happened. The scars were deep, wide, and only a touch off being purple. It looked as though she had been placed belly down on a table saw set to cut grooves a half-inch deep. I tried not to think of those old silent movies wherein the hog-tied heroine barely gets saved at the sawmill.

I took off my name tag completely and said, "I'm Drew Gaston." I couldn't get the tag to stick on my shirt again. "I work for Salty's Showfish."

Mooney Gray came out wearing a blue suit. He took off his coat. He made a big point of ripping off the necktie, as if he didn't trust it. He ripped off his pinstriped blue dress shirt in a way that made buttons fly off onto people seated in the front row. Mooney Gray now stood before the crowd of salespeople in need of motivation wearing his pants and a T-shirt that—from his right to left—had a picture of Moe Howard's face, then a lowercase letter *t* that looked like a cross, and finally Darth Vader's helmeted head.

Lorene said, "I've seen this guy before. It gets worse."

I tried to remember if most children started in a corner box or right in the middle when they played tic-tac-toe.

"I want to start off this morning by telling y'all a little story about two brothers. One was the ultimate optimist, and the other would take bets with complete strangers that the sun wouldn't rise the next morning. You know this second old boy, I'm sure. They had the same mother and father, who fed them the same food, and enrolled them in the same schools, and provided for them the best they could. One turned out eternally optimistic, and the other damned toward pessimism."

I thought, *This is easy.* Cain and Abel. If he asks us if we know who he's talking about, and if I were the kind of man who yelled out answers, I'd yell out Cain and Abel.

Lorene bent over with her pound-sign face and whispered, "If he asks who he's talking about, don't yell out Cain and Abel."

I nodded. I tried to stick my goddamn name tag to my pants leg and wished that I'd gotten coffee so that I'd have an excuse to throw away a Styrofoam cup, or get a refill, or feign scalding myself.

Mooney Gray held one hand up to quiet the crowd of salespeople, all ready to yell out Cain and Abel. "One an optimist, and one a pessimist. Well, these old boys liked to go fishing together, you see. The pessimist would just throw his hook in the water without any bait or anything. He'd say to his brother, 'I ain't gone catch nothing noways.' And then he'd stand there on the bank watching his brother bring in fish after fish off his wormy barb, you know. Bream. Shellcrackers. Sunfish. Cats. Crappies."

Lorene scratched her chin. She said to me, "You're in the fish business. Which one would you hire?"

I said, "Look at my leg," and pulled my pants up to the knee. I showed Lorene a birthmark the size of a small pancake. A woman on the other side of her leaned over and looked, too. I said, "Sometimes this itches, y'all, really bad. I don't know why."

Mooney Gray walked from one side of the foot-high stage to the other. He looked at the ceiling. "The pessimist brother never said a word until, one day, the optimist caught a fish so big that it doubled his rod in half. He pulled and reeled, and pulled some more. He'd snagged a grass carp somehow. Finally the fish freed itself, causing the hook to fly back out of the water at a speed so fast not even Superman could've detected what flew toward the optimist brother's face. That hook ended up embedding itself into this old boy's right eyeball, and it blinded him completely. Soon thereafter it got a serious infection, and the doctor had to take his eyeball out with a spoon."

I put my pants leg back down. I didn't look at my seatmate but thought about how the perfect nine squares on her face resembled the shell of a box turtle. Then I could only think about how cruel this motivational speaker was to tell a story with such a maimed woman in the audience. I knew for certain that Mooney Gray saw Lorene in the audience—that's what motivational speakers did best, wasn't it? They noticed faces and memorized names. I said out loud, "I think I'm in the wrong place." I leaned to stand up, but Lorene turned my way, uncrossed her legs, and kept them apart as if she practiced holding a kickball between her thighs.

Mooney Gray said, "The pessimist brother said one thing. He looked at his brother in the hospital room and said, 'You can buy fish in a market these days, buddy.' So there you go."

Some people clapped. Once they began clapping, everyone else outside of Lorene and me nodded or laughed.

I looked at Lorene and said, "I didn't get that story. Did I miss something?" I figured my mind had wandered up her dress or whatever.

Lorene said, "You don't have to show me all of your inadequacies. Don't think you have to show all of your scars and blemishes. There's no way you'll catch up, dearie."

I picked one eye and focused. I said, "I'm sorry. I'm trying not to look up your dress. I'm that way."

Mooney Gray yelled out, "I see all of y'all nodding your heads and acting like you know what I'm talking about, and that's what I'm trying to tell you is the worst thing about your salesmanship. That story I just told made no sense. But y'all didn't want to look stupid. Here's rule number one: If you're lost while listening to a client, ask for a road map as soon as possible."

I was about to continue my apology for staring at Lorene's disfigurement, but she raised her hand and said, "Mr. Gray, this man here didn't have a clue as to what you were talking about. He didn't get it." She held her left hand up, her index finger down toward my scalp. When the rest of the seminar-goers turned around, though, I saw how they could only stare at mangled Lorene.

I KNEW THE rudiments of a filtration system better than any-one in America. I talked to prospective clients about how fish defecated in their own environment and couldn't live long if no one came around to clean out the tank. That's not what sold the product and services, of course. I had statistics concerning restaurants and bars without aquariums and the same establishments' grosses after installing walls of glass, water, and sea bass. I provided legitimate telephone numbers for people to call in case they didn't believe my claims. More often than not I dealt with ex-surfers, ex-Northerners, ex-husbands. I didn't see many switch-blade victims.

And I dealt with local oceanfront women who hung out at places like Blowfish Aft up in Murrell's Inlet, sat with elbows propped on a foot-wide bar staring at miniature toy scuba divers, said things like, "I picked out that hammerhead all by myself." I wasn't prepared for the remainder of the world that lived and thrived on dry land.

Mooney Gray stalked the tongue-and-groove boards bending beneath his penny loafers. He jutted his chest and wagged one finger left and right as if to a James Brown song. "You've learned to make eye contact. You've learned to shake hands with a firm grip. You've learned to shake hands and make eye contact before giving your spiel. So what? So what?! I have a dog that shakes hands and makes eye contact."

Lorene wore no underwear. I let my right hand fall to the side.

It wasn't ten o'clock in the morning yet.

"Listen," Mooney Gray said. "Listen, I got a story for y'all. This'll mean something. This ain't no trick."

Lorene said to me, "He's going to start this whole thing, and then he'll call for a break. Don't get too wrapped up in it."

"What happened?" I asked, pointing to her face. "I don't want to be rude, but I have this problem with needing to know things."

"Listen up," Lorene said. She took my hand and set it on her small lap. "Even a man more worried about fish than anything else might want to know what this is all about."

I wasn't sure if I then underwent my first petit-mal seizure or what, but my middle finger twitched uncontrollably for the first time ever. It went in X's and O's, as if I were playing tic-tac-toe on Lorene's face. I felt the same warmth on my hand that I might have felt if petting a black poodle in the sun.

Mooney Gray continued. "My daughter joined a gang when she was fifteen years old. We lived in Anaheim, California—you know, right next to Mickey Mouse and Goofy. Gangs don't emerge out of Never Never Land. That's what me and the missus thought. Well, my daughter didn't take much stock in all that. She joined a gang, and as in all good gangs there was an initiation. She didn't have to go out and kill anybody, thank God. No sir. Don't get me wrong, but sometimes I think what she had to undergo was even worse. She had to self-mutilate herself."

I put my hand back on my own lap. I crossed and re-crossed my legs and pretended to cough. Looking back on it all, I kind of figured things out at about this point.

Mooney Gray shook his head over and over, then turned his back to the audience. "Living so close to Hollywood, these gang members thought that they should scar up their faces as a protest to—" he turned around and made quotation marks in the air "'—the beautiful people.' They got box cutters and sliced open their faces. One girl made an X right across her face. She could've been a model before her decision. One girl made like Frankenstein and just put incisions every whichaway."

I turned toward Lorene. "This is your father?"

Mooney Gray pointed at Lorene and said, "My daughter in the back of the room decided that she wanted to stay young forever, and to do so she needed to slice a children's game on her face."

This was Lorene's cue. She stood up, walked past me, and joined her father on stage. Lorene said, "You would think that I would have no sales ability whatsoever because of my face. Let me tell you that last year I cleared almost a half million. And you know that if I can get clients to buy my product without looking at my face, then you can sell whatever it is you sell."

For the first time in my life I thought about how I wished I'd married a woman who taught first grade. I didn't want to sit around motivational speeches ever again. Somehow I knew that whatever Lorene would say, it would end up with me either buying her product out of pity or feeling a guilt known only to biblical characters.

Mooney Gray said, "We're going to take a break for those of y'all who smoke and/or drink coffee. When we reconvene my daughter will tell you everything she knows about selling audiotapes and Braille books to the blind."

I KEYED MOONEY Gray's Lincoln down the driver's side, from front wheel well to mid-back door. I rounded my own car, got in, and drove straight to a place called the Halibut Inn near Neptune Beach, thirty minutes away, where I'd once sold a wall aquarium to a joint that served mostly bikers. The aquarium kept clown fish only, seeing as they held the same colors as the Harley-Davidson logo.

Inside, I ordered a draft and said to the barmaid, "I'm the guy who sold y'all the aquarium." I pointed behind her.

"That's not enough to get drinks on the house." The barmaid had her hair pulled back in a French twist. She wore leggings and a T-shirt that read IF YOU CAN'T LAUGH AT YOURSELF, THEN MAKE FUN OF EVERYONE ELSE.

"I wasn't looking for free beer. I got money. I was just saying."

She said, "I remember when you came in here a couple years ago."

I said, "Drew Gaston," but didn't shake her hand or offer her a business card.

This biker sat down next to me at the bar and said, "Gaston. Gassed on. Son, you must come from a people who got farted on. That's how last names come about. People named Baker come from people who ran bread shops. Smiths are from horseshoers."

"We don't need no more aquariums," the barmaid said. "I can't say that this one does us much good. The owner's gone crazy and talks to the fish most nights."

I looked behind the woman at their hundred-gallon tank—a small one compared with what I'd sold to places like Dale Ray's Delray Bar and Grill, which only held skates and mantas, or what the locals grouped as devilfish. "I been to some kind of motivational-speaker thing I had to go to. I'm not selling today."

I looked at the barmaid's perfect face and thought, *There's something missing*. She placed a glass of beer in front of me. "I've seen those people on TV when I get home at three o'clock. In the middle of the night. That what you're talking?"

I watched the clown fish, which seemed to be healthy. "I don't know what I'm talking," I said. I looked at the biker, who wore an upside-down tattoo on his left arm that looked like a woman's privates but ended up being the devil's goateed face.

He said, "My daddy was a motivational speaker of sorts. He ran the local KKK. Oh, he talked and talked and talked. Then somebody shot him in the eye and killed him. Up in a South Carolina prison."

I looked at the barmaid. Her jaw didn't drop.

"This man I went to see brought along his goofball daughter as a sidekick. She had scars from here to there." I zigzagged my hand like Zorro across my face. "I don't get what people are saying about anything anymore, man. I have no idea what anything has to do with selling what I have to sell. I'm thinking about moving to South Dakota or someplace."

Six clown fish wavered toward the biker and me in such a way that made me think of synchronized swimmers. The barmaid stood before us. She said, "My best friend in high school got cut up while diving down in some of those underground caves over near there." She pointed west. "She was lucky it didn't snag her oxygen. She got cut up on coral or limestone. She got scraped like she got throwed from a motorbike onto pavement. To this day she looks like she had a bunch of skin grafts that didn't quite take."

The biker waved at one of the clown fish, a tiny wave, as if to a newborn human baby. I looked at the barmaid, stood up, and dropped my pants. I showed her the scaly patches of psoriasis on my upper thighs. "Did it look like this?" I asked her. "Look at me. I'm a goddamn skink, motherfucker."

The biker left his beer unfinished and said he needed to rough up someone for money. The barmaid said to me, "Maybe you should lay off beer and drink pure water only. I read something about dehydration one time. And about water that's ninety-nine percent free of lead and other toxins."

I ordered a bourbon and water.

⇒ ⇐

I CALLED MY voicemail from the car. My boss had left one message for me to get in touch with a woman up in Savannah who owned a basement bar called Carpal Tunnel, which was supposed to be geared toward after-fiveo'clock secretaries. "Seeing as 'carp' is part of the name, Drew, well, you can figure out how to talk them into an aquarium." Salty left another message that went, "I didn't pay all this money for y'all to get motivated properly only to have you drive around town listening to your messages." That was it.

I drove back into Jacksonville. I parked at the far end of Mooney Gray's scarred sedan. Somewhere between the bar and the Ramada I had decided to ask Lorene out for a date that night, maybe take her back to the Halibut Inn. Maybe I'd ask the rest of my sales force colleagues to go there, too, seeing as the Brunswick-to-Fort Pierce section of the Atlantic coast wasn't their territory.

I opened the trunk and pulled out an unopened pint of bourbon from beneath some Salty's Showfish brochures, stuck it in my back pocket, and entered the Azalea Room meeting space just as Mooney Gray said, "I hope y'all had a good lunch. Before we break up into groups I want to tell y'all a little story, seeing as that's what I get paid to do."

I sat in my original chair. Lorene wasn't around, but there was a piece of folded-over paper on her seat. She'd written FISH GUY on the top. I took it and read, "I hope you don't think I tricked you or anything. I didn't intend to trick you. After my father got me to an anti-gang intervention expert one of the first things I had to learn how to do was quit tricking people." She signed it *Sincerely*.

While Mooney Gray went into a long story involving people who die to plan and those who plan to die, I shoved the note in my pocket. I got up and went to the reservation desk and said, "I know there's a bar in here open somewhere."

"Yes sir. Second floor." The clerk pointed up. "You can either take the elevator and then a right to the end of the hallway or climb those stairs at the end of this hall and it'll spill you out where you want to be. Whichever's easiest."

I found Lorene at the bar, drinking something that involved a paper umbrella. Most of the Salty's Showfish sales force sat at a round table at the other end of the room. "Mind if I join you here, lady?" I said, pulling a leatherbacked stool out.

"You get my note?" In the near-dark Lorene's scars blended into her face naturally. I wanted to run my hand over her visage, either for security or to make sure Mooney and Lorene hadn't pulled some kind of makeup job to gain sympathy.

"Nothing against you and yours, but I can't take these motivational seminars. The last one I went to involved everybody holding hands and singing, 'If you're happy and you know it, clap your hands,' which wasn't easy, seeing as we were told not to let go of our partners on either side." I pointed at the draft beer dispenser. The bartender poured a pint and slid it over. From behind me I heard Mike Cobb bragging about an aquarium he'd sold to Dollywood when he was on his vacation, far from his Wilmington-to-Norfolk territory.

Lorene tipped her glass in a toast. "I don't travel around with Daddy often. We just happened to be in the same area. There are more than a few blind people in Florida, let me tell you. They want books on tape. They want Braille. I know he's my father and all, but let me say that Mooney Gray is a moral person. He's not like us. He genuinely wants people to succeed in what they do, and he believes in what he espouses."

I thought, *Espouses.* I would use that word from then on out. "That's a true story about the gang? What were you people thinking?"

Lorene ran her index finger down the alluvial chutes of her face. "I wanted to be queen of the gang, pretty much. Hell, any kind of self-etched disfigurement allowed a girl to join in. Some of my friends only scratched an inch-long crease into their forehead or wherever." She took the umbrella and straw from her drink. Lorene set them aside on a clean paper napkin. She slugged down the mixture like a shooter. "It's not easy living in such close proximity to women who can afford perfection long after their looks decline."

I turned to my friends. Danny Clement was in the middle of a story about how he went through some picayune town called Forty-Five somewhere in the Carolinas, how he sold two hundred-gallon aquariums to a man who owned the local cotton mill, how the man only stocked them with fishing lures he'd bought over the years at estate sales when his spinners, doffers, and weavers died. Mike Cobb caught my eye and gave a thumbs-up.

I RETURNED TO the seminar alone. I got in a group of five other men and a woman. Mooney Gray told us to close our eyes and envision anything that might make the world better that didn't involve money. Mooney Gray said, "You can't think about turning slums into condos, seeing as that would take too much money. You can't think about feeding kids in Appalachia or Rwanda, seeing as rice, flour, and wheat cost money. You can't even think about cleaning up the environment, seeing as it'd cost money to filter out what toxins we pour into the Mississippi and places."

I closed my eyes and thought of Lorene's scars. I tried my best not to think, a world without low self-esteem, a world without women who know that they can't compete with what advertisers put in magazines and on television so that said women feel as though they need to lose anywhere from ten to a hundred pounds in order to look like an air-brushed woman midway through a two-hundred-page magazine with ten pages of actual text. I tried not to think, If people still had gills.

"Okay. Now I want everybody to tell their secrets. Y'all vote on which one you think's best in your group, and then I'll vote on which one's best overall. I believe I got another—" Mooney Gray reached into his waist-band "—set of complimentary drink tickets for upstairs."

My group members stared at each other. One man said, "Well, seeing as you're in the club, why don't you start off," to me.

"I ain't in the club. I don't even know what the club is. I sell fucking aquariums."

"I'm in golf balls," another man said.

The woman in the group said, "My boss sent me here because I couldn't talk people into two months' worth of suntan sessions. We live in St. Augustine, by God! Who needs suntan sessions?"

I said, "Eeny-meeny-miney-moe," and went around until it ended with the guy next to me. "You start."

It was worthless. Every salesperson said something that would've cost money—free cars for every American, free groceries, obligatory armed service. One guy said, "To make the world a better place I'm thinking maybe we could all move to space stations and live above it all." He sold air purifiers door-to-door.

I wrote down every suggestion on the lined memo pad provided in each participant's packet. When it got to my turn I said, "The world would be a different and better place without mandatory motivational speeches to attend." My team members stared as if I'd piped up about how Jesus was a gay man who couldn't decide which of the twelve disciples to date seriously.

"That's just plain mean-spirited," said a man who sold a cleansing agent called Scour Power. "Go with the flow, man. Do you know how lucky you are to be able to spend a day not knocking on doors?"

I stood up and looked at Lorene's father onstage. I yelled out, "It would be a better world if we wouldn't have to go to motivational speeches, man. It would be a better world if parents could understand that their children cry out for help in ways unknown to the live-bearing population." It just came to me. I nodded twice hard, turned, and walked out of the room all slumpy and boneless, as if I wore a pimp's costume.

LORENE SAID, "I'M not ragging on your car or anything, but it would be nice to have a convertible right now." I'd gone back up to the Ramada bar, taken the scarred woman by the hand, and led her outside. We drove to the Halibut Inn.

"When you first sat down next to me at nine o'clock this morning, did you intentionally show me your crotch? I want to know. It doesn't matter if you did or didn't. What I'm thinking is, a person with a, well, blemish of some sort might subconsciously redirect another person's line of sight. I'm trying to figure some things out about the human condition."

Lorene adjusted the passenger-side mirror in a way that allowed me to see only the roadside ditch clearly. "We couldn't rob banks when I was in the gang. It was too easy for a witness to give clear descriptions. What we did, though, was hang out down in Beverly Hills and find ways to fuck movie stars. Men or women. I can give you a list of leading men to character actors to sitcom women who will never forget me. I'm etched in their minds, so to speak."

I got behind a slow-moving truck with WORLD'S LARGEST ALLIGATOR printed on the tailgate. I didn't switch lanes and pass it. "What?"

Lorene studied strip malls. She kept her face turned away from me. "Listen. I met a man who opened a New Age bookstore. He had this big gay-and-lesbian section. He had an entire wall of books on holistic healing, and another on how to garden without using any pesticides or insecticides. This was in New Mexico. You'd think that he'd've made a killing. This was in Santa Fe, where all those rich people come buy bad artwork to fill the walls of their new vacation homes up in Taos or wherever."

I listened to Lorene, but what I really wanted to know was if the world's largest alligator was in the back of the pickup truck. It was one of those wide-bed trucks with four tires on back. I wanted the alligator— which certainly had to curl itself in half if it was the world's largest—to raise its head.

"He had a slew of those self-help books, from finding your inner child to finding your soul to finding your perfect mate. He had books on how to read tarot cards. You could even buy books on how to read crystal balls. There were books on discovering souls you didn't even know that you had, like from past lives and whatnot. In the philosophy section he had everything from Plato to Shirley MacLaine." The world's-largest-alligator truck turned off Highway 10 toward the Regency Square Mall. I fucking followed it. "I want to see this thing," I said. The truck pulled into a Citgo gas station.

"Well, this guy who owned the bookstore went out of business completely. As a matter of fact, he didn't average selling more than a book a day over a six-month period."

I put my car in park. The driver of the pickup truck pulled to the pumps and got out. I yelled, "You got the world's largest alligator in back?"

Lorene pulled me by the arm. "Listen. This is important to me, man. You need to listen to what I have to say."

The guy pumping gas said, "I *did*. You ain't seen her, have you?"

Lorene pulled and pulled. I said, "Goddamn. I wonder if that thing escaped."

"It ended up that this man with the bookstore had all of his feng shui books in the wrong spot. He had them in the wrong corner of the room, and pointed in the wrong direction. Faced the wrong way."

I looked at Lorene and imagined what her tears would do should she cry. *She needed a gutter hanging off of her chin*, I thought.

"She's loose? Wait a minute. You lost the world's largest alligator?" Lorene asked.

I stared straight ahead. "That guy lost her." I put the car in drive and took off. "Now that's bad feng shui. He won't be able to espouse his find anymore."

Lorene said something about how she appreciated how I listened to what she had to say. "My father never listened until he had no other option, and then he only used what I said in his speeches across the country."

I turned back onto Highway 10. I turned up the radio. There was a local talk show going on. The guest and the disc jockey spoke of changing weather conditions. The guest was some kind of avant-garde meteorologist. He said it wasn't impossible to imagine the earth reverting to another Ice Age. Likewise, it wasn't farfetched to envision total water. I thought about saying how my business would probably go downhill if the world went all water. I stuck my tongue out and said nothing. Lorene turned toward me. She closed her legs intentionally and said something about how she got tired sometimes of dragging from one spot to the next.

A MAN WITH MY NUMBER

THE MAN INSISTED THAT I NEEDED STICK-ON NUMBERS. He carried a special case that looked like a shrunken steamer trunk, with one handle and three large metal clasps. By *large* I mean the length and width of a playing card. I didn't check the thickness of each clasp. Most clasps aren't any bigger than the ones on old lunch boxes, or maybe briefcases. These were big clasps. I became enamored with them, and thought about buckles on the shoes of Puritans. I remember thinking to myself, This guy should be out selling *clasps*, not stick-on numbers. Clasps like that—hell, you could keep roofs from flying off during tornado or hurricane season with some clasps like that.

The man himself looked normal enough, if standing five four and being thin enough to crawl into ductwork without grunting is normal. I was glad that I noticed this feature of him later. Also, it looked as if he combed his hair after a careful diagnosis from a slide rule, T-square, and micrometer. He had the eyes of a tent revival preacher, part blank and part bloodshot. I said, "Say that all again, man."

This was at the front door. No one ever came to my front door. Hardly anyone ever came to the side door either, except for the mail lady when one of my machetes, oversized boots, or special bolt cutters finally arrived. Or the UPS guy. Or someone with a stray dog saying it showed up at their house and everyone says it's probably mine—which it never has been seeing as I keep my dogs under control. If I had some kind of running-off dog, I could use one of the stick-on numbers guy's trunk clasps to reinforce the dog's collar and chain.

But my dogs never feel the need to roam. People who know me—people who don't show up unannounced with a stray wondering if it's one of mine—know that my dogs somehow understand boundaries. They show up at my house for a reason, then settle in. Dogs seem to sense things we cannot fathom. They know fear, sure, that's all been documented. But they also know what kinds of people won't feed or pet them if they (the dogs) run out into the road or chase birds on a whim. Dogs know good music when they hear it, too.

The man said, "I notice you don't have any street address numbers out there on your mailbox, or anywhere on the side of your house. So it's your lucky day. I'm here to show you some stick-on numbers that won't rust, peel, bleed, fade, or become compromised by the elements. You ever seen that number ten over there in London, where the prime minister lives? They've been showing that entrance with the number ten now since Winston Churchill. Those are our numbers."

I said, "The nursery's closed. I'm out of plants right now. But I'll have some cypresses in the next few weeks." I had kind of presupposed, I suppose, what the man came for. When it wasn't dogs or lost people or the mail lady, it was people confusing my one-man nursery across the street with my private abode. I said, "Wait. I have numbers on my mailbox and right there on the side entrance so in case there's a substitute mail lady or UPS driver they'll know that they're at the right place to bring my machetes, oversized boots, or bolt cutters."

From the front door, you can't see the side of my house. It's around the corner. There's a jut. "I hate to contradict you, Mr...." This guy was good. This guy had something else going for him besides the mesmerizing buckles. He had a clipboard that he could hold in such a way that I couldn't tell if he really had any names written down, in up-and-down-the-road order, standing for the people who lived on Snipes Road.

I said, "Beaumont." It was the fake name I used when I needed to use fake names when people showed up. People always felt non-threatened, at first, around anyone named Beaumont. It was the last name of the actor who played Mr. Ward Cleaver.

The stick-on number guy said, "Here it is. Beaumont."

So I was *on* to him. Ha! To me he wasn't much of an authority on the stick-on numbers game anymore. I kind of wish I hadn't mentioned the things I collected, should he be one to collect the exact same things and want to come back and break in. I said, "Or when the mail lady or UPS driver brings me one of my many assault rifles and booby traps bought from down in South America." I looked way out at the mailbox. I faced it directly, so couldn't see if the numbers might be missing. I said, "What's your name, man."

He placed his clipboard down atop the trunk. He reached in his shirt pocket and produced an ID that can be bought at about any flea market worth its while. I had about twenty of the things I carried around with me at various times when I went out. He said, "Mack Morris Murray. Three M's. That's one of the reasons I always knew I'd be perfect for this job. 3M, like the company that makes the best adhesives going around. People call me Mack Morris."

First off, I thought, *Who would come up with a fake name like Mack Morris Murray?* Me, my fake IDs weren't all that different than John Smith, John Jones, Joe Smith, Joe Jones, Mike Smith, Mike Jones. People like to make the acquaintance of people with easy fake names. People don't like other people with either A) a bunch of names that're all first names like "Mack" and "Morris" and "Murray," or B) a bunch of names that're all last names like "Pinckney" and "Calhoun" and "Sanders." Dogs don't like people with those kinds of names, either. Go introduce your dog to someone named Mack Morris Murray or Pinckney Calhoun Sanders and see what happens. Growling dog, that's what happens.

I closed the door behind me, not thinking. Looking back on it all, that's another reason not to trust people with three first or last names in a row. They get a person too distracted.

I walked out into my front yard, which was four narrow acres, on a slant, until I noticed that, sure enough, someone had stolen the numbers off of my mailbox. There's a place where I can look through the pine trees, winter or summer.

I walked around the jut of the house, stood on the gravel driveway, and learned that the same thing had happened to my house numbers. In my mind, walking back to this fancy-clasped salesman, I remembered what my numbers looked like in both places. I foresaw his opening the trunk, my seeing my numbers that he'd stolen some time in the past couple days, and then my going inside to get one of the machetes.

I said, "I don't have a lot of patience, Mr. Morris."

"Murray. Mack Morris Murray. Please call me Mack Morris," he said. "I don't know if it's the law around here, but in some towns it's the law to have visible and easily identifiable house numbers. For the fire department, you know."

I said, "Uh-huh. Well, 'Mr. Beaumont' might sound like a real nice guy, but he isn't always. You can ask his sons, wife, or that kid Eddie Haskell."

I kept eye contact. So did Mack Morris Murray. And he smiled one of those smiles everyone's seen. In Australia, smiles are frowns and frowns are smiles. I figured this Mack Morris Murray man to be Australian. He could disguise his frown just by living north of the equator. Mack Morris said, "I'm not so sure I follow you. Maybe it would be best I come back at another time."

A couple of my dogs barked inside. There were more in the back, behind the Leyland cypresses I planted myself, which hid the stone wall I built myself, which hid the cedar plank privacy fence I built with the help of a man named Guillermo some years earlier when the dogs started showing up.

I said, "No, you stay right here. Why don't you open up that fancy trunk of yours and let's you and me take a close inspection of what kinds of numbers you got for sale. I got a long address number, you know. It's nineteen, thirty-three, seventeen. It's one, nine, three, three, one, seven."

Mack Morris said, "I got you. It's a hundred ninety-three, three hundred seventeen."

"It's one hundred ninety-three thousand, three hundred seventeen," I said as fast as possible. I'd practiced it before. Sometimes I like to give out my telephone number like that, too.

He said, "We don't offer any discounts on big numbers, if that's what you're asking. I can sell you one number at a time, though, if you're hurting for money right now. I can come back every month and sell you a number." He unclasped his trunk, right there on the brick walkway I also built myself. "They're two dollars apiece."

Mack Morris Murray opened the case full, and leaned the top of his trunk against the side of my house jut. Sure enough, there were about six different styles of numbers in there—the best ones were tile, the worst thin metal numbers cut on an angle. I didn't see any of my own, though. I said, "You got these numbers over at Monkey Grass Estates, didn't you. I know these numbers. All the big houses over at Monkey Grass Estates have these kinds of numbers, on their special stone mailbox holders, and on the exterior of the stone houses."

I used to live way out in the country. Within about a ten-year period a bunch of children and grandchildren of farmers inherited their family land, then sold it off without conscience. Land developers took that opportunity to either A) build subdivisions made up entirely of houses that weren't under 5000 square feet, or B) plop down house trailers that had been repossessed. There were no zoning laws, is what I'm saying. And evidently there had never been any kind of special course the land developers could take on How to Name a Subdivision. The rich places on down Snipes Road had names like Monkey Grass Estates, The Rookery, and Neck of the Woods Acres. The trailer parks had signs leaning out on the road advertising Camelot, Belle Meade, and Vista Bella. It never made sense to me. Snipes Road ran a long way, too, unfortunately. You'd think the goddamn land developers would hurry up and make me an offer for the land where my nursery stands. Hell, those old boys could sink a good sixty or thousand trailers down on the two acres I own across Snipes.

He closed the lid to his trunk. Mack Morris said, "I guess I could get you a two-for-one deal. Or a six-for-three deal. That would come out a dollar apiece."

In his eyes I could see that he wanted to take off running. Where was his car? I wondered. I said, "How did you get here? Where did you come from?" I started laughing. "You walk down the road in one direction at night, stealing people's numbers, then come on back through in the opposite direction, trying to sell them back."

"I'll just give you some numbers," Mack Morris said. He reopened his trunk.

Listen, I've never had anything against scam artists and practical jokers. Me? I'm the man behind going out at night in boots four sizes too big, with a machete and bolt cutters—and sometimes spray paint—changing signs so they read Monkey Ass Estates. Neck Acres. The Nookery.

I said, "Are you a drinking man, Mr. Mack Morris Murray? Let's you and me go inside and partake of some schnapps I got holed up for a special occasion. I like your style, man. Or some brandy."

"I'd like just a plain old can of beer, to be honest."

"I got beer," I said.

Then I turned around to learn that I'd locked myself out of the house. I rang my own doorbell and both Now and Later showed up wagging their tails and barking at the long pane of glass beside my front door. One thing about non-running, boundary-knowing dogs, you can't teach them how to unlock a door. They can be kind of lazy.

"Is the side door open?" Mack Morris asked me. I shook my head. I held my finger up for Mack Morris to wait right there, and I jogged out on the gravel driveway, checked the knob, then jogged back.

I said, "I think the back door's closed, too, but there's a window I got that's unlocked. Thing is, I got one of my bolt cutters lodged in such a way that the window won't open but about ten inches. Let me give you a leg-up over the stone fence and the cedar fence, you go back there, lift the window, shimmy in, and come to the front door and unlock it."

Mack Morris said, "That's not the first time you've mentioned bolt cutters. Why do you have so many bolt cutters?"

We walked toward the side yard and wove through the Leyland cypresses that now touched each other side-by-side and stood twenty feet high. I said, "Cut bolts, what else?" I didn't say how sometimes I used them on my dogs' toenails.

When I got the number stealer balanced right so he could see my backyard, he said, "I ain't going over this thing. How many dogs you got, man? Those things will tear me apart."

I pushed him over. I'm no strong man, but like I said, Mack Morris Murray couldn't have weighed two big bags of cheap dry chow. My outside dogs barked, but they ran off to the far corner of the property, scrambling through a variety of potted azaleas, Leylands, boxwoods, wisterias, crabapple, and whatnot that weren't quite ready for me to take over to the nursery. I had a three-month rule when it came to people's—or at least land developers'—memories as to what plants got sold to them, stolen, then sold again. I'd like to say that these particular dogs were good judges of character, or that I trained them such, but, to be honest, they were mostly pussies. Mack Morris Murray called over to me, "Goddamn you. You better have two cans of beer in there."

Then I thought, What if he gets inside my house and starts stealing things? I thought, I'm an idiot—a man who steals numbers off of mailboxes isn't exactly trustworthy roaming around inside someone's house. I looked through the cracks in the fence and said, "Hey. Hey, wait a minute."

He said, "I found it. This window here? I found it," and I heard the window go up a little. Then I heard him slide right in, and close the window behind himself.

So I ran around to the front of the house, grabbed his trunk of numbers, touched the giant clasps all three, and thought about how at least I had this thing for ransom until he came out. I figured that if he found my machetes and came out the front door swinging, I could block some of the blows with the trunk.

But he opened the door presently. Now and Later stood there beside him, practically smiling, wagging their tails. I set down the trunk, and went inside. I said, "Thanks, man."

"You got to buy some numbers after all that. That's only fair," he said, stepping aside.

I said, "Uh-huh," and walked the long way around toward the refrigerator, inspecting everything to make sure nothing had been slipped into Mack Morris Murray's pockets.

Mack Morris sat down at the kitchen table. I pulled out four cans of beer and set them on the table. I reached into the cupboard and pulled out half a bottle of peppermint schnapps and half a bottle of peach schnapps. Mack Morris looked around the kitchen and said, "I can tell that your wife left you. Mine, too. That's why I'm doing what I'm doing, trying to get by. Yours take you for everything, too? Maybe they're together, living it up."

I tried to imagine the wife of such a small, slight, perfect-haired house number salesman. I said, "It's been a while. I still don't talk about it much." I didn't say, "Especially to strangers." To be honest, I'd only talked to the dogs about it, and most of them were either too young to remember my wife, or they hadn't been thrown out of moving cars yet, abandoned.

Mack Morris opened a can of beer. He scooted back his chair, leaned back, and extended his short legs. "I'll tell you my story if you tell me yours. First off, my wife—let's call her Barb, seeing that's her name—Barb was a churchgoer. Hell, so was I. We went to church. You can't condemn a man for going to church and believing that the Ten Commandments are a good thing. Or the Golden Rule."

I unscrewed the plastic top from a bottle of Mr. Boston Schnapps. I didn't even look down to see if it was the peppermint or peach. Sometimes I did this. Well, every day I did this. It was my little game. I looked up on the wall at two machetes displayed, and wondered how long it would take me to get up, grab one, and take a hundred-and-eighty-degree swing at full force. Answer: two seconds. I'd timed myself often, over the last few years, when all the dogs were out back and out of harm's way. I needed to know how fast I could cut off one of Mack Morris Murray's arms should he stick it out with a Bible attached, wanting to pray for me, this house number selling only a ploy to offer testimonials to the unsuspecting. I said, "Okay."

"Let me make it clear that it was a regular church. It was Methodist. Then out of nowhere Barb started thinking that everyone concerned about the Greenhouse Effect was some kind of Satanist. She thought they had some kind of made-up agenda in order to make money. Why would a bunch of scientists make up such stuff about glaciers disappearing? There were pictures and videos of it! Why would they go to the trouble of faking videos of ice melting on both ends of the planet, that's what I ask you. And what I asked her."

I called Now, but not Later. I said, "Come here, Now." He did. He sat down by my side and stared at me. I could tell by the look in his eyes that he wanted me to put on some blues music. Now liked blues. Later liked Miles Davis and Miles Davis only. Some dog psychologist could explain it all, I'm sure.

"So Barb decided that God meant for everything to be. She took the notion of no free will to extreme measures. She said, 'All actions are Good. It's how God wants us to be. "Good" and "God" are close together in spelling for a reason. If He wants me to drive around throwing

Styrofoam containers out my car window, then it's because He invented Man, who invented Styrofoam, and we can do with it what we will. God invented the earth six thousand years ago, and He did so understanding that we would go through cycles in climate.' I tell you what, when she said it to me, Mr. Beaumont, it was if a zombie spoke. She had a blank look. Her voice came out not unlike what a hand-turned sausage grinder sounds like with, I don't know, maybe paperclips shoved down the funnel."

I opened and drank from the beer. There was no way I was going to tell my story. And at this point I didn't trust Mack Morris Murray yet. I never promised to tell my story, even though he volunteered his. I said, "It makes you wonder." I had no clue what else to say.

"It makes you wonder, it does!" Mack Morris Murray said. He threw back his head and laughed in a way that I couldn't tell if it was fake or not. I know this: He opened his mouth wide, and I noticed for the first time that he had a large black spot on his tongue. He had a spotted tongue in the same way that a half-Chow, half-Lab does. At first I thought maybe he suffered from tongue cancer, and that he sold house numbers in order to pay for radiation, or chemo, or amputation. He reached for the peppermint schnapps.

I pulled back the bottle. I said, "You shouldn't be drinking this stuff. I think it might've gone bad. You shouldn't be drinking it." I felt bad, but I didn't want a tongue cancer victim putting his lips to my bottle. Or a possible mixed-breed devil.

"No, I shouldn't. I have a bunch of people to meet this afternoon," he said. He looked up at the two machetes, then turned around and looked into the den where another dozen were displayed on the walls. "They say a crow can tell if a man's armed with a pistol or not. They say a snake knows if someone walking nearby has a machete in his possession. What's the fascination with machetes, Mr. Beaumont? You afraid of snakes?"

I said, "My name's not really Beaumont. I made up that name."

Mack Morris Murray showed that godawful spotted tongue again. I'll give him this, though—his tongue wasn't forked, at least not physically. He said, "Your name's Leonard Scott, but people call you Pinetop. Somebody told me. That guy in the house down the road told me. Don't worry, it happens all the time. I should write one of those baby name books using only the fake names I've come across in this line of work." He reached for the schnapps again, and I let him take it.

I said, "They call me Pinetop? What does that mean?"

Mack Morris Murray pushed the bottle back my way. "It's not a secret, from what your neighbor said. You go out at night and destroy, or at least maim, the trees in the new developments. Then you go back later and try to sell them clippings from your Leyland cypresses, seeing as they can be grown from sprigs, or clippings, or whatever you call them. I steal numbers, you steal the lives of trees. So what? My wife would think that what you do is God's plan. Me, she'd think it was God's plan only if He invented numbers and wanted us all to abuse the things."

I said, "Come here, Later."

Mack Morris Murray said, "I used to have a regular job as a teacher. I know you probably won't believe half of what I tell you, but I used to be a teacher. This wasn't that long ago. I taught math. Hell, I even worked as a scorer for one of those national education testing services, you know."

I said, "Your tongue looks like my dog Later's tongue. Are you all right, or did you just chew up some licorice before you came over here? What's that stuff—did you chew some clove gum before you came over here?" I said, "I thought all those tests were scored by a computer."

"I did one of the other tests. I scored one of those tests that matter more. I scored one of the tests that gives out partial points even if the final answer turns out wrong." Mack Morris Murray closed his mouth hard. He stared down at both Now and Later. The dogs didn't seem to want to growl at him, like I thought they would, which could've only meant that the guy didn't really have three first names. Mack Morris Murray nodded his head a couple times, almost imperceptibly. He said, "I've always wanted to own a nursery, though. Nurseries kind of run like math. You have two plants, you have four plants, you have sixteen plants. I'm talking about hybrids now. Like your Leyland cypresses."

I said, "I wonder what your ex-wife thinks about hybrid cars. Why would God let Man invent a hybrid car if we were all meant to use up gas and oil and throw Styrofoam and used tires out the car windows."

"I never finished my story," Mack Morris said. "I got sidetracked. It's not your fault—I get sidetracked more and more these days. You're right.

All that stuff about all that stuff. Yeah. So Barb took all the money we had in the bank and moved off to one of those places, and gave it all to one of those preachers. At least that's what I've gathered."

I said, "My wife's name was Audrey. It's not the same story. My wife left me because she said I was too..."

My dogs started barking all at once. I got up and went to the side door to look out and see if someone else had showed up, maybe to sell me gutters he'd stolen off the house while Mack Morris and I talked at the kitchen table. No one stood outside, though. There was no car. I walked around to the front door and only saw the mini-trunk with the beautiful clasps. I opened the door, made sure it was unlocked, went outside, and retrieved the box of numbers. I brought them inside—a mini-trunk of numbers weighs more than you'd think—and was going to set it down on the kitchen floor, but I came in to find Mack Morris Murray holding my two kitchen machetes in each hand.

"You were too what?"

"Trusting," I said. "Put those back on the wall, please." I'd never timed myself dropping a mini-trunk of numbers in the kitchen, running into the den, and wielding two of those machetes off the wall. The only reason why I kept so many machetes, I understood, was to prove to Audrey that I wasn't too trusting, and so on, should she ever return.

Mack Morris Murray said, "I'm just messing with you. I could've cut your head off twice if I wanted to, but I'm not that kind of man. Like I said, Gold Rule. Barb would probably cut off your head and say with a straight face that God meant for her to do it, you know."

I still held the trunk. Mack Morris Murray put one machete back on the wall, ran his thumb down the blade of the other, then placed it below the first. I said, "Goddamn you. I have to go pee." I went outside and looked through the kitchen window to keep tabs on his movements. He placed his head on the table, forehead and nose straight down. Back inside I said, "So that's my story. She said I let people take advantage of me. She said I sold plants too cheap, or believed people when they said they would come back on Friday to pay me in full. Then she left. Last I heard Audrey worked for a tax filing outfit. Last I heard, she dressed up like either the Statue of Liberty or Uncle Sam and tried to flag down taxpayers driving down the road between January first and April fifteenth."

"It's all about inventory. It's all about inventory with women. Well, no, maybe not women. With your ex-wife and my ex-wife. Speaking of which." Mack Morris Murray opened his second can of beer. He took his trunk of numbers from me and set it on the table. I unscrewed the peach schnapps and took two slugs. Mack Morris said, "I have to do this. It'll mean good things will happen to me later." He pulled out two ceramic 1s, two 3s, a 9, and a 7. He lined them up to read *193317*. "Here," he said.

Then he took all the other numbers out and asked me to help him divide them up into style, and number. We stacked them up. He had a lot of ones, as it ended up, which made sense seeing as every street block needs ones. We went on down the line. He had more ceramic numbers than metal, more metal than plastic. When we finished I said, "That's kind of weird that you only have three sixes."

He stuck out his tongue and showed me that black spot.

I pulled out my wallet, dug out twelve dollars, and handed it over. I would've given him a tip, but I realized that I'd need to drive over to the closest hardware store and buy six or eight new bolt locks for my doors. Mack Morris Murray said, "Between you and me, it's a despicable world out there." He pointed with his chin. He refilled his mini-trunk haphazardly.

I said, "It can only get better," which I didn't quite believe, but tried to.

"Nice doing business with you, Mr. Beaumont. Or Leonard. Or Mr. Scott," Mack Morris Murray said. "Or Pinetop. You ain't no different than I am. Don't go around thinking that you're any different."

And then he left. I checked the door so it wouldn't lock behind me, and watched as he clomped through the middle of my front yard, appearing to know where I'd dug holes and covered them with pinestraw and switches. He took all the right veers, and high-stepped in exact places. At Snipes Road he looked both ways, then took a right hand turn toward the residential developments. Because it's the country, and because sound travels, I could make out his whistling from afar. Was it "Onward Christian Soldier"? Was it "Amazing Grace"? Was it that song I didn't know the name of that everyone heard when a bride walked down the church aisle?

Back inside, I opened the silverware drawer. My wife's wedding band and engagement ring were gone. They no longer rested where Audrey placed them before she left, each inside silver napkin holders we had never used.

THIS ITCHES, Y'ALL

A S A CHILD I STARRED IN WHAT I CONSIDERED THE LEAD role of an educational television-produced documentary on head lice. To this day I can remember my entire monologue: "This itches, y'all." The man playing my father was a veterinarian by profession, but he had several community playhouse credits down at the Aiken Little Theatre. My mom in this affair was a Charleston ex-debutante who might've made it on Broadway had she not developed a loss of feeling in her left foot, which caused her to gimp around, slapping her sole down sporadically. Later on she starred in a documentary involving cockroaches and silverfish, from what I understand. The doctor was a regular pediatrician, or so he said. This was 1970. The entire nation transformed itself. At the time, though, no one talked about anything else outside of the head-lice epidemic that infiltrated our South Carolina schools.

"I don't know why we can't say that there's a direct reason why these lices showed up on our white children's heads at the same time our schools took in the others," my TV mom said during a break. I sat in makeup; a woman took a red Magic Marker and plowed long furrows on my scalp. She parted my towhead six or eight times sharply, then pulled the felt tip backwards, exactly opposite of how a Boy Scout den leader might teach.

I thought, *This itches, y'all.*

The regular pediatrician—who got a number of lines involving the history of bloodsucking, parasitic arthropods—rolled up and funneled his script. "I don't know how to tell you this, but it's true. Black people don't serve as hosts to the head louse. A louse is white. It needs to camouflage itself. So they don't go to black scalps. I don't know anything about people in between, like Arabs or the Chinese, but this is a white man's problem here in the South, lady." He tapped the top of his head.

I thought, This *itches*, y'all. *This* itches, y'all. This itches, *y'all*. "There's a black girl named Shirley in my class who showed me the bottom of her feet and the palms of her hands. They're white," I said. I kind of liked her. I kind of thought of her as my girlfriend, really, unless she had head lice on those places.

The guy running the little operation said, "That's enough. Okay. Do we have the kid ready? Let's get this thing done. It's not brain surgery. Hell, it ain't even manual labor."

I'd gotten the part because I raised my hand when Mrs. Waymer asked who knew the difference between ticks and tics. She wrote it out on the board, and asked what each one meant. I knew both. My father owned what would be later on known as Tourette's Syndrome. So I raised my hand and explained it all. Mrs. Waymer never said anything like, "Who wants to be considered for a head lice documentary that might be aired over ETV?" or, "Who wants to be considered for a movie that might be shown in ninth grade across the state when we teach everyone about sexual intercourse, too?" She only said, "Bennie Frewer wins."

I signed a document, my parents got all excited and signed another document, and the next thing I knew I sat in a room in our state capital, along with a dozen other no-experience actors, ranging from fourth to eighth graders. This was a Saturday morning. Everyone else considered had black hair. They gave us our lines, and I have to admit that almost everyone, except for this boy from Due West with a slight speech impediment, got out, "This itches, y'all," perfectly.

They introduced us to the ex-debutante, who at the time I thought was a hundred years old, seeing as she was at least forty, and they brought out the veterinarian who would be my father. They shook hands with each of us and acted as if we should've asked for autographs. Maybe they'd starred in other state-supported documentaries, outside of their community work in *Guys and Dolls, Oklahoma, The Sound of Music,* I don't know.

The pediatrician playing the doctor came out and pointed at me. "It has to be this boy," he said. At the moment I thought he'd accused me of being the only person available who had a strong chance of having hosted head lice at one time in his life. He looked at me with his head bowed down somewhat, as if he knew I'd later on tell people I grew up so poor that I could only afford ringworms for pets.

My parents drove around Columbia, South Carolina, looking for a warehouse that sold condiments at wholesale prices. My father wanted to get some different barbecue sauce, mayonnaise, and mustard. As he dropped me off he said, "When we come fucking back and you fucking win that head fucking lice part I want to fucking have a fucking big fuck party for all the fucking neighbors, fuck." To this day I can't watch a good Hollywood mafia movie without thinking how my daddy missed his own special roles in life.

I walked into the sound room. I left my competitors in their sad queue. A couple of them cried when they didn't get the head-lice part; more of them said, "I didn't want it anyway," all crybaby.

I didn't skip my way inside, or point and ha-ha-ha. I shrugged my shoulders and followed the real doctor. I said, "This itches, y'all," that's it.

After my head got liced up realistically I sat in a barber's chair. This story line wasn't even close—somehow it went that I showed up for a haircut with both my parents, a barber saw the head lice, and a doctor happened to be hanging around waiting for his own haircut. Another little theater actor played the barber, a man who taught drama at a college down in Greenwood that eventually should've lost its accreditation. I caught this fake barber guy kissing my documentary father in the wings soon after the shoot, but that's another story.

I'M NOT ONE of those people whose facial features change drastically twice or more in a lifetime. I'm not one of those people who looked one way before puberty, another directly after sprouting hairs and changing voices, then another, say, at ages twenty-one, thirty, and so on. If I lived to be 150 and my classmates did so, too, I could go to a high school reunion and look exactly like I did in the yearbook. So the entire time I lived in my hometown of picayune Forty-Five I had people come up to me—my age and older, then way younger as the years went by—and ask about my scalp. They said things like, "You done good getting them lices off," or, "Hey, I know you—you the man with what clamps down finally toward the skull bone."

I'm talking that I dealt with these pallet-heads who couldn't understand the difference between movie characters and real life for the rest of my days in Forty-Five. I'd be willing to bet that anybody in my graduating class who ever saw Night of the Living Dead or whatever thought that zombies traversed our planet. If one of them ever saw *Forrest Gump* he probably tried to sue the movie company for telling his own life story.

So, needless to say, I didn't get any dates throughout my high school years, seeing as—I'll give my hometown people this—the notion of a willing suspension of disbelief worked too well. Every girl I ever encountered who'd seen the documentary thought that certainly I had head lice as a child and probably would harbor crabs as an adult.

Sometimes I wished that educational television had cast me in a movie concerning aliens, rich kids, dapper horse breeders, and so on. I often wished that I took part in a documentary about voodoo children and the spells they're able to cast. Only now can I understand how I wish my parents would've seen what happened to other real child actors, how their lives turned into horrendous escapades involving drugs, crime, violence, bouts of depression, and severe second-guessing about forsaking public education for the set of a show that revolved around dissimilar characters stuck under one roof.

I had no choice but to study hard, score well on standardized tests, and leave the entire state for college. I took off from my parents and didn't think about what small biannual residual check came their way when my head-lice documentary got shown on ETV-sponsored distance learning channels across the junior highs of South Carolina.

Don't think that I don't know how there's not been a whole lot of dialogue in my story up to this point: most people tell a story and there are all kinds of antagonists—or at least one good one—and they have to have some kind of talk in order to build up what scholars might call "rising action" or "conflict" or whatever it is that scholars talk about. Understand how this is how alone I had been, from the lice documentary on up until I started anew out of state. I went to school, I sat two desks from everyone else, sometimes my almost-friends Mendal Dawes and Compton Lane made eye contact with me, and then I came home. I grew up hearing only, "Ben Frewer's got head lice" from people I spent the day with, and "Fucking fuck-fuck" from my father, and "We're having Hungarian goulash," from my mother. People always talk about dreaming in black and white or color. Me, my dreams never included sound, except when tiny insects closed in on my ear canals to say, "We're having Hungarian goulash for supper tonight, you fuck-fuck-fucking Frewer with head lice," I promise.

IT DOESN'T TAKE a psychologist to understand how I went off to college in Minnesota, far from the South, in order to take a major in anthropology and minor in P.E. Baby, I wanted to understand from which gene pool I hailed, and I wanted to build tri- and biceps so large that should I ever run into a school chum in an airport it wouldn't take much to beat the shit out of him or her. I'd've gone to college in Canada had my high school counselor not told me that there was no university system up there. Anyway, I met and married a woman named Gabrielle who—though self-conscious and unsure of herself—might've understood the stigmas I endured as a child should I have ever told her. It's Gabrielle I blame for the second half of my life.

"I think it'd be rude if you didn't show up to your high school reunion, Bennie," she said the morning after I'd gotten an invitation from Libby Belcher! Who said it'd be major fun! And that we'd have a big old dance! To music we loved in the seventies! "I mean, Christ, they've probably had one every five years and you haven't been to any of them."

I had taken my degrees in anthropology and physical education and put them to good use over a twenty-five-year span. I refinished furniture in Colonial Williamsburg, and some days worked as a town crier when the regular guy—a man with a master's degree in anger management—had to take off work. Gabrielle wrote little skits about frontier life or whatever when she didn't don the costume of a bread-baking woman, waiting for tour groups to watch her shove loaves in a wood-burning oven.

"I have no interest in what my old classmates have done in life, because I already know," I said. "That sounds conceited, I'm aware of that, but it's true. A couple of them maybe ventured off as far away as Clemson to get an education, then scurried back home to take over the one law firm, or the Mr. Quik Fried Chicken, or the bank, or the army-navy store. A couple actually got out of there like I did, and I know they won't be going to any reunion. The boys married the only girls they'd ever had sex with, and the girls never evolved into the kind of women who second guess their boring lives to the point where they drink alone in the afternoon and down Valium at will. The best a young woman can do in town is marry a dentist. It's sad."

We sat in a house we built ourselves on some land we purchased through luck after one of Gabrielle's skits got bought up by the people who run summer productions near Plymouth Rock, the Lost Colony, and the Cherokee Indian reservation, among other places. She'd found a formula so that John Smith could become Francis Drake could become Chief Skyuka, and so on. She tried to make the skit fit Brigham Young's life, but that never worked out.

Gabrielle took off her apron and bonnet. "It sounds like a good town to bring up children in. You turned out all right. Go back to Forty-Five with a notebook and do some research, Bennie. Go there and figure out why your hometown has turned into an island in and of itself, you know."

My parents had moved to Florida when the local county council banned cursing in public, during my junior year in college. The sentence for anyone blurting out, say, "fucking fuck-fuck," was either thirty days in jail or eight hours picking up trash alongside the railroad track that split Main Street in half. My mother wrote me a letter saying that she and Dad would be leaving in the middle of the night for Tampa, seeing as he had amassed either a year-and-a-half jail time or eighteen straight days with a nail-stick in his hand. My mother wrote to say that all of this had occurred in a two-hour period of time when she and my father had gone to an indoor movie that finally opened in town, had sat in front of a woman who owned the Debs and Brides shop and who kept calling out to everybody how she planned to order "this dress" or "that coat" for the next season. The movie was *Star* fucking *Wars*, and my father couldn't take it.

I reached over Gabrielle to pick up a Swiss Army knife in order to scrape beneath my fingernails the homemade stain I concocted out of plug tobacco and alcohol. Sometimes I used rusted nails and rainwater. I said to Gabrielle, "You know, you might have a point. Maybe I need to go in order to bury some deep-seated animosities or whatever."

"I never wanted to say anything about it, but you do yell in your sleep at night more often than not, and I'm sure it's because you have some wounds that need closure."

I took my knife and scraped a dry patch of skin beneath my wrist-watch. "This itches," I said.

This itches, *y'all*, I thought.

NOT THAT I have any advanced degrees in anything, but I would bet that there's something wrong—and telling—about an entire town of adults who still have first names ending in -y, -i, or -ie. No one of voting age should still call himself Tommy, Jimmy, Wendy, Windy, Windi, Wendi, Wendie, Windie, Jillie, Sammy, Freddie, Bobby, Johnny, or Libby, especially if they've developed stretch marks or been the contributing factor in them. Billy the Kid's all right, but the rest don't work.

Understand that Gabrielle only called me Bennie, I was sure, because that's how I introduced myself back at a freshman get-to-know-you party between a foosball table and Flipper pinball machine in the student center. To everyone else I was plain Ben, the furniture refinisher.

My wife and I took some personal days off in June in order to attend the Forty-Five! High! School! Class of 1977! Reunion! held—get this—at the National Guard Armory. We walked up the walkway between a row of Civil War cannons, and from maybe fifty yards away could hear one of those disco bands singing loudly about roller coasters of love.

Gabrielle, under oath, will attest to the fact that once we stepped through the doors a coagulation of people parted, stepped back, and stared. Wendy Teed said, "I'll be doggone. Bennie Frewer." She seemed surprised at her own voice, as if she'd not spoken with a cheerleader's fervor since seventh grade or thereabouts. "We didn't think you'd show up."

I said, "Wendy. This is my wife, Gabrielle."

Let me make it clear that Gabrielle came from a gene pool unknown to my people—my wife had Scandinavian blood, mixed with one of those other Germanic tribes. She stood tall and lean and naturally blonde, her hair not puffed up as if some kind of nuclear explosion had taken place on her forehead. Gabrielle had not emerged from a cotton mill-owning family who intermingled only with another cotton mill-owning family, or doffers who only married doffers. Her coat of arms showed something other than a cotton ball, a shotgun, and a car engine hung from a tree limb.

Wendy Teed said, "Well. We heard that Bennie got married, but we didn't realize. We just didn't realize. Do you go by Gabby most of the time?"

My wife laughed and laughed. She hit my arm. "Never."

I looked at the Jimmys and Bobbys, the Kennys and Donnies, took my wife's hand, and said, "Y'all got any fucking booze here or fucking-fuck what?"

I led Gabrielle through streamers hung from the armory's I-beamed rafters. We walked toward a wall of blown-up yearbook photographs, of various Jennys, Timmys, and Kathis, all of whom were in attendance, all of whom either played football or waved flags and/or pom-poms.

I noticed not one African American person in attendance, though our high school must've been split fifty-fifty percentage-wise between blacks and whites. I led my wife toward the bar, thinking about the only people who ever spoke to me back then: Cheryl Puckett, Jacquelyn Sanders, Robert Perlotte, R.C. Threatt, Willie Goode, and Shirley Ebo. I turned and said, "Where are our black comrades, anyway?" One of the Larrys from the group following at a safe distance behind said, "They have they own reunion, Bubba."

Then he asked who'd like to go out in the parking lot and have a foot race.

I looked at my wife and said, "Did you hear that? 'They have their own reunion.' Just like before segregation. I told you. I told you that time's stopped here. I told you that this poor place ain't changed whatsoever."

My wife looked over her right shoulder, away from me. A group of my old classmates started dancing to a Bee Gees song. "At least he called you Bubba. He didn't call you Bubby, or Bubbie, or Bubbi." She didn't need to point out how she meant different spellings.

I looked at the bartender and said, "Bourbon, bourbon, bourbon."

MY WIFE AND I sat alone at a table for four. We sat in the corner of the Forty-Five National Armory, amid pictures of my old classmates sporadically placed between photographs of World War II generals, tanks, and antiaircraft machinery. My ex-non-friends danced and danced; they formed lines and kicked their legs outward, is what I'm saying. I thought about my blacksmith friend, Amos, back in Williamsburg—he once worked for the Pentagon—and how he'd missed his chance in the mid-seventies to work as a drummer for any disco band that toured America. Gabrielle finally said, "We can leave, if you want," maybe an hour into the situation.

"I want you to see the finale," I said, even though I wasn't sure what would happen.

Libby Belcher got up on the makeshift stage and pointed for the disc jockey to cut it down. "Now, like we've done every year, we're going to give out awards. Our panelists are the 1977 class of senior cheerleaders!" The judges let out a war cry. "Okay. Most Successful again, is Mikey Self! Y'all know him because he runs the Mikey Self Pharmacy!" Mikey Self stood up and waved. He didn't approach Libby, seeing as there wasn't a trophy, plaque, or certificate for him to pick up.

Libby Belcher went on through Most Changed, Best Preserved, Most Hair Lost, Most Children, Longest Married—which had a forty-seven-way tie, seeing as everyone got married the first weekend out of high school—forever.

I cringed every time she opened her mouth. She said, "Our Traveled the Furthest Award would've gone to Bennie Frewer, who came all the way from Williamsburg up in—" she stopped, and her face let us know that she didn't know the state "—a long way away. But Johnny Russell says he left home and flew around the world to come back. So, for traveling something like a couple hundred thousand miles—the award goes to Johnny Russell!" who lived next door to the armory.

Johnny Russell's father always ran the drive-in movie theater, right next to his TV and stereo shop, and Johnny went off to study mechanical engineering for about a year before returning home and taking over his dad's business. I hated the little shit from third grade onward, even before my lice documentary. Johnny Russell had the IQ of an empty box of popcorn, and made—I imagined—six figures a year.

"That's not right," my wife said.

"I told you. But that's not the least of it, I bet. You keep watching, baby doll."

Wendy Teed got up on the stage and listed out Most Dogs, Most Cats, Most Spectacular Vacation, Best Dressed, Most Likely to Succeed Late in Life, Best Turnaround, whatever. Then she said, "Our final category for Most Famous won't be a surprise to anyone who's been in attendance over the last four reunions." I turned around to see who might've found a cure for cancer or developed a better penny wrapper. "Well, it might be a surprise to the boy who'll get the award for the first time in person."

And then this old film clip came on behind Wendy Teed, of me saying, "This itches, y'all," seated there on a barber's chair. Gabrielle said, "How did you not win the Least Changed award? You look the very same then as now."

I said, "I told you. I told you. These people have something against me still, I swear. You saw it."

I didn't imagine a hush over the crowd; my wife later said that there was that "eerie silence" usually associated with meteorologists or scholars talking about a writer's response to anything involving symbolism. I whispered over to Gabrielle, "What's going on?"

She said, "They didn't sit apart from you because they thought you had *lice*, idiot. They thought you were a movie star. They revered you, you hammerhead."

Wendy Teed, I realized later, paused a few times before introducing me. Finally she pointed my way from the podium and said, "I can't believe that Bennie Frewer's here, can y'all?"

There wasn't a spotlight or anything, but the way she pointed my way let me know that I should stick my arm up in the air. I did for a moment, then I brought it down on my scalp and reflexively scratched at the crown of my head.

When Gabrielle and I were asked to lead the next dance—which happened to be "Free Bird"—I could only wonder if I'd made up everything throughout my life regarding these people. I thought, *Could it be that I might've been laid every day of my life back then should I have wanted to? Was I just another snot-nosed one-shot child actor?*

I dipped my wife during the first guitar solo, naturally.

People clapped and encircled us, but I swear to God by the next song everyone was doing some kind of made-up dance wherein they scratched their scalps as if rubbing flint for spark.

My WIFE AND I moved further south by the end of the summer. We drove from Virginia to Atlanta where I got a job restoring furniture for a number of antebellum plantations within a hundred-mile radius, all of which were on some kind of tour that people could take if they had a couple days to spare. Gabrielle and I drove to North Carolina, then took a sharp right at the South Carolina border, followed it until we hit Tennessee, then drove down from Chattanooga. I vowed to never pass through my home state again, much less Forty-Five.

"I still think you're overreacting," Gabrielle said when we crossed into Georgia. "It was a coincidence, that dance that they did. And Wendy didn't pause as much as you think. Who were they going to give Most Famous to—the guy who got acquitted for stealing a truckload of carbon paper?"

I said, "Look. Forget about it. It's a new life we're starting. You know, that old guy who wrote Uncle Remus stories was from somewhere in Georgia. You might could take up storytelling, like you used to do. In between writing plays or whatever."

Gabrielle pulled her legs beneath her in the passenger seat. "I'm thinking about going over to CNN and seeing if I could get anything there."

Because we sold our large, open house and acreage in Virginia, we had enough money to either buy a small town house in the city or a twelve-hundred-square-foot house an hour away, next door to a primitive artist named R.A. Miller who made a living selling tin cutouts with "Blow Oskar" printed on the top.

We stayed in the city, and I traveled against rush hour traffic each morning, on my way out to places like LaGrange, Winder, and Jefferson. I stripped down southern dining room tables only when necessary and spent most of my time finding ways to support legs invisibly.

It wasn't a week into our new lives when Gabrielle announced, "I didn't get the job at CNN, but I got one with Channel Forty-five. It's one of the public-access stations. Something just clicked, and the guy said I had the perfect face and voice to do human interest stories. And public service announcements."

I said, "No more free bread?" and kissed my wife. I could tell immediately that we would never again argue, that maybe we'd have a child in these, our later years, and that I might be able to bury whatever demons I may or may not have conjured up myself.

When the Atlanta area became infested with cooties some month later, Gabrielle was the first on the scene, interviewing elementary-school nurses, nursing home directors, and everyone in between. Me, I picked up head lice for real from a house where Jefferson Davis once slept, all the way over in Athens.

If I'd've known the politics and procedures of publicaccess stations, how their clips get bought up from bigger stations and so on, I wouldn't have sat down with my wife and her cameraman to talk about how I might've taken a nap on a mattress where Jeff Davis slept, that I didn't know of another place where I could have come in contact with the parasites. I had pet a horse that was from the same bloodline as Davis's horse, but that seemed improbable.

Gabrielle said, "Cut the camera, Gary. Hey, honey, what about you show everyone how to use a nit comb? The station will pick up the tab. I can go into an in-depth report about how to wash clothes and whatnot."

Gabrielle had never liked playing the bread-baking woman back in Colonial Williamsburg, I knew. I said, "Because I love you, and because you finally made it to where you want to be, I'll do it. How many people watch Channel Forty-five anyway, like the six people who don't have cable?"

My wife and her cameraman took close-up shots of me scraping away tiny eggs above our bathroom sink. They showed me stripping our bed and sticking sheets into the washing machine. Gabrielle thought it might be fun if I said, "This itches, y'all," right into the camera.

When my mother called a couple weeks later she said something about how she got all confused, that she didn't know if the nightly news on NBC somehow enhanced my early, early performance in grade school in a way to only make me *look* bigger. Gabrielle's coworkers, of course, took her out that night in celebration of one of the networks picking up her human interest story. Me, I sat at home knowing that I'd never enter another mansion, never be hired to mask any scratches a demi-lune, drop-leaf, or gateleg table might suffer through accidental contact. I knew that I would get a telephone call later from my hometown, either to take away my award or give me another.

FOUR-WAY STOP

G. R. PRIDED HIMSELF ON BOTH HISTORICAL AND TRA-
ditional figures. He felt as if he knew quite a bit about pop culture, too, at least movies and music. This was Halloween at his
and Tina's front door, far from normal suburban neighborhoods. He'd
already pointed at masks and said Batman, Iron Man, Superman,
Spiderman, Incredible Hulk, and common zombie. Clown, ghost,
Pocahontas, ninja, Iraqi War Special Forces SEAL. He'd correctly
identified Reagan, Bush, Napoleon, and Rush Limbaugh. Ballerina,
pro wrestlers (André the Giant, Lex Luger, Ric Flair, The Undertaker,
Macho Man Randy Savage, Hulk Hogan, Dusty Rhodes, Rey Mysterio
Jr.). Football players (Cam Newton and Peyton Manning). G. R. waved
at parents waiting on the roadside in cars, gave a thumbs-up, said how
he liked the way their little Lady Gagas looked, their Mileys, their
MacBook Airs and cans of Red Bull. "Goddamn, how many miniature
Snickers we got left? We got any of those Reese's Cups?" G. R. said to
his wife. "I don't remember Halloween being like this the last few years.
The churches must've quit having parties. I thought parents got scared
off by razor blades and white powder."

Tina sat in the den, with the door open to the living room where her
husband stood at the front door. "I told you to wear a bloody bandage on

your head like some kind of Civil War amputee. That might scare some children away," she said. "We already spent almost fifty damn dollars. Please don't tell me I got to go back out. They aren't even from around here. Some of them aren't even kids." She picked up the channel changer and moved from one Food Network program to another. She went from a tips-on-vinegar-barbecue show to one on noodle making in Southeast Asia. Tina wore flannel pajama bottoms with giraffes printed on them, and a T-shirt advertising WSPA because she called first to the station one morning when she knew the trivia answer, which happened to be "avocado-green shag carpet."

"We might," G. R. said, and then looked out the door and said, "Jesus! Jesus! Two Jesuses! Are y'all with each other?" Two young men limped up the walkway, both burdened with crosses fashioned from four-by-four lengths of pressure-treated pine normally used for flowerbed edging.

G. R. yelled out, "Jesus and Jesus! Y'all are the first biblical characters we've had tonight. Good job, boys!" He focused on the teenagers, but handed over a couple small Butterfingers and Milky Ways to a young hobo and Snow White who elbowed in. They didn't say "trick or treat" or "thank you," but he didn't mind. To the two Jesuses he said, "Man, this has to be tough," for they had to hold their arms out to the side, with plastic orange pumpkins strapped to their wrists, which were strapped to the wood.

"We're not Jesus," the kid on the left said. "I'm Impenitent Thief."

"Penitent Thief. Sorry," said the other kid.

G. R. looked at them and thought, *Did a Mormon family move nearby? Are these boys Jehovah's Witnesses?* He said, "Say all that again, what y'all just said?" He didn't say, "Aren't y'all a little old to be trick-or-treating?" but thought it. He also thought, *It's almost ten o'clock*, and remembered seeing a news item one time about how the last visitors on Halloween often case a house.

The thieves' father slid out of the shadow of the tea olive bush and said, "It's what they wanted. They wanted to go out one last time. What can you do as a father?"

G. R. said, "Jesus. Jesus Christ. " He said, "I doubt I have anything y'all might want," and he stared. "I mean, I got candy, that's it." The father had long brown hair and a beard, and when he stood between his boys it looked like a painting G. R. saw one time in a book in the emergency room's waiting area. "We ain't got no manna, or silver."

"I'm allergic to peanuts," said Impenitent Thief.

G. R. dumped what he had left in both boys' candy receptacles and turned off his porch light once they trudged back to the road. He didn't think, at first, about how he didn't see a car out there for them, and the next house stood a quarter mile away. He tried not to think about how his own son kind of looked like Penitent Thief.

AT TEN O'CLOCK Tina went to bed without saying goodnight, leaving G. R. in the den. He turned to the early local news on the right-wing channel he watched to stay in tune with the enemy's movements. The anchorwoman came on saying, "Some people are calling it a Halloween miracle," then went on to say she'd get to that story right after the weather forecast.

The weatherman said, "It's forty-five degrees outside now, and I got your miracle right here, Amy—it's going to be in the mid-seventies tomorrow, but rain will be moving in over the weekend, with lows near freezing. Near freezing! So much for global warming!"

"Thanks, Pete. That sounds wonderful. As you know, I was brought up in Portland, so a little rain doesn't bother me at all."

G. R. wished he hadn't poured out all the candy. He got up, went to the refrigerator, and thought about eating whatever Tina cooked earlier in the day that involved diced kidneys. He took out two cans of beer and heard Amy say, "And now for the Halloween miracle."

Back in the den, he looked at the TV screen and saw Jesus and the two thieves. He yelled to Tina, "Hey, those guys were here," but she didn't respond.

"They was here, and then they wasn't," a woman being interviewed said to a reporter. "I seen them, and then they vanished. Like, I don't know, I thought maybe I blunk my eyes, but Vanessa here seen them, too, and she says she didn't blunk none either."

The camera swung to the woman's daughter, still in her costume.

G. R. said out loud, "Vampire."

"I come back from my boyfriend's momma's boyfriend's party, and they was standing right dare," said Vanessa, pointing to the stoop. "I said, 'Y'all ain't right,' and took me a picture using my cell phone." She held the phone up close to the camera.

Her mother said, "I normally don't do Halloween, you know. Something tode me this year, though, to go out to Big Lots and get me bunch of them little Skittles packs. We had a bunch of kids show up, and then right at the end come Jesus and them two robbers, you know. I gave them one Skittles pack each—well, two for Jesus—and then they disappeared. We all lit up out here! Ain't no way to just take off without no one noticing."

The camera turned to the reporter. He looked, to G. R., like the kid on *The Addams Family*. G. R. couldn't tell if the guy wore a costume or not. "Amy, I'm on Old Roebuck Road—and three other people say they had the same experience, but they didn't want to be on camera. If anyone out there witnessed Jesus and the two thieves, we'd like to hear about it. Back to you."

G. R. said, "I witnessed it," to himself, then louder to Tina in the bedroom. "I witnessed it. Hey, I might've witnessed a Halloween *miracle*, honey."

He drank his beer and accidentally hit Last on the channel changer. A man wearing a toque looked straight at G. R. and said, "Never, *ever*, underestimate the remarkable flavors of sweetbreads."

G. R. called the station to say he'd seen them, too, but the line was busy for five minutes straight. He finished his second beer, went back to the refrigerator, extracted the rest of the six-pack, and went out to his truck. He looked at his watch and tried to remember when his last trick-or-treaters came by—9:45, he figured. Now it was 10:20. He knew that people walked about three miles an hour because Tina's doctor had put her on a regimen. G. R. thought that anyone sporting a cross couldn't make more than a mile-and-a-half an hour at most, and if they stopped at houses working a late-shift Halloween, it wouldn't even be that far.

He thought, *If I can find these guys and deliver them to the station, maybe I'll get on the news. What would Tina think about that? What would she think about turning on the television in the morning to see G. R. standing there next to Jesus and the two thieves?*

He thought, *Maybe I can tell our story.*

≋ ≋

NEAR THE END of Old Roebuck Road, a quarter mile before it teed into 215, stood a useless four-way stop. On three corners stood pastures, and then there was a cement-block convenience store where sheriff's deputies hung out waiting for people to ease through without holding their brakes properly. G. R. had his window down. He'd called out "Jesus! Jesus!" about every fifty yards, driving twenty miles per hour, his high beams on.

At first he thought he heard the pop-pop-pop of a pistol from behind the store, but then realized the sound to be planks of lumber dropped upon one another. He sat at the four-way a good half minute longer than needed, an open can of beer between his legs, before releasing his clutch and rolling into the store's shallow parking lot and then around back, where, sure enough, Jesus and the two thieves stood around a fifty-five-gallon drum, the crosses standing upright in it, Jesus holding a lit Zippo in one hand and some wadded newspaper in the other.

G. R. pulled up beside them and turned off his headlights. The three men stood motionless. "Y'all was on the news just now," G. R. said. "They said anyone could find y'all, call up the station and let them know."

"We haven't done anything wrong," the father said. "We were hungry. Candy isn't the best for a body, but it's better than nothing." The boy who introduced himself as Penitent Thief apologized again, but his brother said, "And then we'll eat this crap, get cavities, get diabetes, and die."

G. R. got out of his truck. He said, "Is the store closed? What time does this store close? I don't come down this way very often anymore." He thought, *Certainly they'll have cans of sardines or something inside better than candy.* He thought, *I don't have enough beer to share.*

"Name's Darmon. You can have your candy back if you feel like we duped you," the father said. He lit the newspaper and dropped it into the drum. His two sons stepped closer and held out their palms.

G. R. put his beer can on the roof of his truck. "Okay, listen. You men were at my house. I don't know if I looked away, or what, but you disappeared. And then this woman came on TV and said y'all disappeared from her. People out there think you're really Jesus and the two thieves."

"People see what they wish to see," Darmon said.

G. R. said, "Yeah, I know what you mean." Without the crosses on their backs, and without the porch light providing a shadow, these three looked like normal unemployed construction workers. They looked like hobos, grifters, Irish Travelers. If they had shown up without the *accouterments*, G. R. thought, he would've pointed at all three and yelled out, "Welder," or, "Landscaper," or, "Shriner."

"It's a long story," said the father. "Last year we had a roof over our heads. Now we don't."

"Mom does," Penitent Thief said. "She's at the shelter, but there wasn't enough room for all of us."

Impenitent Thief reached into one of the plastic jack-o'-lanterns and culled out the packs of M&M'S. "We got to remember she likes these best, tomorrow."

G. R. reached into his truck bed and wrestled out two logs he'd picked up where Duke Power workers had trimmed trees that neared electric lines. He had prided himself on not buying half-cords of delivered wood for three years. He said, "Wait a minute. I could give y'all this, and you'd have heat for the night. Or I guess I could drive you around and show you how to find wood, so you can have heat for a lifetime. Ha-ha-ha. You know what I mean?" Then he dropped the tailgate and held out his right hand to help both Penitent and Impenitent into the back. Darmon got in the passenger side, after sliding the beer over.

For a couple seconds G. R. thought about taking them straight to the TV station. He thought about saying, "Don't worry. I was never a soldier."

At the four-way stop he lingered, again, too long. Darmon said, "You got it both ways."

G. R. said, "This is right where our son got killed three years ago."

AFTER HE PULLED out the push mower, riding mower, edger, leaf blower, and then the stacked rakes/shovels/post-hole diggers/limb cutters/rolled-up extension cords/rolled-up extra garden hose/boxes of Christmas decorations, there was enough room inside his storage shed to house three stray men temporarily. G. R. manhandled a roll of hurricane fence he didn't need, and a roll of barbed wire he thought he might need some day, then humped out a number of clay flowerpots Tina said she'd one day use to plant lemon trees and ficuses. He moved bags of potting soil, pine-bark mulch, playground sand, and lime. "I'm embarrassed that we have all this shit," he said.

"You have a nice house," said Darmon. "What you got here, two acres?"

G. R. said, "One and three-quarters acres. Y'all can sleep here tonight. But you'll need to leave before my wife gets up. She just won't understand, you know. It's one of those things. Hey, who wants to eat some kidney pie?"

G. R. went tiptoeing back inside the house, picked the casserole dish out of the refrigerator, opened a drawer for three forks. He placed the dish on the dining-room table, got a roll of paper towels out of the closet, and listened for Tina's snoring. He said, "Tina," in a normal speaking voice. She didn't answer. The bedroom television aired nothing, which meant the remote's timer had shut it off. As he stepped out on the back porch he heard one of the boys say, "That wouldn't be right," which made G. R. wonder if his father or brother had just said, "We can break in later."

"I heard all that," G. R. said when he approached the shed, a hundred steps away, in hopes of calling a bluff. "Don't get any ideas about breaking in later. I have no money hidden."

Penitent Thief said, "What? We were talking about what to do if we needed to use the bathroom. Peeing won't be a problem, but in case one of us has to go number two. I was saying it wouldn't be right to use the wheelbarrow."

"We can use one of the jack-o'-lanterns," Darmon said.

"And these paper towels," said G. R., handing over the kidney pie. "Here, my wife said for y'all to eat this," he lied. "Well, anyway, stay warm. Put some charcoal in that hibachi and light it up, but keep the thing outside the shed. I wouldn't want y'all to asphyxiate."

Darmon said, "We appreciate everything. Listen, I'm sorry about your son. I appreciate what you're doing for mine. For me and mine."

G. R. said, "There's a pull cord for a light in here. Let me go back inside and see if I can find some blankets." He started, then turned and said, "There's a smashed-up car over on that side of the property. Don't sleep in it."

"This kidney stuff ain't bad," said the Impenitent son. He said, "Is there a hose out here? Would you mind if we drank some water?"

"Right over there. Help yourself."

G. R. HAD NOT stood in his son's bedroom more than a half-dozen times since the accident. Tina sat at the desk daily. G. R. couldn't. He sat outside—no matter the season—from dawn until dusk most days. Although he didn't have to return to work after the settlement, G. R. wouldn't have gone back anyway. He ran through images of his boy turning a double play in high school, throwing a stick to the dog, sitting down at the desk to work out algebra problems. G. R. knew that he would've ended up just like Jesus and the two thieves had the insurance company not agreed to pay seven million dollars for their client's negligence. Seven million didn't seem like all that much money, G. R. and Tina thought, but they agreed with their lawyer that they didn't want to fight longer. If Sam had lived to be eighty, that would mean a hundred grand per year and some change. Good money for something like a minister or teacher. Not much for what Sam could've done in life had he indeed made the pros.

G. R. went into his son's bedroom and stripped the mattress. Then he opened the closet and pulled out an extra folded-up blanket.

"THE WATER'S RUNNING," Tina said at five o'clock. She nudged G. R. "Did you turn on the washing machine or dishwasher?" G. R. didn't answer. She said, "Someone's outside running our hose." She sat up and elbowed him hard in his upper ribs.

G. R. opened his eyes and stared at the pebbled ceiling he had wanted to scrape smooth since buying the house. He felt Tina looking at him. G. R. thought, *Work*, and then remembered he didn't have to show up at Kohler. He didn't need to check the kiln's temperature. He didn't need to tell anyone not to mess up.

And then he remembered. *I got Jesus and his two thieves out back!* G. R.

thought. From Halloween. I should've called the TV station about this. I could've gotten on there and said some things about Sam.

The running water turned off. G. R. said, "It was the refrigerator. It was the freezer, making ice."

"No it wasn't," Tina said, throwing off the covers and getting up. "I know that noise. I know every noise this house can make. I remember the ones it used to make, too." She grabbed her bathrobe.

G. R. turned on the bedroom television to drown out what sounds a thirsty thief or son of God might likely emit from the business end of a tangled hose. That same chef came on talking about the organs and glands of farm animals. By the time G. R. got out of bed, his wife had turned on the porch lights already and grabbed a flashlight she kept in the china cabinet. "Wait a minute, wait a minute," G. R. said. "Let me go out first," but she'd opened the back door and stepped out, shining a beam.

"It's just a homeless man and his boys," G. R. yelled out too loud. "They're just staying for the night, honey. I felt sorry for them."

Tina held the light on the three men. She said nothing, and they stood motionless, twenty feet away, all three with their hands above their heads—though the two boys held theirs out to the side. Darmon said, "We couldn't sleep, and we thought we'd water your plants. If you water things at dusk they tend to get mold. What time is it, anyway?"

Tina turned and looked at her husband. She kept the flashlight pointed toward Darmon and his sons. "What the hell are you doing to us? Why can't you do anything right? First Sam, and now this. And everything that's happened in between."

"That was a fine casserole you baked," one of the sons said. "We appreciate the food you cooked, ma'am."

Tina stared at her husband. She said, "What?"

"I gave them your kidney pie," G. R. said. "They were hungry. I couldn't let them live off of Skittles and Snickers, you know. Didn't you hear me yell out to you to turn on the news and see the Halloween Miracle? It was these fellows here I was talking about."

Tina asked G. R. how much he'd had to drink and went back inside. She turned off the back-porch floodlights. Darmon said, "We didn't mean to get you in trouble." His Penitent Thief son said the same.

"Y'all have to forgive her. She doesn't know how she comes off sounding. I keep waiting for her to turn a corner, but it doesn't seem to be happening."

Darmon said there was no need to explain. He asked if G. R. needed help putting the mowers back in the shed, and thanked him for his kindness, and said they should be walking toward the shelter, anyway, in order to give some candy to his wife. The Penitent Thief handed over folded blankets and linens and apologized for any scuff marks. G. R. said he'd be looking out for them as the evenings got colder, and reminded Darmon to look for already-cut firewood beneath power lines.

G. R. returned inside and went straight to his son's room. He unfurled the sheet and blankets, then lay atop the bed. G. R. fell asleep praying for his wife to revert back to being the gamesome woman she'd been before the accident. He pushed his head deep into his dead son's pillow and wondered what kind of willpower it would take to suffocate himself.

Four hours later he heard the doorbell. Tina answered. Before he could get up he knew already that a merciless and committed person stood there—if not the Impenitent Thief, then another. He thought about how he would finally be able to tell his family's story to anyone watching the early local news.

JOHN CHEEVER, REST IN PEACE

E'D NEVER READ A JOHN CHEEVER STORY, SO THAT couldn't have been the reason he traveled, dead of a massive heart attack, across his neighbors' backyards aboard the Bolens seventeen-horsepower, forty-two-inch-cut riding lawn mower. And no one could explain later how Owe Posey's machine veered inexplicably from swimming pools, gardens, overgrown pergolas, gazebos, kiosks, birdbaths, scuppernong vineyards, ancient and unused swing sets, the occasional mean barking tethered pit bull. It happened on one of those midsummer Sunday mornings when no one in Gruel, South Carolina, performed manual labor—for it was the Lord's day—and everyone either drove twenty miles to the nearest church or hid their cars so people thought that they'd gone to Sunday school and eleven o'clock services.

Owe had turned the key without telling his wife, Carla, that he would only cut the one-acre backyard, that Monday after work he would finish up the front yard and weed-eat around the shrubs, crabapple trees, hand-placed brick walkway; and their own birdbath, kiosk, pergola, unused swing set, and vacant koi pond. The night before, Owe and his wife had celebrated their twenty-fifth anniversary at Roughhouse Billiards, on the square, and both of them drank too many cans of Pabst Blue Ribbon. Owe, for what it's worth, had said, "I swear to God on our thirtieth anniversary I'm going to splurge us with a night up in Greenville at the Holiday Inn Express, right on Main Street. They's a New Orleans-style restaurant within walking distance we can go eat shrimp."

He pronounced it "srimp."

Jeff the owner said, "Twenty-fifth anniversary's silver, right? Well these PBR cans are mostly colored silver."

Carla said, "Do you have any Goody's headache powders back there, Jeff? I got me a headache."

Owe's parents named him Owen, but some kind of snafu at Graywood Regional Memorial caused the birth certificate to come back "Owe Posey." His parents saw it as a sign and never fought the defect. Throughout his life, upon introducing himself, people thought he couldn't finish a sentence beyond pronoun and verb. Owe would say, "I'm Owe," and they'd expect him to continue: "I'mo go into town for a while," or, "I'mo buy me a flyswatter and put some entomologists out of business," or, "I'mo get me a beer—you want one?"

He'd gotten to be a local hero back when Ed McMahon yelled out "Hi-owe!" loudly to Johnny Carson on *The Tonight Show* whenever someone said anything a touch racy. In the 1970s, particularly, "Hi, Owe!" could be heard as he walked across Gruel's tiny square.

Jeff the owner shook his head. "We can't get aspirin anymore. Gruel Drugs got some, I hear, but they're closed." He turned to two men attempting trick shots at the pool table. "Any y'all got a aspirin for Ms. Posey?"

"I know it's our anniversary and all, Owe, but I need to go home. My head's banging. I just want to sleep, and sleep in tomorrow."

Owe wanted more booze. It wasn't but eleven o'clock. He said, "Sure, honey." To Jeff he said, "You think I can buy a few mini-bottles of bourbon off you? Me and Carla might have to celebrate in the morning, you know."

Jeff said, "This is the time when it's good to live in South Carolina. You go up to a place like New York where the bars sell drinks out of a regular quart bottle, you can't buy for take out. And I read the other day *you can't smoke up there in a bar.*"

Owe Posey said, "Goddamn." He looked at his watch. "Goddamn. I'm glad it ain't midnight. That would make it Sunday."

The Poseys drove two blocks home and parked behind their house. Carla went upstairs to bed. Owe said he wanted to draw out some preliminary plans for some preliminary plans down in the kitchen. He kissed his wife for the last time, then alone and convinced that Carla slept, tried to direct his satellite dish toward a Dutch channel he'd discovered one time wherein women tended their gardens in the nude.

BOTH OWE AND Carla worked at Park Seed Company, he as a horticulturalist and she in the catalog department. He watered everything from snapdragons to habaneros mostly, and Carla took care of mailing. Owe pulled off dead leaves. Carla took care of telephone orders. They lived in Gruel because disrepaired antebellum houses in a town gone bust since the mid-1960s could be bought for less than thirty grand, even in 2004. They got theirs—a two-story, ten-room house with hardwood floors and two bathrooms—in 1980 for fifteen. The foundation crumbled, the walls held termites, the attic housed a bat colony, and the yard seemed to be a mole/vole/shrew breeding ground, but Owe insisted that he could set aside some of his paycheck each month and, inevitably, resurrect the place. "I'm betting we can refurbish this house by 2005, and resell it for forty, fifty thousand," he said back in 1980. "Maybe more. If Graywood County ever grows and gets some industry, people will flock here. They'll want to live in the suburbs of Forty-Five. Who wants to live in a big city?"

And he was right, outside of industry coming into Graywood County. Owe had saved his money, re-mortared the foundation, and so on. Each year they paid more taxes due to their house's tax assessment.

"We have the best life possible," Owe said to the TV screen in their kitchen. "We have a better life than even you women picking tulips." He twisted off a one-and-a-half-ounce plastic Jim Beam bottle and held it upward, toward Carla directly above him. "What does anyone know."

Owe high-stepped out the back door, walked through the mudroom, and exited to his old empty koi pond. He sat on the rock edge and set his feet down in a melange of unripe, fallen pecan husks, wild morning glory, and tulip poplar pods. His fish disappeared one day, and word was either some frat boys at Anders College over in Forty-Five underwent some kind of scavenger hunt or one of the poorer citizens of Gruel got hungry. It didn't matter to Owe. He just knew not to restock only to become disappointed.

In the moon- and star-light it looked like his feet rested in an olive-green, orange, and purple swamp—as if he stood ankle-deep in his own septic tank. Owe looked to his right. An embankment of slightly tamed kudzu stood between his property and that of an abandoned house where, supposedly, Jefferson Davis once slept, a place owned by a man named Seabrook Pinckney who sent his kids up north. When the father died, no one returned to claim the house.

Owe looked to the left and thought, *I could take my car out of park and let it roll all the way down to Gruel Normal School, if I wanted.*

He opened another mini-bottle, then a third. He said to no one, "Why don't these people ever admit that they drink a glass of wine every once in a while? What else could they do in Gruel? Some wine. Some claret. A gin and tonic, or julep." His wife turned on a bedside lamp upstairs for about two seconds—enough for Owe to see a bat flit close to his face—then she switched it off.

An hour after dawn, when Owe Posey woke up on the ground with his feet still in the ex-koi pond, he became oriented and thought, *I want my wife. It's our anniversary!* He thought, *I'll start up the lawn mower and it won't seem like I woke her up on purpose.*

PAULA PURGASON NEXT door said that he waved to her as he left behind a forty-two-inch path through her crab-grass and clover. She said, "Oh, Owe had his head on the steering wheel, but I thought he only kidded around. You know how he was sometimes! I remember one day he told me about a stray cat that came around and drank a cup of gas that he used with a toothbrush to clean the carburetor of his lawn mower. He said that cat lapped up some gas, then ran around in circles until it fell over stiff. I asked Owe, 'It died?' He said, 'No, it only ran out of gas.'"

Dr. Bobba Lollis, the pharmacist at Gruel Drugs, said, "He came by here long before we went to church. We go to church, you see, and we leave at 8:30. Anyway, I was out back putting sunflower seeds in the feeder, and Owe went by in a giant crescent, completely missing our little grandbaby's wading pool. I thought he was only being neighborly, you know, cutting everyone's grass. I thought he maybe thought it was Saturday."

"He's lucky I didn't shoot him," said Victor Dees. "I got me some Lugers from down at my army-navy store. Shit, man, I seen him coming across from over Bobba's house and the first thing I thought was *head shot*. Then I thought, *No, just go for his tire*s. But I drank my morning coffee. They's things I won't stop to do when I'm drinking the morning coffee."

Bekah Cathcart shrugged. "I thought at first my ex-husband had come back to haunt me. Not that he's dead that I know of. Of which I know. I'm merely glad that Owe Posey didn't disturb my Zen meditation garden. I yelled to Owe, 'Hey, you dumb SOB, don't run over my Zen meditation garden!' like that. In a weird way it looked like Owe tried to perform the cobra or sun salutation yoga pose. I have this sand pit, too, where I sweep circles. Some people use a rake, but I like to use a regular straw broom I bought from the Lions Club. Anyway, he drove around my special places. I didn't know Owe Posey all that well—he kind of kept to himself and declined joining the Gruel Association to Sanctify History like the rest of us who hoped to improve the town. But looking back, that doesn't make him a bad person. I think he was only shy."

Owe Posey ambled his way through a dozen backyards, up and down hills, then crossed Old Augusta Road. He cut hay dead for a good quarter mile through land no one claimed, and, finally, ran into a cement ex-silo at old Gruel Sand and Gravel, which now housed, partly, the Gruel Normal School.

After headmaster Derrick Ouzts shook Owe Posey—and everyone in town wondered why Ouzts would be at Gruel Normal on a late Sunday morning—he called an ambulance. Ouzts also called Carla Posey and said, "I hate to disturb you, Mrs. Posey, but Owe showed up here on his lawn tractor and we needed to send him to the hospital."

Before he could say, "He seemed to've had a heart attack and didn't know where he was," Carla Posey said, "You sure it's Owe? Lawn tractor? He only had a Bolens seventeen-horsepower, forty-two-inch-cut riding mower."

"Well, he showed up slumped over the steering wheel. That's all I know. He lodged himself accidentally up against the old sand silo."

Carla looked out of the upstairs bedroom window. She saw a serpentine strip of cut grass heading east.

And she laughed and laughed, though her head still throbbed.

AT FIRST, OWE thought he'd been shot in the chest. He wondered if one of Victor Dees's purported hand grenades lodged within his own rib cage and detonated. The coroner would later tell everyone down at Roughhouse Billiards that he'd never seen a heart that exploded such—that fragments of heart tissue catapulted into Owe's spleen, liver, and lungs. In actuality it wasn't quite the truth, but no one questioned the coroner's expertise.

In the split second between Owe Posey's heart attack and his head's subsequent thud onto the mower's steering wheel, he thought, I shouldn't have drunk that last mini-bottle; *I shouldn't have fantasized fucking that Dutch girl in her tulip garden; the capital of Louisiana isn't New Orleans; I forgot to put Sevin dust on the Bigger Boy, Better Boy, La Rossa, Beefmaster, Early Girl, Mountain Delight, Early Cascade, and Sixty-Five Day VFFNT Hybrid Whopper tomato plants in greenhouse one, wilt, nematodes, wilt, nematodes.*

He thought, *Carla deserved better than what I ever offered, and in his death ride he didn't so much envision bright light beckoning from afar as he foresaw a long, long, forty-two-inch wide path where the citizens of Gruel could skip and frolic and forget about all the pressures of a meaningless life.*

THE GRASS NEVER grew back. When viewed from above it looked like a thin river Styx meandered between Owe Posey's back porch and the center of Gruel Normal. At first all of Carla Posey's neighbors wanted to sue her, or at least ask that she bring back some fescue from Park Seed. Then someone started the rumor that a man on his way to hell will leave a scorched mark on the earth at the point of his demise. Before long another rumor spread that Carla Posey practiced witchcraft, that she and Owe poisoned plants on their job, and that a bevy of hitchhikers could be found buried beneath their crawlspace.

"I don't give a damn if she's a witch or serial killer," Paula Purgason finally said at an impromptu Chamber of Commerce meeting. "We can use Owe's dead path as a tourist attraction. Do y'all remember back thirty years ago when that little baby's headstone glowed at night over in Forty-Five? Everybody thought it meant that child was another messiah. They had people showing up from three states away to witness that thing. Hell, a busload of Mexicans showed up, and they're used to discovering Virgin Mary statues crying blood all the time."

Jeff the owner said, "I remember that tombstone. It ended up having some kind of phosphorous in the granite. The moon and nearby streetlight caused it to glow."

"We owe Owe," Paula said. "He might be frying in Hades right now, but instead of castigating Carla we need to get her on our side. Maybe we can hire her as a tour guide of sorts you know, tell visitors all the bad things her husband did in life even if he didn't do them. It would be like one of those ghost tours in Charleston."

Victor Dees, dressed fully in camouflage, shook his head. "First off, Owe Posey was a decent man. He worked hard, paid his taxes, and didn't grow marijuana in his backyard even though he had the botanical abilities. Second, that death path to hell goes through my property, and I don't want no witch and her tourists traipsing across my place. Maybe I got some old claymore mines planted back there, y'all don't know."

Dr. Bobba Lollis said, "Oh shut up, Victor. I traipse around your backyard all the time when my dog gets loose. I vote we talk to Carla. I made the motion."

Paula seconded, and everyone in the makeshift unofficial Chamber of Commerce voted Aye except for Victor Dees. He said, "Nolo contendere," the only Latin term he'd ever used.

In John Cheever's story "The Swimmer," as any college English professor teaching a sophomore-level course in Literature of the Supernatural can point out, Neddy Merrill's journey through the neighborhood pools goes from the Westerhazys' pale shade of green all the way to icy, icy water at the Gilmartins' house, then the Clydes' pool where he could only keep his hand on the curb. In between Neddy found himself in sapphire-colored water, a dry pool, the murk of a public pool, opaque cold water, cerulean water, and so on. Any college English professor worth his or her sheepskin will point out "symbolism" five minutes into class discussion, and how Neddy Merrill's awkward and visionary escapade imitated the stages of human life, et cetera.

But if the members of Gruel's volunteer Chamber of Commerce, or the larger contingent of the Gruel Association to Sanctify History, had taken the time to consider Owe Posey's half-mile adventure they might have noticed how his backyard remained shaded to the appearance of dusk even at noon. And where he ended up, after the hay field, was a white sand-covered lot. In between were various shades of dark green, olive-green, pale green, then yellow. Oh, if only one of the Gruel citizens had paid attention in college—or *gone* to an institution of higher learning that boasted an English department—then he or she would have no other choice but to sit in a corner and wonder if a philosopher might ever offer up any kind of valid epistemological answers in which to believe.

Luckily for Carla Posey, she took that sophomore-level course. She studied *Frankenstein*, and "Young Goodman Brown," and "The Swimmer" at Anders College. She understood that the townspeople's rumors were off base. Carla took a six-month leave of absence from Park Seed—her good boss said that he'd call it "maternity leave" since she'd never used one, since she'd been a loyal, committed, and trustworthy employee—and while grieving her husband's sudden and untimely death she took to reading again. Sometimes she took *The Stories of John Cheever* to Owe's grave site, sat on his non-illuminating tombstone, and read aloud. More than a few people noticed.

When Paula Purgason showed up finally with a platter of brownies baked by Maura-Lee Snipes at Gruel Bakery, Carla Posey's place was dark. The door was ajar, though, and Paula let herself in, chiming out, "Yoo-hoo, Carla? Are you home?" She thought, *Has Carla gone to bed and forgotten to lock her door? Has she gone somewhere for supper?*

But she heard foreign voices emanating from the far left side of the house, and walked toward the kitchen. Carla Posey sat on the floor, surrounded by only cabinets and appliances.

The TV set on the floor, too. Paula looked at the screen, which showed naked women, their hair in pigtails, tending to what looked like an island of blooming tulips. Paula said, "Carla? I brought you a little get-well something. I'm sorry it's taken me so long."

Carla didn't turn. She leaned forward and stared at the television, her face two feet away from it. Paula pounded on the doorjamb, but got no response. The women on television seemed to be talking about life and death, the way they held tulips upright, then turned them upside down. "We have a great proposition for you," Paula Purgason said. "It's a way for Owe to live forever. We want to give something to Owe."

Carla Posey didn't acknowledge her neighbor. She got up, turned off the TV, pulled her dress off above her head in one motion, and stood still there in the dark.

The next day Paula Purgason wouldn't say how she left the brownies balanced atop the staircase newel. She'd go to Roughhouse Billiards, order shot after shot of bourbon, and say how she could no longer sleep.

CAULK

ELAINE INSISTED ON MORE SILICONE, AND I STOOD MY ground at least twenty-four hours on how she didn't need it. I said there was a reason for honest ventilation, for breathing, and that too much silicone would hamper this process. I mentioned how it would be obvious to her both winter and summer, when everything unnatural in the world either contracted or expanded. This was fall—late October— in South Carolina. At noon the temperature got up to the mid-seven-ties, but the humidity was a low sixty percent. There existed no other time to paint a house.

"If you don't caulk right then you'll have to do the job again before the year's out," Elaine said. "I know what I'm doing, Louis. Remember—I lived in Mexico City the spring semester of my junior year in college."

I didn't get the connection. We stood outside. I held a caulk gun in my right hand, with about half of the tube gone. It was the first one of the third case. I turned the lever down so no silicone spilled out, so caulk didn't exude out on my beat-up noname-brand tennis shoes, making me undergo flashbacks of a time at the Auto Drive-In with my first high school girlfriend who almost gave it up. I said, "I've caulked every goddamn seam, Elaine. I've caulked boards that were welded together— that were petrified, by God—and needed caulk about as much as a goat needs a can opener."

Elaine held nothing. She stood with her hands on her hips and looked at the soffit and fascia. She looked at a point twenty feet off the ground and said, "You didn't smooth that bead down. You missed a spot."

This was near dusk. Elaine had come home from work hoping to find me—I know—not working on the house like I'd promised. Sometime earlier in the week I'd been drinking, and as drinkers might be wont to do I'd said the house needed painting unless we wanted someone like Andrew Wyeth hanging out in the front yard thinking we lived in a weather-beaten barn, and that I didn't have much else to do, seeing as I'd gotten mad at my last boss and quit a job driving oxygen canisters around to hackers and wheezers. Elaine said, "It needs to be scraped and caulked hard, Louis. Why don't you let me hire someone to do the job right. There's no need to even talk about it if you don't feel committed to do the job right."

Of course I took all her talk to be a challenge, and didn't understand that she knew how to wind me up like a cheap metal mouse that skitters across linoleum floors. I said, "Why would a complete painting stranger care about how this house turns out?" I felt my one eye starting to travel off. We stood outside, still. I pretended to check the soffit and fascia, too. I said, "Personally I think I'm ready to paint tomorrow. If you want, I'll go over the whole house again with caulk."

And I meant it. In my mind, a person scraped flaked paint and caulked up holes, buckled seams, roof flashings, door casings, and paid special attention to window frames. That's what I did the first day. The god-damn house was airtight, but if she wanted more caulk, then I'd do it.

Elaine said, "You weren't drinking up on that ladder, were you?" She took my caulk gun, turned the lever 180 degrees, and shot an invisible indention underneath one of the living room windows. Elaine rubbed it four directions, then handed the tube back.

"There's no telling what somebody might charge to paint this place. I don't even know anyone who knows an honest painter. They say to never let a roofer around your wife, and never let a painter near your liquor cabinet." I felt my eye wander back even with the other. I'd drunk about half a good bottle of Old Crow during the day. There are two theories: don't drink and don't fall off the ladder, or go ahead and drink hard so it won't hurt so much in case you do fall.

I've tried both in the past. The second's best. When I worked construction one summer in college sober, I pulled back a shutter where a small but nervous clan of bats nestled daytime. They flew out. I fell off. This is no lie: on the way down the entire history of French literature passed before my eyes. When I hit the ground I got out the "Bo" from "Baudelaire," but nothing else.

MOST TIMES WHEN Elaine went off on two-day business trip seminars in order for her to push what she pushed, namely new and improved kitchen accessories—there are more conventions held on blenders and whatnot than the average person thinks—I'd either find a way to get time off from my job delivering oxygen, or I'd stay home looking out the Venetian blinds to see if Elaine hired a detective to see if I left or invited dancing escort women over. But this last time I didn't get an invitation, even though I'd quit my job and had the time.

"We're doing a fair in Atlanta," Elaine said. "We got I don't know how many rooms downstairs at the Omni to show off the new products. They're saying every new micro-brewery pub is sending someone to check out our line of mid-sized Hemingway sampler stemware."

I said, "Huh. Not to mention the zucchini thing." What else could a caulking boy say? Elaine's company had developed a slicer/dicer/skinner mechanism that worked so clean and easy they thought it might change Americans' attitudes and diets. Me, I couldn't tell the difference between zucchini, cucumbers, or dill pickles. I didn't care to cook or eat any of them, either. As far as the Hemingway line—I'm glad Elaine's company didn't market a set of *shot* glasses.

I said, "Well, you have a good time, dear. Don't go down to Underground Atlanta all by yourself. Don't show up at the Cheetah 3 with your friends just because women get in a strip joint free."

Elaine rolled her eyes. She said, "I won't have any time off, Louis. And if I did—like maybe if there's a blackout and we can't showcase our wares—I'd find a museum."

"If there's a blackout it might be hard to look at art," I said. It just came to me, fast. Sometimes I thought that maybe those oxygen canisters leaked and gave me extra brain cells or something.

Elaine said, "Caulk. Don't start painting until I get back. I'll call you when I check in at the hotel."

She kissed me on the mouth, but didn't mean it. This happened once a month. I knew she had cutlery on her mind. Me, I could only get out, "If you're going to talk the talk, you better caulk the caulk," like an idiot.

I'D STILL BE married if it weren't for the weather. In a way, Canada's to blame. If that big Arctic swoop they show during the weather-map section had moved south of Appalachia while Elaine worked in Atlanta, then we'd still be together, I'm sure.

Whereas it got down to the low twenties in places like Johnson City, Tennessee, it stayed in the low seventies in the Upstate of South Carolina.

As any reputable caulk tube will point out, caulk cannot be used at temperatures below 5 degrees centigrade, which is 40 degrees Fahrenheit. Hell, the tubes I used even had directions written in French—which I'm sure had something to do with that Canadian Arctic jet stream, seeing as I've never seen actual French people caulking their field stone houses out in the countryside near Dijon or wherever.

Elaine went off, and I got to work. I finished the last eleven tubes of the third case, and then I called a local hardware joint and got them to deliver another dozen cases and put it on Elaine's bill. I brought Jason the delivery boy inside and we feasted on canned smoked oysters and Bloody Marys before I got to work on the house.

I said, "My wife seems to think an entire wooden house needs a layer of caulk before it gets painted," and handed him some ground habanero peppers for his drink. Jason looked like a college kid going to a Baptist school, but this was a Friday morning and he wasn't in class. Later on I thought how he looked a little like someone I saw on television who was a member of a white supremacy militia group.

"A lot of people use primer," he said.

"Exactly! You prime the wood, and then you paint it," I said. This is no lie: Jason poured a quarter teaspoon of ground habanero on his thumb, then snorted it. Jason said, "Pain. Pain's good so you remember pleasure. That's one of my mottoes."

I poured another drink and put it away. I poured another drink and put it away. I'd made a pitcher, and made a mistake. I didn't want a delivery boy dead on my hands with hot peppers up his nose. I said, "Prime, paint."

"Well, technically, you only prime new wood, man. Or new sheetrock. After your house's been painted, I wouldn't prime it again. Maybe that's just me," Jason said. I looked across the table at him and thought, *How can a twelve-year-old get a job as a delivery boy?* Jason said, "I only work weekdays, you know. I help out my friends doing jobs they're doing—not as a gofer, either. If you need help caulking and you're willing to pay, I'd be glad to help you out. I can get you references." He nodded up and down ten times.

I poured the last of the pitcher and said, "Am I the only delivery you have today? Here." I handed Jason ten bucks for a tip. I said, "No. This job is something I have to do myself."

Jason sat there with his first drink still full and a red powdery stain on his upper lip. He said, "I understand, dude."

I said, "Say, do you have any other mottoes?"

He didn't blink. He said, "Paining others gives pleasure, too."

That night I slept without my wife. Every light, television, radio, and appliance stayed on. The evening low was fifty-two degrees.

I CUT HALF of the nipples down two inches, and the others only a half centimeter. I needed thick, thick beads and I needed ones so thin I could've worked Hollywood as a make-up artist for villains and swashbucklers. I put the twenty-foot extension ladder up at the far gable and set my stepladder up against the front of the house. There was no need for drop cloths.

When I got four feet down the house in wide rows, I'm sure the bees showed up only because they thought it was the biggest albino hive ever. There are different caulks, I'm sure, but I stuck with siliconized acrylic white. If I'd've used a gray color, then wasps would've shown up, thinking our house was one big paper nest.

My right forearm hurt and pulsed like the furthest moon of Jupiter, and at times I thought the four triggering fingers I used might cramp into a claw so hard no middle-weight boxing champion would have a chance with me. I did not think of Elaine flirting with men from Minnesota who owned slight restaurant chains, with men who didn't come so much for the spectacular as they came for the spectacle—let me say now that I know my wife got hired for her physical attributes more than she did for her culinary or home ec prowess. Elaine majored in anthropology, for Christ's sake, and I know for certain she spent her first year in college as a pom-pom girl.

Our house was thick and white, is what I'm saying, by Sunday night when Elaine came back. She only got a sweeping glimpse of it when she turned her car into the driveway. At the door I said, "Hey! You got back safely. You cheated Death again."

Elaine said, "There must've been too many cars coming my way in the opposite direction. You didn't paint the house all white, did you?"

I grabbed my wife's suitcase. I shuttled her inside as quickly as possible. This was the exact moment when I thought maybe I'd gone too far, out of meanness. I said, "Did people like y'all's products?"

"The house looked really white," Elaine said. She tried to turn around, but I pushed her toward inside. "I could see our house from way far away," she said. "There's a glow."

"Life in the big city," I said. "Boy, that really seems to change your way of looking at things. Of seeing things. Of your outlook on what is real and what isn't."

I held my wife's suitcase. She held a handful of her company's pamphlets. Ten minutes after I closed the door it got steamy in the house, for reasons other than a wife returning from a business trip.

ELAINE SAW NOTHING wrong the next morning. When I awoke due to a cramp in my forearm, Elaine stood above me in her robe at an hour past dawn. She held an eight-inch-wide brush in her hand and said, "You can start now." She had on her robe, and held a blazer outfit she always wore to work, as if she went out to either sell real estate or lead a group of drunks from intervention to committal.

I said, "It's supposed to rain today." It's the first thing that came to me.

"No, it's not. I just watched the local news while I dried my hair. It's supposed to be warm again." Elaine brushed something invisible from her coat.

I said, "How could you hear the weather report with a blow-dryer on? I think you heard wrong. There's no way you could hear anything right with a blow-dryer on."

Elaine smiled, but didn't show her teeth. She grinned. She said, "I went outside to get the paper. I bet it's ninety degrees out now."

Lookit: I swear it doesn't get ninety degrees at dawn in South Carolina during October. There might be ninety percent humidity. It might get to ninety degrees by two o'clock in the afternoon, but not before sunlight. One time my grandmother on my father's side said it reached 110 and rained simultaneously on Christmas day, 1950, but at that point she'd gone through both radiation and chemotherapy—she liked to pull the top of her dress down and show the cavity where one breast existed, then say how smoking was bad for you.

I got up and said to my wife, "Did you look at the house?"

"I'm so happy you gave in," she said. "Let me say now that I thought I'd come home and find that you hadn't done anything since I left. I'm sorry. I didn't think you'd caulk the house right." Elaine walked into the laundry room.

I stood in my boxer shorts sober. I said, "It's a joke, you idiot! I caulked every square inch of the house. It looks like a Dairy Queen treat from the road. Yesterday an Eskimo family happened by and asked me the name of our contractor—they said they'd been looking for an igloo like ours ever since they left Lapland, or wherever."

Understand, I caught myself hyperventilating, and my bad eye strayed off even though it was morning and I'd not partaken yet. Elaine came back in the room wearing a pair of bicycle shorts so tight she showed camel-lips. I didn't realize that everything was out of sync. Why did she take a shower and wash her hair before exercising? Elaine held five-pound weights in her hand and said, "What? One-two, one-two, one-two," et cetera.

I CAME INSIDE from almost painting to find Elaine on the telephone with her college roommate Amy. They planned their tenth reunion. Elaine laughed too much, I thought, as I came up from behind her. Elaine said, "Well, I wouldn't know how to react to an uncircumcised man, either. I've only seen one once." I tried to step back out of the room, but made a noise. The floor creaked, is what I'm saying, and you'd think somebody who lived there—namely my wife Elaine—would've thought to have caulked the area.

Elaine hung up without saying goodbye or anything. She just put down the phone. To me, my wife said, "Hey," and smiled. She could've done a commercial for toothpaste or dental floss.

I said, "Is there a problem with the phone lines? If you want me to do it, I'll call the telephone company and say our phone's gone out."

Elaine stood up erect. She'd put on the business suit. "That's okay," she said.

"I couldn't call the telephone company if our line was out, stupid!" I said.

Elaine said, "Louis, there're men who don't play this game always. I thought you were outside painting the house."

What could I say? I knew there were other men out there—younger, better-looking men—who didn't have the advantage of taking a logic course on the college level. I don't want to come off as superior or anything, but I've noticed how people without four-year college educations tend to buy more mobile homes percentage-wise, and how people like me have noticed that acts of nature, viz. tornadoes, knock over trailers.

Of course they didn't scrape, caulk, and paint wood, granted.

I said, "So you're looking for a man who ain't circumcised, is that what you want? I guess that's what you want." I'd put minibottles in the gutter the night before. I said, "Four fat men stopped by thinking our house was a pilgrimage to the Michelin man. Did you, by any chance, know that the word caulk comes from the word caucus, which means just a faction of a political party? It's Greek. It means the whole goddamn house doesn't need doing."

This wasn't exactly true, but it sounded right. I was pretty sure the word caucus came from some Greek word.

Elaine said, "You're full of crap. Caulk comes from a 304-smilliliter tube, which is approximately ten-point-three fluid ounces."

I said, "Does Amy have a ten-point-three-fluid-ounce uncircumcised caulk tube she's worried about? Is that what y'all were talking about, Elaine?"

My wife actually giggled. She turned her back toward me. She said, "Uh-huh." Then she went to work, finally, running late.

IT'S IMPOSSIBLE TO roll paint right, across concentric horizontal loops of siliconized acrylic caulk. After Elaine left I put the brush aside and rummaged around in the garage until I found an old roller with a nap used for rough surfaces. My wife wanted the house a hue the paint company paint-namers tabbed Saharan Winter Sand, which most sane individuals outside of the house-painting business would call "tan." I took my roller and pan outside, my aluminum extension handle, and the long ladder. The beads of caulk were stuck so thick it felt like driving over a Walmart parking lot of speed bumps paved one after another. It didn't take me one hard roll up and down to have a flashback of little league baseball, and that feeling of bees in the hands when you swing and hit a pitch in on the handle. The sound that emanated was not unlike a stick drug across an expensive, tightly cropped picket fence.

"That's a nice mural of the Riverside dirt track stands after a muddy Saturday night," some guy in a Camaro yelled out at me as I stood in the middle of the front yard not admiring my work. I turned around and waved. I laughed, and even thought deep down how this guy probably knew exactly what I did to get back at a wife. I watched him ease by slowly, and paid attention to his gravity-prone mouth sag, and thought to myself, *Now there's a man who's had destiny knock on his forehead more than once before he thought about answering the door.*

I thought how maybe the same could be said about me, too, for about three seconds. Then I looked up at the sky for rainclouds, and wondered if rain might wash down Saharan Winter Sand over caulk lips over and over until one smooth facade showed that might satisfy wife, real estate agent, and prospective buyer alike.

A thunderstorm wasn't in the forecast, just as Elaine told me.

I yelled back, "Come here and tell me that," like fighting words.

I knew this guy—I'd seen him over at Compton's store—and he always meant business one way or the other. He was one of the Shirley boys who ran an auto body shop nearby, pushing and pulling dents out of car panels and hoods. Ray Shirley also ran dirt track at Riverside, of course, in the modified division. One time I took Elaine over there and everyone jumped out of the stands holding their faces. I said, "Someone farted."

What happened in fact was that there was a drunk guy raising hell below us, and there was this old woman who had a canister of mace, she blew the thing in the drunk man's direction, and then all hell broke loose. Much like that Canadian Arctic wind not showing up on the weather screen, this woman didn't understand how the wind blowing toward her might send spray backwards.

That's what happened. Elaine and I stood there while everyone ran from the bleachers. Elaine said, "What the hell?" like that.

We smoked cigarettes, too, and didn't smell or feel a thing.

This old guy in a wheelchair up top with us shook his head and said, "Again. It's happened again. When will people understand stock car racing?"

I thought about the double-amputee when I returned to the ladder, after the Shirley boy drove off. I thought to myself, *There's a way caulk might make his life bearable, if one of those companies came up with a more pliable prosthetic limb.*

I got up on the ladder and got my face close, is what I'm saying. This is no lie: I caught myself wondering why a Supreme Being didn't invent regeneration for human beings. And at that moment something picked me off the ladder and threw me to the ground.

I almost broke my first hip at age thirty-three.

"YOU DID IT all on purpose, Louis. Don't lie to me," Elaine said when she got home. "What'd you do, jump off the ladder? I bet you had to go up that thing ten times and dive off to get a swelling that bad."

I was in a tub of Epsom salts with an ice pack on the side of my ass. It had been years since I'd bruised myself, and I couldn't remember if heat or ice came first. One time ten months before, I crashed the oxygen delivery van into the front of some old guy's house and tore up my knees. This was winter and I'd lost control going down his driveway. He came outside with his walker and handed me two Darvons. I sang in the ambulance, later.

"Is it raining outside yet?" I asked Elaine.

"What did you do to paint the house? Did you get out a little water-color brush and draw lines?" she asked.

My ice melted. For a second I wondered if I could create a thunder-storm in the bathroom with enough ice and hot water. I said, "I used a roller instead. Then on top of the ladder I looked up and saw these buzzards circling. They thought they'd found a dead polar bear rolled over, I bet. I leaned back, and then fell off, I swear. Help me out of here."

Elaine walked away. I struggled around, then finally slid out over the edge. When my wife returned she said, "Good. I found six Fine Red Sable brushes from when I took that painting class in college. Fill in the gaps, Louis."

I think she might've meant that in a double-entendre kind of way, now.

SHE DID. ELAINE didn't come back that night, or even the next morning to pick up clothes for work. I waited until noon the next day to call her at work, and then only got an answering-machine message about what number to call to order the new chinois with beech-wood dowel and stand. Of course I went outside with my tiny brushes and started filling the white indentions by hand. I knew later that the job wouldn't be so difficult if I'd've only used the eight-inch brush and painted from horizon to horizon.

Ray Shirley came by and said, "I seen you fall off the ladder. I seen you in the rearview mirror and felt it was part my fault for breaking your concentration."

I said, "My foot slipped." I felt like an idiot holding the artist brush.

Ray Shirley said, "You aim to fill in every spot you missed with that little thing? Goddamn, boy, I didn't think you'd be good on detail work, what with the way you caulked the whole place."

My hip hurt. I'd put Icy Hot on it earlier, which burned my fingertips, which made it hard to hold the brush, which felt like a thin branding iron in my hand. I said, "Originally I only planned on teaching my wife a lesson. I think she left me, though."

Ray Shirley stood on the ground, looking across the street. His Camaro idled chugging in my driveway. He said, "I'm on my third. The first two didn't understand racing. Third one's half blind. She don't get scared watching me, ever."

I started to say how I could've used a blind wife—and even got my mouth open to say so—when some hand reached down again and pushed me. I almost broke my second hip, then. Ray Shirley stepped out of the way without looking up. He got me to my feet and held my arms over my head so I'd get my breath back. "You seem to be the kind of fellow what needs a job on the ground, son. Hell, you need a job below the ground, like a miner, or a grave digger."

I tried to say, "Or a cave guide," but couldn't get it out.

OUT OF MEANNESS I finished painting the fouled front of the house, then the rest of it with the regular paint brush sideways. The place looked pretty good when I finished. From afar the ripples weren't even noticeable—like maybe two miles away—and up close it only looked like I'd bought wood from a lumberyard with dull and wiggly band saws.

This process took me less than a week; I forget meteorological lingo, but it may have been Indian summer. What I'm saying is, it was the end of October and early November, and still warm enough to paint at night. There was no need for spotlights. I'm no geologist or chemist, but I bet siliconized acrylic caulk has some kind of phosphorescent properties that make it glow in the dark. I almost needed a welder's mask to see what I did and where I'd been.

In my mind I saw Elaine driving by the house at dawn, checking to see if I covered the caulk adequately. When cars passed by I never turned around for two reasons—I didn't want to make eye contact with my wife, and both my hips seemed fused to the point of petrification. I think there's some kind of toy where this guy goes up and down a ladder, stiff, and I could've modeled for it.

I didn't turn around, but I did yell out, "Dead man caulking," more than once I swear.

Understand, I didn't call Elaine up at work, and made a point not to look in her closet to see if somehow she'd returned while I went out for booze or cigarettes so she could scavenge up all of her low-cut blouses and slit skirts. I didn't pace back and forth, seeing as how I couldn't. Not once did I get on the telephone and call Elaine's parents, her boss at home, various clients I knew she kept an ongoing customer relationship with, the police, or that guy who has a show on TV about missing persons. Somehow I knew maybe Elaine underwent a seven-year itch thing known usually to people like me, and that she'd return in time all apologetic, spiritual, calm, and ready to patch up anything wrong in our relationship. I felt certain she'd saved vacation and sick days up in order to meditate in New Mexico, or Nag's Head, or some real ashram over in real India.

She didn't.

I never called Elaine's old roommate Amy, on purpose. Already I knew my wife had given up and left her job—that she'd learned from me. I thought about that poor kid Jason with his mottoes, and wondered if he knew Elaine.

My wife called once and I said, "Hello," and she hung up, not knowing we'd gotten that star 69 device. Elaine had left everything we'd accumulated in order to live with Amy, the woman worried about what uncircumcised people might mean to her future. My wife had moved to Delaware, of all places.

I sat in the living room alone like a man alone in his living room. I thought about how this house now stood caulked beyond what full-time caulkers might agree upon.

Ray Shirley finally showed up again and I waddled to the front door and let him inside. He said, "I got people working the pits who don't care as much about life as you do."

I sat inside my house steamed for two reasons. I said, "What?"

"I want to ask you if you're working any more in a real job," Ray said. "I know you're not working a real job getting paid and all."

I'd been thinking about oxygen. I'd been thinking about how someone out there needs to start up a business as an oxygen-tent caulker, just in case. I said, "I'm working. I don't get paid, but I'm working. It's hard to explain, man."

Ray Shirley looked out the front window where my eight-foot step-ladder still stood. He said, "I have one word for you." I said, "Uh-huh."

"Pitman," he said.

My whole life flashed before my eyes, with the exception of the time Baudelaire came to me in college. I said, "Right, pal."

Ray Shirley said, "My boy I had working for me down at the garage just quit. He worked Saturday nights when I raced, too. I think you're the man I need for the spot he left."

I nodded. There was no way I could afford my tan igloo another year without a job. I'd called my oxygen boss, drunk and begging, but he'd found someone stupid and reliable to fill my place. I said, "I don't know anything about cars."

Ray Shirley shook his head sideways. He mentioned how I needed to get over Elaine, and nothing could do it better than learning the intricacies of carburetors, pistons, valves, and timing chains. He said there weren't enough people out there who could fill holes left wide and inviting by people who ran fourway stop signs, or followed too closely. I limped each step outside toward his car, on my way to find my new job, the one he said God called upon me to do.

These days I sit on an upside-down dry-wall bucket, waiting for customers to offer their dinged and dented vehicles. Let me say that I'm not the first person to notice how modern science should've invented a Bondo of sorts by now, to smooth over damage we've done to what still flutters on beneath the rib cage.

WHEN CHILDREN COUNT

T
HE ONLY THING MADAME TAMMY SAID THAT MAY HAVE been overheard went something like, "Oh, hell, it doesn't matter—I'll take paper." She stood in line at a regular check-out aisle in a Winn-Dixie halfway between Charlotte and Atlanta. Fifty customers stood in the 10 Items or Less line. Tammy only bought a roll of paper towels, some fingernail polish remover, Jewish rye, and pimento cheese, even though she stood between two women with full carts. She held a twenty-dollar bill. It was noon, and Tammy had just read a hundred palms at the Monday-Thursday Chesnee flea market near the North Carolina border, in peach and apple country.

"You sound exactly like my dead sister," this woman said, pushing her full cart into Tammy's backside. "I ain't never heard nothing like that. Say this: 'I will never, ever order a club sandwich here with bacon again, what with the ptomaine.' Say it. Say."

Tammy turned around and smiled. She still wore the black turban, the black smock, the golden spangles and half-moons. She stood six feet tall, and raised one eyebrow for emphasis. The woman behind her kept putting groceries on the belt: white bread, frozen dinner rolls, a slew of Vienna sausages, potted meat, Spam, diapers for both kids and adults. "Club sandwich ptomaine," Tammy said.

"Well I'll be damned," the woman said. "It's as if my sister spoke from the grave." The cashier gave Tammy her change. "It's the last thing I ever heard her say. She ate a bad sandwich over at this little place best known for its barbecue, she made herself known how she felt about the food, and then she died later on that afternoon."

The cashier said, "Do you want one of the game pieces in order to see if you can win a million dollars instantly, or save them up for weekly bargains?"

Madame Tammy said, "I don't believe in playing games at the store. I don't like getting my hopes up." She stepped forward and took her one sack.

The woman behind Tammy held out her hand for the little perforated cardboard square. "Listen, I'll pay you to let my little niece call you up and say something. If you'll just talk to her a little bit. She keeps wanting to call up her momma in heaven and all, and me and my husband—we got custody now—we don't know how to handle it. We don't know how to handle it. We just don't know. We don't. It's hard explaining some things." Tammy turned around and nodded, although she just wanted out of there.

The cashier looked back and forth between them. She slid items across the scanner. Between blips she said, "My mother died when I was twelve. I'd just about forgotten what she sounded like until one day the TV was on and this lady was doing a commercial for getting your credit fixed. It sounded just like my momma. I hope to hell that woman doing commercials don't make it in Hollywood, seeing as I couldn't take hearing that voice oncet a week or nothing. It was just a local commercial, though."

A two-for-a-dollar frozen pizza didn't connect. The cashier kept running a flat box of sausage-topping over the eye. "Well," Tammy said. "I'm not around much. And my brother's coming to stay with me awhile. What would I say?"

The woman said to the cashier, "They're two for a dollar. Just ring the goddamn thing in! It's written on a big orange thing there. Just ring it in."

"Store policy," said the cashier. She had braces, and some boy's high school ring on her index finger. Tammy thought she didn't look more than twelve at the time, and remembered how she felt when her own father left some three decades earlier.

The pizza clicked finally. Tammy said, "Sure. Tell your niece to call me up." She reached in her pocketbook and pulled out a business card. It had an eyeball on an open palm. "Since I'm not there most of the time you might tell your niece that the pay phone's pretty busy up in Heaven, in case she can't get through."

The woman said, "Her name's Edwina, but we call her Eddie. She's a special child. We call her Special Eddie. Listen. You ain't got an answering machine, do you? That might confuse her—why her momma won't pick up and all. Hey, do this if you don't mind: change your message. I'll pay you and all."

Tammy nodded. She didn't ask the woman how they would get together for payments, and so on. "I'll do what I can do. And I can do, I promise." She didn't go into details about how she searched every day for her own father at flea markets across America.

MADAME TAMMY DIDN'T want a roommate, wayward brother or not. She had enough problems, and a list of needs longer than a desert turtle's lifeline. She had to buy rubber-soled boots, seeing as a man selling stolen rebar at the table next to her got hit by lightning last Wednesday down at the Pickens County Flea Market. She needed to hire a new gofer—the school year had started and she no longer had a fifteen-year-old to depend on—to scour the various markets she worked, in search of old men selling used golf balls. Madame Tammy needed to take the only snapshot she owned of her father, Shorty, and get it touched up by one of those photographers who filled in cracks, tears, and fades. Over the years she had felt certain that her father didn't do stunt work in Hollywood like he wrote in those couple letters thirty years earlier; although she wasn't a true psychic she felt certain he still dove into dark, still, nighttime water hazards, retrieved duffers' errant approach shots, and cleaned them up for resale more than likely.

Madame Tammy needed complete silence at night so she could sit in a chair and replenish herself with hope. Her father could've died from cancer, stroke, or heart attack by now.

"I don't have room for anyone, Lamar," she told her brother. "I live in a little place. I'm hardly here, too. Hell, I live in the back of my van more often than not." Right away Tammy thought about how most people might've said, "If you're hardly there, then you'll hardly notice me." It wasn't that she felt embarrassed about her living conditions between flea markets—she owned a vertical, three-story, fifteen-hundred-square-foot house on top of Tryon Peak, near the South Carolina/North Carolina border. Some days she referred to the house as the Tower. After particularly fruitful flea-market days she called it the Steeple, and on bad days the Finger.

Lamar used a phone card to call her. He was already in Opelika, trying to stay off Interstate 85, on his way. He said, "This thing only lasts ten minutes. Look, I just need a few days—a week at most."

Madame Tammy wasn't embarrassed about working flea markets, either. She knew that most people—especially wives—thought she said things like, "For twenty dollars I can tell you that you'll get your next blow job in five minutes." In reality, perhaps it was better than her real modus operandi, namely finding answers about family, commitment, and medical history, among other things. Madame Tammy heard adults walk past her table at various Southeastern markets, not able to whisper, "Whore," or, "Nutcase," or, "Gypsy."

"If you come up here for a week then you better bring something to sell," Tammy told Lamar. "I'm not going to put up with another free-loading man who wants to spend time in my Tower while I work my tail off holding fat, callused hands in the heat and humidity. All the while I tell goners they got a happy long life ahead of them."

Lamar said, "We haven't seen each other since you moved up there for good, Sis."

Tammy looked out her front window. In the winter, sometimes, she swore she saw the Atlantic Ocean, some four hundred miles away. "Why aren't you teaching? Shouldn't school be starting down there by now? I lost my boy who used to look around for me."

The mechanical operator came on and said, "You have one minute."

Lamar said, "Parents in Montgomery, Alabama, don't have much sense of humor. There aren't any students left in all of America who understand sarcasm or irony, either."

The telephone beeped a series. Tammy said, "Well come on, then. If I'm not here, then I'll leave a note where you can get me. The door'll be unlocked."

She heard no answer from Lamar, realized that she'd spoken to dead air, and hung up. Tammy waited ten minutes for the phone to ring— long enough for Lamar to go buy another phone card from Opelika, Alabama—it didn't, and she went out the door. She carried two pictures with her that needed refurbishing. One photo showed her mother and father together, in front of a DeSoto. Her mother wore a regular cotton dress with some kind of pattern on it. Her father wore suspenders and had his hair slicked back in a way that heightened the receding hairline.

The other photograph was a black-and-white close-up of her father's palm, and the scar that ran from the meat of his thumb to between his index and middle fingers. Initially it was supposed to be used as evidence in some court case involving an inferior and spastic spinning frame in the FortyFive Cotton Mill where Shorty worked, later as some kind of documentation for workman's comp. Tammy's father left town before he could find a lawyer to help him out. He left after shooting a wealthy man in the groin, at a public golf course, probably on purpose.

The details didn't matter. Tammy and her brother got out of Forty-Five. After college, and after two misguided husbands, Tammy decided to find her father, and not because of every other human being on one of the afternoon talk shows. She would know him by his scars, only. She read a book on the finer points of palmistry, and rented five-dollar flea-market tables soon thereafter. When a desperate client had a mal-formed series of lines, Tammy made up only good news, smiled, and told the person he or she had nothing to worry about whatsoever.

She had made up good news for her brother, too, when he took a job teaching tenth-grade geometry in Montgomery. And though she didn't truly believe in her own fake psychic abilities, Madame Tammy knew she would have to lie to Lamar again. Then there would be the problem of offering the truth, too.

"SEEMS TO ME Jesus of Nazareth could've done better than turning water into wine. Seems He could've done something a little more spectacular, for a miracle. Rock into wine, maybe. Poison ivy into wine. Hell, why didn't He turn Satan into wine?—all your people say that booze is the devil's doing in the first place." These are the words that got Madame Tammy's brother, Lamar, fired from teaching tenth-grade geometry in Alabama.

"I don't understand why you'd bring religion up in a math class," Tammy said to her brother. He'd not had time to even bring in his couple suitcases or the boxes in the back of his car. Lamar didn't arrive until three days after calling from northern Alabama. Because he couldn't think of anything else, he spent nights diving into country club golf course water hazards and collecting golf balls to have something to sell at the flea markets next to his sister.

"Beats me, too," Lamar said. "I'll tell you this: the parents didn't understand, obviously, and down there no one thinks to ever have a respectable hearing, trial, or closeddoor conference. I said that shit about Jesus on a Friday afternoon, and the principal and district superintendent came to oversee me pack up my classroom on Saturday morning."

"Like father, like son, as they say."

Lamar reached in his pocket and pulled out a hip flask. "You can do better than that, Tam," he said. "All that goddamn comparative-lit education you got, you can come up with something better than a cliché." He laughed, took a swig, and handed the flask over.

Tammy shook her head no. "Okay. Where the salmon spawn and die, there the next generation spawn and die. Whatever. Listen, you can either sleep on this couch, or on the floor, or in the hammock outside. You can stay a month. Then you have to go back home. That's the law around here. I read it somewhere. No one can stay with his or her grown sibling for more than a month."

Lamar said, "I didn't come to get lectured. And I have enough money to move, once I get my retirement. They'll hold it somewhere between thirty and ninety days. I don't have to wait until I'm sixty-five or anything like in some of the backwards, unrelenting, selfish states. I don't want to be a burden. I just needed to get out. I'll tell you later."

Madame Tammy said, "I hope this doesn't have anything to do with one of your students, Lamar."

"I thought you were some kind of psychic. Shouldn't you know?" He drank from the flask. "I'm only kidding. It's Fermat's Last Theorem. Some pinhead figured it out, so there's no more reason to live in mathematics, as far as I'm concerned. Computers, too—there's no need to stand in front of a chalkboard. Some people think the universe is governed by mathematics and whatnot. When I said all that stuff about Jesus in class, it was my way of being mathematical. Just like when I talked about the closest distance between two points, I was being religious. Fuck it."

Lamar brought up his clothes. He took his sister down the mountain to eat at a family-operated pool hall/bar/pizza joint called Shots and Slices. Right after Tammy beat him in their first game of nine-ball Lamar said, "I guess living up here kind of insulates you from undergoing another bad marriage."

Tammy said, "I like these people. It's also a central point for flea markets between mid-Florida and northern Virginia. I made a big mistake going out to New Mexico one time, lost my mind, and came back. Don't give me shit, especially after all you've done."

Lamar re-racked the balls while Tammy went to order a large, odd pizza—anchovies and pineapple. Lamar looked at the walls, pictures of people standing in front of wooden tables, everything from milk glass to measuring devices in front of them. When Tammy came back he said, "I know it's your business and all, but instead of reading palms why don't you take some notes and write some kind of scholarly work about it. Why don't you write something with an anthropological slant? I bet it'd sell. I don't know. Give it some kind of racy title. Call it *Hand Jobs in America* or something."

Tammy broke, and the nine ball swerved into a side pocket. "You owe everyone in here a drink. That's the house rules. Listen, I only want to find our daddy one last time. It's not so much that I feel unwhole because he left us early on. I can't explain it."

"What'll you do if you find him?"

"Shoot him twice," Tammy said. "I'll have a scotch and Dr Pepper. Don't make fun of me or I'll tell you the truth about your love line."

TAMMY'S LOCAL FRIEND Fagen placed two quarters on the table. He said, "Are y'all'ses playing for fun or money or both or neither?"

Fagen wore a coonskin hat without the tail. He kept a knife attached to his belt.

Tammy said, "Hey, there, Clarence Fagen. How you doing today?" She slipped up on the pool table and let her legs dangle.

Fagen smiled halfway. "Same old same old. Man's got to do what a man's got to do. Can't complain."

Tammy pointed at Lamar and said, "This here's my brother the mathematician. Or the ex-mathematician. He ain't quite the same as us. To him, six hours equals six hours."

Lamar didn't know what that meant. He stuck out his hand to Fagen and said, "I'm Lamar. Good to meet you."

Fagen said, "Fagen." He nodded. "Say. If you're a mathematician then I guess you know that one-hundred-to-one odds is pretty good. I'll bet you a thousand dollars to your ten that you'll have to pee before I do. You think on it." Fagen turned to Madame Tammy and said, "Any luck with your daddy's hand, finding it?"

Lamar didn't like his sister's choice of lifestyle, friends, or secrecy. Tammy said, "Don't bet him, Lamar. Fagen wears a drainage bag and pees down his leg all the time into the thing. He acts like he never has to pee."

Lamar thought this: x times y equals xy. He thought, 3.14159265, but could go no further.

Fagen said, "Damn," and took his two quarters off the table. "If you going to be that way, then I don't want to play no more."

"Fagen sells pelts," Tammy said to Lamar. "He sells pelts and keeps an eye out for his daughter. She'd be about what, now, Fagen—eighteen?"

"Eighteen going on nineteen. Unless she's exactly like her momma. Then she'd be eighteen going on either three or sixty-five, depending on her mood."

"Fagen's wife took off with their daughter ten years ago. The mother had a thing for fur coats, and Fagen here figures, like mother, like daughter. He thinks he'll eventually find her wanting to buy ten or twelve rabbit skins to sew together into something."

Lamar said, "Huh." He rolled the cue ball down to the other end of the table, but not hard enough for it to return. A song came out of the jukebox that sounded like the soundtrack to a foreign wedding—Italian,

Jewish, or Greek—which caused a couple boys to pull out their quarters and get the thing back to country music.

Fagen's eyes rolled back somewhat. Lamar figured the guy was pissing into his bag. "The last thing I heard my wife say was that she wanted to find a man who could set her down on a mink couch, drive her around in a car with sheepskin seats."

Lamar said, "Logic's a tricky thing, but I think you're going about it right. My own dad had a love for selling golf balls at the flea market, and I imagine that Tammy here will find him doing the same one day. It makes sense that you'll find either your ex-wife or daughter looking for cheap fur. Shit, I remember when I was a kid, my father would take me out at midnight and we'd dive into golf course lakes. I'd scoop out balls with my forearms, and then later on he'd clean them up in Clorox. Then we'd set up a table at the local flea market on Saturday mornings with some kind of dirty sign, something like 'Look at These Scarless Balls,' or, 'Our Balls Still Have Bounce.' It wasn't the best time in my life, but I guess it made me who I am today. Tammy didn't have to put up with all that back then."

Fagen drank his beer. He placed the bottle down on a fold-out wooden chair. "The sign said, OUR USED BALLS STILL HAVE DIMPLES. I been knowing your sister now six years. She told me. If I was you, I'd get over it. Seems to me your sister has more bruises than you do about your daddy taking off. You want to help her out, take some balls to the tables and sell them a dollar a dozen. Sooner or later your daddy'll come up to buy you out so's he ain't got competition."

"Come on now, Fagen," Tammy said. "We're out having fun." She racked the balls for a regular game of eight-ball.

Lamar said, "I'm not judging anybody, man."

Fagen said, "You right. I'm sorry." He turned around to select a cue stick. The back of his belt was one of that kind with a name branded into it. His said "LEONARD."

Lamar chalked his cue and raised his eyebrows to Tammy. "I started a tab up there. If you want another scotch and Dr Pepper just go put one on it."

Fagen turned around and looked down his stick for warp. He said, "What do you think the chances are that someone could break, and then all the balls came right back to where they once were? I'm talking, what are the chances that a man could knock hell out of the balls, have them scatter and ricochet all over the table, then land right back where they were racked, in the same order?"

Lamar said, "Not very good."

Fagen said, "I didn't think so." He broke. The two ball went in. Fagen said, "I guess it wasn't meant for me to do it a third time."

"WHEN WE'RE NOT sitting behind flea-market tables looking everybody in the face—or in your sister's case, on the hand—then we're at bars. When we're not in bars, we're at diners—Waffle Houses, Huddle Houses, American Waffles. When we're not eating or drinking, we're watching afternoon shows on TV. The people we're looking for don't go to movie theaters; they go to drive-ins. They don't go down to Atlanta to watch the Braves play; they sit in the front rows of professional wrestling." Fagen kept looking at the side pocket.

Lamar said, "Hey, how come you got LEONARD written on the back of your belt?"

"When we're not in bars, diners, drive-ins, or wrestling matches, we tend to drive up and down roads looking for people with car trouble. And I'm not talking about the interstates. The people we're looking for always take back roads, secondary roads. You ever looked at a Rand McNally and seen those little vacant lines where roads are going to be? That's where my daughter is now. That's where your father is. I'd almost bet that your father is with my daughter. I ought to kill you right now, just for mentioning it."

Fagen shot. The cue ball bounced around and knocked in the seven. He hadn't called anything beforehand. "Bought it cheap from a man down on his luck," Fagen said. "Didn't buy it from a man named Leonard, though. Bought it from a man named Eugene. Eugene got it from a man named Horace. Horace got it from Leonard in some kind of bar fight, I don't know. Horace had a lot of belts he sold to Eugene. He had one that said 'Cassius Clay.' Eugene promised that Horace used to be a real contender, in a way."

Lamar thought, *Maurice Fréchet came up with the idea of metric space in the year 1906.* He thought, *The tree roots of mathematics are algebra, plane geometry, trig, analytic geometry, and irrational numbers. The capital of Alabama is Montgomery.* "I bet that might be worth something. Cassius Clay. I'll be damned."

Tammy came back with a round for everyone. She said, "Y'all didn't wait for me? We could've played cutthroat, the three of us."

With his eyes Lamar said, "We are."

"I met a man one time said he fought Rocky Graziano. Not Rocky Marciano. Graziano. Said he fought him when Graziano was finished, after he'd quit fighting professional. They got in some kind of altercation in a bar, like men do. This old boy had a scar on his face shaped like an arrowhead. I believed him. Graziano had a way to twist his boxing glove twice on the skin before anyone knew what hit. He was one of them people who could pull out your heart while it still beat, I bet." Fagen shot hard into the far bank, hitting nothing. "Take over, Tammy. A couple boys just come in thinking they got good kidneys." He handed her his cue.

Fagen stared down Lamar, then winked. Lamar noticed the arrowhead-shaped scar beneath Fagen's left eye. "Is everyone in the flea market business a scam artist? This is like a foreign film. Goddamn, I feel like subtitles might be lined up at the bottom of my frame," Lamar said.

"Your food's ready, Tammy," someone yelled out from the other room.

Tammy placed her stick on the table. She looked at her watch. "We better take this to-go. It's late. We have to get up at four to get good tables next to each other down in Pickens."

Lamar said, "That's no problem. Sometimes I wake up at three and find myself going over square roots."

Lamar slept on the floor. When the telephone rang an hour into his sleep—when there was a pause before some child asked him if he was God—he said, "What's with you people? Tell your mother to find a reason to live, outside bothering me at all hours of the day and night." He couldn't fathom how they followed his trail all the way from Montgomery.

The child said, "This is Eddie. I'm calling my momma." Lamar sat up and reached for his cigarettes. "This is Eddie. Aunt JoJo said Momma lived here. Are you Jesus?"

Lamar stood up. He said, "This isn't funny anymore, kid," and hung up.

TAMMY TOOK A bottle of vodka down from the shelf and poured it into three flasks. She shook a halfgallon of orange juice, then poured it into a Coleman camping thermos.

She stretched her fingers back and forth.

Lamar rolled over on the floor, five feet away from the refrigerator. "I had the worst dream of my life. I must've woke up every five minutes. I know where our father is. He's in a telephone booth somewhere fucking with us. That's what I dreamt."

Tammy said, "We need to leave in about twenty minutes. If you want to sell golf balls you might want to take a shower. If you want to mill around with people, don't bother. It's going to be hot today."

"Somebody called up last night and messed with me. You can find anybody's movements on the Internet these days. They found me. All my parents down in Montgomery found me. They called and kept asking if I was God or Jesus. You don't have some kind of weird one-nine-hundred number do you? You don't have some kind of sex number where you talk dirty to women and say you're God, do you?"

Tammy put down the thermos. "Fuck. Fuck, fuck, fuck. I forgot." Lamar did two sit-ups and got up. "I met this woman at the store." She went to the phone and hit star sixty-nine.

Tammy memorized the number, called back, and got an answering machine. It was four o'clock in the morning. Aunt Jojo's voice said, "Way to go. You better plain find Special Eddie's momma so she can leave a message for her little girl."

Tammy felt her face redden. She waited after the beep, then said, "Hey, honey. It's been hectic up here. This is Mommy. I'm sorry that I missed your call. Please call me back between five and six o'clock tonight. I'll be here." Tammy spoke as if she tried to lure a stray dog toward her. She looked at Lamar. He shrugged, then took one of the flasks and drank straight from it. "Sometimes the devil is able to tap into our phone lines here, and that's what happened last night. But don't worry about me, and remember that I love you."

Lamar said, "It's okay to drink at the flea market? I don't remember Dad ever drinking behind the table."

"That's the difference between a man who believes in nothing and a man who still has hope, Lamar. Goddamn you, play along with some things every once in a while. The one thing you have to learn at the market is that you have to play along with people."

"What'd I do? What the hell, was that Fagen that called last night?"

"This isn't a good start to the day. I might know that I'm a fake, but I do believe in omens, voodoo, curses, karma, haints, specters, next-lifes, and that what-goes-aroundcomes-around theory. God's going to come down on me for what you've done, Lamar. I bet you a dollar not one person wants a palm read today."

Lamar put the flask in his hip pocket. "Listen. If you multiply two negatives you get a positive. That's all I have to say. When something goes wrong in life, I just try to find another negative. Then everything's back to normal." He bounced his head up and down like some kind of sideways metronome.

Madame Tammy reached down, squeezed his testicles, and said, "This is what our daddy used to do to me back when I wasn't but six years old. It's okay, understand. I'm not mad about it. I just want you to know."

Lamar placed his rolled fist back down. "Well. I guess that's the kind of negative you can't double." When Tammy showered he hit redial on the phone, got plain Eddie's aunt Jojo's answering machine, and said, "This is Saint Peter. I'm the gatekeeper guy. You can see your mother in person at the flea market this morning. I'm in charge of letting people in or out, and your mom's going to be out."

LAMAR DIDN'T THINK to steal egg cartons from behind Bi-Lo, Winn-Dixie, Food Lion, or Harris Teeter so he could display his unwashed balls to the public. The eight-by-four-foot tables at the Pickens County Flea Market weren't made up of anything but one-by-four pine strips, with an inch between the boards. Lamar set his balls down in rows and hoped the wind didn't blow them away.

"You don't know me," Tammy said. She shone her flashlight in his face. "No matter what happens, we don't know each other. If I yell out for help, don't come over the boundary, Lamar." She drug her pointy shoe on the red clay.

Tammy kept a fake crystal ball and real tarot cards on her table. Lamar only had his balls. They were across from Fagen with his pelts, and a guy named Weigel who seemed to specialize in alligator heads and turtle shells. Weigel kept saying, "Snappa, snappa, snappa, snappa," when people walked by shining their own flashlights on his products.

"Golf balls. Golf balls. Balls for golf," Lamar said.

Madame Tammy didn't talk.

"When it's dark, we want light. When it's light, we want cloud coverage," Fagen said. "When the woman comes by wanting table rent we wish we were invisible."

Lamar laughed. He pointed at Fagen and said, "Listen to this one— the summit angles of a Saccheri quadrilateral are equal. Dig: the line joining the midpoints of the equal sides of a Saccheri quadrilateral is perpendicular to the line joining the midpoints of the base and summit."

Fagen held one rabbit pelt in midair before setting it down on his table. "You talk like that to regular people, boy, you won't sell your balls."

Tammy didn't hold her hands together as if in prayer or anything, but she kept her head down and seemed to concentrate. She said, "Lamar, you've turned into an idiot. Please don't tell me that you're an idiot."

Weigel said, "There's a difference between a crocodile and an alligator. I've seen gators. I go down to Florida and kill me alligators every winter. I don't go to Africa for crocodiles. There's where crocodiles live. In Africa. They got different noses and teeth. They're different."

Fagen walked away from his table and said, "This is Tammy's brother. You ain't got to sell him. He knows you ain't ever wrestled a real alligator."

The sun barely labored itself upwards on the horizon. "Twelve balls, one dollar!" Lamar yelled. He'd been to flea markets over the years and knew the going rate was usually four-for-a-dollar, at best. Already people walked the tables, mostly antique dealers looking for cheap yellowware, or stolen service-station signs. Lamar said to everyone who came by, "If you see another guy selling golf balls, tell him I'll sell my entire stock for twenty bucks." It seemed the quickest way to lure his father.

Tammy looked up at the fading stars. Fagen said, "Don't sell off all your stock at once, Lamar. If you do that, you'll just end up sitting in front of an empty table. If you leave, then some asshole wanting to get rid of his pit-bull puppies will show up, and no one can sell with pit bulls in the vicinity, I swear."

Lamar handed Fagen the flask. "Oh, I got more balls in the van. I'm just saying that. I got it under control."

Madame Tammy said, "I'm undergoing a vision wherein you need to go find another job teaching math, far, far away. I'm having a vision that there are geometry-deprived students in Alaska, Lamar."

By EIGHT-O'CLOCK—not two hours into daylight—no other golf ball dealer had taken Lamar's bait. He'd sold a few dozen balls to regular customers, though, and after the woman came by wanting the five dollars for table rent Lamar stood only two dollars in the hole. He didn't respond to Weigel or Fagen when they remarked how it was probably a good thing that he got out of education. Tammy sat in her foldout metal chair and watched the crowd. When this full-time flea-market wheeler-dealer came up to her and said, "I got a proposition—you tell people that their lives will turn around if and only if they go buy a yardstick, slide rule, or micrometer from me, then I'll give you ten percent of the profit," Tammy shook her head no. "I don't believe in measurements. Measurements cause wars, ultimately. I won't have anything to do with that. To be honest, I've gotten caught up in this game before and it just didn't work out."

Lamar looked over to the man and said, "We use a baseten method. But there are cultures that go by base three, or base sixty. Look it up. It's in the history of mathematics."

The man selling measuring devices walked away as Lamar tried to arrange his balls on the table to give a specific example. He was engrossed in showing how some cultures have a counting system that goes, "One, two, two and one, two twos, many," when plain little Eddie and her aunt Jojo walked straight up to Madame Tammy's table.

Tammy recognized the woman immediately, and pulled the gossamer veil over her face—not so much to hide herself from the kid as from Aunt Jojo. Aunt JoJo said, "Special Eddie? This woman here can conjure up your momma. She can use your momma's voice, just like in them seance movies we watch Friday nights."

Lamar looked up. Aunt Jojo's normal voice came out as if she spoke to someone a hundred yards away. Even Fagen and Weigel knew something different and decidedly odd was going on at the flea market that morning.

Tammy said, "I'm doing fine, Eddie."

The little girl looked up. Tammy figured out that Eddie wasn't more than ten years old. She wore a pair of overalls and had pigtails. Her blank, flat face pretty much worked as an advertisement for what her future held: a ninth-grade education at most, two children by the age of eighteen, a single-wide mobile home, and a husband who'd beat her whenever possible. Little Eddie said, "I done good on my spelling test, Momma." She spoke to Madame Tammy in the same way a child speaks to big walking stuffed animals at Disney World or Chuck E. Cheese.

Lamar looked up from his balls. He said, "Spelling's important, but math's best." No one looked his way.

Madame Tammy said, "Run for your life, Eddie. That's all I have to tell you. Move to another state. Stick out your thumb and hitchhike to Iowa or Wisconsin as soon as possible. Don't eat any more sausage, white bread, Vienna sausages, baloney, or bacon. Kick in the television set. Never, ever watch afternoon talk shows. And don't let anyone ever, ever take you to the flea market again."

The girl pointed at Tammy and said, "That's my mommy." She turned and looked at Aunt Jojo. Eddie said, "One, two, three, four, five, six," evenly.

Aunt Jojo lurched across Madame Tammy's table, knocked over the crystal ball, scattered the tarot cards, and grabbed for Tammy's neck. Tammy tried to hold the woman back, tried to use what yoga and tae kwon do knowledge she had to repel the attacker. Aunt Jojo spit, clawed, and yelled, "Don't you talk to your own baby that way. We're doing the best we can do, and not getting no money for it."

Lamar picked up one golf ball and threw it hard. He hit the woman in the left temple and stunned her momentarily. Fagen and Weigel rounded their respective tables and pulled the woman down to the ground. A crowd appeared and circled the area.

Fagen said, "That might run her out of business for good. When a seer can't see trouble right in front of her, she ain't doing her job."

Madame Tammy unraveled her veil. She reached out for Eddie, led her to the van, and drove away.

"I SAW EVERYTHING that happened. I got my table over there, and I saw it all. If you need some kind of witness, I'm the one. I'm Heidi." Heidi stuck out her hand to Lamar. She pointed again toward her table, filled with milk glass. "I've been waiting for something like this to happen here. I'm surprised it hasn't happened sooner."

Fagen said, "Goddamn, Heidi. When did you come back? I heard you moved to California or something. I heard you gone back to teaching college."

Aunt Jojo shook her head twice, looked around confused—kind of like a fainting goat, Lamar thought—and instead of yelling out, "Where's my baby, where's my baby?" like in any ordinary documentary, she only brushed off her pantsuit and walked away. Was she embarrassed? Did she hope that no one saw what happened? Did she think to herself, Well, that's taken care of? When she got about five tables down the row she turned and said, "I was wondering when God was going to let me know what should happen."

Lamar smiled and waved at her. He turned to Heidi and said, "I used to teach. You used to teach? Man, what happened? I was teaching only a week ago."

Heidi said, "That woman attacked that woman."

Lamar said, "No. Not that. I mean, what is it that drove you to work flea markets?"

Fagen walked back across to his table. Aunt JoJo walked out of sight. Heidi smiled and shook her head. Weigel said, "Snappa, snappa, snappa, snappa."

Lamar said, "Somebody's got to give me a ride back. My sister's left me."

Heidi said, "I don't know what happened." Then she said she could take Lamar wherever he wanted to go right after eleven o'clock. She said she'd never sold a piece of milk glass after eleven, that she'd not taken any kind of poll about it or marked down a calendar, but that's the way things worked out. "Plus, that guy selling all of the rulers and whatnot is going to start bothering me pretty soon, if I remember his ways correctly."

LAMAR HAD NO more bags, what with his sister gone. He didn't have his full allotment of golf balls. He stood there watching everyone, content with waiting. Lamar watched Heidi across the gravel walkway and a few tables down. He thought, *I still don't believe in chance, but things aren't looking so bad.*

He thought, *cos a=cos b cos c + sin b sin c cos A*, for no reason in particular. Weigel and Fagen watched him nonstop, and he felt their stares. Lamar nodded at them occasionally, and even told men who came by his table that if they were looking for a deal, they should go buy a pelt, or Davy Crockett hat, or an alligator head.

Now, in the real world Lamar and his new colleagues would've worried about Madame Tammy; they would have packed up and driven up the mountain and found a way for Tammy to either turn herself in or take plain little Special Eddie back to her aunt's house. No one would've put the incident somewhere in the back of his head, only to bring it up later inside a bar where Fagen was conning some frat boy into betting who'd pee first. In the real world this incident of mistaken mother, chance, and loud-mouthed unemployed brother would not end up in the Rolodex of flea market stories on a par with how Frank McNutt and his kid Jacob used to sell Sears Silvertone radios when Jacob crawled into them with his tiny transistor radio, et cetera.

From what everyone understood later, Madame Tammy got the girl home and simply held her for a good twenty-four hours before calling the Department of Social Services and explaining things. On different occasions Tammy would tell people that she told the little girl that there was no God whatsoever, or that God indeed took care of everyone. It's pretty much documented that she made plain Eddie repeat, "The bleak shall inherit some mirth," over and over until she got it right.

In the real world someone would've stayed with Madame Tammy for more than a week, just to make sure she overcame the depression that set in, the extended hours of walking back and forth in her small silent house.

Heidi packed up her milk glass in old newspaper and packed her trunk. She almost skipped over to Lamar and asked if he was ready to go. They left. Ten minutes later a tiny man walked up to Fagen and said, "I heard that some fellow this way sold golf balls cheap. He leave already?"

Fagen pointed at the empty table. "Boy had to go check on his sister. He was selling twelve for a dollar when he was here."

"Damn. I get me four bucks a dozen. Course mine are clean. I scrub mine down with Clorox and all. I use me a toothbrush. I ain't one them men sticks the cuts and scruffs downward in the egg carton."

Fagen nodded. "Good for you. You seem like a real moral man. You should've been here earlier. There were a bunch of teachers who seemed to have problems. Maybe you could've helped them out. You could've been named Mayor of Flea Market."

The man looked at Lamar's empty table again. He said, "I used to be a stuntman out in Hollywood. I've fallen off ten-story buildings, and been drug by wild horses."

Fagen smiled. He asked the man if he drank beer much, if he'd like to see a stunt Fagen could do with his bladder. The man said he couldn't. He said that he'd had to retire, and came back south in order to track down his son and daughter. And although Fagen knew deep down that this man was Shorty—Madame Tammy and Lamar's father—he didn't ask, or offer information. Like everyone else in the flea-market business, Fagen knew that this man might be faking it, that he might work for some branch of the government, that he might be trying to chum up with everyone in order to make a bust.

Fagen looked at Weigel. They packed their wares simultaneously and drove away while Madame Tammy's father pulled out a ripped and faded photograph of two children.

FRESH MEAT ON WHEELS

BEFORE CEREMONIALLY BURNING DOWN A LIFE-SIZED replica of the Calloustown Courthouse—which never existed in the first place—built over the previous year in a field adjacent to Mr. Morse's tree farm and nursery, it was tradition to take every sixth-grader to the various attractions nearby. This included the Finger Museum, where a man had severed digits floating in formaldehyde from all the pulpwood men who had chainsaw accidents over the years. Then we would all go, via minibus, to a taxidermist's place where he'd set up The Safest Petting Zoo Ever. Our sixth-grade teacher, Ms. Whalen, said we were to understand what there is to appreciate about our hometown before viewing what General Sherman could've done if he'd understood Calloustown's meaningfulness, and not veered away on his march between Savannah and Columbia. My heart wasn't into this bastardized field trip because—and it's not like I had ESP back then—I foresaw the possible arguments, fistfights, and one-upmanship that would occur. If I had extrasensory perception back then I would've found my mother in the organic berry field she and my father operated and said something like, "Please tell me the sexual intercourse y'all have told me about is not like sticking your penis in an armpit filled with deep-cleansing moisturizer."

Since the invention of the minibus, sixth-grade boys at Calloustown Elementary spent the night at Ms. Whalen's house, for early in the morning her husband, whom up until this point I'd always thought an otherwise good man named Ben who somehow broke away from local DNA and closed-mindedness, would get us together and drive us around the countryside in order to point out what General Sherman missed by swerving away from Calloustown. The sixth-grade girls, I learned, all stayed at the other sixth-grade teacher's house, a woman named Ms. Harrell, in order to learn about what was going to happen to their bodies soon. I don't know if it's true or not, but before the minibus the Calloustown kids stayed at other ex-teachers' households for the night before embarking on mule-led wagons. And before the mules, those poor Calloustown kids had to plain walk to, say, the Finger Museum, which probably only held one finger on display.

"Do not bring up how we're Democrats, Luke," my mother reminded me as she pulled up to Ms. Whalen's house. "If anyone asks you if you're a Christian, it's best to go ahead and lie. What's it going to matter, seeing as we don't go to church anyway? If your teacher offers you a baloney sandwich for breakfast, just go ahead and eat it seeing as it's not going to kill you much."

I said, "Why am I here again? What's going on?"

My mother put the car in neutral, and then seemed to experiment with reverse and one of the lower gears. She said, "Are they not teaching you any existentialism at Calloustown Elementary?"

I didn't get it. I said, "Tell me again who Sherman was?" It's not like I wasn't from the South—it's just that my parents watched the news at night, and read books written by people who won awards, and they didn't sit around moaning about how things could've been, like my classmates' parents seemed to do. "And go through Jesus again, just in case."

My mother laughed. She leaned over and kissed my forehead and said, "You'll be fine. I got you some special gray flannel pajamas packed up for you to wear so you'll fit in. I tried to draw a stars and bars on your sleeping bag but it just came out a giant X. If anyone asks, say it faded and ran in the washing machine."

I didn't get those remarks, either. I said, "It's Valentine's Day. Do they do this everywhere on Valentine's Day?"

General Sherman burned Columbia, South Carolina, on February 17, 1865. According to the denizens of Calloustown, he should've burned their town on the fifteenth, if he had any sense of the right thing to do, on his way back north.

My mother said, "More or less."

GENERAL SHERMAN DIDN'T consider our ancestors' town worthy of torching, and the consequences, over the next seven or eight generations, weren't unpredictable: a miniscule region of highvoiced men and women whose families intermarried endlessly, producing higher-voiced offspring, ad infinitum, all Yankee-hating, distrustful stump grinders and third-shift health professionals at what still got called the Calloustown Home for the Feeble and Discouraged. I exaggerate, but not much. Beginning in sixth-grade civics class a variety of students would blurt out, "Sherman didn't think Fairview Plantation was good enough to burn! Shows you what he knew! They got them four bedrooms there, and two roomses!" et cetera, their larynxes squealing in such in-credulous-filled manners that at times—say later in South Carolina history class, or eleventh-grade American history when the Civil War section took up two nine-week grading periods—it sounded like one of those trick crystal glass band members wet-fingering a rim ceaselessly. It sounded like the emergency broadcast system's television test most days when the prodigy of Munsons and Harrells wailed out their disgust in regards to William Tecumseh Sherman's notions of aesthetics: "What's so good about Atlanta, Savannah, or Columbia? Sherman was stupid! He said he wanted to march to the sea, and Calloustown starts with a C."

I hate to think that I've always considered myself of a higher ilk than the typical Calloustowner hell bent on grasping worthful arson, but it's true to a degree. My parents arrived at my place of training only after surrendering law practices right before offers of partnership. They cashed in some savings, did some research, bought the cheapest arable land available in Zone 8 in regards to that Hardiness Scale, began an organic farm long before it became commonplace and chic, and then had their only child—me—in their late thirties. By "long before" I might really mean 1981, right after the Iranian hostages got released. Because of the hostages and a certain doomful outlook regarding economic growth and detente, and without doing research on how vengeful their new neighbors had become, my parents settled on a crossroads known neither to blues songs nor sulfurous flame.

I grew up with Munsons and Harrells alike pissed off that someone considered our cows, sheep, hogs, and chickens inedible, our women unattractive, our spring houses tainted. Maybe that's why my mother never allowed me to read the Bible in general, and Job's story in particular. It's a wonder that more than a few of us non-Munsons and -Harrells escaped with self-esteem higher than a collard stalk.

"If they ask you if you hunt, say yes. Fish, yes. Hate everyone north of Virginia, yes. If stupid Bobby Harrell asks you again about your pets, say you own a cottonmouth and a fire ant farm." My mother had a whole list that she went over daily as I shoved books in my backpack. My father started every morning reciting Latin terms he knew by heart before entering his torporous berry patches. "If one of the Munson boys keeps asking you if you've been with a girl, here," my mother would say, pouring Chicken of the Sea tuna water on my palm. "Tell him to sniff your finger."

That was another little action or saying that I didn't get, of course. But the half-feral cats that lived inside the school liked me, which, of course, got me called Pussy.

MR. WHALEN SAT in his living room with a fishing pole. There were bags of store-bought ice all around the hole he'd fashioned into the floor, and the hook on the end of his line descended down into a crawlspace. Bobby, Donnie, Larry, and Gary Munson held poles, too, as did Lonnie, Ronnie, Billy, and Stonewall Harrell. These were my classmates. These were my sleepover comrades the night before the "What Does Sherman Know?" annual festival.

"Get you a pole, there, Luke," Mr. Whalen said. "We're playing a little game called Ice Fishing in Minnesota. We don't got no need to ice fish around these parts ever, so I thought I'd teach you boys a little bit about it."

I said hello to all of the two-syllable-named classmates. None of them said anything back. I said, "Do you have fish in the basement?"

"We're fishing for rats and mice," Ben Whalen said. He patted the lid to a plastic cooler next to him, as if there were caught vermin inside. "Put you a chunk of cheese on your hook and drop it on down."

These were bamboo poles, probably macheted over on the edge of Mr. Morse's tree farm. I threw my line into the hole and squeezed in between Gary and Lonnie. I tried to peer down into the hole, but couldn't tell how deep it was. I said, "Did you cut this hole in the floor by yourself?" because I couldn't think of anything else to say.

Bobby Munson yelled out, "Luke ain't a Christian!"

I said, because I'd been taught to do so, "I'm the only one here named after somebody in the Bible. There isn't a Book of Bobby."

"Boys," Mr. Whalen said. "This is all of y'all, right?" He drank from a plastic cup, and I could smell the booze in it. "Boys, while I got you all here I might as well use this opportunity to tell you about the birds and the bees, it being Valentine's Day and all."

Later on I figured out that because we had no male teachers in the sixth grade, one of the teachers' husbands would have to take over. Over at the girls' sleepover, it probably wasn't so uncomfortable for a woman to explain sex.

I think it was Lonnie Harrell who said, "My grandmother has a beehive in her backyard."

"I got pictures of my grandmother with a beehive hairdo," one of the Munsons said.

"I ain't talking about real birds and bees," Mr. Whalen said. "Let's pretend that I'm talking about mice and, and... I don't know. Let's just say I'm talking about mice, seeing as they reproduce like all get-out." He took a big swig from his cup.

My sixth-grade teacher came in the room carrying a tray. She wore blue jeans, which kind of freaked everyone out, and said, "Who wants some Pepsi?"

You'd think none of the Munson or Harrell kids had ever had Pepsi, which might've been true. Half of them dropped their poles down into the hole and rushed our teacher. They grabbed and kicked each other out of the way. Me, I sat there thinking about something else my parents had told me: "Pepsi Cola" rearranged came out "Episcopal." So I said, loudly, "We drink Pepsi Cola all the time at our house because it's 'Episcopal.' That's what we drink. At my house. Because it's a Christian drink."

Everything seemed to stop. It wasn't my imagination that all of my male classmates shut up and turned to me as if I'd spoken in tongues. Ms. Whalen—I should mention that her maiden name was Munson—said, "What did you say, Luke?"

I said, "I mean, we drink Gatorade."

I didn't think I had said anything blasphemous—in retrospect, I think all these children of Pentecostals had never heard of another denomination, except for maybe Baptist. I was glad that Mr. Whalen broke the tension by yelling, "I got one, I got one, I got one," and then pulling up a fake mouse that, like a blue crab breaking the surface and experiencing air, he somehow got to let go of the cheese and drop back down into the crawlspace.

My sixth-grade teacher screamed and took off running for the kitchen. My classmates brought their Pepsis back, and one of them said, "Hey, Luke, go under the house and get our poles we dropped."

I said, "You dropped them down there. You go get them."

"You scared to go under the house, son?" Ben Whalen said. Yeah, Mr. Whalen. You'd think that Lonnie, Donnie, or Ronnie would've dared me, not my sixth-grade teacher's husband, a man I'd up to that point thought to have escaped inbreeding disasters.

"Luke rhymes with puke," Bobby said.

I don't know why I thought it necessary to prove myself, to say, "Somebody at least give me a flashlight."

I WALKED OUTSIDE the Whalens' house and didn't look back to see if anyone stared at me through the window. I could've walked home—it wasn't but a mile—but I knew my parents would've been disappointed. Somewhere between my father mumbling, *"A fronte praecipitium a tergo lupi"* and, *"Ubi fumus, ibi ignis,"* he always said to me that enduring frost only made one stronger. I walked up to Mr. Whalen's six-wheeled truck—this is why I thought he had escaped the normal Munson/Harrell mindset—a silver refrigeration vehicle that he drove around a few-county area with FRESH MEAT ON WHEELS written on the panels. He offered people ribeyes and filets and hamburger patties, chicken and fish and pork chops, for prices much lower than

Winn-Dixie, Bi-Lo, or the A&P—grocery stores that might be thirty miles from Calloustown.

I went around the side of the house and paid attention not to get snagged by briars or the Whalens' neighbor's pit bull on a long chain, and then the back of the house where a short door led to the crawlspace. I turned on the flashlight and thought, Somehow this is going to *keep me being made fun of.* In a normal world kids would say, "That Luke—he's brave." But in the land of Calloustown, a day before the "What Does Sherman Know?" celebration, it would probably come out that I was one with Satan, what with my non-fear of all things rabid that live beneath our abodes.

I got in and waved my light around. As it ended up, the Whalens' crawlspace was nearly high enough to count as a basement—six feet high, at least, where the hole stood—with a hand-troweled cement floor. I found the dropped bamboo poles right away, and saw light streaming in from above. I took a few steps and heard Stonewall say, "That's not how I learned how it works," then took a few more steps. Mr. Whalen yelled down, "Are you there, Luke?" but I didn't respond.

I walked right to the edge of the bastardized ice hole and heard my sixth-grade teacher's husband say, "That is how it works. It's just like this here hole. The sperm's the cheese, and the hole's the hole, and once the cheese hits the hole it don't take long for a baby to come out of the hole. The rat."

I was twelve. We were all twelve. Mr. and Ms. Whalen didn't have children at this point, and perhaps this was why. I yelled up at the hole, "Here," and started shoving poles upward. Somebody, one of my class-mates, yelled back down at me, "Don't step on any of the babies down there."

Somebody else said something about a stork, and then Mr. Whalen said loudly, "I give up," and, "Monetta, I've done my job here." Then he might've fallen over, for there was a noise, and one of the Harrell kids said, "Are you all right?"

I wasn't paying attention much. I'd come across a cache of Matchbox cars—vintage ones, though I didn't know the difference at the time. Someone had built a miniature Grand Prix road course of sorts, com-plete with barriers, army men onlookers, trees fashioned from those col-ored-cellophane toothpicks, and what appeared to be the Calloustown

Courthouse that never existed in the first place. I might've said, "Hey, can we play down here later?"

Or I might've kept it to myself, thinking that if Mr. and Ms. Whalen ever die in a fiery wreck, I'm coming back down here to get some things before anyone else finds them. Again, my parents hadn't gone over those Ten Commandments at this point, especially the one about coveting your neighbor's 1:43-scale die-cast toy cars.

I walked into the circle of light and looked up at all the little Munson and Harrell blank faces looking down at me. I said, "What's going on up there?"

Mr. Whalen reappeared and said, "Hey, I got an idea. We might as well go through the whole nine-month process," and he told the boys to throw their hooks back down. To me he said, "Hey, Luke, do me a favor. This is going to be fun! Place all the hooks around your belt loops. Go ahead! I won't let you get hurt none."

Ms. Whalen's sixth-grade boys pulled me up through the hole in her den floor. I have no clue what kind of test line they used, or how the bamboo poles didn't break under my weight hanging there in the crawl-space, but Ben Whalen told me to start screaming like crazy, and I did. What else was I supposed to do? I couldn't see any of my unlikely deliverers, for they'd had to back down the hallway pulling.

Mr. Whalen stood there leaning against a bookcase that held a dictionary, a number of ashtrays, some candles, and framed photographs of dead deer. He yelled out, "Okay, y'all run back in here," as I gathered myself on the lip of the hole, surrounded by ice bags.

No one said, "Are you all right?" Ms. Whalen yelled from a back room something about how we needed to settle down so as not to fall back in the hole.

Ben Whalen said, "And that's how a baby is born, but without the ice or clothes that Luke is wearing."

MY TEACHER'S HUSBAND shoved what ice hadn't melted over the hole's lip. He slid the makeshift hatch over his own crawlspace, and covered the exposed wood with a rug that wasn't much bigger than the jagged edges it needed to hide. "I'm going to make a spiral staircase down there one day," he said, apparently to himself.

I said nothing about all the cool Matchbox cars my sixthgrade classmates and I would sleep directly over. I wanted to tell someone about it, but already understood that, if I revealed what I had discovered, somehow a Donnie, Lonnie, Gary, or Billy would label me a big baby for liking toy cars over the real ones that they swore they drove around all the time when their parents weren't home.

My teacher said, "Now, no horseplay tonight, boys. Y'all stretch out your sleeping bags in here and go to sleep. Mr. Whalen will be waking y'all up early-early-early. 'What Does Sherman Know?' is a long and tiring day. I made some special treats for tomorrow in the freezer, so don't go around snooping."

"Goodnight, Ms. Whalen," we said in unison. I have no idea what happened to her husband, but I heard the back door squeak open while our teacher warned us against cutting fool all night.

She turned off the lights. We made no noise. Then Stonewall Harrell giggled. He'd commandeered the flashlight at some point after I got birthed. Stonewall said, "I know what a woman's nookie looks and feels like for real. It ain't like what he told us."

I don't want to say that my organic-farming, ex-corporatelawyering parents sheltered me. But I'd never come across this "nookie" term. I knew poontang, beaver, snatch, trim, twat, quim, muff, quif, box, cooter, and meat wallet, but not nookie.

Lonnie and Donnie said, "No, you don't," and then there was a bunch of uh-huhs and don't neithers.

"I can prove it," Stonewall said. "Y'all cover me. I'm going into the bathroom."

I didn't mean to say nookie out loud, but I did just to get a feel for it. It's not the kind of word, I knew, that I could use daily, like when I said something about a box or beaver.

"Stonewall better not come back in here dragging along Ms. Whalen," Donnie said.

He didn't. No, Stonewall returned with a gigantic blue jar of women's nighttime facial cream. He said, "What I'm about to show y'all is something my cousin taught me last year. Now, everyone slop some of this stuff on your wiener, and then come stick your wiener in my armpit." He slung off his T-shirt and got down on his knees. "You got to close your eyes, though, for it to work best."

I'M NOT SURE what happened after that. This isn't one of those "selective memory" occasions. I'm not being judgmental for what those Munson and Harrell children did the night before "What Does Sherman Know?" but I didn't join in—perhaps because I thought a joke was being played on me. I got up from the floor and grabbed the flashlight. I went to the bookcase and opened up the dictionary to find everything marked out by black Magic Marker. It's like an entire language disappeared, page after page. I turned to the G's to see if maybe they'd left "God" there, but they hadn't. I turned to the J's, for Jesus, but it was marked out, too. I picked up the dictionary—this was one of those Thorndike Barnhart red hardbacks, probably stolen from our classroom at Calloustown Elementary—and went out the front door with it. I walked without paying attention, as if on automatic pilot—which they say General William Tecumseh Sherman mastered above all else—and skirted the briars and next-door pit bull successfully. No noises emanated from the den at this point. I opened the door to beneath the house and found Mr. Whalen seated cross-legged, surrounded by his Matchbox car collection. He had a drop light hanging from a floor joist, and he didn't turn his head.

"You want to play a little game I like to call 'What Does Henry Ford Know?'" he asked me. "You want to play a little game I like to call 'What Does Detroit Got that We Don't?'" I should've jumped, but I didn't. I should've either said yes or no instead of pointing to the floorboards above me and whispering, "They're fucking each other's armpits upstairs with your wife's Noxzema."

Mr. Whalen said, "Now, not everyone likes a tattletale, Luke. I do, though, so you came to the right place." He handed me his plastic cup, told me to take a drink if I wished—I did, only to learn that he partook of Pepsi and George Dickel, a combination I'd had before—and got up from the cement floor without grunting. He whispered, "Unfortunately, your teacher threw away all the boxes to these cars. They'd be worth a lot more money if I still had the boxes. Don't forget that, Luke. Sometimes a box is more valuable than what goes inside it."

Years later I would realize that he still worked on his sex lesson. I said, "Yes sir."

"What're you doing with that dictionary?" he asked me quietly. I shrugged. He leaned in closer and said, "I blacked out every word in there except for *desperation*. Go ahead. Turn to page 275. I keep waiting for Monetta to open the thing up. Maybe she already knows all the words inside."

I drank more from his cup, not thinking.

MR. WHALEN KEPT a stepladder in his crawlspace, of course. I took a theater appreciation class in college my freshman year and learned three things: If there was a pistol on the set, it would be fired at the end of the first act; if there was a telephone on the bedside, it would ring, usually not on cue. I learned, too, that most drama majors were obnoxious and insecure, and that if they didn't make it in a summer rep group they'd go off to law school, eventually get disenchanted should they have any sense whatsoever, then finally give it all up in order to farm berries, sing campfire songs spontaneously, and teach their children most of the euphemisms for female genitalia.

So I wasn't surprised or shocked when my sixth-grade teacher's drunken husband said to me, "Let's stand this aluminum ladder up right under the hole where I'm going to eventually build a spiral staircase." He kicked it open, then tested the floor for balance. Ben Whalen held his index finger to his mouth for me to be quiet, then took his plastic cup of booze from me.

Here's the scariest segment out of the most freakish night in my life up until this time: Mr. Whalen offered no pantomime hand gestures á la high school ROTC members obsessed with semaphore. He looked at me once, didn't smile, and we simultaneously climbed up both sides of the stepladder—he on the DO NOT USE FOR STEPS side, and me on the traditional silver treads—like Olympic-caliber synchronized swimmers, or champion ax men at a logging competition in the Pacific Northwest, or adjacent geysers at a national park. Ben Whalen put his plastic cup in his mouth, we placed our palms up to the makeshift hatch, and shoved hard so mightily and fast that not one Munson or Harrell child had time to react. Listen, these guys never exactly reacted quickly most days—thus all the bruises during baseball season—but you'd think that an eruption of floor below a cheap throw rug might cause four prone Harrells getting faux-screwed in the armpits by Noxzema-slathered Munsons to yelp, run, or fight before their discoverers underwent sensory-based deductions, which could only end, later on, in blackmail situations.

"What the hell you boys doing?" Mr. Whalen yelled out, even before the circle of floor tipped over entirely against the useless bookcase. He emerged into his living space, took two or three determined steps, and flipped the light switch. By the time I came out of the hole all of my sleepover comrades rushed to find their pajama bottoms and hide both erections and tainted, compromised armpits. There would be talk of my being "born again," within the next six months, and—like an iconic unseemly act performed in public by a celebrity—by the time I left Calloustown for good it seemed as though everyone aged twelve to forty had been present and witnessed the occasion. "What the hell you boys doing to each other?"

Before anyone could answer—and I'll admit that I started laughing uncontrollably, which is why I don't play poker—our sixth-grade teacher flew into her own, now corrupted, den. She got that look on her face that meant "I'm calling your daddy," and without raising her voice much said, "Get your clothes back on, boys." She reached down to the floor, picked up her fouled jar of night cream, and said, "Where'd y'all get this?"

Oddly, she looked straight at her husband. Did I mention that he never set down his plastic cup throughout the spooky entrance, or how a pint bottle peeped out of his left back pocket?

"We was just playing a game," one of the Munson boys said.

I quit laughing long enough to say, "Playing Pin the Pecker on an Armpit," and, perhaps affected by a jigger's worth of good bourbon, lost my balance and fell back down the hole, half-sliding down the ladder's stringers.

You'd think that I'd've heard one of the adults say, "Uhoh" or "Are you okay?" I swear, though, between terra firma and the cement floor I heard my sixth-grade teacher say, "No wonder Sherman swerved from this wasteland."

≋≋

I REGAINED CONSCIOUSNESS with my head against a dirt mound built for Matchbox car coasting. Jefferson Davis and Robert E. Lee stood beneath my eyes, and Jeb Stuart covered my upper lip. Ms. Whalen held the three in place, delicately. What would've been our little surprise treats sometime between the Finger Museum and the Stuffed Wild Animals petting zoo—Kool-Aid frozen in ice-cube trays, with plastic confederate soldiers frozen into them to be used as handles—now worked a secondary mission, namely to keep the swelling down from the tumble I took down Mr. Whalen's imaginary ice hole/vagina.

I woke up and said, "What day is it?" like that, like I always had done in the past after getting knocked out.

My teacher shushed me and said, "You're a different kind of Calloustowner, Luke."

Upstairs, though I didn't know it at the time, all the Munson and Harrell boys had been locked up inside the Fresh Meat on Wheels refrigeration truck in order to keep them out of the way and unable to call their parents. Somehow, if I knew the parents of Calloustown, the entire Noxzema incident would be interpreted as the Whalens' fault. She'd get released from her teaching duties, and every Harrell and Munson would go back to eating non-fresh meat bought from a grocery store chain's amateur butcher.

"I called his parents but didn't get an answer," Ben Whalen said to his wife.

I sat up and said, "I like the ambulance best," referring to the Lomas Ambulance #14 Matchbox car that Mr. Whalen—during playtime—had backed beside a #57 fire truck, both of which were in front of a #13 Dodge wrecker, which seemed to be aiding the grenade-throwing army man who had just wrecked his #73 Mercury station wagon.

"You don't need an ambulance," Ms. Whalen said. "By the time an ambulance gets here you'll have healed these bumps and grown new ones." She took Jeb Stuart off my lip and put him in her own mouth. "You're okay, comparatively."

I said, "I think my parents drove down to Columbia to see a movie, that's where they are." I got up and said, "I'm okay."

Mr. Whalen didn't offer me another sip of George Dickel. He said, "I got a good mind to leave them boys in the truck for the rest of the night. We got any Pine-Sol? I need to go scour down the den from whatever emissions those boys made up there."

My teacher leaned in to look at my pupils. I thought she wanted to kiss, but she said, "What's the capital of Florida?"

Immediately I said, "Miami."

"He's all right," Ms. Whalen said, and her husband nodded.

We walked out the crawlspace door. When we passed Mr. Whalen's work truck he banged on the panels hard a few times. Inside the house my teacher put on some rubber gloves and covered the hole in the floor, then the rug, then scooted a table over the hole. She told me to try my parents again, I think just to see if I could remember the number. My mother answered on the first ring. She said she and my father had decided against going to a movie, that they'd been there all night, that the phone hadn't rung. I told her she needed to come get me, and when she asked why I didn't say, "Because I know anatomy," or "I don't fit in," or "There's a chance I'll turn to alcoholism if I stay here much longer," or, "My teacher doesn't know state capitals." I said, "I hit my head when we were playing freeze tag."

Ms. Whalen took the receiver from me, finally, and said to my mother, "Luke was It," among some other things. Again, in retrospect, I think she might've been speaking metaphorically.

So I missed another ceremonial burning of the Calloustown Courthouse. I heard later that Mr. Whalen's minibus didn't start up the next morning and that he had to drive my classmates around in the back of his work truck. Those idiots said they were surrounded by hanging meat for the entire day, by carcasses meant to be bought by their kin. I shrugged a lot over the next six years and lied back at them. I told them my father let me take dates out on his cherry picker once a year to see our hometown fake burn, and it worked in regards to getting girlfriends amorous. When, finally, I told my parents the truth about that one night I had with the Whalens, my father made a point to order a gigantic box of sausage, though he only cooked the patties and set them out for crows to eat, then fly around our hometown fouling windshields and rooftops. My father believed that a modern-day Sherman might act likewise.

LICKERS

THE MAN SAID HE FOUND HIS DOG ON THE FRONT PORCH one November, right before Thanksgiving. He said it was the truth, and that if he wanted to tell lies he'd've said Christmas, or Easter, or one of the other healing holidays. It caught me off guard, certainly, understand. While he went into a description of his dog's capabilities I stood there sockless at my front door trying to capture "healing holidays." Ash Wednesday, maybe? Independence Day probably made people feel better, especially recent immigrants. What about Valentine's Day? Me, I always felt ultimately worthless and destroyed on Valentine's Day—not healed in any human conception. I couldn't pay attention right off. The dog appeared to be part shepherd, part beagle, part Lab. Nothing special. She had long black and brown hair, flopped ears, legs a little too short for her body. The dog made decent eye contact, panted, and let her fat tongue loll out long to one side or the other.

"If you'd like to see some snapshots, I got them. And official documentation," the man said. "I have witnesses and phone numbers."

This was a Saturday morning. I'd lived in Gruel for a good year, trying to fit in. No one seemed anxious to make my acquaintance. The woman I bought bread from down at Gruel Bakery one time said, "You should try my special bread with Jesus crust," and two locals trying to perform trick shots down at Roughhouse Billiards once said thanks when I picked up their errant cue ball. But that was about it.

"I got a picture of a guy who says he zipped his pants up funny on his testicles. Oh, it cut him to pieces. Personally I think he had something else happen to him, like maybe he tried to cross a bob-wire fence one night drunk and cut himself something awful. But that's neither here or otherwise. What matters is I got a picture of his things sliced, and a other of good old Pam licking the sore, and then a other of it healed." He lowered his head and said quietly, "I don't show that picture to the women, by the way."

The man had an old-fashioned army knapsack with him that he pulled off his right shoulder. His hair stood up wild and funny gray on his head, wiry. He dug in and started pulling out three-by-fives. I said, "Your dog's named Pam? Pam?"

"This is Pam. Say hey, Pam."

Pam sat down and stuck out her right paw. I waved, and looked out in the front yard to see if some kind of hidden camera posse stood nearby, like on one of those TV shows. I bent down and shook Pam's paw. "Good dog. Sorry I don't have any kind of sore," I said.

"Here's a picture of a boil, before and after," the man said. He handed me Polaroids of a giant neck pimple and then of smooth skin. I didn't say, "Anyone could take a picture of a giant dermatological abrasion, and then another of someone else's smooth skin." I said, "Huh. How about that."

"Here's some more." He handed over photographs of cuts, scrapes, possible leprosy, oozing sores of one variety or another. Then he had the supposed cured areas in vivid color. He said, "Five dollars. You can't beat that. Try going down to a doctor in Forty-Five. It's thirty-five dollars just to walk into the door. And then you got drugs, salves, and ointments to pay for later. Try going to the Graywood Memorial Emergency Room. You ever noticed how if you turn GMER around it comes out GERM? There's a reason for that."

He wore a T-shirt that read MIRACLES HAPPEN, but no picture of Jesus underneath the statement. I sat down on my steps and pet the dog. I said, "What do you do, travel from town to town, healing people with Pam here? That's kind of cool. Someone should make a documentary."

"It don't matter none my name," the man said out of nowhere. He stood stiff, and had a look on him mostly captured by Confederate soldiers posed brave and defiant. "Let's just say my name's Seth. If I were a real doctor I'd have me a Seth-a-scope, you know what I'm talking?"

I didn't. If I were a doctor named Seth I'd probably try to pick up women by saying, "You want a little of the Seth-a-scope," like an idiot, poking my groin back and forth.

I stuck out my hand and said, "I'm Curt." *It's the first time I'd had the opportunity to introduce myself since moving to Gruel,* I thought. "I'm Curt." My parents might as well have named me Angry or Short-Tempered.

Seth shook my hand and Pam the healing dog stuck out her paw, all reflexes.

"You trying to tell me, Curt, that you ain't got a bruise, some joint pain, a blister, skin rash? Pam the healing dog can fix it all. Hey, I tell you what—you look honest enough—I can have her lick your needs, and then I'll come back the next day for the five dollars. I'll come back tomorrow. All's I'm asking is that you be honest with me."

Please understand that I'm not a sick man, physically or mentally, but for some reason I thought about this: What if I had some bad and persistent hemorrhoids? *Would this Seth fellow allow his dog to lick a man's butt?* I said, "Not a twinge, as far as I'm concerned. Hell, I'll give you five dollars if you're hurting for money, man."

Seth said, "I got pictures of Pam's work on sprained ankles. Tendonitis. This one old boy over in Forty-Five had a nervous tic she licked away, though it can't be documented very well on photographic paper. I needed to get me one them cameras with a fast shutter speed, so maybe the before picture would come out a blur what from the tic. Pam will lick away about anything, except hemorrhoids. I draw the line there. I won't let her lick some stranger's ass, excuse my language."

Can he read minds? I thought. "Okay. Now that you mention it. I was just trying you out, seeing how persistent you were. A long time ago I was a distance runner. This was maybe twenty-five years ago. Right into my freshman year in college. Anyway, I ran and ran, and I'm starting to think that the cartilage in my knees is pretty much worn away. Especially on wet fall days, my knees ache and throb."

"I've seen it before," Seth said. Pam the dog pricked up her ears. "Roll up your pants leg, son. Ready yourself for a miracle."

≥ ≤

I HAVE TO admit that Pam's healing session was more than pleasant. Not that I've ever spent money on a massage therapist of any kind, but I imagined that my experience with the dog was similar in a "non-deep tissue" kind of way. That dog licked and licked for a good hour. Seth walked around my front yard smoking cigarettes. I pet Pam's head and said things like, "You a good girl, aren't you?" Every once in a while she pulled back her lips and kneaded my knees for fleas in that way that only dogs can maneuver.

I said to Seth, "How can y'all live off five bucks a session? There's no way."

He said, "Well, it's five bucks for fifteen minutes, officially. I guess I should've mentioned that. Technically, you owe twenty dollars. But it's up to you. So far, Pam ain't had to take no more than fifteen minutes to heal a wound, you know."

I kind of felt the way I did when I first said, "Oh, hell, yeah—go ahead and give me some cable TV," not knowing that every little religious station added on at Charter Communications' whim would cost me more monthly. I said, "Yeah, you probably should've said something about that."

"But it don't matter. It's up to you. Tomorrow I'll come by, and you'll be honest, and you'll tell me whether or not your knees feel better. And then you'll either pay me what Pam deserves or you won't."

I stood up and rolled my pants legs down. I looked at the dog and said, "Thanks." To Seth I said, "It's been a known fact for years that a dog licking an open wound makes it heal quicker. I mean, when I was growing up and had a scab, my dog Dooley'd lick it."

Seth lit another cigarette. He looked out toward the Gruel skyline, which meant the back sides of four one-story brick buildings. "That's true, Curt. But I've had Pam's salivary glands tested. And I have documentation right here," he patted his wallet, "that states her spit—for some unknown reason—contains higher levels of stearic acid, sodium borate, allantoin, and methyl paraben. The doctor up at Duke who conducted all the tests said she also has a way of secreting acetaminophen that he'd never seen before. Oh, Pam's a medical mystery."

I'm no idiot. I understood that it didn't take much for a man like Seth to memorize the ingredients of any burn cream, plus an extra-strength headache powder. I thought to myself, *In a way that's my job, in a way.* I said, "Well. Whatever. I'd like to talk to that Duke boy. He might've gone to too many basketball games."

"Here you go," Seth said. "Goddamn it. It's true most people I run into haven't even heard of medical research, man. I'm glad to talk to someone who's been around. What're you doing in Gruel, of all places?"

I didn't go into how my wife left me for another man—a high school *guidance* fucking counselor she worked with up in Greenville where she taught social studies to tenth graders who couldn't pass the class in seventh, eighth, or ninth. I didn't say how I threw a goddamn dart hoping to hit Montana or Maine, that I'd made a promise to myself to go wherever it landed, and how the stupid thing landed only fifty miles south. I didn't say how there weren't many places in America where you could buy an antebellum house in need of slight repair for ten thousand dollars. I didn't say, "Fuck, if my dart had landed in the Bermuda Triangle I would've moved there." I said to Seth, "I could live anywhere. I work as a freelance indexer."

Pam sniffed my crotch. I tried not to view this as a sign.

"A freelance indexer. That has something to do with fingers?"

"Nope. Well, I guess in a way it does. Somebody writes a book with a lot of notes. A lot of citations. It's my job to read the book, and then have everything in alphabetical order at the back of the book. You've seen books like this, I swear. I do mostly biographies. Publishers call me up and send me manuscripts, and I filter everything out. You've seen it before. At the back of books."

I didn't go into where I'd made major contributions: books by or about Kissinger, Nixon, Bush, Reagan, Lucifer, and Satan.

"The backs of books. And now you're here."

I said, "With a dog licking my knees."

Seth looked left and right, pulled out his cigarette twice, and exhaled. He said, "Bubba, this ain't much of a town. What do you do in a town like this? What can I do for my dog here?"

I looked across the way. I lived on Old Old Greenville Road, in a Victorian house that...sure, the ceilings fell down throughout, and the roof looked like some giant sat on it, the gutters hung like weird incisors, the floor sagged in a way that made it impossible to walk from den to dining room—but otherwise it seemed a perfect place to freelance indices. I said, "I don't know. Here I am. But by goddamn I don't have a sore on my leg."

"Well."

Pam the dog cocked her head. I thought about doing a couple deep knee-bends, but didn't. I knew that I'd perform such things the next morning. I said, "It's been good meeting you, Seth. Pam."

Seth said, "Uh-huh," and looked at me like I was out of my mind. Index freelancer, you know. He said, "Tomorrow, Bubba. Tomorrow's Sunday." And then he gave me a look that might've said, I'll kill you if you don't come up with the money. Or maybe he gave me a look of You and me could drink some beer together. Sometimes I get those looks confused. I do know that my knees didn't have a hair on either one of them, if that matters, after Pam got done.

I PERFORM MY job the old-fashioned way: I keep a notebook open, I read, and I take notes with a pencil. Normally I place twenty-six little tabs at the top of the pages, A through Z. As I read, I place asterisks in the margins, and go to my notebook to jot down what I've found.

Let's pretend that I'm indexing a biography of, I don't know, Pavlov. I might have to turn to the S's under "Salivation" and write pages 1, 2, 4, 6-120, 122, 124-400, and so on. Under "Temper tantrum" I might only have to place down, "—with dog, 98," "—with wife, 360," or whatever. It's a meticulous job that I never mind, but one that a spouse might find both all-encompassing and anally retentive. As a matter of fact, if my ex-wife indexed my biography she'd probably have pages one to the end marked for obsessive-compulsive behavior. I don't care.

Since I had *moved* to Gruel my job as a freelance indexer was more or less at a standstill. I wouldn't call it a self-imposed hiatus, seeing as the publishing houses teamed together and quit sending me work. Evidently I'd gone too far on three successive books in a row from three separate presses—one on George Wallace, one on Jesse Helms, and another involving the 1994 Republican "Contract with America." Each one had pretty much the same section that began with the letter I. Under

"Idiotic behavior" I listed *every* page of each book. The same went for "Idiotic thought." Then I listed my own name under "Rational thought."

Hell, who knew that someone actually read those indices back at the publishing house? I'd *never* had a copy editor chosen for my own work. As far as I was concerned, I *was* the copy editor, in a way. But then some newly graduated do-gooder from Smith or Sarah Lawrence or Vassar who got a job somewhere between intern and courier decided to take a look at my work, told on me, and so on. I think she's probably senior editor now, at age twenty-three.

But I'm not pouting. You'd think, seeing as Marissa left me soon thereafter and I moved to a town named after the worst breakfast ever invented, that I'd've gone to cutting myself or holding my hands too close to a flame (bad indexer, bad, bad indexer) in such a way that would give Pam the healing dog a challenge. I didn't.

I woke up the next day at four a.m. as normal, and did my routine. In the old days I got out the book at hand and got to work. I know I've always told myself that I'd never be like my father, but I woke up two hours before dawn, got to work, and prided myself on being finished for the day before *The Today Show* finished. Then I could take a nap, watch the noon news, maybe practice horseshoes, most likely play about four thousand games of solitaire, wait for Marissa to get home from her job as a teacher of at-risk teens, listen to her stories about some nineteen-year-old tenth grader confused at there being a Washington, D.C., and an entire state with the same name, prepare supper for us, then go to bed. This occurred in Raleigh, Charlotte, Greensboro, Charleston, and Savannah. Let me make it clear that I could work anywhere, so we always moved only because my wife either "had" to move or "had a better offer." I don't want to start rumors, but I have a funny feeling now that she got "asked" to leave some of those jobs, that maybe she belittled students and colleagues alike. Who knows.

So I got up at four, and walked around the kitchen drinking coffee, putting everything in alphabetical order. I don't want to come off as some kind of seer, but I could feel someone standing on my front porch, so I went out there and turned on the outside lights to find Seth and Pam the dog. I opened the door and said, "What did y'all do, sleep in my front yard?"

"How're those knees feeling, friend?" Seth said. He wore the same thing as the day before. "Do a couple deep knee-bends right now and tell me you don't feel better. I'm serious. If you can honestly say you don't, I'm on my way. If you do, then it's twenty dollars."

I said, "Now I can see how you make a living. If you're waking people up at four in the morning and working till midnight, that makes sense." Pam sat down and wagged her tail, sweeping a couple leaves and a ton of dust around.

I did the knee-bends, and sure enough I didn't feel the tendonitis/arthritis/effects of being thirty pounds overweight that I normally felt. My ligaments didn't feel as though they stretched to the bursting point, is what I'm saying. "Come on in," I said, like a fool.

Seth and Pam ambled into the empty den—or probably the "parlor"—and stood five feet into my house. I went upstairs to find my wallet. When I came back down Seth said, "They's a bunch of gurus living out at the old Gruel Inn. Did you know that? Pam and me went by there hoping to do some healing, and this one yoga fellow bent way over and licked the back side of his knee. It's people like that might put us out of business."

I handed over one of those new twenty-dollar bills that look more like French money than American. I said, "I pretty much keep to myself," but didn't go into the whole I-might've gone-crazy-for-a-little-while explanation.

Seth said, "We appreciate it." He bent down to Pam and said, "Dog food for a month, baby!" and showed her the money. Then he walked backward to the door and opened it.

He said, "You don't know how much this means. Hey, tell your friends about Pam the healing lick dog."

I said, "I will," and didn't go into an explanation about how I knew no one in Gruel outside of the woman with the Jesus crust bread and the trick shot players who said thanks. I said, "Good luck to you and yours," for some reason.

On the porch Seth said, "You know, on our way up here—on our way through your yard—I thought I saw some kind of snake hole you might want to be aware of. It's right out here."

He pointed. I wasn't afraid of snakes, but I'd overheard some people at Roughhouse Billiards talk about how there seemed to be a preponderance of snakes that infiltrated the town lately. I said, "Where?" and followed him out in the yard.

I might've made it five or six steps barefoot before I felt what ended up being broken glass and tacks in the soles of my feet. I yelled out a couple damn-it-to-hells and made it back to the steps on my heels. Because, again, the porch lights were on I could see the blood flowing from the balls of my feet, from in between my toes, et cetera. I said, "Ow-ow-ow."

"Uh-oh," Seth said. "Hey Pam, get to work on this old boy's sores."

The dog approached me on cue.

OF COURSE I knew that Seth spread broken Coke bottles and tacks in my front yard and lured me out there to step on them early morning barefoot. And I didn't hold it against him! He'd probably seen me go out every morning without shoes to pick up my newspapers—the paperboy drove a step van and delivered the local *Forty-Five Platter*, *The State*, and the *Greenville News* in three long swoops as he drove by in a way that made me walk from gravel driveway to property edge to retrieve them all. I figured that I'd only been cased, just like in crime drama movies.

We sat down in the kitchen and Seth said, "That coffee smells good."

I said, "You can have some for twenty dollars a cup, peckerhead," like that. Maybe I wasn't as amused as I pretended.

Pam the dog licked and licked my bare feet in a way that reminded me of my honeymoon, in a way that reminded me of a woman I'd worked with on an early biography of Rasputin. Seth said, "You look like the kind of man who might hold some bourbon around the house. You got any bourbon around the house? I like bourbon in my coffee."

I didn't say, "Here we go," aloud, I don't think, but I thought it. If I were indexing this scene for a book I'd've written "here we go" under "Bourbon request." "Yeah, there's some bourbon in the cabinet over there. By the way, I'm not paying you five bucks a quarter hour for this. I'm on to you, man." I looked at the dog lapping my soles. "I'm on to you, too, Fido," I said.

Seth retrieved a quart of Old Crow and sat down across from me. He got back up, found two jelly jars, and placed them on the table. "To be honest, it's not good for you to drink while Pam's at work. Drinking thins the blood. It's the same with tattoos, you know. My dog can't lick and lick if the blood's going to keep spewing."

I looked over at Seth and noticed how one eye wandered off funny. I'd known people with this affliction before, men and women who were tired, or got drunk, and then that one eye rolled around loose. I said, "Are you all right, buddy?"

"I'm you," he said. "I don't know anything about your personal life, but I'm betting that we're one in the same, if you know what I mean."

I looked down at Pam and said, "Hey, that kind of tickles."

"Don't think that I've always wandered around with a dog licking sores. I've not always been this way."

I nodded. I waited for him to tell me how he once worked on Wall Street or as a lawyer, maybe a lobbyist. I said, "Go on."

"You ain't from around here, are you?"

I said, "No sir. I'm not." *Come on*, I thought, *tell me how you used to be a real doctor.*

"People from around here will tell you about how I coached high school football. That's what I did until I couldn't take it no more. And maybe I wasn't the best coach in the world, but by God I could tape an ankle. I could put a halfback back out onto the playing field with a broke foot and he wouldn't even know it. He wouldn't feel the pain. I could talk a broken ankle into feeling like it only got a slight sprain, you know what I mean?" Seth took a drink of his jelly jar bourbon. The sun rose outside. A dog licked my feet nonstop.

I said, "Huh. That's weird."

"I taught history, and driver's ed, and P.E. And I coached football down in Gig. Then I found Pam. Then I got fired for beating a kid on the sidelines during a game, and some parents didn't like that. It was only a placekicker."

What else could I say but, "Everybody's gotten politically correct about those kinds of things."

My knees felt invigorated. My feet immediately felt better. Seth said, "I'm telling you. I was out of there on a rail. A placekicker! That boy couldn't kick his sister's butt, much less a football through goalposts."

I drank from my own jelly jar and felt good. Not that I'm proud to admit it, but sometimes in the old days I got up at four a.m. and poured bourbon while doing my index work. I'm pretty sure it shows in that one biography I did of Truman Capote. There were things under Q that didn't need to be there.

"Do you know what it's like to pull off a perfect end sweep?" Seth said. "Do you know what it feels like to pull off a flea flicker when the defense has no idea it's about to happen?"

I said, "No sir."

"You ain't much of an athlete, are you? No offense, but you have no clue what I'm talking about, do you?"

I said, "Yes, I do. Fucker. I do. I'd go outside and challenge you in one-on-one basketball or a game of horseshoes, if my feet weren't all screwed up from your little game."

"You got any cards? While we're here we might as well play some poker." Seth threw down the twenty-dollar bill I'd given him earlier.

I had cards right there in the kitchen drawer, next to the couple spoons, couple knives, couple forks. I said, "No."

"You don't seem to be the kind of man who can take it," Seth said. "I've known men like you."

His demeanor certainly had changed since the afternoon before, of course. And I thought about saying, Hey, buddy, I don't know where you come off giving me life lessons, seeing as you travel around with a licking dog. But I didn't. I said, "I've taken more than you could imagine."

"You got any dice? Hey, let's play rock-paper-scissors-dynamite!" Pam the dog kept licking. "Hey, you want to see a picture I got of a woman who lost her eye, and how Pam licked it back into seeing? This might be the scariest thing ever."

Pam the dog withdrew from my bleeding feet. She hacked a couple of times. And then she got up, wobbled away from us, fell over, and died.

Seth said, "If Jesus had a dog hanging around him, those stigmata wouldn't even be mentioned. We wouldn't even have no religion if a dog like Pam were around at that time."

We stood there in my kitchen with a big dead dog. What could I do? I never got trained to deal with such a situation. I said, "Jesus."

"I ain't got no land to bury her. Do you mind putting her in your back-yard? I ain't got no land to bury her, outside of the old football field back in Gig. Right on the fifty-yard line. That would be kind of funny. And fitting."

I said, "Let's just put her down here in my backyard. I would be honored to have Pam in my yard." What else could I say? I didn't mean it whatsoever, but Seth seemed to want to hear such.

I creaked around on my swollen and defective feet, sidestepping the dog. Pam's tongue stuck out funny and her open brown eyes clouded over minute by minute. I said, "Well. There's a shovel outside. We can find a couple sticks of wood for a cross, if you want. Hotdamn." I got the bottle of bourbon and brought it back to the table.

"You're walking better," Seth said. "The least you could do is give me twenty more dollars for your feet."

I looked at him as if he were insane. What did he mean? This big dead dog lay or lied or laid out in my kitchen. "I'm sorry, buddy. I'm sorry that you lost your job as a high school coach. But this ain't my problem. I have enough problems right now."

Seth knelt down to his dog and pet it. He said, "Pam, Pam, Pam," and I have to say that I almost cried right there and then.

I said, "This is weird, man."

"I don't even know you," he said, crying. "I don't even know who you are, Curt. And here I am crying in front of you." His hair flowed around like an old sea anemone. "That's my dog," he said, pointing.

Pam almost looked like she only slept. The dog didn't move, of course.

"Come on," I said. In my mind I thought about how I could index such a scene—Seth crying, Seth weeping, Seth in disbelief—all in alphabetical order.

"What do I do now? What do I do now?" Seth said.

I circled the dog a couple of times, and then approached Seth. "I'm not so sure I can lift her up what with my feet all mangled."

Seth said, "Do you have any good liquor? I don't like this stuff. You got any smooth liquor?"

I heard "Licker" more than anything else. I didn't say it, though. That's what kind of got me in trouble with Marissa—saying what came into my mind at inopportune moments. Somebody should write a book about it—I could do the index. I said, "This is all I got," and pointed toward my bottle of what, by the way, I considered great bourbon.

Seth pointed at my legs, halfway down. He said, "Well, come on."

We grabbed Pam. I took the shoulders and Seth took her haunches. He walked backward out of the house, and down the steps, and into the backyard. We set her down at the foot of a wild fig. I said, "Figs are supposed to be recuperative," just like that. Recuperative! I hadn't used the word in my entire life, even in indexing.

"Well," Seth said. He looked over at an old shed on the back of the property, an eight-by-sixteen tongue-and-groove structure I'd not even figured out what to do with. Up to this point I only kept a shovel and a rake inside. "Hey, there's another house there."

I said, "If I ever get a riding lawn mower that'll be its resting place."

Seth said, "I ain't got a place to live."

I walked over and got the shovel from inside. When I opened the swinging door, though, I envisioned Seth inside, sitting there atop an empty and upside-down drywall bucket. I foresaw myself going to pick him up at night, walking with him to Roughhouse Billiards. We'd get inside and wait out the trick shot players, then spend hours trying not to knock the eight ball in at wrong moments. Whenever I bent over hurting he'd say, "We need Pam about right now."

I said, "Here's the shovel."

He didn't scoop into the earth daintily. I tried not to think of what a healing dog couldn't do with the rest of us treading ground in an uncertain manner.

Seth said, "Good dog. Good dog. I'm sorry. Good dog."

On his way off my property—and I don't know how to convince anyone that I knew how he'd never come back—he let out a low howl. He turned his head to the rising sun and let one loose, not unlike what a bloodhound emits when a fire engine's siren's far, far away. I hobbled my way back inside. Later that day I turned on one of those business channels and stared at what happened with the major indices, elsewhere.

DIRECTOR'S CUT

MY FATHER HAD AN AFFAIR WITH A WOMAN ONCE MAR-
ried to an Irish Traveler—one of those guys who takes money to
seal your driveway, but then skips town. The woman, a Flora
Gorman, ran the Dial-a-Style beauty salon and cut my mother's hair
once a month. The salon, a three-seater, must've been a front for other
things, because it remained hidden way out on two-lane Pick Road,
which dead-ended at a creek that fed the Savannah River. My mother
had to go out of her way to the Dial-a-Style, which probably meant that
she suspected my father's dalliance.

"I lived with a bouffant atop my brain from 1977 to 1979, back when it
hadn't been in style for ten years," my mother told me. "You remember.
Dial-a-Style my ass. Every Irish Traveler's woman down there looked
like that girl on *I Dream of Jeannie*. That girl on *Gilligan's Island*. Jackie
Kennedy. Whoever posed for the Mr. Bubble's box of bubble bath."

This was over the telephone. I'd not talked to my mother since taking my wife down to meet her a couple of days after our impromptu
wedding ceremony, thirteen years earlier. As I've always contended, the
non-communicative nature of our relationship stemmed from Mom's
unwillingness to believe that I knew nothing of Dad's affair, plus her
presumption that no man named Spillman could turn into anything but
a petty and ceaseless philanderer. I said into the receiver, "I remember

that big sign out front of the Dial-a-Style. Like a rotary phone where you could turn to a pageboy, or that haircut that looked like a nuclear bomb exploded your bangs. And then the Peter Pan look."

My wife, Raylou, turned her head toward me and squinched her eyebrows—the international facial expression for "Who's that?" She flipped through a gardening book too fast, as if in search of the plot. I mouthed "Mom" and shrugged my shoulders.

"Yeah. Yeah, like any one of those women married to Irish Traveler scam artists knew how to cut hair. Those bitches didn't know shit."

I calculated my mother's age. She wasn't quite old enough for classic dementia. Maybe she suffered from a post-menopausal syndrome akin to Tourette's. Even when my father packed up and left for New Orleans with Flora Gorman, my mother hadn't gone on a cussing binge. I said, "So, what's on your mind? Raylou and I are still together, by the way, and I don't run around on her. I quit drinking. Raylou has a slew of people across North America and Europe who collect her face jugs. I make sculptures, welded entirely from bolts and hex nuts. You can see them standing in a number of cities, and I just got a commission to weld some giant angels for Birmingham, Alabama."

"Good," my mother said. "Your father and I were married for almost fifteen years before he took to foreign snatch. So you still have time to become a true Spillman."

Raylou set down the book, opened the end-table drawer, and took out a pack of Lucky Strikes that I hadn't touched in two weeks. She held a cigarette lengthwise in her open palm, sprang her arm like a catapult, and caught the thing in her mouth after it had flipped a few times in midair. "What're you doing?" I asked my wife.

My mother said, "I watched a fascinating show on the influx of nutria and armadillos down in Louisiana, which made me think of your fucking father, which made me think of you. Where the hell's this Gone Ember where you live? I called Information about twenty times before the stupid man on the other end figured out I wasn't saying 'sputum,' and then I got you. Then I thought that you'd invite me up, seeing as I'm retired from teaching those goddamn little chalk-eaters. And I've changed my hair. I've convinced myself that if you look me blankly in the face and don't recognize me at first, it's because I have a new hairdo instead of that son-of-a-bitch beehive that made me look like either a linthead working the cotton mills or a punk rock singer."

I veered my eyes away from Raylou and said, "Okay. Well, okay. Can you still drive, or do you need me to come down there and get you?"

I held the phone away from my ear as my mother went into a stream-of-consciousness curse that embarrassed me. She finished by saying, "I got a van, and I got equipment. I got almost enough backers, and I got people."

I told her that I seemed to be missing something in the conversation. I said, "People for what?"

I listened as my mother exhaled smoke—something she didn't do when bringing me up alone as the only white boy within about a two-mile radius. She said, "I've spent the last twelve years studying up on it. Thank God for the invention of the VCR. We never did get a movie house within twenty miles of here, Harp. Anyway, I took a college course in the mail, and after conference calls to my professors at Southern Cal, I've finally figured out how to make a movie."

At that moment I wished that Raylou and I had a speaker-phone feature so that she could listen in. I said, "Wait. You took a film class at the University of Southern California?"

She exhaled again. I heard a Zippo click. "Southern California Junior Film College. I might have those words turned around. Some such crap. Anyway, I successfully completed the program. My major's in directing. My minor's best boy."

MY MOTHER, HER hair buzz-cut a half centimeter all over, hadn't been in our house for more than five minutes when Raylou decided to pipe up. "You know," she said, "I have an idea for you. Why don't you try a documentary on Harp, here? You can do a documentary that'll be multilayered as can be. First off, you get him doing these twelve-foot angel sculptures for the city of Birmingham. Then you get his constant struggle with staying off the liquor. If some of his new friends show up and you get to interview them, I see Sundance Film Festival in your future."

I looked at my wife, and just in case she couldn't interpret my expression, I said, "I'll kill you." But what she had said was true: since I'd quit drinking, quit going to rehab, and quit going to AA meetings, the rehab participants and AA victims had taken to coming my way. Sometimes I thought they were checking up on my progress. But most of the time I suspected they felt safe at our little compound, on a twenty-acre rounded piece of granite far from liquor stores and bars. I imagined a documentary wherein my part-time helper, Bayward, went into detail about how he had tried to perform a tracheotomy on himself so that beer would shoot out his throat—which, of course, it wouldn't—before reaching his bloodstream. I daydreamed about Vollis, Evan, and Kumi—the Elbow Boys—trying to explain how they had discovered a questionable orthopedic surgeon down in Costa Rica who had fused their elbow joints together so that they couldn't bring a drink to their lips. I said to my mother, "You don't want to make a documentary about everyday people doing nothing. It would be boring and a waste of cellulite."

"It's celluloid," my mother said, taking suitcase after suitcase out of her Dodge van. "Damn. First test in history and terminology class." She looked around at the Quonset hut I used for a studio, Raylou's work shed and adjacent kiln, the clear expanse of smooth granite where nothing man-made was standing. "Not many trees around here," she said. "Wouldn't have a problem with lighting." She reached down, picked up a suitcase, and put it back in the van. "Okay. I'd say it's about time for a drink, but I won't do that. When in Gone Ember, you know. I believe Marty would act thusly, too. Marty and Francis Ford. Frank. F. F. Quentin's another story, though."

I thought that if this were a movie, my mother and I would undergo an awkward hug while Raylou looked off at the horizon. "Did you actually get taught by those directors somewhere along the line? Do you know them somehow?"

"This'll work out perfectly," my mother said. "Great idea, Raylou. Listen. I've got to be up-front on this." My mother put some of her luggage in an outbuilding, an eight-foot-square structure that, I felt certain, my wife insisted on having built as a kind of alcoholics' playhouse, for when those forced-upon-me acquaintances showed up uninvited. "I know I said 'When in Gone Ember,' but this old cinematographer could use a drink. Are you sure you quit, Harp? You're named after a by-God Irish lager, among other things."

I said, "We're fresh out. If you brought your own, fine. I won't be bothered."

Raylou grabbed two suitcases to haul into the house and said, "We've got bourbon and vodka, I think, Ms. Spillman. You come on in, and I'll fix you up."

Where? I thought. *Where's the booze?* I hadn't gone on any scavenger hunts since I'd quit, but believe me, I knew every inch of fiberglass insulation and its underside from the old days of Raylou's hiding. I said to my mother, "You were going to say something about being up-front."

We walked a straight line to the house. I didn't point out the snapping turtle pond between Raylou's workspace and our sliding glass door, for fear that my mother, who had suicidal tendencies, might dive in.

We sat in the den. My mother looked surprisingly young for a woman nearing sixty, a woman whose only husband had run off with a jack-Irish Traveler's wife who used to operate the Dial-a-Style, a woman who must've lost all reason to live if she'd spent hard-earned retirement money on the Southern California Junior Film College correspondence course. She'd lost weight, and she looked more wiry than I could remember. Her baldish head made her look like an older and savvy California woman involved in the movie industry.

"I'm neither ashamed nor proud of it. I was going to make a feature film about your father's running away like he did. And I was going to let the guy have it—kind of like a modern-day Job, you know. But now that I see you, Harp—" She held up a see-through square with her thumbs and index fingers, like a camera lens, I supposed. "—and with Raylou's suggestion, I see how I can turn this all around."

Something sounding like an earthquake occurred in the guest bedroom, bottle shaking against bottle. I tried to envision where my wife had hidden the booze over all these dry days. Or months and years. I said, "As long as you don't need my help, do what you want. I have a thing against movies. And I'm not a theater snob. I just have a thing against actors."

Raylou came out carrying Old Crow so old that it came in one of those embossed bottles. My mother said, "You look exactly like your father when he was thirty-eight. As a matter of fact, that's when he left us. Oh, I can see all kinds of possibilities in a documentary, sort of a cross between *Fahrenheit 9/11* when it comes to showing how stupid you are—I mean your father was—and, oh, I don't know. Let me think back to the syllabus we had second semester." My mother did those fingers my way again. "I can see a multilayered before-and-after, then-and-now, the-acorn-doesn't-fall-far kind of movie, with a ton of voiceovers provided by yours truly."

I didn't like the sound of this, of course. It's not how I ever imagined a reunion with my odd, obsessed mother. My wife said, "The bourbon's old, but the mixer's new. What'll you have with this, Ms. Spillman?"

"I've got it! A cross between that and maybe a little-known film we saw on Rube Goldberg and his ways." To Raylou my mother said, "I'll take it straight out of the bottle, if no one is joining me. And please call me Ansel."

Raylou walked a wide half circle from my reach and handed the un-tapped Old Crow to my mother, a woman whose name I'd always known to be Margaret. Margie. Peggy. Peg.

MY WIFE CONVERTED to Quakerism. She hosts her fellow parishioners in the eight-by-eight outbuilding on Sunday mornings, and asks that I tiptoe, that I don't fire up the MIG welder, that perhaps I use this time to take a long, long, quiet walk far away from our house. Raylou and her pacifists require a boatload of quiet. I brought this up when my mother—or Ansel—said that she wanted to work in seventy-two-hour cycles with one day off in between. I mentioned that we couldn't work on Sundays. "I don't have much use for Quakers," my mother said. "I'd've liked to've gone to a Quaker school, though, just to beat everybody up. You have to understand, I like action!"

I asked myself how long doing this documentary could take. She would watch me weld for a minute or two, and ask some questions; watch Raylou form a face jug, ask some questions; and then maybe assume that ubiquitous voiceover to rant about how her husband, my father, never had any ambitions beyond grading eggs and peaches for the South Carolina Ag Department before he ran off with a younger woman who couldn't dial but one style.

My mother said, "I really need to hire someone to run a second camera, or at least hold a boom mike." This was kind of late on that first night, and the booze didn't seem to have affected Ansel.

Raylou said, "You know, we could do this between the three of us. When you're shooting Harp, I could hold the microphone, and vice versa. On top of that, Harp and I both learned how to run a camera and do lights back in college. You don't need a rocket scientist." Raylou kept talking to a point above my head. I wasn't sure, and tried to retrace the evening backwards, but she might've excused herself to the bathroom and smoked some pot in there.

Maybe she had hit a bowl or two, probably with a ceramic pipe she'd made between face jugs, which took her thirty minutes to form and she sold for upwards of three hundred dollars. Back in my more politically incorrect drinking days I might've pointed out that slow kids, too, grew up to fetch top dollar on their face jugs. I said, "I have enough to deal with right now. I'm not even sure I'm all that hip to someone's putting my mug on film. Some people out there might be looking for me, you know."

My mother didn't say, "Oh, come on and humor me." She didn't say, "Well, this is a fine welcome after all these years of silence." She got up from her seat and said, "Well, this little cinematographer needs to visit the editing room to unreel a spool."

I looked at my wife when Mom got out of earshot. "You've been smoking pot again, haven't you? I can tell. Don't try to hide a high from an old drunk, Raylou."

She giggled. She said, "First off, do you think your mother's film will ever be seen by anyone? Give it a break, Harp. This might be the highlight of her life. And you want to take it away? Check your ego in the Green Room, man. And second, your mom gave me the pot, back when you were pretending to need something in the room where I had the bourbon hidden. The latest etiquette books say that smoking dope is proper and right if it's offered by an older family member. Family sharing keeps everybody from feeling uncomfortable."

I looked at my wife. I'd forgotten that her eyebrows kind of arched up like a clown's, like a McDonald's sign, like the wings on my giant welded angels, when she got stoned. I said, "I'll love you tomorrow, but I want to go on record as saying this is trouble."

My mother came back and said, "False alarm." She grabbed her bottle and sat back down. "Oops, there it is again. Take two." She walked faster to the bathroom this time.

"A big mistake," I said.

I UNBOXED A new crate of shiny steel nuts from Southern Hex, stood back, and stared at the frame I'd built of rebar. My mother stepped in closer to me and said, "Unlike most artists, Harp Spillman doesn't hold his thumb up to the work in progress."

I laughed and said, "Cut!" I said, "That's just stupid, Mom. Can you go back and add the commentary later? And let me know what you plan to let out of your mouth?"

Raylou lowered the boom mike to rest on our granite lawn. She said, "That was kind of dumb, Ansel, I hate to say."

My mother made no promises but said, "And...action!" like she'd seen in the movies, I supposed. I pulled the trigger on my MIG and beaded a nut down low, and then another and another. In the distance wild dogs barked, and a flock of ducks passed over. I sensed the camera angling up toward the sky. I said, "The trick to these things is getting them heavy enough to remain sturdy, but balanced so they don't tip over while I'm working. And I want enough negative space to create the illusion that the angel is nearly airborne."

This time my mother yelled, "Cut!" She said, "Okay. You weren't good at direction when you were a kid, but I let you slide, seeing as your father was to blame. But you're an adult now. Hell, you're old enough to leave your wife."

Raylou said, "Thanks." I said, "See? I told you."

I circled the half angel, and my mother operated the camera about two inches from my face, which luckily couldn't be seen for the welder's mask. She said, "So. When your father left you for that skank gypsy, what did you think, Harp? Was that when you decided to become an artist—because your brilliant mother supported you, and helped nurture your talent, and urged you to follow your dream, even though she couldn't afford to get her hair fixed right in a proper hairdo?"

I said, "Most of that's correct. I think my mother really only wanted to see the pretty colors all swirl together while she smoked dope in secret."

My mother said, more quietly, "Yes. Yes. That'll keep an audience riveted." I pulled the trigger again. Over the hiss my mother said, "How's about that father of yours? Do you think you received your alcoholism through him genetically, or did you start drinking hard early on in life as a means of trying to forget what an asshole he was and still is?" I didn't answer. I continued working, reaching down for new nuts, standing back half crouched, trying not to think about how I would soon invest in a series of massage therapy sessions, or at least a case of Doan's backache pills. My mother said, "I'll take that for a yes."

Raylou kept the mike above my head, and my mother shot for a good half hour in silence. Finally I set the MIG down and pulled up my mask to get a look at the sculpture. My mother turned off her handheld camera. I said, "Maybe it would be a good time to go film Raylou. I'll hold the mike. You probably have enough footage that you can cut and splice together."

We went through the same format, pretty much. I held the mike, Raylou sat down at her electric wheel, and my mother said, "Raylou, do you truly believe that Harp received his alcoholism genetically, or that he began drinking at the age of thirteen because his father left a stable household in order to navigate the strange choppy waters off the Gulf of Poontang?"

I leaned the microphone up against Raylou's groundhog kiln. She started laughing. I said, "Are you intent on making an X-rated film? You need to watch your language a bit, Mom, if you ask me. I don't care what those correspondence-course directors say, even art-house movie joints have some sense of decorum, from what I hear."

"Cut," my mother said. She set the camera down on the hard rock of our acreage. "Don't y'all have any friends or anything?" She swept her arm around. "I need some people to tell me some stories, man. Y'all obviously can't do it."

She left her equipment on the ground and walked back to the house as if marching toward a spank-needy child. I said to my wife, "I told you this wouldn't work out. She was kind of nutty way back when. That kind of behavior doesn't reverse itself."

Raylou shrugged. She said, "I'm betting she won't need another twenty-four hours to understand she can't find a story here."

Those same ducks, I was pretty sure, flew back overhead in the opposite direction. My mother yelled out, "What the hell are these things?" and I looked to see that she'd almost stepped into the snapping-turtle pond.

I said, "Never mind those things. It's a long story that involves Raylou's getting too involved with rescuing animals she thinks are being tortured by biologists."

"Biotoxicologists!" Raylou called out. "Hey, now that might be—"

"Hurry up and bring the camera," my mother yelled. "Leave the microphone for now. Hey, when these things have their necks stretched out, they kind of look like...good God, man, talk about your father." She said, "I got a whole new idea. Take one, baby, take one!"

What my mother decided to shoot ended up—I'll give her this—was kind of a good idea. She took a real liking to the six snappers—now weighing in at about twenty pounds apiece, their necks able to stretch out nearly a foot—and filmed them burrowing down in the mud, gnawing on chicken necks, sticking their heads out of the water like prehistoric periscopes. My mother said, "I think I could just dub some Bartok over the film—maybe some Shostakovich—and then market this documentary to schools, so they can get their students to understand biology and music. I'll call it something like, damn, what're those words for a turtle's shell? One for the top and one for the bottom."

My wife said, "We have copperheads around here, too. A few rattlesnakes. You'd have to go farther south to find cottonmouths. I'm thinking you could do a whole series of shorts involving, you know, God's scary creatures of the South."

I said, "We got fire ants, and the neighbor down the hill tried to smuggle in some anteaters from Central America or someplace, but they all got loose. Two of them, from what I understand, are now mounted, looking down from some confused hunter's mantel."

We sat in mesh chairs that Raylou got somewhere; they rolled up and fit in a bag. We sat in the Quonset hut, surrounded by what angels I had finished, drinking coffee. My mother and Raylou ate dry, dry homemade scones that I wouldn't touch, because I figured they'd remind me of the days of pretzels and beer. My mother said, "You know, it's really not all that bad here in Gone Ember. I don't see the hustle and bustle like where you were brought up, Harp." My hometown might've held two thousand residents. Maybe nothing is more selfish than a committed drunk become a committed recoverer, which may explain why I said, "Don't think about moving up here."

Raylou said, "Harp. That's not very nice." To my mother she said, "You can come up here any time you want."

"Hollywood East," my mother said. She rubbed at her scalp a few times, the way a kid might rub a balloon to create static. "No, I was just being polite. I'll keep my home base right there near the Dial-a-Style, so I can remember every day why I'm on this planet."

I cleared my throat. I got up, rummaged through a drawer of old washers, and found a pack of Camels I'd stashed for mornings when I felt lost without bourbon. I said, "Is your reason for being on the planet that you want to make sure everyone knows what Dad did twenty-five years ago? I mean, that first documentary you started—the one about how I looked like him, and I was destined to act like him—to be honest, I thought it was plain mean-spirited. And kind of presumptuous."

Raylou got up and said that she wanted to throw a couple dozen face jugs, that she needed to chop oak for the kiln, that she'd bought a new shingle hammer she thought might work best for cracking up the old porcelain plates she used for scary teeth. I think she felt uncomfortable. I think she thought my mother and I had to have some kind of long-time-coming talk, in which my mother might admit to some shortfall in her child-rearing skills, or I might confess that I should've initiated contact years earlier, before the era of correspondence courses, when my mother had no hobbies or use for family members.

When my mother opened her mouth wide, I thought she was going to acknowledge some shortcomings on her part, or say that she admired my overcoming the Spillman family's drinking problem. The sound that came out of her throat, though, sounded like what happens when you use one of those trick cellophane-and-cardboard discs that kids put in their months to talk like the speech-afflicted. Or it sounded like a death rattle.

I said, "What?"

My mother pointed at her chest twice. She pointed at half a scone—and later I would observe that outside of a cheap way of killing yourself, scones were better used as door stops—and then at her throat. She got up out of her chair and walked quickly to my twelve-gallon wet-dry Shop-Vac. She made that noise some more and stamped her feet. On her face I read...frustration? Discomfort? Some kind of existential dread? Finally she eked out, "Choking."

She was the one to turn on the switch. I jumped up like a good son and tried to figure out how to perform the Heimlich maneuver without touching my mother's breasts, because, well, I had enough nightmares.

My mother shoved the black nozzle in her mouth, tightened her lips around the business end, and unclogged her air passage. The image was one I knew I would never escape, even with daily visits to a certified psychoanalyst with training in hypnosis to eradicate Oedipus complexes. I screamed for help, but by the time Raylou showed up, the vacuum's hose was snaking around on the floor, a chunk of scone stuck to the plastic attachment, and I stood there cradling my mother's abdomen from behind. Raylou said, "I knew y'all would patch things up. I wish I had this on film. I didn't want to say anything before, but you don't need all the cursing and violence."

I let go of my mother. Later I would think about how most people would thank a son for having a Shop-Vac at the ready, for my at least attempting to heave at her diaphragm. "Lucky thing I don't wear dentures," my mother said. She went back to her chair. "If you end up with your teeth falling out someday, Harp, you can blame it on your father's gummy side of the family. Maybe that's why he ran off with Flora Gorman. It wasn't for her hair, believe me. Maybe her having retractable teeth played a part in it. I saw it before. I saw her in the Dial-a-Style. I saw her have to apply another strip of that gum glue." My mother laughed and laughed. She reached into her pocket and pulled out a four-inch clay pipe that I supposed Raylou had given her. "Now that I think about it, your daddy's mistress looked about like those snapping turtles when it comes to smiles."

Then, like any good sniper, she left the premises. Raylou went back in the house, and I stood in my studio making a mental list of what I needed to do next. My mother packed up her van and drove straight through Gone Ember, without so much as an invitation to come see the final cut of whatever it was she had shot. I realized that in the movies I would probably have a voiceover saying, "What just happened?" or, "I hope to hell this is all a dream," or, "This isn't good for my recovery."

I locked the door to the Quonset hut. At the snapping-turtle pond I tried not to think of my father's mistress from years ago. Inside, while my wife took orders for her face jugs over the Internet, I turned on the television. One of those cable channels was showing a *Three Stooges* marathon. Another was showing a Marx Brothers film. The Atlanta station had Laurel and Hardy, and the cartoon channel offered up *Road Runner*.

Nothing seemed funny.

I turned to the Independent Film Channel. A German man and woman, their faces in close-up, talked about the good and essential symbiotic nature of termite mounds, with subtitles. I think the man tried to make some kind of connection with Schopenhauer. I turned to Animal Planet, and—God or Satan will insist that something more powerful than I had planned this all along—a man was doing a voice-over explaining the many differences between land tortoises and aquatic turtles, but declaring that both depended on sturdy plastrons and carapaces. A woman pointed out that although it's not common, snapping turtles have been known to be monogamous, and one pair stayed together more than fifteen years.

I thought about post-acute withdrawal syndrome. I turned back to the cartoon channel.

PROBATE

W
E DIDN'T CARE, REALLY, ABOUT THE TRAVELING EU-
thanasia vet's failed marriage. We didn't care about why
this woman showed up nine hours later than she said she'd
arrive. I can't say all of this for certain. I'll admit that I'm making some
suppositions. I'd like to say that I could call Miranda and fact-check
this whole night, but she took off two days later without leaving much
of a note, and certainly not a new address. Her voicemail's full, so I can't
leave a message, saying, "Call me back so I make sure I don't go around
telling this story wrong." I can't even remember the vet's last name,
though I remember her showing up, trailing along a rolling hard-shell
case of dog biscuits, sedatives, and animal heart-stoppers. She came in,
didn't make eye contact, and said her name was Dr. Nancy. She was
one of those kinds of vets—like a pediatric oncologist who took one too
many humanities courses, or a fearful dentist specializing in adolescent
pulpectomies, or a questionably intelligent recent seminary graduate intent on teaching a group why evil, famine, early death, spina bifida, mul-
tiple sclerosis, tainted water supplies, dwarfism, cystic fibrosis, asthma,
and muscular dystrophy exist in the world (not to mention AIDS, war,
domestic violence, neuropathy, club feet, polio in the old days, death by
handguns)—who think it necessary to go by first name only. Dr. Nancy.
Like Cher or Madonna. Oprah, LeBron. Jesus.

"Hey, I'm sorry I'm so late, but I got stuck on the phone with my therapist," this vet said. Miranda and I stood in our kitchen, where our dog Probate, lying sideways on the floor, panted, squealed, yelped, and practically pleaded, "Put me down now." Probate's real name happened to be Max; we'd inherited him when Miranda's mother died seven years earlier. Probate seemed to be a mix of Chow and pit bull, he lived to at least fifteen years old, and his hips didn't respond daily. He was so black that no one would adopt him other than us, we knew, what with that fact about black dogs left forever at the pound. He had three tumors on his belly, which meant when I tried to lift him he bit me. "I'd do the same thing," I said to Miranda.

Probate had responded to his new name right away. You could say, "Come here, Max," or, "Come here, Probate," and he'd do so. That fucker would stare at me nonstop until I finally said, "You want to go to the recycling center?" I'd say, "You want to go see Robin at the liquor store?" I'd say, "You want to drive over to Señor El Perro Caliente and get a wiener?" He loved me, and I him.

A good dog, is what I'm saying.

If Miranda were here, she'd admit that the dog'd quit eating a week before. Anyone with a rational side, or a heart, would understand that it was Probate's time.

My dog Probate!

Miranda's momma died at Hospice Care of the Lakelands, which meant she got lung cancer, didn't want to leave her own house, never told anyone. Nor did she confide to Miranda or me about all the bins of *What Doctors Won't Tell You* and *Miracle Cure* pamphlets and books she kept shoved beneath beds. She never let on that she possessed hoarding tendencies. It's not like Miranda and I visited, then found it necessary to open closet doors to find stacks and stacks of Bradford Exchange "limited edition" collector plates; post-1992 Donruss, Topps, Upper Deck, and Leaf baseball cards from when the market got flooded; Beanie Babies; electroplated "coins" produced by the British Royal Mint in conjunction with the Columbia Mint in Washington, DC; every canceled check since 1965, and so on.

We visited often, but didn't go snooping around, I guess. And Miranda's mom came to live with us on a number of occasions. We lived ninety miles away only. Miranda's mother showed up after hip surgery, and after that time when she fell down and dislocated her shoulder, and the ER doctor said, "I can pop this back in," and then he sheared the ball right in half. Miranda's mother—her name was Evelyn—came to live with us that time when she thought she might want to hurt herself with the drugs she held left over. She brought poor old Probate with her. He lifted his leg on the dining-room table, on end tables, on both couches. He walked right up to the front door and lifted his leg, then trotted to the back door and did the same. He went up the stairs, jumped up on the guest mattress, and licked himself in ways that ruined the queen-size bedspread.

Probate!

"He's the only thing my mom had to love," Miranda announced more than once. Personally, I think it was a slightly passive-aggressive thing for her to say. I mean, I guess I should've gone ahead and blurted out, "No, she had you, Miranda," but I rarely followed through. Sometimes I got out, "She had the entire Atlanta Braves lineup, in order, stacked tightly in those little boxes, or in plastic-sheeted notebooks, from about 1990 until her death."

Her momma sank and fizzled and occupied our time, then she died, and then we went through probate. And we got good Probate, who put up with us until we needed to call the traveling euthanasia woman.

As an aside: Miranda hired out an auctioneer. Me, I didn't care about the estate's worth, but my then-wife seemed upset that her mother's collections didn't bring in more than two thousand dollars, after the twenty-five percent, after the thousand dollars charged for sending out mailing-list postcards to people who, obviously, didn't care to clog their homes with Beanie Babies, baseball cards, collector plates, or fake coins. Even the Hospice Thrift Store people didn't seem all that excited about garnering the leftovers that no one bid on: a console stereo, circa 1968, that weighed about four hundred pounds, for example. That Hammond organ with the special piccolo/flute/timpani keys. Maybe thirty stuffed vipers, all coiled in a lifelike way, that Evelyn kept after her husband—an amateur herpetologist—took off for one of the southwestern states when Miranda went to college. As it ended up, we filled most of our attic with useless "collectibles."

≥≤

Besides not making eye contact, Dr. Nancy showed up dressed in what appeared to be some kind of damsel-in-distress costume. I'd never met a traveling euthanasia veterinarian in the past, so it didn't occur to me that, perhaps, he or she should wear scrubs, or at least blue jeans if the euthanasia involved a horse or goat. I'd left the back porch lights on and had told her—some eleven hours earlier, when she said she'd show up at noon—that the driveway would lead her to the back of the house. I heard her big Suburban growling onto our property, spitting pea gravel, and went to the door.

I should mention that Probate had howled, probably in pain, for all this time. Miranda spent most of the hours petting the dog's head, or crying, or finding ways to go outside and perform tasks that could've been accomplished later: raking pine needles, filling the Yankee feeders with sunflower seeds, cleaning the gutters, checking the tread on our two cars' tires with a Roosevelt dime.

My wife started digging a grave in the red clay that might've measured six inches deep until later I went out there with a real spade, and an ax to cut through roots and tendrils. I rifled through every drawer we had, but could only find aspirin, Benadryl, and half of what I figured might be Lortab from when Miranda suffered her last bout of kidney stones. I discovered a sliver of what might've been oxycodone, and residue from about six separate one-hitters I'd stashed on the bookshelf behind *The Confessions of Jean-Jacques Rousseau*. When the vet hadn't showed up by two o'clock, I placed a speculative concoction on a glob of peanut butter, lifted Probate's flews, and scraped the homemade sedative behind his upper back teeth. He bit at me, sure, and then continued his horrific howl-whine.

It just occurred to me that "howl-whine" sounds like "Halloween." Maybe there's a reason. Add that to Dr. Nancy in her costume, at our door. She wore a corset, a floor-length dress made of velour-like material, lace sleeves, the whole getup. Dr. Nancy sported a Robin Hood hat with a feather spouting out the side, which I thought, in retrospect, kind of veered from the rest of her attire. I don't know what kind of brassiere she sported beneath, but it influenced her décolletage mightily.

She dragged that suitcase and said to me, "Please tell me you're the Stinsons."

I nodded. I said, because I wanted to know, "Does your therapist have a dog that needs putting down?" Of course I knew the answer. Dr. Nancy harbored unrelenting neuroses and spiteful daydreams and more issues than the Library of Congress's newspaper and magazine stash.

"No," she said. "No. I just need to talk to her when I'm spiraling. My husband left me after nineteen years. You ever have any foot problems, Mr. Stinson?"

I said, "Call me Charlie." I almost said, "Call me Mr. Charlie." I said, "I'm Charlie, and this is Miranda." Probate lay on the kitchen floor panting, whining, yelping. I said, "I've never had any foot problems."

"My ex was a podiatrist. You probably know him—Walker Posey. I think he's been named Best Podiatrist in the County going on about ten years now, according to the *Spinning Around* Readers Poll." That was the local newspaper's weekend supplement that came out on Fridays so people would know all about the crummy things people like Miranda and me wouldn't do on Saturday night. *Spinning Around*'s readers named Olive Garden as Best Italian Restaurant, Walmart as Best Sporting Goods, Subway as Best Ethnic Food because the place offered ciabatta bread.

Miranda said, "Probate's got all his shots. Our regular vet's Dr. Gagliardi. We couldn't get Probate into the car, so we called you."

"I know Dr. Stefanie," Dr. Nancy said. "I think I used to work there, maybe about ten or twelve years ago." She pushed up her boobs with both hands. She pulled back some kind of near floor-length cape that accented the costume. Who doesn't remember where he or she worked at some point? Me, before I signed on with Piedmont Consumer Pulse because the previous vice president lost it altogether and quit—which *hadn't* gotten voted Best Marketing Firm in the County—I had a number of both full- and part-time jobs throughout high school and college, then afterwards. I worked at a pharmacy (mistake on their part), drove a water truck, washed dishes as part of work-study, spent six days as a roofer, worked at a Budweiser warehouse (another mistake on my employer's part), waited tables during that one semester of law school, delivered newspapers in the middle of the night, cut and delivered firewood from my daddy's tree farm, sold Christmas trees from my daddy's tree farm, married Miranda, worked for her father's Consumer Pulse of the Carolinas, then went out and took the VP job with the competition. Who doesn't remember jobs?

Probate let out a noise that almost sounded like "Help," I swear to God.

Miranda said, "You can just call up your therapist like that? Does she charge you by the hour even over the phone?"

I kind of wanted to know the answer, too. Dr. Nancy said, "It's okay. It's okay, buddy. It's just your soul trying to leave your body."

It took me a second to realize that she talked to Probate, not me. Miranda said, "Probate's real name is Max. Charlie renamed him Probate."

Dr. Nancy had been stooped down in her damsel-in-distress costume until this point. I'm not proud, but I could look down and see her boobs easily from where I stood. I'm not proud, but I kind of wanted Probate to stop whining and breathing erratically for an hour, just so Dr. Nancy could remain crouched, considering her options.

"Oh," Dr. Nancy said. She stood up. "How old did you say Max is?"

"Fifteen," Miranda said. Maybe I should mention that Miranda wore those Spandex things I see more and more running women wear, plus a T-shirt that didn't go much past her navel. She said, "Well, we don't know. Probate came from the Humane Society, and then my mother had him for about eight years, and we've had him for six or seven. I'd say he's between fifteen and seventeen, really."

"There's no telling," I said, because I couldn't think of anything else to offer. "We never fed him onions or chocolate! I pride myself on knowing what dogs can and cannot consume. We made sure he never ate pork, or any of those other things that make dogs sick or poisoned!"

Dr. Nancy said, "Renaming animals can be very confusing for them, and make them feel worthless. Some scientists speculate that that's what happened to the dinosaurs."

SO THE VET shot my dog up with a sedative, Probate went to sleep, the vet shaved a spot on Probate's left foreleg, then she swabbed it with alcohol. I didn't say, "Why did you sterilize the spot on my dog's leg? It's not like an infection's going to bother him later."

Miranda shook her head sideways as if she underwent a petit mal seizure, held her mouth wide in a stifled cry, and excused herself to the bedroom.

The vet injected pentobarbital, I stroked down Probate's spine, and his pains—the cancer, the failed hips, the probable long-term mourning for my mother-in-law—vanished within a minute. Dr. Nancy got up and, without asking if I possessed any allergies, pulled a stick of incense from her bag, lit the end, and waved the smoldering thing over my dog. She held a stethoscope to Probate's chest, then pulled back and said, "Okay. His spirit has lifted. This is just your dog's body. His spirit has risen." She spoke calmer than a golf announcer on CBS, or someone trying to coax fish toward the shoreline.

I feel bad, but I started laughing. I mean, I bent over and slapped my knee. I said, "Is that sage? What's that scent?" But I tell you, I couldn't stop laughing. I said, "Oh my God. Oh, Jesus, you're something. Hey, do you go to Burning Man every year? Oh man oh man oh man. Hey, what's with the getup? *Spirit has risen*. Goddamn."

Dr. Nancy saw no reason for my humor. She said, "Do you have any other animals living in the house who need to say farewell to their friend?"

That made me laugh even more. I yelled out, "Miranda! Miranda, get in here!" I looked down at Probate, whose eyes were open, staring at that little vent at the bottom of our refrigerator. I said, "Myrrh? Sandalwood? Frankincense?"

Miranda yelled back, "I can't!"

I said, "No, we don't have any pets who need to offer their bon voyages." Then that made me laugh. I said, "'Bon voyages!' Like we have a cadre of French pets upstairs. Miranda!" I screamed out too loudly. I said to the vet, "No, no pets. Probate had a special relationship with some squirrels and chipmunks out in the yard, but I don't think that they held the same feeling of camaraderie."

"Will you be wanting me to take the body to get cremated? Do you want a paw print cast? Now would be a good time for me—or you, if you feel strong enough—to cut some of Probate's fur off, for a keepsake. You can put it in a jar. I've had clients frame their dog's fur."

The vet's eyes went all cockeyed at this point. She looked all over the house. I thought maybe she'd made up stories about an ex-husband, and she would come back later with her spouse and rob us. "You could put Probate's hair in a little amulet and wear it around your neck."

Like I said, Probate was part Chow and part pit bull. He kind of shed. I looked over at the corner and saw a swirl of his hair gathered. I said, "No, that's okay."

"That's okay to not get cremated?"

I said, "How much do I owe you?" and pulled a checkbook out of my back pocket. "I already dug a grave, right beneath a tulip poplar. It was Probate's favorite place to sit and listen to the songbirds on crisp spring mornings."

And then I bent over and started slapping my knee again. I leaned down and pet my dog over and over. I got out, "Songbirds!" I got out, "Your spirit has lifted!"

I got out, "God*damn* it, Miranda, grow up and *get out here.*"

"Some of my clients have been fiber artists. They've incorporated their pets' fur into works of art," the vet said. She stared up at the ceiling, and at the floor simultaneously.

I glanced down at her boobs, one of which had kind of fallen out of the weird, encumbering costume. I caught myself thinking of moats, and flaming arrows, of Trojan horses, and then Trojans. I said, "It's weird that your ex-husband is a podiatrist, and his name is Walker. Did he always know that he was going to be a podiatrist?" Maybe it was the marketing side of me, but I thought it necessary to say, "Did your ex-husband ever think he might want to go into physical therapy?"

"I'll help you carry Probate to the grave," the veterinarian said. "Let me help you. Probate's going to be heavy and cumbersome."

"No. I need to do this myself," I said.

Miranda opened the bedroom door a crack and said, "Is it over?"

I looked back toward my wife. For some reason Dr. Nancy thought it necessary, at this moment, still holding the incense, to hug me hard and stuff her face sideways into the nape of my neck. She kind of wailed a little, too. She made a noise that didn't sound unlike a dry heave. I didn't think Miranda could hear it, but I'm pretty sure the traveling euthanasia vet said, "I wanted to meet a knight at some point tonight."

I waited about two seconds before saying, "That rhymed."

She said, "It has come to this."

Miranda opened the door and strode toward us. I held my arms out in that way that people do to prove they're not hugging back. I held my arms out sideways in the international sign for Hey, This Isn't Me Doing This. My dog Probate lay dead—or at least his body was there, seeing as his spirit had scrammed the entire scene. Dr. Nancy said, "It is all for the best," and, "He is in a better place now," and, "We are not supposed to understand the meaning of Death, or of Life, for that matter."

My wife—now ex-wife—said, "Do you have any more of that drug by any chance?"

THE ELEVEN O'CLOCK news came on. Dr. Nancy stubbed out her incense in the sink, then put what was left over into a special pocket of her suitcase. She took out a bottle of spray Clorox, got down on her hands and knees, and encircled Probate's body with disinfectant. I got a roll of paper towels off the counter and handed them to her. She said, "Probate might've emitted invisible microbes, and I don't want y'all breathing them in."

I shrugged. Miranda started crying again, covered her face, and went out on the back porch. I said, "Do you have a regular clinic, Dr. Nancy? I mean, in case we get another dog, can we bring it to you for rabies shots?"

She shook her head. She said, "I couldn't take it anymore. Too sad."

Too sad? I thought. *Sadder than traveling to strangers' houses and putting their pets down daily? Or nightly?* I said, "Huh." I said, "Look. I'm not going to let you leave here without telling me why you're dressed up in such Renaissance festival attire."

"Corpse-dew. I believe that I have eradicated any possible corpse-dew."

I said, "Good. Maybe I'm wrong. Do you dress like this every day?" From outside, I could hear my wife sobbing uncontrollably. I heard her call for her mother. In retrospect, maybe I should've gone out to comfort her.

Dr. Nancy said, "It's my therapist's idea, really. She says one of my problems is that I wish, too often, to conform. She says my ex-husband drilled it into me I should conform, and before that time my own parents wanted me to be a debutante, and before that time I needed to be a cheerleader, and before that time I had to win the spelling bee. Spelling bee, cheerleader, debutante, wife who acted stupid in front of her husband's friends." She kind of let out a heh-heh-heh. "Do you know how much harder it is to graduate from vet school than med school, or at least med school to end up a foot doctor?"

Again, we stood there right beside my dead dog. I didn't think it was right. I said, "I have to work in the morning. I better get Probate in the ground, then cover the grave with a big piece of roofing tin I got out earlier. And some cement blocks."

Miranda sounded like she had dry heaves. She couldn't hear the veterinarian, I didn't think, but I thought about how she'd shown me photos of her own self winning a spelling bee, being a cheerleader, being presented to society the summer after her first year of college. Did she think that I made her act stupid in front of my friends? Did I, unintentionally?

The vet placed both her hands on Probate's chest, held them there ten seconds, stood up, and said, "The spirit has definitely lifted." She said, "On my way out I'll talk Miranda into coming back inside while we bury your friend."

I said, "No. I mean, yes, talk her into coming back inside. But like I said, I want to bury him by myself."

"He's heavy," the vet said. "You're going to need my help."

I said, "I can handle it." I still held the checkbook.

She said, "It's five hundred dollars, made out to Dr. Nancy, DVM."

Finally, I stood above my dead mother-in-law's dead dog for five minutes before Miranda came back inside. She walked straight to the bedroom and, without turning her head, told me to get the sheet she'd set aside earlier to wrap Probate's body. In another five minutes I heard Dr. Nancy's big Suburban crank up, and she backed out of the driveway at about forty miles an hour.

I don't want to admit that the traveling euthanasia vet held some knowledge in the situation, but Probate's corpse didn't feel like any fifty-pound bag of dog food I'd ever hefted over my shoulder. It felt like what some of those He Man competitors endured. I don't know what the spirit weighs, but it couldn't have been much.

I could've plain dragged my dog out the door, down the couple steps to the pea gravel, then continued toward the tree where I'd fashioned his deep red clay-walled grave. Or I could've gotten a flashlight, roamed around the backyard, found the wheelbarrow that I never kept in the same place two days in a row, returned, and so on. But in the end I bent down, remembered to use my thighs instead of my lower back, and cradled my now-ex-wife's still-dead mother's mixed breed after I wrapped him tighter than a specialized burrito in a bedsheet Miranda used only when my friends from college showed up needing to spend the night.

Anyway, I got the dog out there and set Probate down on the edge of his final resting place. Hours earlier I'd had the foresight to leave my spade against the tulip poplar—I'll go ahead and say that the tree died within a year, maybe from my having to cut half its roots. I picked up Probate's body in two clenched fists of percale, leaned over slowly, and eased him into the ground. I'm not one to be religious or spiritual, seeing as I'll go to hell for misleading people in the ways of marketing and advertising, but I thought it necessary to say aloud, "You were a good dog, Probate. You were good as Max, and you were good as Probate. I hope we meet in the afterlife, buddy."

I shoveled hard clay on top of his body, then shuffle-stepped a few times to tamp it down, then placed that piece of roofing tin over the bruised and tender earth-breach, plus six cement blocks I'd sequestered over the years for such a moment.

At this time I cried.

Maybe I stood out there and looked through the branches toward the sky for thirty minutes. Maybe I wondered if it was too early to consider driving down to the Humane Society at some point within the month, picking out a young stray, and naming it for the first time. I can't remember. I sat down on a compromised wood-slatted bench nearby and tried to imagine a traveling euthanasia veterinarian's nighttime dreams. I thought of Miranda inside, and envisioned her opening and closing drawers, in search of pain medication. Somehow this would all be my fault: Probate's demise, the vet's tardiness, the inappropriate cleavage. The long-buried reminder of Miranda's own life-filmstrip: spelling bee, cheerleader, debutante, unhappy spouse. I envisioned my wife pulling open our filing cabinet upstairs, finding our wills, making a note how she needed to change hers. Or did she ricochet around our house, gathering useless mementos, readying them for one of the local thrift stores so that, later, we wouldn't encumber each other with needless keep-or-trash decisions?

I returned the shovel. On the back porch, after standing too long trying to compose myself, I turned the knob and tried to remember if I had locked the door behind me, out of habit.

SHOW-AND-TELL

I WASN'T OLD ENOUGH TO KNOW THAT MY FATHER COULDN'T have obtained a long-lost letter from famed lovers Heloise and Peter Abelard, and since European history wasn't part of my third-grade curriculum, I really felt no remorse in bringing the handwritten document—on lined and holepunched Blue Horse filler paper—announcing its value, and reading it to the class on Friday show-and-tell. My classmates—who would all later grow up to be idiots, in my opinion, since they feared anything outside of South Carolina in general and my hometown of Forty-Five in particular, thus making them settle down exactly where they got trained, thus shrinking the gene pool even more—brought the usual: starfishes and conch shells bought in Myrtle Beach gift shops, though claimed to have been found personally during summer vacation; Indian Head pennies given as birthday gifts by grandfathers; the occasional pet gerbil, corn snake, or tropical fish. My father instructed me how to read the letter, what words to stress, when to pause. I, of course, protested directly after the dry run. Some of the words and phrases reached beyond my vocabulary. The general tone of the letter, I knew, would only get me playground-taunted by boys and girls alike. My father told me to pipe down and read louder. He told me to use my hands better and got out a metronome.

I didn't know that my father—a "widower" is what he instructed me to call him, although everyone knew how Mom ran off to Nashville and hadn't died—had once dated Ms. Suber, my teacher. My parents' pasts never came up in conversation, even after my mother ended up tending bar at a place called the Merchant's Lunch on Lower Broad more often than she sang on various honky-tonk stages, waiting for representation by a man who would call her the next Patsy Cline. No, the prom night and homecoming of my father's senior year in high school with Ms. Suber never leaked out in our talks, whether we ate supper in front of the television screaming at Walter Cronkite or played pinball down at the Sunken Gardens Lounge.

I got up in front of the class. I knew that a personal, caring, loving, benevolent God didn't exist, seeing as I had prayed that my classmates would spill over their allotted time, et cetera, et cetera, and then we'd go to recess, lunch, and then sit through one of the mandatory filmstrips each South Carolina elementary school student underwent weekly on topics as tragic and diverse as Friendship, Fire Safety, Personal Hygiene, and Bee Stings. "I have a famous letter written from one famous person to another famous person," I said.

Ms. Suber held her mouth in a tiny O. Nowadays I realize that she held beauty, but at the time she was just another very old woman in front of an elementary school class, her corkboard filled with exclamation marks. She wasn't but thirty-five, really. Ms. Suber motioned for me to edge closer to the music stand she normally used on Recorder Day. "And what are these famous people's names, Mendal?"

Ricky Hutton, who'd already shown off a ship in a bottle that he didn't make but said he did, yelled out, "My father has a letter from President Johnson's wife thanking him for picking up litter."

"My grandma sent me a birthday card with a two-dollar bill inside," said Libby Belcher, the dumbest girl in the class, who later went on to get a doctorate in education and then become superintendent of the school district.

I stood there with my folded document. Ms. Suber said, "Go on."

"I forget who wrote this letter. I mean, they were French people."

"Might it be Napoleon and Josephine?" Ms. Suber wore a smirk that I would see often in my life, from women who immediately recognized any untruth I chose to tell.

I said, "My father told me, but I forget. It's not signed or anything," which was true.

Ms. Suber pointed at Billy Gilliland and told him to quit throwing his baseball in the air, a baseball supposedly signed by Shoeless Joe Jackson that none of us believed in, seeing as the signature was printed, at best. We never relented on Gilliland, and later on he plain used the ball in pickup games until the cover wore off.

I unfolded the letter and read, "'My dearest.'"

"These were French people writing in English, I suppose," Ms. Suber said.

I nodded. I said, "They were smart, I believe. 'I want to tell you that if I live to be a hundred I won't meet another man like you. If I live to be a hundred there shall be no love to match ours.'"

The entire class began laughing, of course. My face reddened. I looked at Ms. Suber, but she concentrated on her shoe. "'That guy who wrote that "How Do I Love Thee" poem has nothing on us, my sugar-booger-baby.'"

"That's enough," Ms. Suber belted out. "You can sit down, Mendal."

I pointed at the letter. I had another dozen paragraphs to go, some of which rhymed. I hadn't gotten to the word "throbbing," which showed up fourteen times. "I'm not making any of this up," I said. I walked two steps toward my third-grade teacher, but she stood up and told everyone to go outside except me.

Glenn Flack walked by and said, "You're in trouble, Mendal Dawes." Carol Anderson, who was my third-grade girlfriend, looked like she was going to cry, as if I'd written the letter to Ms. Suber myself.

Ms. Suber said, "You've done nothing wrong, Mendal. Please tell your daddy that I got it. When he asks what happened today, just say that Ms. Suber got it, okay?"

I put the letter in my front pants pocket. I said, "My father's a widower."

MY FATHER WAS waiting for me when I got home. Like everyone else, he started off in textiles, then gave it up. I never really knew what he did for a living, outside of driving around within a hundred-mile radius of Forty-Five buying up land and then reselling it when the time was right. He had a knack. That was his word. For a time I thought it was the make of his car. "I drive around all day and buy land," he said more than once, before and after my mother took off to replace Patsy Cline. "I have a Knack."

I came home wearing my book bag, filled with math homework and an abacus. I said, "Hey, Dad."

He held his arms wide open, as if I were a returning P.O.W. "Did your teacher send back a note?"

I reached in my pocket and pulled out the letter from Heloise to Abelard. I handed it to him and said, "She made me quit reading."

"She made you quit reading? How far along did you get?"

I told him how I only got to the part about sugar-booger-baby. I said, "Is this one of those lessons in life you keep telling me about, like when we went camping?" My father taught me early on how to tell the difference between regular leaves and poison ivy, the year before, when we camped out beside the Saluda River, far from any commode, waiting for him to gain a vision on which tract would be most saleable later.

"Goddamn it to hell. She didn't say anything else after you read the letter?"

My father wore a seersucker suit. He wore a string tie. I said, "She called recess pretty much in the middle of me reading the thing. This is some kind of practical joke, isn't it?"

My father looked at me as if I'd peed on his wing tips. He said, "Now why would I do something like that to the only human being I love in this world?"

I couldn't imagine why. Why would a man who—as he liked to tell me often—before my birth played baseball for the Yankees in the summer, football for the Packers in the winter, and competed in the Olympics, ever revert to playing jokes on a nine-year-old son of his? "Ms. Suber seemed kind of mad."

"Did she cry? Did she start crying? Did she turn her head away from y'all and blow her nose into a handkerchief? Don't hold back, Mendal. Don't think that you're embarrassing your teacher or anything for telling the truth. Ms. Suber would want you to tell the truth, wouldn't she?"

I said, "Uh-huh. Probably."

"Uh-huh probably she cried, or uh-huh probably she'd want you to tell the truth?" My father walked to the kitchen backwards, pulled a bottle of bourbon from the shelf, and drank from it straight. Twenty years later on I would do the same thing, but over a dog that needed to be put to sleep.

I said, "Uh-huh. I told her you were a widower and everything. We got to go to recess early."

My father kept walking backwards. He took a glass from the cabinet, then cracked open an ice tray. He put cubes in the glass, poured bourbon into it, and stood staring at me as if I had told secrets to the enemy. "Did she say that she's thinking about getting married?"

I said, "She didn't say anything."

I wondered if my mother stood before a group of men and women drinking house beer, if she sang "I Fall to Pieces" or "Crazy" or any of those other country songs. It wasn't but three-thirty in my father's house. There was a one-hour time change, at least, in Nashville.

"I'VE GOTTEN AHOLD of a genuine Cherokee Indian bracelet and ring," my father said the next Thursday night. "I ain't shitting you any on this one. Your mother's father gave them to us a long time ago as a wedding present. He got them when he was traveling through Cherokee County up in the Cherokee country. Your grandfather used to sell cotton, you know. Sometimes those Indians needed cotton. They traded things for cotton. That's the way things go."

I said, "I was thinking about taking some pinecones I found." I had gathered up some pinecones that were so perfect it wasn't funny. They looked like Christmas trees built to scale. "I was going to take a rock and say it was a meteorite."

"No, no. Take some of my Cherokee Indian jewelry, son. I don't mind. I don't care! Hotdamn I didn't even remember having the things, so it won't matter none if they get broken or stolen," he said. "This is the real thing, Bubba."

What could I do? I wasn't but nine years old, and early on I'd been taught to do whatever my elders said, outside of drinking whiskey and smoking cigarettes when they got drunk and made the offer, usually at Sunken Gardens Lounge. I thought, *Maybe I can pretend to take my father's weird jewelry and stick it in my desktop. Maybe I can stick a pinecone inside my lunch box.* "Yes sir."

"I won't have it any other way," he said. "Wait here."

My father went back to what used to be my mother's and his bedroom. He opened up a wooden box he'd fashioned in high school shop, and pulled out a thin silver bracelet, plus a one-pearl ring. I didn't know that these trinkets once adorned the left arm of my third-grade teacher, right before she broke up with my father in order to go to college, and long before she graduated, taught in some other school system for ten years, and then came back to her hometown.

I took the trinkets in a small cotton sack. My father told me that he'd come get me for lunch if I wanted him to, that I didn't need to pack a bologna sandwich and banana as always. I went to the refrigerator and made my own and then left through the back door.

Glenn Flack started off show-and-tell with an X-ray of his mother's ankle. She'd fallen off the front porch trying to run from bees—something the rest of us knew not to do, seeing as we'd learned how to act in one of the weekly filmstrips. I got called next and said, "I have some priceless Cherokee Indian artifacts to show y'all. The Cherokee Indians had a way with hammering and chiseling." My father had made me memorize this speech.

I showed my classmates what ended up being something bought at Rey's Jewelers. Ms. Suber said, "Let me take a look at that," and got up to take the bracelet from my hand. She peered at it and then held it at arm's length and said, "This looks like it says 'sterling' on the inside, Mendal. I believe you might've picked up the wrong Indian jewelry to bring to school."

"Indian giver, Indian giver, Indian giver!" Melissa Beasley yelled out. It wasn't a taboo term back then. This was a time, understand, before we all had to say Native American Head penny.

I said, "I just know what my dad told me. That's all I know." I took the bracelet from Ms. Suber, pulled out the ring, and stood there as if offering a Milk-Bone to a stray and skittish dog.

Ms. Suber said, "I've had enough of this," and told me to return to my desk. I put the pearl ring on my thumb and stuck the bracelet around the toe of my tennis shoe. Ms. Suber said, "Has your father gone insane lately, Mendal?"

It embarrassed me, certainly, and if she had said it twenty or thirty years later, I could've sued her for harassment, slander, and making me potentially agoraphobic. My desk was in the last row. Every student turned toward me except Shirley Ebo, the only black girl in the entire school, four years prior to lawful integration. She looked forward, as always, ready to approach the music stand and explain her show-and-tell object, a face jug made by an old, old relative of hers named Dave the Slave.

I said, "My father has a Knack." Maybe I said nothing, really, but I thought about my father's Knack. I waited.

Ms. Suber sat back down. She looked at the ceiling and said, "I'm sorry, Mendal. I didn't mean to yell at you. Everyone go on to recess."

AND SO IT continued for six weeks. I finally told my father that I couldn't undergo any more humiliation, that I would play hooky, that I would show up at school and say I had forgotten to bring my show-and-tell gimcrack. I said, "I'm only going to take these stupid things you keep telling me stories about if it brings in some money, Dad."

Not that I was ever a capitalist or anything, but I figured early on that show-and-tell would end up somehow hurting my penmanship or spelling grade, and that maybe I needed to start saving money in order to get a head start in life should I not get into college. My father said, "That sounds fair enough. How much will you charge me to take this old, dried Mayan wrist corsage and matching boutonniere?"

I said, "Five bucks each."

My father handed them over. If the goddamn school system had ever shown a worthwhile Friday filmstrip concerning inductive logic, I would've figured out back then that when Ms. Suber and my father had had their horrific and execrable high school breakup, my father had gone over to her house and gathered up everything he'd ever bestowed upon her, from birthday to Valentine's Day to special three-month anniversary and so on. He had gifts she'd given him, too, I supposed much later, though I doubted they were worthy of monogamy.

But I didn't know logic. I thought only that my father hated the school system, had no trust whatsoever in public education, and wanted to drive my teacher to a nervous breakdown in order to get her to quit. Or, I thought, it was his way of flirting—that since my mother had "died," he wanted to show a prospective second wife some of the more spectacular possessions he could offer a needful woman.

He said, "I can handle ten dollars a show-and-tell session, for two items. Remind me not to give you an hourglass. I don't want you charging me per grain of sand."

This was all by the first of October. By Christmas break I'd brought in cuff links worn by Louis Quatorze, a fountain pen used by the fifty-six signers of the Declaration of Independence (my father tutored me on stressing "Independence" when I announced my cherished object to the class), a locket once owned by Elmer the glue inventor, thus explaining why the thing couldn't be opened, a pack of stale Viceroys that once belonged to the men who raised the American flag on Iwo Jima. I brought in more famous love letters, all on lined Blue Horse paper: from Ginger Rogers to Fred Astaire, from Anne Hathaway to Shakespeare, from all of Henry VIII's wives to him. One letter, according to my dad, was from Plato to Socrates, though he said it wasn't the original, and that he'd gone to the trouble of learning Greek in order to translate the thing.

Ms. Suber became exasperated with each new disclosure. She moved from picking names at random or in alphabetical order to always choosing me last. My classmates voted me Most Popular, Most Likely to Succeed, and Third Grade President, essentially because I got us ten more minutes of recess every Friday.

I walked down to the County Bank every Friday after school and deposited the money my father had forked over in a regular savings account. This was a time before IRAs. It was a time before stock portfolios, mutual funds, and the like. They gave me a toaster for starting the account and a dinner plate every time I walked in with ten dollars or more. After a few months I could've hosted a dinner party for twelve.

ON SATURDAY MORNINGS, more often than not, I drove with my father from place to place, looking over land he had bought or planned to buy. He had acquired a few acres of woodland before my birth, and soon thereafter the Army Corps of Engineers came in, flooded the Savannah River, and made my father's property near lakefront. He sold that parcel, took that money, and bought more land in an area that bordered what would become I-95. He couldn't go wrong. My father was not unlike the fool who threw darts at a map and went with his gut instinct. He would buy useless swampland, and someone else would soon insist on buying that land at twice to ten times his cost in order to build a golf course, a subdivision, or a nuclear-power facility. I had no idea what he did between these ventures, outside of reading and wondering. How else would he know about Abelard and Heloise, or even Socrates and Plato? He hadn't gone to college. He hadn't taken some kind of correspondence course.

We drove, and I stuck my head out the window like the dog I had owned before my mother took him to Nashville. We'd get to some land, pull down a dirt road usually, and my father would stare hard for ten or fifteen minutes. He barely turned his head from side to side, and he never turned off the engine. Sometimes he'd say at the end, "I think I got a fouled spark plug," or, "You can tell that that gas additive's working properly."

He never mentioned people from history, or the jewelry of the dead. I took along Hardy Boys mysteries but never opened the covers. Finally, one afternoon, I said, "Ms. Suber wants to know if you're planning on coming to the PTA meeting. I forgot to tell you."

My father turned off the ignition. He reached beneath his seat and pulled out a can of beer and a church key. We sat parked between two gullies, somewhere in Greenwood County. "Hotdamn, boy, you need to tell me these things. When is it?"

I said, "I forgot. I got in so much trouble Friday that I forgot." I'd taken a tortoise to show-and-tell and said his name was John the Baptist. At first Ms. Suber seemed delighted. When she asked why I had named him John the Baptist, I said, "Watch this." I screamed, "John the Baptist!" When he retreated into his shell and lost his head, I nodded. She had me sit back down. None of my classmates got the joke.

"The PTA meeting's on Tuesday. It's Tuesday." I wore a pair of cut-off blue jeans with the bottoms cut into one-inch strips. My mother used to make them for me when I'd grown taller but hadn't gained weight around the middle. I had on my light-blue Little League T-shirt, with Sunken Gardens on the front and 69 for my number on the back. My father had insisted that I get that number, and that I would thank him one day.

"Hell, yes. Do I need to bring anything? I mean, is this one of those meetings where parents need to bring food? I know how to make potato salad. I can make potato salad and coleslaw, you know."

"She just asked me to ask if you'd show up. That's all she said, I swear."

My father looked out at what I understood to be another wasteland. Empty beer cans were scattered in front of us, and the remains of a haphazard bonfire someone had made right in the middle of a path. "Maybe I should call her up and ask if she needs anything."

Although I didn't understand the depth of my father's obsession, I said, "Ms. Suber won't be in town until that night. We have a substitute on Monday, 'cause she has to go to a funeral somewhere."

My father drank from his beer. He handed the can over and told me to take little sips at first. I said, "Mom wouldn't want you to give me beer."

He nodded. "Mom wouldn't want you to do a lot of things, just like she didn't want me to do a lot of things. But she's not here, is she? Your momma's spending all her time praying that she never gets laryngitis, while the rest of us hope she does."

I DIDN'T KNOW that my father had been taking Fridays off in order to see the school secretary, feign needing to leave me a bag lunch, and then stand looking through the vertical window of my classroom door while I expounded on the rarity of a letter sweater once worn by General Custer, or whatever. When the PTA meeting came around, I went with my father, though no other students attended. Pretty much it was only parents, teachers, and a couple of the lunch ladies who had volunteered to serve a punch of ginger ale and grape juice. My father entered Ms. Suber's classroom and approached her as if she were a newspaper boy he'd forgotten to pay. He said, "I thought you'd eventually send a letter home asking for a conference. I thought you'd finally buckle under." To me he said, "Go look at the goldfish, Mendal. You've always liked aquariums. Maybe I'll get you one."

I looked at the corner of the room. My classmates' parents were sitting at tiny desks, their knees bobbing like the shells of surfaced turtles. My third-grade teacher said, "I know you think this is cute, but it's not. I don't know why you think you can recount me however many years later after what you did to me back then."

My father pushed me in the direction of the aquarium. Ms. Suber waved and smiled at Glenn Flack's parents, who were walking in. I said, "Can I go sit in the car?"

Ms. Suber said, "You stay right here, Mendal."

"I might not have been able to go to college like you did, Lola, but I've done good for myself," my father said. I thought one thing only: *Lola?*

"I know you have, Lee. I know you've done well. And let me be the first to say how proud I am of you, and how I'm sorry if I hurt you, and that I've seen you looking in the window when Mendal does his bogus show-and-tells." She pointed at the window in the door. Mr. and Mrs. Anderson walked in. "I need to start this thing up."

My father said to me, "If you want to go sit in the car, go ahead." He handed me the keys, leaned down, and said, "There's a beer in the glove compartment, son."

Let me say that this was South Carolina in 1968. Although my memory's not perfect, I think that at the time, neither drinking nor driving was against the law for minors, nor was smoking cigarettes before the age of twelve. Five years later I would drive my mini-bike to the Sunken Gardens, meet one of the black boys twirling trays out in the parking lot, order my eight-pack of Miller ponies, and have it delivered to me without conscience or threat of law.

I pretended to go into the parking lot but circled around to the outside of Ms. Suber's classroom. I stood beneath one of the six jalousies, crouched, and listened. Ms. Suber welcomed the parents and said that it was an exciting year. She said something about how all of us would have to take a national test later on to see how we compared with the rest of the nation. She said something about a school play. Ms. Suber warned parents of a looming head-lice epidemic. She paced back and forth and asked everyone to introduce himself or herself. Someone asked if the school would ever sponsor another cake-and-pie sale in order to buy new recorders. My father said he'd be glad to have a potato-salad-and-cole-slaw sale. I didn't hear the teacher's answer. From where I crouched I could only look up at the sky and notice how some stars twinkled madly while others shone hard and fast like mica afire.

BY THE TIME I reached high school, my mother had moved from Nashville to New Orleans and then from New Orleans to Las Vegas. She never made it as a country singer or a blues singer, but she seemed to thrive as a hostess of sorts. As I crouched there beneath a window jutting out above boxwoods, I thought of my mother and imagined what she might be doing at the moment my father was experiencing his first PTA meeting. Was she crooning to conventioneers? Was she sitting in a back room worrying over panty hose? That's what I thought, I swear to God. Everyone in Ms. Suber's classroom seemed to be talking with cookies in their mouths. I heard my father laugh hard twice—once when Ms. Suber said she knew that her students saw her as a witch, and another time when she said she knew that her students went home complaining that she didn't spank exactly the way their parents spanked.

Again, this was in the middle of the Vietnam War. Spanking made for good soldiers.

My third-grade teacher said that she didn't have anything else to say, and told her students' parents to feel free to call her up should they have questions concerning grades, expectations, or field trips. She said she appreciated anyone who wanted to help chaperone kids or work after school in a tutoring capacity. I stood up and watched my friends' parents leave single file, my father last in line.

Fifteen minutes after I'd gotten back in the car, five minutes after everyone else had driven out of the parking lot, I climbed out the passenger side and crept back to Ms. Suber's window. I expected my father to have Lola Suber in a headlock, or backed up against the Famous Christians of the World corkboard display. I didn't foresee their having moved desks against the walls in order to make a better dance floor.

My father held my third-grade teacher in a way I'd seen him hold a woman only once before: one Fourth of July he had danced with my mother in the backyard while the neighbors shot bottle rockets straight up. My mother had placed her head on his shoulder and smiled, her eyes raised to the sky. Lola Suber didn't look upward. She didn't smile either. My father seemed to be humming, or talking low. I couldn't hear exactly what went on, but years later he confessed that he had set forth everything he meant to say and do, everything he hoped she taught the other students and me when it came to matters of passion.

I did hear Lola Suber remind him that they had broken up because she had decided to have a serious and exclusive relationship with Jesus Christ.

There amid the boxwoods I hunkered down and thought only about the troubles I might have during future show-and-tells. I stood back up, saw them dancing, and returned to the car. I would let my father open the glove compartment later.

THE NOVELS OF RAYMOND CARVER

O NCE I FINALLY GOT TO EXPLAIN THE FAMILY DYNAM-
ics of my childhood home life back thirty years earlier—I'm
talking I started with my first memory of tracking sand into a
Myrtle Beach motel room on summer vacation, and ended with my
waving an invention covered in flypaper for my father in order to clear
dust motes and imaginary speckles from the air the day before I left for
good—the magistrate only sentenced me to 180 hours of community
service for attempted grave desecration. The security guard and subsequent sheriff's deputy believed wrongly that I wanted to steal my dead
father's rings, watch, or lucky change he insisted fill his postmortem
pants pocket. They didn't notice my recently deceased mother's crema-
tory ashes balanced atop the headstone. This was two in the morning
on the outer edge of Gruel Cemetery on the first day of spring—a day,
traditionally, that my father made Mom and me scrub the entire house
with ammonia, then Clorox, then Texize pine cleaner: walls, furniture,
appliances, floors, even ceiling. Back when I had an indoor dog named
Slick, it was my job to vacuum him every morning before school, every
afternoon at feeding time. Slick took to watching the front door endlessly, and finally escaped through the legs of two Mormons one summer day. He never returned.

"What you're saying is, your father had a phobia against germs," Judge
Cowart said as I stood before him without a lawyer two weeks after the

incident. "There's a name for that kind of behavior now." Judge Cowart wasn't a real judge seeing as magistrates got voted into office, either Democrat or Republican. In real life he owned Gruel Modern Men's Wear, one of the last businesses on the square to evaporate.

I said, "Yes sir. And he was plain mean, too."

The deputy and graveyard security guard had stood at the other desk to recount their version of events. There was no jury, but the magistrate's courtroom was packed. My arrest made the weekly *Forty-Five Platter* newspaper, the next town over. The deputy, a boy I grew up with, named Les Miles, pretty much went over everything that happened in his life on up to taking me to the Graywood County Detention Center. I think Les liked having such a large audience.

Say "Les Miles" real fast. It's one of those names like Mike Weir. Or Derrick Rapp. Ben Dover. Mike Hunt. I hadn't noticed growing up that maybe it built up inside him so much that his only options in life appeared to be cop, professional gambler, or sad mime.

Judge Cowart said to the deputy and security guard, "What you're saying is, he only got a good two feet down in one spot. It wasn't like he popped chalk down and dug up the entire site."

"We measured it out to be a two-foot-by-two-foot piece of sod," said the security guard, an older man named Niblock who moved down to Gruel from somewhere in Pennsylvania with his wife in order to semi-retire. I couldn't imagine how bad his life must've been up there to make such a drastic choice. "I keep a measuring tape on my belt at all times," he said. "Sometimes I get time to build bluebird houses up in the office during my shift."

I remained seated until the magistrate asked if I would like to question either man. I stood up and said, "Everything they've said is true," which brought about a massive gasp from the pewed spectators, followed by accusations of my being a Satan worshipper and ungrateful son. I said, "All of that is true, but it was for a good, moral, spiritual, ethical, bighearted reason." I had practiced my speech ever since posting bail.

Judge Cowart said, "Let's hear your side of things. Go ahead and loosen that one hundred percent silk tie bought over at Gruel Modern Men's Wear on the historic square, unbutton your Botany 500 sport jacket, and let all us in on what's of a higher purpose."

Of course I wasn't about to say that I wanted to pour my mother's ashes into my father's grave so that he would have to live forever covered in a fine dust. No, I went through my daddy's stories of germ-free insistence, how he one time covered the entire exterior of our brick house in Saran Wrap. I told the judge, cop, guard, and seated guests about the times my father installed window fans in every room, blowing out, until our electric bill from Duke Power came in at over four hundred in 1968 dollars. None of these stories were false or exaggerated. I offered midstream to take a lie detector. Some time after I left Gruel for good my father got it in his mind that Mom's skin peeled off microscopically in their bed, and he bought a neoprene diver's suit for her to either wear at night with him or sleep in the guest bedroom with the door closed. He'd gone so far as hanging transom-to-floor thick clear plastic flaps at every entranceway in the house—the kind usually found in warehouses, drive-through car washes, and between where a butcher cuts his loins and meets the public in case he needed to hole up by himself.

Judge Cowart finally said, "This is all very interesting in a woe-is-me kind of way, Mr. Cary. I'll give you exactly two minutes to find a point."

In retrospect I think I should've requested a jury. Swaying the gawkers wouldn't matter, I supposed, but I followed through with my plan. "My father got electrocuted while trying to rewire a central heat and air system backwards so it sucked dust out of his living space. That happened some fifteen years ago. My mother believed that caskets and funeral plots cost too much money, and she requested to be cremated. I followed through with her desire. On the night that I got arrested in Gruel Cemetery, I only wanted to pour her ashes on top of my father's final resting place. I knew that they needed and wanted to be together. Nothing else. She had already sold the plot directly next to Dad. That's it."

Luckily no one called me on the lie detector test; the final section of my defense—and I got my voice to crack a few times—was not quite as sentimental or melodramatic as the truth, like I said. I really only wanted to envelop my father so he'd be bothered and distracted for eternity.

I'm pretty sure that I heard more than a few women behind me go, "Ahhh," like that. Judge Cowart wrinkled his brow and looked at Les Miles and Mr. Niblock. They shrugged in unison. "Well. I got to say I have no precedent to work with. I believe you, Mr. Cary. But we, as a democratic society, can't allow people to take up shovels at their whim." He went on and on, said something about both King Tut and the remains of Confederate soldiers trapped inside the Hunley submarine, banged his gavel, and gave me community service.

I should mention that I came back to Gruel completely alone, that no woman will ever marry me. My first name's Ellis, so it comes out one of those names like Les Miles, Mike Hunt, all the rest. It's an old-fashioned South, and exactly zero women want to be called Mrs. Ellis Cary, wife of a desecrater. I'd have a worse chance in a land of Cockney women. At least that's what I've always told everyone.

IT TOOK MY English department chairman four semesters to completely understand my great scam, a series of sophomore-level courses approved by a six-person curriculum committee, then approved by the stupid dean, a clutch of hands-on busybody trustees, and the president of the college. For all I know our state legislators and governor, too, thought it utterly fantastic and unselfish of me to teach five classes per semester while my colleagues took on only four.

"I don't know how you do it," Donna Mickel, a Faulkner scholar who got a master's degree from Clemson and doctorate from the University of Alabama, said to me more than once. She'd been at Anders College since its 1975 inception as a state institution. "Some of us kind of wish you'd slack up, Ellis. You're making us look bad." Donna Mickel liked to tell a story about how she *almost* had a paper accepted one time in *College Writing, College Reading!* It was a section of her dissertation entitled "William Faulkner, Closet Merchant Seaman: The Feminist and Oceanic Politics in the *Collected Stories*." Then Donna Mickel gave up altogether, and took up the clarinet.

What else could I ever say to her but, "These first-generation students need to know"? "Call me obsessed, but there are works of literature that I think will only make them stronger citizens, no matter what fields of expertise they choose later on in life."

My ex-department chairman once said—I swear to God—"One of the best classes I took in graduate school was the novels of O. Henry.

I wouldn't mind teaching it myself if anyone else could take over my Hardy Boys and Postmodernism course." Dr. Blocker went to one of those Ph.D.-by-mail outfits. "I got to tell you, Ellis, we're happy and proud to have you on the faculty here. Keep up the good work."

The first-generation students got it, though: They knew that my made-up course in the nonexistent novels of Raymond Carver meant that they would have nothing to read, that they would have no major papers. They showed up faster than Eskimos at a handwarmer giveaway. What started out as my teaching only one Ray Carver's novels class and four sections of English 101 ended up being five identical courses, each jammed with thirty students. I handed out blank sheets of typing paper for my syllabus.

"Your students really love the Raymond Carver novels class," every one of my colleagues told me during the course of each semester. "I wouldn't mind sitting in on it myself."

I didn't fear that ever happening as much as I feared some pinhead real scholar finding a Raymond Carver novel locked up inside a Syracuse, Iowa City, and/or Port Angeles basement, of the treasure being reported in *USA Today* or on *Entertainment Tonight*—how the very first novel ever of Raymond Carver was found by a snooping grad student, and a bidding war continued between publishing houses up in New York. Then I'd have to admit how I met with my students during their Monday-Wednesday-Friday or Tuesday-Thursday sessions and we basically talked about real-life problems concerning love and hate, conformity and rebellion, innocence and experience—the regular themes in all of Carver's short stories. I'd have to admit that although I urged my students to read all of the writer's stories, I never tested them, or offered up themes, or graded a paper over a two-year period. Everyone made an A as long as they showed up for class. It had been my contention long before that grades didn't matter in the history of the universe.

"It has come to my attention that you haven't actually taught any of Raymond Carver's novels since developing the course," Dr. Blocker finally said. "Could you explain this to me?"

We sat in my office. I turned off my computer so he couldn't read the screen where I was writing up another set of fake courses on the novels of Ring Lardner. I looked out the window at two of my students trying to catch a Frisbee in their mouths. One of them, I knew, would grow up to be an administrator. I said, "What are you talking about?"

"I think you know what I'm talking about. I was going over our majors' exit questionnaires, and more than a few of them mentioned how they learned more about life in your class than any other, even though there was nothing to read." I should mention that I already knew that my mother was dying, that her oncologist's prognosis was for her to be gone in three months tops, and that I would probably have to ask for a leave of absence in order to tend to her limited estate. So it wasn't like I was brave or anything when I said, "You fucking idiot—Raymond Carver wrote zero novels. If you people here knew anything whatsoever, you'd know that when I made up the course it was only a joke. I thought for sure somebody would say, 'Hey, that's funny, Ellis Cary—that would be like teaching a course called the Poetry of Ronald Reagan.'"

Dr. Blocker sat forward. "Well, as a matter of fact, I brought this up with Dr. Mickel and she said that it would be like teaching the poetry of William Faulkner."

I didn't say, "You bunch of fucking morons, Faulkner's first book was poetry." No, I said, "Listen. Let me tell you about my father." I went into everything, exactly as I would have to do soon thereafter with Judge Cowart, from Myrtle Beach motel sand in the carpet to the giant flypaper swatter catching microbes in the air. Then I said, "In some kind of genetic bad luck, I am highly allergic and fearful to chalk dust. Y'all are lucky that I haven't sued the college for workmen's comp, or for not establishing a safe workplace for the handicapped. Anyway, I made up the Carver course because I knew it would keep me from having to write on the chalkboard, thus saving my life."

Dr. Blocker leaned back in his chair. "I'm going to have to fire you for insubordination. There's an insubordination clause in your contract. I can only classify you as being insubordinate."

I said, "Nancy Drew wouldn't have had anything to do with the Hardy Boys, in case you're interested. Now, *she* was postmodern."

I trashed everything in my computer, outside of a little song I'd written about the English department, and boxed up my books, and left town. My mother died within the week, but not before telling me that she wished to be cremated and scattered in places that I thought she'd be most beneficial.

≥ ≤

My community service involved literally painting the town red: fire hydrants on the square, two brick alleyways, the base of Colonel Dill's statue across from Victor Dees's Army-Navy Surplus, a wooden house on Old Greenville Road where, supposedly, Jefferson Davis slept while his troops got massacred in a variety of fields to the northeast. Get this: My parole officer was a kid named Buck Hammond who underwent my first Novels of Raymond Carver class two years earlier. I met with young Buck and said, "I take it you're familiar with what went on in court."

He said, "No one's ever mentioned where your mother is now. Where's your mother now? I mean, if you didn't finish the deed of pouring her onto your father's grave site, then what happened to her?"

I taught him well, I thought. "She's still in the little snapshut plastic container that they gave me at Harley Funeral Home over in Forty-Five. She's on the mantel back home."

Buck said, "I know I didn't take any psychology courses over at Anders. I majored in sociology. But I learned enough in your Raymond Carver class to know that you still want to spread her ashes on your daddy's grave. Am I right?" He wore a suit that came from Gruel Modern Men's Wear, I could tell. The lapels could've been torn off and used for curtains. "Understand that I have to tell you what you have to do, and what's right, and all that. I have to tell you not to return to your daddy's grave armed with a dead mother, you know. I got to tell you never to dig up any ground in a graveyard, no matter what you think's for the best in the long run."

I said, "Hey, Buck, if I finish everything y'all tell me to do before a hundred and eighty hours is up, do I get to leave? Or will y'all find more things for me to do? Should I spread out my time, or work my butt off?"

Buck Hammond had a photograph of the president behind his desk, beside a framed miniature reproduction of the Bill of Rights. Off to the side was a needlepoint Lord's Prayer. "I trust that you would know what to do. Do the same thing any of those characters in a Raymond Carver novel would do."

I said, "I got it," and winked without winking. I smiled, but then wondered if it was all some kind of trick. Did I accidentally give Buck a B? I wondered.

"I think we have us something like two or three other men and women doing community service here in Gruel right now. Picking up trash on the roadside. Talking to teenagers about the dangers of smoking pot— that's the easiest community service there is right now seeing as there aren't but about two teenagers left in all of Gruel. Next time you decide to confront the law, you might want to get caught for smoking dope, Mr. Cary—you can get done with your community service in about thirty minutes."

I said I'd keep that in mind. I said, "What do I do, check in with you or someone every morning? I'm staying over at my parents' old place while all of this is going on. Hell, I guess I'll be staying there after it's done, too, seeing as I don't have a job."

My ex-student the parole officer said, "Ellis Cary. That kind of comes out like a complete sentence, don't it? Noun, verb, adjective. Is scary an adjective or an adverb? I was always taught that adverbs come right after verbs."

I shook my head. I wondered where my father's specter drifted at the moment, whether he spooked a germ-free lab or hovered above the crystalline air of Mount Whitney. Did my mother feel trapped within her plastic confines? I said, "There are too many rules in language, and there aren't enough at the same time, Buck. It's one of those things. I can't explain it all." He handed me a can of paint and a four-inch brush. "You might as well start with the hydrants, I guess." He said, "Listen, I can bring in Les Miles and that graveyard guard on the pretense of asking them questions, if you want. I'll let you know. I'll call them in, and then you can go spread your momma anywhere you want without them putting you in jail."

I told Buck Hammond that I should've given him an A plus.

I walked off from the office like Michelangelo, thinking but one thing: Raymond Carver could've written a novel if he'd only given the main male character the same name throughout every story. Sure, the guy would've had a different wife every chapter, and a different job or lack thereof, but pretty much it would have held the same voice. I walked to the first hydrant, right in front of Roughhouse Billiards, and set down my can. It wasn't eight thirty in the morning. Some fellow came out and bet me a dollar he could put a cue ball on the sidewalk, strike it hard with his eighteen-ounce stick, and get it to bounce off my can of paint and balance, finally, on the fire hydrant. He said he was training to be the best trick shot player in history, and that people were out there already writing novels about him. I suggested that he talk to a man or woman somewhere in the vicinity doing community service lectures about the evils of drug usage.

I WORKED DILIGENTLY until noon and had all of Gruel's fire hydrants sparkling red. I thought to myself, one hundred seventy-six hours to go. I walked back to Buck Hammond's office for another can of paint to say that I would start the alleyways, but he was at lunch. One of my community service comrades sat in Buck's office—the woman—and I said, "I'm betting you have to talk to people about pot." She wore a tie-dyed skirt and matching bandanna, a torn tank-top shirt that exposed her belly button ring, and a tattoo on her left bicep that looked like a bull's-eye, like a target.

"That's the other guy. I'm doing community service for throwing an apple core out the car window. The judge didn't believe me that an apple core will disintegrate into roadside compost. He got me for littering. Either a month in jail and a thousand-dollar fine, or two hundred hours of cleaning up the town." She slid her index and middle fingers beneath her nose and I thought for a second that she'd give me the secret Phi Beta Kappa handshake presently, but she didn't. "Are you the guy painting? I'm supposed to follow around behind you and clean up any drips you leave."

I introduced myself quite clearly: "My...name...is...Ellis...Cary," so she wouldn't hear "Hell-is-scary."

She stuck out her hand. She looked about the age of some of the first students I ever taught at Anders College, maybe thirty years old. She said, "Wow. Weird. I'm Cashion," She stuck out her hand. She didn't say her last name. And it was Cashion who said, "Hey, if I married you my name would be Cashion Cary. Like some kind of grocery store."

I don't know if it was because I was the kind of man who could figure out ways to get paid in full to teach textless classes, but I was way ahead of her. As soon as she said "Cashion," I had spelled it correctly in my mind, figured out what people would call her if we became betrothed, and in my mind's eye foresaw how we'd decorate my inherited house in Gruel. I said, "Yeah. Yeah. I get it. Is Cashion some kind of family name? I get it."

She nodded. "I wonder what time this guy's coming back. I need to see if I can take tomorrow off. I think I have the town pretty cleaned up. You haven't dripped a bunch of paint, have you?"

Ding-ding-ding! I thought. I thought, *I will from now on.*

I said, "What's going on tomorrow?"

"For some reason I decided to go back to college after all these years. It's a long story that involves wanting to follow The Dead around straight out of high school, you know, but then Jerry died. I followed some other bands around, but it wasn't the same. I made enough money selling ginseng I probably wasn't supposed to dig up in Tennessee, but nothing felt right. So I came back home here and enrolled in a couple classes over at Anders. I either want to become a nurse or a financial planner. I want to help people."

Please never come back, Buck Hammond, please never come back, Buck Hammond, I thought. I said, "You're having to take all those general education requirement courses, I'm guessing. I used to teach there."

Get this: Cashion Cary-to-be said, "The dean said I could come in as a sophomore due to life experiences. I mean, I'm having to pay for everything myself—I didn't get any scholarship money—but I'm not having to take English comp and all that. Maybe I should have. I'm kind of having trouble in this course called the Novels of Raymond Carver. Dr. Blocker said we're supposed to find out what we're supposed to find. Every day he sends us to the library to do research, but I have no clue what he really wants."

The Novels of Raymond Carver! I thought, setting down my new paint can. "You have to believe me when I say that I can help you immeasurably," I said. "I haven't been this serious since I told my father that it wasn't healthy to take a bath every hour. But that's another story. Listen, if you want help on the novels of Raymond Carver, then I'm your man. I'm the idiot who designed that class. You either have to hand him twenty blank pages stapled together at the top left or you and I can come up with a fake paper that'll make him scurry around trying to check your citations for the rest of his life. I'm willing to write the fake paper for you, if you want. I can do it in a second. We just have to come up with one or two made-up titles. This'll be fun. This'll be easy."

I waited for Cashion to say, "You're my hero, Ellis Cary. How can I ever repay you?" She didn't.

Buck Hammond walked back from lunch and I yelled out, "Tell this woman how much I taught you in my Raymond Carver novels class. Tell her. Tell her this very instant! Tell her now."

I TOOK THE paint can home and poured half my mother inside. Listen, I stirred her in. I whipped those ashes, no matter what. At one point my paint stick popped the sides of the can in a way that sounded like "Froggy went a-courtin' and he did ride, uh-huh" over and over. I pureed. As I figured it, my mother would infiltrate and dust up Gruel full-time should my mean weird father decide to revisit his homeplace.

"He seemed to write a bunch of short stories," Cashion said from the dining room table where she spread out a slew of blank pages. "I read, I think, all his stories—some of them seemed to be the same, with only different endings or beginnings. And he wrote some poems, too."

"You damn right," I said. I wore a pair of goggles in case my mother's ashes flew up in my face. I'd read and taught Sophocles enough to know better. "Listen, tomorrow when I go to paint, I promise you I won't spill anything if you promise not to leave me alone. Litterbug."

"Grave robber."

"Weird hippie who can't predict a band member's death."

"Loser."

Oh, we went on and on. I got all giddy and found myself daydreaming about discovered lost manuscripts of Raymond Carver, or of taking the time to write an entire novel about a wife who leaves her husband for smoking too much dope, and the blind man the husband brings in as a boarder. Or maybe a novel about a man who runs a drying-out facility and all of the funny-sad stories he hears from clients and visitors alike. I thought of a novel told from the point of view of a scared, scared divorced man who takes to carrying a gun at all times, eating rat poison on purpose, or maybe a guy whose wife leaves so he puts all their furniture out on the front lawn, arranged perfectly.

And so on. I fantasized about a life with Cashion, one where we would travel far from Gruel to live out our days. I would come back yearly, at night, to visit my parents' remains. "You're not really going to paint your mother in town, are you?"

I said, "My mother became attached to the town after Dad died. Her neighbors slowly accepted her when they found out she wasn't afflicted with germophobia. It seems logical to me. As a matter of fact, that should be a law—that every dead person get painted to a storefront or alleyway. Make kids think they're being watched all the time. Kind of like animism."

Cashion continued to sit at my mother's dining-room table and printed her name in the dust. She said, "I was only kidding earlier about being a nurse. I'm not freaked out by molecules, but—still—there's no way I could see people dying all the time."

I finished sieving Mom thoroughly. Would I keep the other half of her remains in a glazed clay vessel for the rest of my life? Would I come back in a year and risk getting caught by Les Miles and Mr. Niblock again? Cashion picked up one of Raymond Carver's collections and opened it up in the middle. Fifteen minutes later she said that the characters came across a dead woman in the river, but did nothing. She didn't think it right. I said it was only a story, it was only made up.

We stared at the paint can for too long, then walked over to the pool hall an hour before it unofficially closed. Our parole officer never said we couldn't offer toasts to one another and to those surrounding us. I didn't say anything like, "Here's to my spending more than my allotted time cleaning up this town." I didn't say, "Here's to a woman destined to clean up after my mistakes." The bartender slid two shots our way. He said that he'd met more desperate people in Gruel, that we shouldn't get optimistic.

OUTLAW HEAD AND TAIL

NORMALLY I COULDN'T HAVE MADE THE TAPE THAT Saturday. Right away, right there during the job interview a few weeks before, my soon-to-be-boss had said, "Ricky, is there anything about this job that you have a problem with?"

I didn't say, "I can't work for a man who ends sentences with prepositions." I couldn't. It was a job bouncing, or at least talking. I was going to be something called a "pre-bouncer." If some guy came into the Treehouse and looked like he meant trouble, I was to go up to him and start a little conversation, and let him know this wasn't the kind of place to throw a punch without inelegant and indubitable consequences.

I have a way with words. I'm synonymous with rapport.

I said to Frank, "Well, I'd rather not work Saturday days, 'cause my wife has to go to temple and I have to drive her over there. I don't go to temple. Hell, I don't even go to church," I said. "I don't mind working Sundays, but I'd really like it if you could get someone to work afternoons on Saturday for me. Night?—Saturday night—I'll be here. The only thing I ask of you is that I don't work Saturday afternoons, say, until six o'clock."

Frank said, "You know, you talked me into it. Man, what a way with words! It's a deal. You're a godsend, Ricky. I lucked out getting you as a pre-bouncer."

Frank had opened the Treehouse a year earlier, but didn't hire a bouncer or pre-bouncer right away. About the same time his insurance agent told him his payments would soon double, though, he hired me and a guy named Sparky Voyles to keep things down. During his first year, Frank put in claims for a whole new set of glasses, from shot and snifter to the special two-foot beer glasses he ordered, plus twelve tables, sixteen chairs, another tree stump to replace the one that caught on fire and caused smoke damage to the ceiling, and forty-two stitches to his own head one night after a fearful brawl erupted over whether Chevys or Fords would dominate the circuit in the upcoming season.

Frank bought the Treehouse because of insurance, ironically. He'd worked in the pulpwood trade and one day a load of logs slipped off a truck he stood behind, came rolling right off like a giant wave, clipped him behind the knees so hard they said he could run as fast backwards as forwards there for a few days. Of course, he couldn't run at all, and had to get fake knees installed. His lawyer also got him another quarter-million dollars or so due to a lifetime worth of pain and subsequent nightmares. Frank took most of that money and made the Treehouse, a regular small warehouse he furnished with tree trunks from floor to ceiling, so if you blindfolded someone and took him inside the bar, then took off the mask and showed him around, he'd have the feeling that the whole building was up above the ground, built into the forest.

So during the first year there were fights and insurance claims, but the second year started right off with me and Sparky there to quiet things down. Frank didn't want us to be too heavyhanded, though. He didn't want the bar to end up so quiet it looked like a flock of mute birds built their nests in the Treehouse. He only asked for stability.

Sparky went the same route as Frank—he worked at the railroad before becoming a bouncer, getting paid under the table because he took in disability checks from when both of his thumbs got cut off between two boxcars that clanged together and weren't supposed to, and he erroneously thought he could prevent it from happening. He couldn't. Sparky had been a brakeman originally, out of Lexington.

Anyway, I worked hard pre-bouncing, and kept up with what I had to know, which was mainly words. This is how I get back to the tape and that Saturday. What I'm saying is, because I'm so conscientious about my job, it could've killed my marriage.

On the previous Thursday, Jessie went in to her doctor's office to have him finally go ahead and do that sonogram thing. She couldn't wait to know what our first baby was going to be, building her argument around the fact that we didn't make all that much money, and if it was a boy we needed to pinch even harder and save up for his circumcision.

Jessie works as a freelance interior decorator. She got her degree in art history and felt like it gave her the right.

I took Jessie down to the doctor's office, but she couldn't get an appointment before four o'clock in the afternoon. I got clearance from Frank to get off work on Thursday, but that meant I had to come in Saturday morning at eleven 'cause the guy who normally worked Saturdays needed to go to a wedding anyway. It ended up a simple and clean swap. There didn't seem to be that much of a problem.

So I took my wife to the doctor and she did what she had to do, but the doctor still couldn't even take a stab at it, for the baby kept turned around the whole time. I was hoping it'd be a girl. I never have seen myself as being the father of a shy son.

Two days later I drove Jessie to synagogue. I drove back home in time to throw in a tape and set the VCR so I wouldn't miss *Bonanza*, which showed in syndication every Saturday on one of the cable channels. I set the station and time to record, then left for the bar.

I WATCH *BONANZA* every week. That's where I get my ways. That's where I get my ability to talk people out of starting fights. One time this burly truck driver-type came in and seemed upset that a white guy came into the Treehouse with an African American woman. There'd been a similar episode on *Bonanza* one time when Hoss piped up to a stranger, "Well, would you rather be blind and not have to see the ways of the world?" He said it to a redneck, of course. *Words of wisdom*, I thought right there and then. I'd thought "words of wisdom" on more than one occasion while watching Ben Cartwright bring up his boys the best he could. I remembered watching *Bonanza* when I was a boy, too, and how I admired the way Little Joe and Hoss and even Adam handled themselves in town. My father, though, used to throw beer cans at the television set and say, "What them boys need to use a little more often is their trigger fingers, not their tongues."

It's that kind of thinking that makes it almost amazing that I grew into being a pre-bouncer. If I'd taken my father seriously back in the sixties, I'd've ended up being something more secluded and self-centered, something like a bookkeeper, or a jockey.

I said to the burly guy, "Hey, there's two things that can happen here: either you can learn to understand that love is blind, or I can get Sparky to come over here with his eight remaining fingers and blind you himself, so you don't have to live with seeing interracial dating in your midst. *Comprende, amigo?*"

I pointed at Sparky. Without his thumbs it looks like he could use his fists as skewers. The truck driver looked over at Sparky, back to me, then to the white guy and black girl. He said, "Well, okay then," just like that. I stood my ground and tried not to shake. The little voice in my head kept thanking the Cartwrights over and over.

So I put the tape in the VCR, and I set the station and time, and drove off to the Treehouse. The bar doesn't open until noon, but I got there at eleven in order to help Frank clean up from the night before and to set out our specials in the plastic stand-up signs for each table. Frank said, "How goes it, Ricky?"

I said, "Okay, I guess. You?"

Frank said, "Uh-huh. Fine." He said, "You know, we didn't really get to talk last night. I mean, I heard you say that you still didn't know if you'd have a little boy or a girl, but what else did the doctor say?"

I wiped off a table. Friday night had been pretty slow at the Treehouse. Down the road there'd been a yearly festival with a battle of the bands and a tractor pull. I said, "He didn't say much. He asked if she'd been taking care of herself, whether she'd quit drinking and smoking. She said she had, which is true—and, goddamn, it ain't fun around the house, by the way. And then he said he thought her delivery date might need to be changed about a week early. Not much else went on. He dabbed some goo on her big stomach and we saw this little crooked Vienna sausage-looking thing on the television screen. Then he gave us the tape."

Well, no, I said, "The *tape!*"

I didn't say goodbye to Frank. I didn't tell him I'd be right back. I just left the Treehouse, got in my car, and drove fifteen minutes back to my house.

It was too late. Right over the image of my as-yet-sexless child, the floating little thumb-sucking thing inside Jessie's body, Hoss now talked to Little Joe about how skittish the horses seemed to be all of a sudden.

SPARKY SAID, "WELL, it could be worse, Ricky. At least she still has the baby. One time when I was working Amtrak, this woman came screaming out of the bathroom saying she'd miscarried in the toilet. We were flying down the track about sixty miles an hour, you know. I had my break and was eating an egg salad sandwich in the dining car. I remember all this 'cause I had a mouthful of egg in my mouth when this woman made the announcement."

I nodded my head and shoulders quickly, trying to get Sparky to finish the story. I needed to make some phone calls, or talk to some of the customers.

Sparky said, "She came running out of that bathroom saying the thing came out of her, she thought, but she wasn't sure. On a train, you know, it goes straight down to the track, and at sixty miles an hour you don't have time to exactly check what came out in the bowl underneath you. One time I had a kidney stone and I was supposed to be pissing into a strainer, but I kept forgetting. So I have a stone in between the tracks somewhere from Lexington to Danville."

I nodded hard, waving my right hand like a paddlewheel for Sparky to finish up. A group of four women came into the Treehouse, all of them in their mid-thirties. I needed to find a way to talk to them.

"This woman on the train—her name ended up being Brenda—had a nervous breakdown right there and then. She fainted. Two men who were afraid of airplanes and traveled on business trips up to New York all the time got up and grabbed her, checked her heartbeat and breathing, and put a pillow behind her head. I said, 'Damn, you don't see this everyday on an Amtrak train, do you?' Well, as it ended up, we took her off the train at the next stop and sent her to the local hospital. That would be Gaffney—we were doing the run down to New Orleans—and then on our way back up she waited there at the station for me. She got on board and said, 'I want you to tell me exactly where we were when I miscarried. I want you to take me to the spot so I can give my baby a proper burial.' I told her that by this time—a couple days had gone by—surely her miscarriage was gone. But she got on board the train and took it up to Charlotte, and then we got out and started walking back south on the tracks. My boss said I had to do it, and that I'd probably get a raise for the whole thing."

Two more women walked into the bar. I waved my arm faster for Sparky to get to the moral of the story.

"We found about twenty turtle shells," said Sparky. "You would not believe how many turtles get stuck in between the tracks, especially snapping turtles when you're near a lake or in the swamps. We found turtle shells, and that was it. I wasn't even sure what I was supposed to be looking for. And if I did run across anything that looked like a baby, I didn't want to see it, or point it out to Brenda. So as it ended up, after I finally convinced her that we'd gone past the spot where she miscarried, she walked over into the woods and got some sticks. She borrowed my shoelaces and fashioned a small wooden cross, stuck it a few feet from the track, and said she felt better. And an hour later this gandy dancer came from the station to pick us up to get us back to the station. I wonder whatever happened to old Brenda?" Sparky asked, like I'd know.

He walked off with his hands in his pockets, straight down like trowels were attached to the ends of his arms. I lost all pride and any bashfulness whatsoever and started asking women if they had any of their sonogram videotapes around their houses.

I offered a hundred dollars to buy one of them.

TERESA SMILEY SAID she'd be right back. Teresa Smiley said she kept hers on her bookshelf, stuck between a 12-Step program book and a Stephen King novel. Since her husband had gotten custody of their little boy, she got depressed thinking about it, but said, "A hundred dollars! Hell, I won't sell for less than *three* hundred."

It was one of those occasions when I didn't have time to check out the going rate for sonograms on the black market. So I said, "One fifty." I said, "Lookit, unless you had your sonogram on Thursday, there's going to be a different date down there on the screen. I mean, I'm going to have to go to great lengths of finding out a way to forge the video."

Teresa Smiley stared hard at me, then sat back down at her table, a table filled with women who worked third shift at the mill. Teresa said, "The memory of a child is worth more than a hundred and fifty dollars, Ricky. And your wife won't even notice the wrong date down there. We women are interested in the baby, not the time of day. I'm insulted, and I think you should be really ashamed."

"A minute ago," I said, "you were saying how you got depressed even knowing the tape was around. Come on, Teresa, you don't know how much I need this tape." I told her my story, but didn't explain about *Bonanza* over the image of my baby. I told her it was professional wrestling, so she could understand why I might be a little distraught about having to work on Saturday in the first place.

Teresa said, "Two fifty," I said, "Two," and she left to get the tape. I didn't even ask her if her child, too, was turned away from the camera, and if it wasn't turned away, was it real obvious as to the sex of the child. When I saw ours, I wasn't even sure where was the head and where was the tail. To me, Jessie's sonogram looked like a picture of an ulcer or something on her stomach wall. I couldn't make out a meaning whatsoever. I didn't have that art background that Jessie could boast about.

Sparky came over to me a few minutes after Teresa left and said, "You might have some trouble coming at you, but I'll be there for you."

I said, "What do you mean?" The worst thing that could happen, I thought, was for Jessie's meeting to be canceled and her coming to the Treehouse to spend the day.

Sparky said, "What I'm trying to tell you is, don't turn around immediately, but there's a guy down at the end of the bar staring a hole through you. It's Teresa's ex."

I didn't turn at all. I could feel the guy staring straight into my brain. The Treehouse had its regulars who came in every day—house painters, self-employed body shop men, the disabled, people who only really worked on Wednesday mornings over at the flea market—but there were people who came in haphazardly, maybe once a month, to sit by themselves and get over whatever it was that stuck in their craw. I never had to pre-bounce any of those people. First, it wouldn't matter—if they wanted to fight they'd fight no matter what I had to say. Second, most of them were so consumed with whatever bothered them, they didn't have the energy to actually get off the barstool and start a fight, though they'd probably like to see one.

I said to Sparky, "The one who got custody? Are you talking about Teresa's husband who ended up with the kid?"

He said, "That's the one. Name's Ted, but everyone calls him Slam. He won the state wrist wrestling championship four years in a row, and the Southeast tournament twice."

I said, "Goddamn it." I thought, *If only I'd taken the time to look at the videotape before I threw it in to tape* Bonanza. I thought, *If only the baby had turned around so we'd know the sex of it.* I thought, *If only Jessie hadn't gotten the appointment on Thursday,* and almost caught myself thinking, *If only I'd put on a rubber that night.*

Sparky said, "I arm wrestled him one time, but it's hard for me to get a grip, what without a thumb. Hell, it was hard for him, too. I kept sliding right through his hand."

"Shut up, Sparky," I said, and walked straight over to Slam. I said, "Your ex-wife's about to save my life, man. I screwed up and taped over my child-to-be's videotape inside the womb, and Teresa's going to get y'all's so I can make a tape of it." I said, "My name's Ricky."

Slam said, "Wife."

I said, "Excuse me?" He didn't look my way. He seemed to keep staring at where I stood talking to Sparky.

"Not ex-wife. Wife. Just like a piece of paper can't make a marriage, a piece of paper can't end one, neither," said Slam.

I said, "Are you Catholic?"

This is no lie. Slam said, "I'm an American and it's the American way of being."

I said, "Oh. Well, then your *wife* is about to save my skin."

Tape the *tape,* I thought. I thought, *You should've asked her to tape the tape.* I mean, there wasn't a reason for me to pay so much to more or less swipe hers. I tried to think of a way of getting to her before she even got inside the Treehouse so we could at least renegotiate.

Slam said, "What?" He held his beer in a way I'd not seen before, a half-inch from his face and a quarter-inch to the right. At first I thought he used the can as a mirror to check out someone who walked up behind him. Being a pre-bouncer, I notice things like that.

I said, "Your wife's saving my ass."

There's this look that only certain people can give. There's this look some people can give that's somewhere between smoke in their eyes and hand grenades in their pockets. Slam had that look. I turned my head toward Sparky but he'd already started punching a guy named Hull who came in drunk and wanted a piece of another guy named Dayton for not painting his house evenly earlier in the summer.

Slam said, "Well, I guess that's better than *humping* your ass, Bo." He said, "Glad to hear it," grabbed his beer, and left the bar, either unaware of the law, or unconcerned about the police that regularly parked across the street.

Sparky came over and said, "You got a way with words, Ricky. Whatever it is you said, you did it, man."

I sat down on the barstool next to Slam's and concentrated so as not to actually pee in my pants like in the cartoons.

As soon as Jessie had taken that one-minute-and-you-know-if-you've-really-missed-your-period test in the bathroom, she pulled a Walkman out of the bedroom closet, put in new batteries, and slipped a tape of Mahler's Fourth Symphony in the cassette holder. She pulled the earpieces of the headset as far apart as possible, strapped them around her sides, and put the volume on full blast. Jessie said, "We're going to have a baby, Ricky."

I'd just been watching her from the other side of the room.

I didn't even know about the bathroom test. I sat there on the side of the room reading my thesaurus. "A baby?" I said. "Are you sure?"

She said, "I have this theory. I believe that if you play music inside the womb, the fetus absorbs it and when the baby comes out, instead of crying and screaming, it'll make noises similar to an orchestra."

I said, "What?"

She said, "The reason why a baby always wails is because it absorbs the noises of the outside world for nine months. In the city it hears horns honking, people screaming, the conglomeration of people's conversations all going into one big drone, dogs barking, cats crying out in the night, the hiss of a teapot."

She had a list of every possible noise, it seemed. She finally finished her dictum with, "So if I keep playing classical music, when the baby's in pain or wants a bottle, we'll be serenaded with French horns and oboes, and violins. Bassoons!" She said, "Bassoons! And piccolos and flutes and cellos."

Hell, to me it didn't sound like all that bad a theory. I mean, it's logically possible. I said, "Why don't you order some of those books on tape, and then at night the baby can tell *us* stories."

Jessie put another Walkman on her own ears and left the room. She kind of left the room a lot during her pregnancy, for that matter. I'm not sure why. I've always tried to be sensitive to her needs.

TED, OR SLAM, whatever, kept standing outside the Treehouse. He was waiting for his ex-wife Teresa, I knew. Just about the time I started to go outside to tell him I wouldn't make a tape of his pre-born child, she tapped me on the shoulder. Like every intelligent woman with a lunatic ex-husband in her life, she sensed danger. She parked the Buick a few blocks away and took the back entrance. I said, "Ted's here."

She looked around. She said, "Ted was in here earlier but I don't see him now."

I said, "Out front."

"Oh. Well. Good," she said. "That'll be two hundred dollars up front, no check."

I only had a check. I said, "Hey look, I got this better idea. Why don't we find another VCR, and do a tape-to-tape so you don't have to lose yours totally. I mean, someday you might want it back." I kind of saw a big confrontation ahead, like when birth mothers arrange for adoptive parents, then change their minds in the delivery room.

Teresa said, "I won't change my mind, believe you me. I've had it. I want a new life, Bubba. As a matter of fact, I've already contacted the paper to advertise a yard sale for next weekend. I'm getting rid of my old high school yearbooks, too."

I said, "Well, okay." It was nearly three o'clock and I couldn't take the chance of Jessie getting a ride home from the synagogue with one of her friends, slipping in her tape, and fainting when she came to believe that her baby had suddenly gained a clear and distinct shape and form which looked like Hoss. I said, "Hold on a second."

I bought Teresa a drink on my monthly tab and walked over to where Sparky stood in the corner of the bar, scanning the slim crowd. "Sparky," I said, "look, do you have one of those teller cards by any chance? I lost mine in the machine—not 'cause I didn't have any money—because the back strip got dirty or something and it's Saturday and the bank's closed and I need two hundred bucks right now to buy the tape. I can give you a check today, or if you wait until Monday morning I can go over to the bank and get cash for you."

Sparky said, "I hope you remember this when you go and name your child."

I said, "I can't name my kid *Sparky*."

Sparky said, "I wouldn't expect you to." He reached into the wallet he kept chained to his belt loop and pulled out two hundred one-dollar bills. He said, "My given name's Earl. Earl for a boy, Earline for a girl."

I don't know why I said okay, but I did. I figured if I could get Sparky drunk later on in the evening, maybe he'd forget the promise.

"Here you go," I said to Teresa. She handed me the tape. She handed me her own personal sonogram videotape of the only child she'd ever had and said, "I hope I picked up the right one. Slam and me did some amateur strip stuff one night, but we never sent it off to any of those programs on cable."

I asked Sparky to cover for me, told him to use the word "discretionary" or "castigatory" should a fight seem eminent, and I took the back door out, too.

THERE IS A supreme being. Someone powerful exists, or at least existed for me that afternoon. I pulled out my tape filled with *Bonanza*, plus a half-hour special on the NASCAR season at the halfway point, and pushed Teresa's baby's video in my machine. It didn't need rewinding. I wondered if she'd ever really watched it.

It wasn't her strip show. Right there on the screen, in brilliant shades of gray, was a form. I couldn't make out eyes or genitals. There was no way possible Jessie could see the difference between her womb and that of a woman who grew up and lived in a mobile home.

I felt good about living in America.

The Supreme Being stayed on my side, 'cause while the tape still played, in walked Jessie, home from what ended up being a committee meeting of a group called Sisters of Bashemath, Ishmael's Daughter. She said, "I thought you had to work."

I moved closer to the television screen, down on the carpet, and held my forearm parallel to the date and time logo down at the bottom. I said, "I went and got things going, but I started feeling a little nauseated."

Jessie came up to me, all smiles, and put her hand on the back of my neck. She said, "That's so sweet. You have sympathy pains."

I knelt on the floor in front of the TV screen. I could hear Mahler's First Symphony playing out of the cassette attached to Jessie's stretched sash. I said, "Well, yeah, I had some pains alright, but I'm feeling much better now."

Jessie asked me to rewind the sonogram. I clenched my teeth, re-wound it, prayed to all the superior beings ever invented for her not to notice the difference.

And she didn't. While I watched Teresa's child float around in her belly, Jessie lowered the volume on her Walkman and pushed her chin in toward her stomach. She said, "We're watching you right now, honey."

I didn't say anything about any kind of name recognition, like, "We're looking at you, Earl or Earline."

I sat and watched. And I thought to myself, *Certainly I want my own child to grow up and be happy and famous and healthy and intelligent.* I thought, *I want to be able to spend time with my kid, go to games, teach him or her how to communicate, take long trips across the country to see how different people live.*

And deep down, oddly, I kind of wanted the kid I watched on the television screen to end up a bandit and a folk hero. I wanted that obscure head and tail I saw on the screen to grow up and be an outlaw of sorts, a fugitive. At that very moment I knew that I'd always keep up with Ted and Teresa's boy, and help him out whenever it seemed possible. I'd tell him to keep moving, always, in order to stay content, and to talk to strangers, no matter how scary it may seem.

I COULD'VE TOLD YOU IF
YOU HADN'T ASKED

ESMOND WANTED TO MAKE A MOVIE CALLED *CHICKENS*. He wasn't sure if he had the imagination to pull it off, and he had no hope of grants or investors. The one thing he did possess was a beautiful but crazy wife, though I didn't know about her right off.

I had no money, either, of course, but was getting some notoriety as a visionary what with the patch of gray hair on the back of my head that looked just like an eyeball, added to the fact that I'd predicted three Kentucky Derby winners in a row, the date of Black Monday, and Hurricane Hugo's strength, time, and place of landing.

I could see, understand.

Desmond said, "Weldon, I know what I want to do will be a big seller. I just want you to give me the green light, guy. I call it *Chickens* for two reasons. First off there will be chickens in every scene—somewhere strutting in the background, maybe. Second, I want to train the camera on people and ask them about what they fear more than anything else. I want a man to look into the camera and say, 'The gang violence around here is scaring me more than cornered rats.' Meanwhile he'll be eating a piece of fried chicken. That's subtext, man. I want to see a kid riding a homemade go-cart in circles around his parents' shack, going through a herd of chickens."

I said, "I don't think it's a herd. I think it's a clutch, or a brood. You might want to get that down before trying to approach investors. It's a bed of clams, and a cloud of gnats, and a sounder of boars. It's a troop of monkeys and a knot of toads—that's my favorite, a knot of toads." I'd memorized *The World Almanac*, 'cause it had this kind of information.

Desmond stood there in the small kitchen of my small cabin. I drank Old Crow mixed with ginger ale and milk thistle to help replenish my liver. I'd been sitting there almost nonstop—not always drinking, of course—since getting fired from my job a year earlier at Coca-Cola in Atlanta. I had worked in an advisory and public relations capacity, but I'd been on a downward run with the higher-ups ever since I said publicly that the new Coke they wanted to market wouldn't work whatsoever. Desmond said, "You know I'm not as smart as some people think I am. I'll admit that. You know my wife wants to leave me because she has fulfillment issues. She says I'm not performing to what she saw as my capacity when we married."

I said, "You're going to have to give me a minute to think this one out. It might take me some time to puzzle out what Hollywood wants, and what the people want."

Desmond said, "I need some time to write out the script anyway."

He wore a pair of khakis that didn't quite fit anymore. They hung down low, and his stomach stuck out like a silhouette of Stone Mountain down in Georgia. Desmond and his nutty wife moved from New York down to Christ Almighty, North Carolina, about the same time I made enough money to move up and buy a summer cabin, long before I understood that I might have to move there for good. Desmond thought he'd absorb some of the South for the bestselling novel he planned to write, but the South absorbed him.

Desmond pulled out the chair across from me and sat down. I said, "There's a job down in Tryon with First Realty. They're looking for someone to put up For Sale signs. I think they pay ten bucks to put up a sign, and five for pulling it down once the house is sold. Here's what you do: Get the job. Put up the signs. At night drive around and knock the signs down. They'll ask you to put the signs back up and you'll get paid twice. Let's say you only have ten signs a week. That's only a hundred dollars a week. But if you keep knocking them down, you could make fifty bucks more. Plus you get the five dollars for what sells." I mention this conversation to show that, contrary to his subsequent claims, I told him all these scams before I ever laid eyes on his wife.

Desmond said, "I want to make movies. Films, dude. I've given up writing novels about upper-middle-class people trying to find out about themselves in new and exciting ways."

I got up and made another drink without as much milk thistle because I felt dangerous. I said, "After you make the money by peckering around with real estate agents, go put down money on a lush apartment. You put down one month's rent and the security deposit. Pay in cash. Lie about your name. Then place a want ad in the papers for the apartment for about half what you pay."

Desmond said, "Weldon. I don't want to go to jail."

"You ain't going to jail, man," I said. "You're a filmmaker. How many filmmakers are in jail, outside of that guy who can't come back to America for what he did with an underage female?"

Desmond held his head funny. I told him to get some nice furniture, tell prospective renters that he'd gotten a one-year job somewhere and wanted to keep the apartment. I told him to get a post office box and a telephone his wife wouldn't know about.

Desmond said, "Five people a day come in for one month. I show them the apartment, say it's furnished, and take their money?"

I said, "Ask for cash. Say you don't believe in checks. Give them receipts. In no time you got enough money to make your movie." Before Desmond could think about it I said, "Three hundred dollars for the first month, three hundred for the security—that's six hundred. Six hundred times a hundred and fifty people. That's ninety thousand dollars. Hell, rent out three or four apartments and you can go beyond documentary-style black-and-whites. Goddamn, boy, I see a major motion picture in your future."

Desmond said, "My wife's not a patient woman, Weldon. This has to happen fast."

I said, "Go rob a bank. Rob a bank, then make your movie. I wouldn't, but you might."

Desmond shook his head. He pulled his khakis up, then combed his hand through where he wanted more hair. Outside, a hawk circled above Lake Christ Almighty. I tried to think about people in a theater, watching a movie with chickens in every frame, but couldn't.

≳ ≴

I FOUND DESMOND'S wife dumping ice deliberately, a ritual I'd heard about but taken for myth. Desmond's wife went in the back door to their added-on house and brought back one of those Styrofoam chests for transporting good meats or vital organs. She stepped softly. She was wearing padded bedroom slippers. I didn't speak, because what she was doing looked a lot like what I imagined ancient Asian religious folks did during their somber ceremonies, or how a talented seer might act outside in times of rare planetary alignments. Desmond's wife sprayed Numz-it first-aid medicine between her ice mounds.

"Are your soles soft rubber?" she asked with her back turned. I swear to God this is true. What I'm saying is, this woman was both cosmological and ontological somehow. She may have been teleological, too, but I don't remember all my metaphysics from college.

I said, "I just wanted to come and see if Desmond was doing okay. I just wanted to see what he's working on these days." I wasn't sure if he'd told his wife about *Chickens*. I didn't want to give any secrets away in case he kept plans to himself. It's a male code.

Desmond's wife stood there holding the Styrofoam. She wore a thin cotton print skirt that let light flow through—her upper thighs could've been used as sturdy, solid thin masts, is what I'm saying—and a T-shirt that read VOTE YOUR UTERUS. It kind of gave me the creeps, but I swear I couldn't keep my eyes off it. She had big knockers. Desmond's wife said, "The earth is our mother. Walk softly. I'm about to plant a garden, and I don't want my mother to hurt whatsoever. I'm numbing her skin before I dig. I'm numbing the dirt before I dig or hoe or scrape."

I couldn't say anything except, "Shew—I don't want to hurt the earth none. I wouldn't also want to disturb a grist of bees or a down of hares." What the hell.

Desmond's wife said, "You didn't major in geology, did you? I hope you didn't major in geology."

I about told her I never went to college. I said, "No. I majored in philosophy in undergraduate school. Then I went on to law school and quit before the year was over. I never was good at the sciences, really."

"Geologists become miners. Miners end up drilling holes in the earth. You wouldn't go to a dentist and have him drill into your teeth without any kind of pain killer, would you?"

I said, "Tell Desmond I came by and I'll try to get in touch with him later." I started to walk away, back around the cold shallow lake to my little cabin. I kept thinking how men down here pride themselves on not coon-dogging what's already been treed. We don't actively pursue a married man's wife, is what I'm saying. We kill the husband more often than not, or at least get him in a situation that involves a long prison sentence. Thinking about it almost made me have a Pentecostal fit, all thicktongued and spastic.

"You ever been to a proctologist?" Desmond's wife asked me. She didn't seem to squint as much as she seemed to want to cry, or pass two stones the size of a bad carpenter's thumbs.

I said, "I just sit in my room and think, ma'am. I work as a freelance consultant these days, when admen can't come up with ideas and don't want to lose their jobs. Please don't judge me or anything, please."

Desmond's wife said, "My husband went down the mountain to do some work. He won't be back until way past ten or eleven tonight." This was a Sunday. Realty offices were closed. I knew what Desmond was doing. I laughed and said, "Hey, do you cover your land in sheets of plastic when it hails?"

Desmond's wife took out a little memo pad notebook from the elastic band in her skirt, and wrote down something. She smiled, and raised her eyebrows. She looked like God let her down on a handmade sunbeam.

I didn't understand until later that maybe women from up north kept track of when their husbands returned. Maybe I'd gotten too caught up in my own ways to realize Desmond's wife was sending me a signal.

I LEFT DESMOND'S wife and went home until the sun went down. Then I made my way backwards toward every sign I'd seen lately from First Realty, knowing he'd be nearby in stocking cap and black gloves, sweating from the humidity. I found him hidden halfway down in a carport adjacent to the sort of solid cedar-shake shingle house admired and purchased by people who have a thing for armadillos and alluvial outcroppings.

I said, "Desmond! Get out of there, man, it's me!"

Desmond shimmied goofily, holding his hand up against my pickup's beam. He said, "Weldon, you scared the shit out of me."

I said, "I meant to. Your wife said you wouldn't be back until late, so I surmised that you got a job doing what I said."

"Well," Desmond said. "I got to do what I got to do in order to do what I want to do, you know."

I said, "Uh-huh."

We shook hands. He'd already thrown down the For Sale sign a good twenty feet from where he had planted it earlier.

Desmond said, "You didn't tell me to wear different-sized shoes when I did this. But I'm wearing different-sized shoes. I went down to a Salvation Army place in Spartanburg and bought three pairs of boots ranging two to four sizes too big than what I wear. I wear a normal ten. I figure no one would be able to trace it back to me—unless they open the woodbin where I keep them during the day."

I said, "There are no cops in Christ Almighty, Desmond. I think you're pretty safe."

He said, "You didn't tell Fiona where you thought I might be, did you?"

I thought, *Fiona*. I had never met a woman named Fiona, but it seemed like a Fiona would be either the kind of woman who'd numb the earth before digging into it or the kind who welcomed strays. I said, "When she told me you wouldn't be back until ten or eleven tonight, I told her you probably drove all the way to Charlotte looking for a strip joint. Now don't go committing suicide with that post-hole digger."

He said, "Okay."

"It's a joke," I said. "I didn't tell her anything, you idiot."

"You don't know my wife, Weldon," he said. "I'm not real proud of it, but I have a girlfriend back in New York. I tell my wife I'm going back to deal with an agent or editor. Actually I lost both my agent and my editor. It's a long story that involves a favorite uncle and his cousin's wife's daughter."

Desmond laughed. I tried not to make eye contact and found myself staring at his chin more than anything else. I said, "That's okay," though I didn't think it was. Listen, I took those marriage vows seriously—even my ex-wife would have to back me up on that one.

We stood while two jets flew overhead, almost side by side. In the brush beside this house a doe rambled, bedding down. I thought about my ex-wife in my ex-city, living not so far from my ex-job. I handed Desmond a beer out of the bed of my truck and said, "There are no chickens living nearby. What're you going to do about that?"

"When I wrote novels I didn't care about truth," he said. "I published a novel about Vietnam and the women's lingerie industry. To be honest, I didn't know squat about either. I'm from Brooklyn. All you need to know applies to both subjects—camouflage only works for so long."

I did not say how it was the same thing in advertising. I didn't say anything because it looked like we were bonding in the dark, and that scared me. I said, "*Chickens.*"

He said, "I put ads in some magazines up north for the apartment. People come down here in the winter, you know. I even said it was a condo."

It would've been a good time to tell Desmond that I was only joking, that I made everything up about how he could make money. But his wife worried that the earth hurt, and I worried that she hurt, too. That's all I could think about there in the dark, with one For Sale sign down and another fifty or so scattered around the mountain. No comet, or shooting star, or UFO showed itself. No Dodge Dart skidded around the curve carrying a trunkload of moonshine. I did not smell marijuana burning anywhere, though I felt hungry and responsible, as always. "Desmond," I said. "Desmond, Desmond, Desmond. I may have made a mistake by telling you how to make money to support a movie. Don't you have any family that believes in you?"

I turned the lights off in my truck and left the engine running. I barely saw him, is what I'm saying. Desmond said, "My dad's dead and my mother thinks I'm still going to write the great fucking American novel. I can't let her down." He shuffled a foot in sparse gravel and said, "I don't have any brothers or sisters, and I wasn't that popular growing up."

I didn't ask if Fiona had anyone. I kind of knew. I said, "Fiona numbed the earth so she wouldn't hurt it any when she planted a garden, or something. Have you thought about keeping the camera turned on her? I don't want to make any judgment about you and yours, but I bet a documentary about your wife would be interesting. Hell, all you'd have to do is buy some security cameras and set them up."

Desmond took a draw from his beer and threw it back into the bed of my truck. He said, "That might be an idea, paisan."

I said, "When's the last time you saw a movie about a person who did things a whole lot differently than anyone else?"

"I don't remember offhand," Desmond said. "I could've told you if you hadn't asked."

With that response I knew Desmond needed to go back up north. No one in his or her right mind below the Mason-Dixon line answered questions with "I could've told you if you hadn't asked." It didn't even make sense. If it did, people would just walk around aimlessly spouting out answers like, "Carson City is the capital, not Las Vegas or Reno!" or, "Robert Duvall played Boo Radley!" or, "Jupiter's equatorial diameter is eighty-eight thousand miles," or, "Tonga's chief crops are coconut products, bananas, and vanilla."

I said, "Goddamn, if you got such a hard-on for chickens, maybe you can buy a couple roosters and keep them on your property so they'll show up in some scenes with Fiona."

I did not, of course, mean this in an odd, poker-night, jokey way. Desmond took off his watch cap, wiped his forehead, and laughed without thinking about how it might be heard all up and down the mountain, through two valleys, past his job at the real estate agent's office, and into whatever apartment he rented there at the foot of Mount Christ Almighty on the Pacolet River, "Where Retirees Can Enjoy the Splendor of Country Mountain Living."

I DO NOT know the cost of spy gadgetry, and didn't ask Desmond how many signs he set up, knocked down, and reset over a two-month period. He bought his chickens first, over the complaints of the home association, and later set up cameras one at a time when Fiona drove down the mountain for ice, Bactine, gauze, Neosporin, and whatever else she used to help heal the mother on which we live.

I know I found myself looking across a quadrant of lake water too often. I used binoculars, hoping to see Fiona bent over in a less-than-modest dress. I thought about how my wife was long gone.

The first time I met Fiona she knew I was watching her numb the soil, so I should have known she could feel me watching her two hundred yards away. One morning she knocked on my door and I answered. When she said, "You want a telescope?" I could only hope that I heard wrong.

"Hey, Fiona. Come on in for some coffee," I said.

She said, "Is it one of those flavored coffees? You know those flavored coffees have chemicals in them that they don't advertise on the box."

I said, "It's regular coffee. I have some bread, too. I was just about to have breakfast. Come on in."

She stood there wearing the only skirt I'd ever seen her wear, the one that sunlight ravished without much effort. Fiona said, "Weldon, right?"

I said, "Uh-huh."

She said, "I know when you're watching me, Weldon. You aren't doing anything weird up here, are you?"

I said, "I'll confess that I watch you. I've never seen anyone care about blemishes so much. I apologize, and I'll quit, but I promise I'm not doing anything perverted. I've had a wife and I've had girlfriends. Not at the same time, either—I took a course in ethics one time in college."

That wasn't true. I mean, I had not taken a course in ethics, which I figured gave me the right to tell a lie. Fiona said, "Did you use any preservatives in your bread?"

I told her I washed my hands between each knead.

WHEN WE FUCKED daily for the next six weeks we did so slowly. Fiona wasn't sure about my cabin's pilings—whether or not they were planted loosely—or whether our rhythm might tamp down into her mother like the misstroke of a blunt-ended toothbrush that jabs your gums. I did not tell her about her husband's uncle's cousin's daughter. I did not break male code in that way. And there was no love between Fiona and me, at least that first week: We only whispered about the earth moving, often.

But I said more than once in her ear, "Where were you when I thought I should get married?"

"Probably getting married. Or in Santa Fe learning massage therapy," Fiona said to me more often than not.

DESMOND CAME OVER finally in midsummer. I felt uncomfortable, of course. We hadn't spoken since I told him to scrap *Chickens*. Desmond said, "Weldon, I've been thinking. I don't want to be nosy, but how do you live? You don't work in advertising anymore, do you, Weldon? You don't have a home office upstairs so you can just fax what you're thinking, do you, Weldon?"

Desmond seemed to have something to say.

I said, "I saved money well and invested okay. I work as a consultant sometimes but don't seek it. I don't like to brag or anything, but people in the industry know me, and when they're out of ideas they get in touch and offer me money. An adman without an idea is an ex-adman in about a thirty-second spot."

Desmond said, "Huh."

I said, "I thought you'd be wearing a beret by now. How's it going?"

"Oh, I'm set, amigo," he said. I poured bourbon. "I ain't got a story line or anything but figure I can do it through editing. Are you sure this'll work out?" Desmond didn't sit down when I shoved the chair out for him.

I couldn't lie. I said, "Well. Maybe your wife's not as quirky as I thought."

"So you're saying Fiona's not odd enough to star in my film, is that what you're saying? You saying my wife's too average to care about? I don't think you know what you mean, Weldon."

Desmond had a different edge to him. He bowed up on me good. People in the South sometimes think Northerners display a certain curtness, a certain broad and blatant cruelty toward other human beings. It's a misconception that thrives with others—such as how dead blacksnakes on fence posts end droughts, or crossing a downhill stream will stop a specter. People from the Northeast are kind, really. Unlike me—and the people I know—they don't constantly scheme at ways to kill friends, acquaintances, and relatives.

I said, "I'm saying I don't know what I'm saying." Desmond held his fists at his sides. In this short time I'd already considered throwing him off my porch headfirst, taking the fire poker to his temple, even rigging a clipped and frayed electrical wire from an outlet into my toilet so when he peed out his bourbon it'd shock him hard. When I stuck up one index finger and shook it like a scolding mother from a fifties movie, Desmond evidently thought I foreplayed a shot to his nose. He decked me quick, then. He said, "I know about you fucking Fiona, Weldon. I got movies and I got a lawyer."

I've REALIZED THAT the more isolated a person attempts to be, the more people know about him. I'm sure everyone on Mount Christ Almighty, and the valley towns of Tryon and Columbus, even smaller Lynn and Green Creek, knew that I had a scalp condition that required dandruff shampoo. Or that I had the occasional bout with athlete's foot when I worked in scawmy conditions, or that I had hemorrhoids from worrying too much about my goddamn feet. People knew these things because I could do my grocery shopping at one place only—a family-owned store down the mountain called Powell's.

When this buzz-cut kid handed me a subpoena to show up at Fiona and Desmond's divorce proceeding, he held a handkerchief to his mouth. I said, "Have you got a bad cold or something? I took a bath this morning."

"I don't want to get the tuberculosis," he said.

"I ain't got TB."

"Well, you had to go down to the doctor last week, and you haven't bought any cigarettes since, and you had a coughing fit down at the Waffle House," the kid said.

"Oh. Oh, yeah. It's not tuberculosis, man," I said. "It's rabies." I took two quick steps his way so he jumped clean off the porch, eight feet off the ground.

I'd gone to the doctor to get some shots because I'd been hired to check out the chances of a Disney project in Kuwait. I told them to save their money, but they didn't. That Gulf War thing took place soon thereafter. There you go.

I lied in front of the judge and jury, in front of the packed house at the Polk County courthouse, in front of Fiona, Desmond, and their respective lawyers. I said, "No sir, I never had sex with her in my house. It's true she came over as the films indicate." Then I said, "On more than one occasion Fiona came over looking for Bactine, Neosporin, and gauze." I made it sound like Desmond beat her or something, but I didn't care. Desmond had the brains to point one of his little cameras toward my front porch. The jury saw something like forty-two clips of Fiona walking in my front door, all but one of me hugging her there. When Desmond took the stand he swore I'd told him about my scams just so I could lure his wife over my way. He'd put his hand on the Bible and everything, and looked the jury straight. Obviously they believed him. Luckily, no chicken followed Fiona over or we might have been sentenced to the electric chair. This was the South.

Of course she lost everything. Juries from the mountains of western North Carolina don't care about mental cruelty or impotence or abuse. It's as if "Stand By Your Man" is piped into the chambers.

The prosecutor asked me, "Do you know what kind of person you are, breaking up a marriage?" I sat silent. "You're nothing but a coward, lying like this. Do you know the meaning of coward?"

I tried not to shake. I didn't look up or down, or sideways back and forth haphazardly, like an animal confused by rain.

I didn't mention to Desmond's lawyer how the mountains of North Carolina are filled with garnets and rubies and emeralds and mica. I didn't say how one day when Fiona came over she made me lie naked in the sun, and placed semi-precious gems on what she understood to be pressure points on my body.

I understood, too. I'm talking sundial—she put a rock right on the end of my pecker. Fiona said, "I'm trying to learn the proper and beneficial uses of magnets, but I don't feel sure about myself yet."

In the distance we heard Desmond's roosters crow. Fiona put rocks on herself, and we both fell asleep. I got a sunburn, and when I woke up it looked like someone had written tiny O's on my body. I'd never felt better in my life—when Fiona rolled over on me our white marks fit like pistons, I swear. Let me say right now that it was at this point that I knew I loved Fiona, and could work as the conductor on her trainload of neuroses. Call it luck or predilection on her part, but those stones made me feel different about myself and the rest of the world, and the way things would end up in the future.

The prosecutor said, "Boy, I believe you got some Sherman in you, what with the way you burned a marriage with a perfect foundation." He pointed over at Desmond and said, "What else could you have done to this poor man?"

YEARS LATER ON, reading about how *Chickens* won those independent film competitions, I had all kinds of reactions, most of which involved duct tape, a hard-backed simple chair, a pistol butt, and a smile. I read that in France the movie was called *Les Poulets*, of course, and audiences considered it some kind of classic. In Holland or Denmark the film went by plain *Peep-peep*. Because Desmond won the divorce, he also got the house and half of Fiona's worth, enabling him to back himself on his own project. Fiona came from a wealthy family, too. What I'm saying is, I damn near forgot that women named Fiona either numbed the ground when they walked, or took in strays, or had a trust fund the size of influenza.

We live quietly these days and we compromise. Sometimes Fiona circles that gray patch on the back of my head as if she were mixing a drink with her finger. She says I'll come up with a vision for us both. I don't make fun of her when she goes outside at night and cries with the stars and moon. And unlike most people, I'm now allowed to stomp on this earth.

HOW TO COLLECT FISHING LURES

MOVE OFF OF THE FAMILY FARM, GO TO A STATE UNI-
versity that offers a degree in textile management, get a job at
a cotton mill that will eventually fail during the Reagan years,
marry a woman who will go back to college later on in life then leave
you for three states south, have one son named with only initials—like
V. O.—and try to get him to understand the importance of moving out
of the textile town, get fired so that the company no longer has to pay a
pension, and spend too many days sending out resumes to other failing
cotton mills that have no need for a forty-seven-year-old midlevel executive. Send your son off to college and wonder what he sees in literature,
history, philosophy, art, and Eastern religions.

Try not to think about your lungs looking like kabobs of half-eaten
cotton candy. Go to the unemployment office in your small South
Carolina town and feel worthless, useless, lost, and emasculated. Spend
time watching programs that have more to do with collectible trea-
sures and less with world, domestic, regional, or local news. Watch infomercials into the night. Go to a bookstore where too many young
people hang out without touching books, find the section of antique
price guides and memorize the names, photographs, and prices of jigs,
topwater plugs, spinners, spoons, minnow tubes, and frog harnesses.
Decide to take a scuba-diving course that won't cost more than one (1)

unemployment check. Learn to cook and eat macaroni and cheese, spa-ghetti, ziti, rice, and mashed potatoes. Remember the documentary you saw on carbo-loading.

Invest what extra money you don't have into a wet suit, oxygen tank, mask, and flippers. If, for some reason, you did not acquire forced shal-low breathing (FSB) from the mill, invest only in goggles and snorkel.

Drive to the nearest man-made lake and walk it. Step off distances. Practice at home using a yardstick so that your steps equal thirty-six (36) inches with each pace. Take extensive notes as to where men older than you fish for largemouth bass. Make a map of the place. Point out points, coves, creek mouths, beaver dams, and where the men in boats—usually the men a level above you at the cotton mill, or their sons—drop anchor or troll.

Realize that just because an antique-price guide claims that a Clothes Pin Minnow goes for two to three hundred dollars ($200-$300) doesn't mean that anyone in Forty-Five, South Carolina, might pay that much money for it at an antique show, flea market, or yard sale. Just because someone in New York, California, or Colorado might be willing to lay down two to three thousand dollars ($2,000-$3,000) for a Flying Hellgrammite Type II, manufactured by the Harry Comstock Company out of Fulton, New York, in 1883 before being bought out by Pflueger Enterprise Manufacturing Company in Akron, Ohio, doesn't mean that everyone will offer only five bucks ($5) for the thing in Atlanta, Charleston, Charlotte, or Raleigh.

Go to the closest bars, roadhouses, and bait shacks and talk to every human being possible. Pretend to be interested in how they caught their biggest bass. Secretly tally who used live bait, who used rubber worms, and who used lures that you want.

By this time, too, it should become apparent that you should no longer tell friends or relatives about your latest ambitions. They will insist that you go to the local psychologist and take a battery of examinations rang-ing from the Minnesota Multiphasic Personality Inventory (MMPI) to the Barriers to Employment Success Inventory (BESI), with everything in between—vocational interest tests, career interest inventories, the John Holland Self-Directed Search, the Myers-Briggs Type Indicator (MBTI), and a dexterity test that involves pegs, washers, and caps.

You've already withstood these tests one long afternoon instead of standing in line at the unemployment office.

Buy an underwater flashlight, a mesh cloth bag, and some needle-nosed pliers. Take the first dive somewhere near a cache of sunken Christmas trees. After you find your first Surface Tom, King Bee Wiggle Minnow, or Hell Diver, stick it in your bag and resurface. I don't want to make any broad generalizations or cheap jokes, but you'll be hooked. Go buy a johnboat immediately.

You'll need the boat in order to go out past dusk—using the flashlight—and drop heavy objects into the water where you know men and women fish. Cement blocks work well, as do long bent pieces of rebar, old front fenders, spools of barbed wire, and certain cement statuaries (lawn jockeys). Leave these in place for at least two months before visiting the scene. What I'm saying is, be a patient farmer—harvest, sow, re-harvest. If you have searched all of the likely lost, snagged, and badly knotted fishing lure regions of a particular lake, then go to another lake, map it out, talk to locals, and so on. Allow Lake Number One (#1) to repopulate itself with the bait you will find later.

Remember: Scuba diving is not an inexpensive mode of transportation. It's better to take two or three trips down for a hundred lures than a hundred trips for a hundred lures. For those who've retained Pink Lung and chosen simple snorkeling, no one knows for sure about the Bends, really.

Now that you have a good collection of rare vintage fishing lures in various stages of wear, think about presentation. Stick them haphazardly in a shadowbox. Attach them to mesh bags similar to the one you use while on a pilgrimage. Gently stick them into the yardstick you own if that yardstick has some kind of maritime theme, viz., Shady Grady's Bait 'n' Tackle—We'll Give You Worms; or Gene's Marina—All Size Slips. Either clean the lures until they look unused and put them in a fake original box, or dirty them up more so.

There are people out there with large vacation houses who will buy the latter option. It might not be bad to purchase a few bobs, run them over with a car, then reglue them nearly together. The vacation-house people will buy anything to give themselves a sense of doing something dangerous and near-tragic when they grew up.

As did your wife three states away.

If you choose to sell off duplicates—and you will—and if a day comes when you feel a full-lunged breath release from your body for the first time since losing the job, maybe send your ex-wife a cheap Ball Bearing Spinner, plus a note saying that y'all's son is well, and that signs of panic and danger diminish with each new morning. By this time she'll know about your irrational hobby. Write, in detail, complete lies about snapping turtles, gar, water moccasins, a big sale of Wilcox Wigglers and the women who bought them.

Or get in the johnboat, turn off all lights, ride as fast as possible until you hit an exposed stump, and sink.

SET YOUR ALARM clock for four o'clock in the morning on Saturdays and Sundays if you live within a half hour of a flea market. Otherwise set it accordingly. Make a thermos of coffee the previous night. Sleep in your clothes if at all possible. In the winter, wear a watch cap. In warmer weather wear a sleeveless shirt and pants with at least one (1) hole in them. Either wear old Converse tennis shoes or comfortable hiking boots. Pick up the morning paper at the end of the driveway.

Be sure to have a pocketful of case quarters only.

Don't wear a goofball cap that reads "I COLLECT FISHING LURES" on the front. Take along a flashlight and a bag that isn't mesh or plastic. If people selling good old lures at a flea market see you coming with the hat, they'll jack the price about four (4) to ten (10) times what they originally wanted. There's been documentation. If they see a bag that they think contains lures, they'll at least double the original asking price. You have only quarters because if someone's asking, say, two dollars ($2) for a lure, automatically say, "Will you take a quarter for it?"

Let's say y'all dicker until it gets to a dollar, a fair price for a Rhodes Wooden Minnow seeing as it books between fifty ($50) and seventy-five dollars ($75). Then say you forgot to take your quarters, and pull out a twenty-dollar bill. The seller might be likely to either, (A) not sell you the lure; or (B) kill you.

Nevertheless, do not take a loaded pistol with you, especially if someone plans to tag along.

I'll explain this later. Go alone whenever possible, of course.

Now. Get to the flea market and focus on lures. Take out the flashlight—it'll still be dark when you arrive—and shine it on tables. Stray from people who sell figurines, baby clothes, pit bull puppies, rebuilt lawn mowers, action figures, fast food restaurant toys and giveaways, Pez dispensers, yellowware, silverware, socks and underwear, baseball cards, chickens/rabbits/goats, heart pine furniture, shot glasses, phonographic equipment, Rottweiler puppies, used books, VCRs, computers, advertising yardsticks, and hippie decals.

Look for tables filled with fishing rods, cigar boxes, used tools, guns, and tackle boxes. Look for tables filled with a mixture of everything. Shine your light on wrinkled men who might be selling off their oxygen tanks, flippers, masks, snorkels, needle-nosed pliers, and whatnot, men who've given up altogether on the fishing-lure collectible craze because they didn't map out lakes, talk to old men, plot strategy, sink cement blocks, and everything else detailed in Part One (1) of "How to Collect Fishing Lures."

When you come across a table or display of everything from Gee Wiz Frogs to Arrowhead Weedless Plugs, keep your beam on them for exactly one nanosecond (onebillionth of a second). Pretend that you have no interest in the fine Celluloid Minnow or the Jersey Expert. Look over at the AK-47 on the table, or the Zebco rod, ball-peen hammer, and socket-wrench sets. Feign disinterest, is what I'm saying. Go, "Oh, man, I ain't seen one them since I grew hair south," or something.

Say a personal mantra that the man doesn't know what he owns. Over and over in your head say, "Quarter-quarter-quarter-quarter," and so on.

Here's the worst scenario: he says, "Yeah, the T.N.T. number six-nine-hundred was real popular. It's going for upwards of seventy-five dollars on the market, but I'm only asking thirty for it."

Do not walk away. Don't nod in agreement. Don't shake your head sideways, either. Slowly direct your flashlight's beam into the man's face and, using all common sense and knowledge of the human condition, measure how desperate he is. Don't blurt out, "Will you take a quarter for it?" Maybe say, "I'll check back with you later," or, "Good luck," or, "It's supposed to be a nice, sunny day."

After you have picked through all the tables—if this particular flea market has indoor booths and outdoor tables you need only concern yourself with the tables—go back to your pickup truck, turn on the overhead light, and read through the Garage/Yard Sale section of the Classifieds. Circle the ones that'll be near your drive home. Also, look under Antiques and see if anyone sells a large quantity of vintage lures at rock-bottom prices, which won't be there. But you have to look, seeing as you've gotten to the point of obsession.

Drive slowly past the front yards of strangers and make educated guesses as to whether they'll have any lures. The formula is about the same as the flea market—if you see an inordinate amount of baby clothes heaped up on card tables, drive on. If you see a table saw and leaf blower, stop. Yard-sale lures run cheapest, but after factoring in gasoline and wear and tear on the pickup truck it might end up about the same as the sixty-two-and-a-half-cent (62.5¢) average you keep at the flea markets.

It's now seven thirty or eight o'clock in the morning. Stop and get a six-pack of beer. Carry what lures you nearly stole and catalog them immediately. Write down name, price you paid, and what the particular lure books for.

Open the first can of beer. Change the truck's oil. Cut the grass. Rearrange all of your lures in alphabetical order, followed by price, followed by oldest to latest model. Watch one of those fishing programs on the same channel that showed infomercials back when you didn't know what to do after becoming unemployed. Give your dogs a bath.

At exactly noon drive back to the flea market and find the man who wanted thirty bucks for the T.N.T. number six-nine-hundred. He'll be sitting on the tailgate, probably staring at the ground. Go ahead and say, "I'll give you five dollars for this lure." He'll get offended but eventually sell it, seeing as it's exactly what it cost him to rent the table. If you want, on the drive back home, tally up what you bought and what you spent—nineteen lures for seven-sixty ($7.60) and one for five bucks ($5). That comes to twelve-sixty ($12.60) for twenty (20) vintage lures. It comes to sixty-three cents (63¢) on average, I promise.

Finally, the reason why you're alone and without a pistol is because a friend, son, spouse, or significant other is always apt to walk ahead of you, find a cheap and rare lure, hold it up, and yell, "Hey, here's what you've been looking for!"—which will cause the seller to jack the price times fifty. Then you'll have to shoot your passenger.

Prisoners can't keep lure collections in their cells, what with the barbed hooks. So that means more for you. As always, you want more.

There will be days when you find no lures beneath the surface of natural lakes, man-made lakes, farm ponds, or slowmoving murky rivers. No one at flea markets in a tri-state area will have any on display. A traveling antique roadshow might come through the area and nobody there will have a single common lure, much less overpriced Paw Paw Spoon Belly Wobbler Minnows, Paw Paw Spinnered Plunkers, and Paw Paw Sucker Minnows. You will wonder if your chosen field of expertise has bottomed out. You will think back to the supply-and-demand lecture you heard years earlier in college. If the drought turns into a month, you'll find yourself seeking a palm reader. On a good day she'll tell you all about how long some scientists dedicate themselves to a specific disease, virus, or birth defect without giving up hope. On bad days she'll laugh at you and say, "Fishing lures? You collect fishing lures? Good God, man, get a life—there are three million homeless people in America."

It might cross your mind that idiotic dictum that goes, "Give a man a fish and he'll eat for a day; teach him how to fish and he'll eat for a lifetime." If this occurs as a soothsayer tries to make sense out of the lines in your palm, remember this one: "Find yourself a lure and you got the beginning of a collection; carve yourself a lure and chances are some moron from New York City will think of you as a primitive artist and want to represent your work."

Okay. It is my belief that you won't find lures for extended periods of time because your body tells you that it needs a rest from either, (A) staying under water too long; or (B) because you're about to lose your temper at a flea market and thus get shot by a seller without a sense of humor or patience. It is at these times that you need to go find an old-fashioned dollar store, a five-and-dime, a Woolworth's, they're still in operation. Buy a bag of wooden clothespins. Buy some plastic eyeballs at a hobby-and-craft shop, and eyelets. Buy red, yellow, and green enamel car-model paint and a thin, cheap brush. Go get some three-pronged trebles at the nearest three-pronged treble outlet.

Because you own a pickup truck and have been in textile management most of your life, you will have a nice folding knife. Thin the midsections of each clothespin, between the head and the two line grippers. Whittle away. Paint the things differently, so it doesn't come across as assembly-line work. Make spirals and polka dots. Paint racing stripes down the legs and think up cool names like JumpaToad, JumpaFrog, JumpaSkink, JumpaMander, JumpaCricket, JumpaHopper, JumpaMinnow, JumpaMouse, JumpaBlowfly, JumpaShiner, JumpaWobbler, and Jumpa-Wigwag-Humdinger-Smacker. Break off some of the legs of every other lure so you can add "Junior" to the title.

With your needle-nosed pliers, open up the treble hooks, insert the free end into an eyelet, close the circle back up, and screw the eyelet into the clothespin's end.

Always screw last.

It is too hard to paint the lure afterwards. To make an authentic homemade primitive lure might cost as much as a dime (10¢). You have two options: either go to the flea market and try to sell them for fifty bucks ($50) each, in hopes of selling one or two to men who also collect fishing lures and haven't been able to find any of late, or for two dollars ($2) apiece, in hopes of selling the entire lot in one sweltering summer day out on the jockey lot.

I've done both. Because you know about men and women with a pocketful of case quarters, it's easier to wait out for wealthy people traveling from elsewhere who think they've found a regular idiot-savant craftsman.

I'm not sure, but I think it's how Bill Gates and every televangelist got started.

No matter what, do not think about your life prior to collecting and selling fishing lures. Forget that your ex-wife gave up on her wrong-headed singing or acting career and is about to marry a cattle-and-citrus tycoon down in Florida. Forget that your son writes folk songs about check dams, culverts, and the silt of humanity when he's not making a hundred grand a year getting hired out as an anti-PR idea man. Don't remind yourself that the neighbors are about to start up some kind of homeowners' association and they'll write a letter about your yard presently, seeing as when you came home from flea markets as outlined in "How to Collect Fishing Lures," Part Two (2), you never cut the grass.

Remember the hum and drone of the spinning room, before the government lifted sanctions, tariffs, taxes, and whatnot on Southeast Asian countries. Smell the linseed oil barely solid on wooden loom-room floors, and the older doffers, weavers, and spinners who spoke of textile-league summer baseball games as reverently as they spoke of their mothers and friends without fingers.

Think about how you don't want to be remembered merely as a human being who crunched numbers and yelled at workers for not getting yarn and cotton thread perfect.

Understand that there's something magical in a fishing lure—between two-and-a-quarter (2 ¼) inches and five (5) inches long, single, double, or triple—trebled, reversible metal discs and wings, with or without bucktail, propellers, belly weights, joints, week guards, head plates, side hook hangers, and nickel finish. Revel in the mystery of how such a device could, without pheromone or promise, attract descendants of the first living creatures worth noticing.

Admire the notion of symbiosis. Think of how the lost, snagged, sunken lure needs you as much as you need the lost, snagged, sunken lure. On good days, think of yourself as a lure of some type, only half-human.

COLUMBARIUM

NOT UNTIL MY FATHER WALKED INTO THE POST OF-
fice—or perhaps it was a few days earlier at the bastardized crematorium—did I understand how much he despised my mother's constant reminders. For at least fifteen years she substituted "No," "Okay,"
or "I'll do it if I have to," with "I could've gone to the Rhode Island
School of Design," or "For this I gave up the chance to attend Pratt," or
"When did God decide that I would be better off stuck with a man who
sold rocks for a living than continuing my education at Cooper Union?"
I figured out later that my parents weren't married but five months when
I came out all healthy and above-average in weight, length, and lung
capacity. To me she said things like, "I should've matriculated to the
Kansas City Art Institute, graduated, and begun my life working in
an art studio of my own, but here I am driving you twenty miles to the
closest Little League game," or, "I had a chance to go to the Chicago
Art Institute on a full scholarship, but here I am trying to figure out why
the hell X and Y are so important in a math class," or, "Believe you me,
I wouldn't be adding pineapple chunks, green chilies, and tuna to a box
of macaroni and cheese for supper had I gotten my wish and gone to the
Ringling School of Art."

I went through all the times my mother offered up those blanket state-
ments about her wonderful artistic talents usually by the fireplace while
she carved fake fossils into flat rocks dug out of the Unknown Branch

of the Saluda River there at the post office while my dad and I waited in line. She sold these forgeries down at the Dixie Rock and Gem Shop, or to tourist traps at the foot of Caesars Head, way up near Clingman's Dome, or on the outskirts of Helena, Georgia. My mother's life could've been worthwhile and meaningful had she not been burdened with motherhood; had she not been forced to work as a bookkeeper/receptionist/part-time homemade-dredge operator at the family river rock business; had she not met my father when her own family got forced to move from Worcester, Massachusetts, because her daddy was in the textile business and got transferred right before my mother's senior year in high school. There were no art classes in the schools here; she could only take advanced home ec and learned how to make fabric and dye it, just as her father knew how to do at the cotton mill, more than likely.

"I could've gone to the School of the Museum of Fine Arts in Boston had I not been forced to take an English class that I'd already taken up in Massachusetts and sit next to your father, who cheated off my paper every time we took a multiple-choice test on *The Scarlet Letter*. I blame all of this on *The Scarlet Letter*, and how your dad had to come over on more than one occasion for tutoring," my mother said about once a week.

I didn't get the chance to ever point out to her how Nathaniel Hawthorne lived in Massachusetts. A year after her death I figured out the math of their wedding date and my birth, and didn't get to offer up anything about symbolism, or life mirroring art, et cetera. My mother died of flat-out boredom, disdain, crankiness, ennui, tendonitis from etching fake fossil ferns and fish bones into rocks, and a giant handful of sleeping pills. Her daily allotment of hemlock leaves boiled into a tea probably led to her demise, too, if not physiologically, at least spiritually.

According to my father, the South Carolina Funeral Directors Association didn't require normal embalming and/or crematorial procedures should the deceased have no brothers or sisters and should said dead person's parents both be dead. Looking back, I understand now that my father made all this up. At the time, though, I just sat on the bench seat of his flatbed, my mother in back wrapped up in her favorite quilt inside a pine coffin. "We're going up to Pointy Henderson's, and he'll perform the cremation. Then we'll scatter your mother down by the river so she can always be with us."

Mr. Henderson was a potter and president of the local Democratic Party. About once a year he came down from the mountains and enlisted Young Democrats—and we all joined seeing as once a year, too, he held a giant shindig that included moonshine for everyone willing to either vote right or, if underage, at least put yard signs up.

"Cremation takes two to three hours at 1400 to 1800 degrees," Henderson said when we got there. "I did the research long ago." He got his two daughters to heft my mother off of the truck and carry the box to the groundhog kiln, which appeared to be dug into the side of an embankment. "My fire reaches near two thousand degrees on a good day," he said. "After Mrs. Looper cools, I'll go to ashing down the hard bones, if that's all right."

My father nodded. He'd done his crying the night before, as had I. "We'll come back in a couple days," my father said.

"You and me's kind of in the same business, I guess," Henderson said. "You take rock and sell it to people want paths to their front doors and walls to keep them out, and I take clay and sell it to people who want bowls on their tables."

I didn't get the connection. I guessed that clay was kind of like ground-down rocks, to a certain extent. I looked at Mr. Henderson's daughters, who were my age, and were so inordinately beautiful that no one spoke to them in school. If Homer came back to Earth and met the potter's daughters, he'd've had to rewrite the Siren section of *The Odyssey*. One of them said, "Sorry."

I said, "I'm a Democrat," for I could think of nothing else. "I'm thinking that some laws need changing."

The other daughter said, "Sorry."

My father and I drove back home, as they say, in silence. Right before my mother slumped over in her chair dead at the age of thirty-three, she had set her last pancake-sized rock, a fake millipede etched into it, down on the stool. For her carving tool she'd been using a brand-new single-diamond necklace my father bought her. I don't know if her engagement ring, which she normally used for such forgeries, had worn out or not. My father had bought the necklace as a way to celebrate a new account he'd won—as the sole river rock supplier for an entire housing tract deal down in Greenville that would include a hundred patios and driveway-to-front-door paths.

I sat at the kitchen table reading a book about three out of the four ancient elements. My mother had just gotten up to go to the bathroom, I assumed. She said, "I could've gone to the Maryland Institute College of Art. Here I am walking to the bathroom one more time."

Those were her last words, as it ended up. "Mom's last words were, 'Here I am walking to the bathroom one more time,'" I said. My father, without offering a reason, performed a U-turn in the middle of highway 108 and drove back to Mr. Henderson's. I said, "I guess she didn't know those would be her last words."

"Maybe she was a visionary. Maybe heaven's just one giant toilet, Stet. I don't mean that in a bad way." I knew that he did mean it that way, though. My father didn't cotton to there even being a heaven or hell. In the past he had said, "If there was a hell in the middle of the planet like some idiots believe, I think I'd've seen a flame or two shoot out from as deep as I've dug for rocks over the years."

We drove back up Mr. Henderson's rocky driveway not two hours since we first arrived. He had already shoved my mother into the chamber. My father told me I could sit in the truck if I wanted, which I did at first until I realized that I had something important to say to the potter's daughters, something that might prod them into seeing me as special. Something that might cause both of them to be my dates at the prom in a few years. I got out and stood there. Mr. Henderson explained something about the firing process, about the wood he used, something about how he can perform cremations cheaper than making his own pots because there's no glaze involved. His daughters walked up and stood with us twenty feet from the kiln door. I said, "My mother was an artist."

They said, in unison, "Sorry."

Smoke blew out of the kiln's chimney and my father said, "Well I don't see any smoke rings going skyward. Which means I don't see a halo. Come on, son."

Not until I had graduated from college with a few degrees—my father had told me to get my fill of education before coming back to run the family river rock business—did I understand the backtracking to

Mr. Henderson's makeshift crematorium: My father wanted a sign from the Otherworld, just in case his final plan bordered on meanness or immorality.

I'm not sure what we spread down by the Unknown Branch of the Middle Saluda River. It's not like I shadowed my father for two days. I imagine he flung plain hearth ash down on the ground. At the post office, though, my father told Randy the post office guy, "They all weigh the same. You can weigh one, and the postage will be the same on all of them."

There were six manila envelopes. Randy said, "Don't you want return addresses on these?"

"I trust y'all," my father said. "I trust the postal service."

To me Randy said, "You applying to all these colleges?" He sorted through the envelopes. "I guess you are, what with all these admissions departments."

I said, "Sorry," like a fool, for the words of the Henderson girls rang in my ears still. I'd learned long before not to contradict my father. A man with a river rock business doesn't keep many belts around. I could go throughout life saying my father never spanked me, but I couldn't say that I'd never been stoned, in a couple of ways.

Driving back home my father said, "She got her wish. She finally got to attend all those art schools." Then he pulled off to the side of the road, past a short bridge. Beneath it ran a nameless creek. I got out, too, and together we took drywall buckets out of the back of the truck, trampled our way down the embankment, and scooped up smooth rounded mica-specked flagstone, each one the size of an ice cube, each one different in glint.

VACCINATION

MY DOG TAPEWORM JOHNSON NEEDED LEGITIMATE
veterinary attention. It had been two years since she received
annual shots. I read somewhere that an older dog can overdose
on all these vaccinations, and I have found—I share this information
with every dog owner I meet—that if you keep your pet away from rabid
foxes, raccoons, skunks, bats, and people whose eyes rotate crazy in their
sockets, then the chances of your own dog foaming at the mouth diminish drastically. I also believe that dogs don't need microchips imbedded beneath their shoulder blades if you keep the dog leashed or in
the house, or with the truck windows rolled up when you drive around
showing the dog farm animals living in pastures. I brought this up to
Dr. Page one time, back four years earlier when Tapeworm Johnson
was somewhere between eight and nine. Tapeworm showed up at my
door one morning, back when I was married and living in a regular
house, her ribs as visible as anything you'd order down at Clem and
Lyda's Barbecue Shack off Scenic Highway 11, her paw pads split open
from, I assumed, days traveling from wherever her conscienceless owner
dropped her off. Tapeworm looked coon or bird dog mostly, though
she'd never pointed over the years I've known her, which might explain
a stupid hunter letting her loose, without a collar, and so on. Seeing as
nothing seemed hopeful in the marriage, I let the dog inside, took her

to Dr. Page's ex-colleague Dr. Lloyd Leck—who overdosed on horse tranquilizers a while back, though people in the community say they were only ostrich tranquilizers seeing as Dr. Leck dealt with the more entrepreneurial ranchers who'd moved in to raise emus, llamas, and the like—and Dr. Leck said the dog had tapeworms. When I had signed in I put "Jane Doe" down for Tapeworm Johnson's name. When we scheduled a second visit for a month later, so the dog could put on weight and get vaccinated for diseases I felt sure got made up by either the American Veterinary Association or the Dog Pill and Serum Manufacturers of the United States, I told the vet to put down "Tapeworm" for a name, what the hell. There are worse possible names. The dog could've been diagnosed with some kind of blocked urethra, or mange.

I have a medical doctor I call Bob. I have an ophthalmologist I call Henry. There's a chiropractor who lives a mile down the road from me in one of those fake log houses built from a kit. I call him Snap-Crackle-Pop when I come across him at the barbecue shack. I refer to professors as teachers, which seems to piss them off. I went to college with our governor, and I call him Fuck-twig now, just as I did back then. So in case anyone thinks I disparage veterinarians—who have to know all the bones of about every animal ever invented, not just the two hundred six of humans—understand that I call Dr. Page Dr. Page, and before he couldn't take it anymore and offed himself with giant bird tranquilizers, I called Dr. Leck Dr. Leck.

Tapeworm got out of my truck without any aid, and she led me to the clinic's door. One woman sat in the waiting room. She said, "Look, Loretta, you have a friend! Look at the pretty doggie!" in a high-pitched voice normally used by mothers talking to non-verbal babies, or school nurses to special ed first graders who shit their pants and wished that they hadn't. We have a lot of problems these days, and I think that making it a felony to speak in such a manner might eradicate gun violence in the future.

When I signed in I looked down to read "Holly" for the owner's name, and "Loretta" for her dog. Under Reason for Visit Holly had written "Toenails." Under Tapeworm's Reason for Visit I wrote down "Change Oil Filter." I figured someone later would see it, and then ask Dr. Page if she could check the Jack Russell's oil.

I felt Tapeworm tugging toward Loretta, and when the two dogs' noses touched they wagged their tails. Holly said, "See? They can be friends."

I said, "That's good."

Holly said, "Janie said she's running late. She's back there in surgery. Somebody's dog got shot in the eye. Can you imagine? Janie said it's an emergency, and that she's going to have to amputate the eye." Holly looked normal and friendly enough. She might've been late-thirties, and wore hippie clothing that somehow matched—a thin cotton lavender skirt, a black and gray tie-dyed sleeveless blouse, those sandals that cost way too much money because they supposedly offer arch support. If I ever meet a podiatrist I think I'll call him or her Sole Brother or Sole Sister, like that.

I didn't think "amputate" was the correct term for an eyeball, but didn't say anything. Holly wasn't wearing a bra. She didn't shave her armpits, which didn't bother me seeing as the majority of women living on this planet—contrary to popular American Christian belief—didn't shave anywhere, just like most men. Holly had her hair braided three times in long pigtails, which made me scared that she might have been one of those Second Ready people who'd moved into the area, ready in a second for the Second Coming. I figured a Second Ready woman might keep three braids in homage to the Trinity.

"Homage" might not be the correct term. For some reason, I said, "I've known one-eyed dogs and they get around fine. They adapt." I sat down on the bench perpendicular to Holly. Our dogs continued to be friendly.

"I'm Holly and this is Loretta," she said.

"Hey, Holly. I'm Edward Johnson. This is Wanda." Who's going to tell a braless woman you got a dog named Tapeworm? Wanda was my ex-wife's name.

"I've never seen you here," Holly said. "You look like a level-headed person, and I'm always on the lookout for level-headed people. By level-headed, I mean people who love animals and maybe don't record reality TV shows to watch over and over."

I thought about fake-speaking in tongues, but the last time I'd done that as a joke somebody called 911 and said I underwent an epileptic seizure. This happened at a hardware store when an employee told me that if God wanted a nut and bolt to rust together beyond loosening, then I shouldn't interfere with WD-40.

"It would be kind of a coincidence if you and I came into a vet clinic at the same time more than once," I said.

Holly said, "Ed or Eddie? Or Edward, all the time?"

"Edward all the time." I didn't say how Wanda wasn't Wanda all the time. I kind of daydreamed way ahead to Holly calling for Tapeworm— "Wanda! Wanda! Wanda! Come here, Wanda!"—and how I'd have to say how the dog must've lost her hearing.

Holly slid over on her bench in my direction. Tapeworm began panting, and then jumped up beside me. I looked over to the counter and wondered if Dr. Page no longer had a receptionist, then figured that maybe she needed help in the surgery room. Holly said, "Edward. One time I was with my boyfriend—I don't have a man in my life anymore, maybe because of what I'm about to tell you—and I called him Edward out of nowhere, just like in that Led Zeppelin song, you know, about calling out a different guy's name. I didn't even know anyone named Edward back then. Maybe I was having a vision about the future." She smiled. "I got a tattoo of two dung beetles going up the back of my thighs. Maybe one day I'll go to Africa and see some real ones."

I made a mental note to open my dictionary to the "non" section when I got home so maybe I'd finally learn the correct spelling of "non sequitur."

I said, "I got one of a chameleon, but it keeps changing colors and blending right in with my skin."

Dr. Page—maybe every veterinarian in the world—didn't have much taste or imagination in art. She'd gotten a new Norman Rockwell reproduction, her ninth, and it involved a dog and a little boy, like the others. If I were a veterinarian I'd nail Jackson Pollock posters on the wall so people would think, Well, at least my dog didn't look *that* bad after getting hit out on the highway. There were also rows of Hummel-like dog figurines placed in a shallow figurine display case, *DogFancy* and *Bark* magazines scattered about, and a Canine Weight Guide chart tacked to the door that led into the examination rooms. The TV remained tuned to Animal Planet. An upright plastic holder housed pamphlets for lost pet medical insurance.

"We should go out and get some coffee afterwards," Holly said. "We could drive over to Laurinda's diner. We could sit in the parking lot and let our dogs play together."

I had work to do. I said, "Okay."

"We should go out and get a *drink*." Holly looked at her wristwatch. "I'll be in there five minutes. How long will it take for Wanda? As long as she's not getting an operation, let's say fifteen minutes. And then by the time we get to, say, Gus's Place, it'll be eleven. That's not too early. Gus lets dogs come inside."

Dr. Page came out wearing a surgeon's shower cap. She said, "Hey, Edward. Hey, Tapeworm Johnson." She looked at Holly and said, "Come on back. Now, who is this one?"

Holly didn't say anything about the Tapeworm Johnson reference. She drug Loretta into the back. I stood up, let go of Tapeworm's leash, and went outside to look in Holly's car. She drove a VW Bug, of course. She left the windows down, which meant—in my mind, at least—it was okay for me to look in her backseat floorboard and glove compartment for pharmaceutical evidence in the way of lithium. I found dog hair. I'm no forensic evidence expert, but I felt pretty sure that I discovered wiry white hair, long copper hair, short black hair, short gray hair, long liver-colored hair, and so on. It didn't all come off of Loretta, is what I'm saying. Did I want to spend an afternoon with a crazy dog woman? That was the question.

I found Grateful Dead cassette tapes and CDs. At first I thought I discovered a roach in the ashtray, but upon smelling it—then eating it—I learned that it, more than likely, ended up being the remnants of a hand-rolled American Spirit cigarette. Did I want to get involved in any way with a woman addicted to the evils of nicotine—like I'd been addicted with cigarettes all the way up until the day after Wanda took off, leaving me alone with Tapeworm?

I wanted to find a grocery list, but didn't find one. I wanted to find a couple books. If she had a copy of *Don Quixote* I'd've thought that I'd finally met my soul mate. If she had a number of those self-help books, or memoirs written by the brainwashed cast of aliens involved in the Bush administration, I'd've known to've brought a wooden stake along with me to the bar. But I found no reading material. Did I want to sit around in a bar with two dogs that might've been as literate as Holly?

I got out of the Volkswagen, reached the veterinarian's front door, turned around, rolled the windows up all the way on my pickup, and locked both doors so no one could rifle through my belongings. When I got back inside the waiting room I found Tapeworm stretched out on her back legs, eating all the dog biscuits in a bowl between the registration ledger and a doorknob used to tether a dog. Tapeworm turned her head, kept her mouth open, and looked at me with bird dog eyes that said nothing but, "You caught me. I'm sorry, but this is who I am."

I said, "Bad dog, Wanda."

HOLLY CAME OUT with Loretta and right away I noticed not as much clacking on the tile floor. *That Dr. Page must be the queen of clipping dog nails*, I thought. Holly said to the vet, "I'll see you next week to do the hind nails."

"Okie-dokie," said Dr. Page. She didn't wear the shower cap anymore. To me she said, "Come on back, Edward."

I said, "I owe you some Milk Bones."

"I'll be at Gus's Place. Come on down there, Edward," Holly said. She leaned in and kissed me on the cheek—Who does that? When did women start kissing strangers on the cheek?—and patted Tapeworm on the head. The dog Loretta licked Tapeworm on the muzzle.

I tried to say, "I might not be there seeing as I have some honeysuckle to gather," but couldn't get it out. I'm no psychologist, but maybe I didn't want Holly to know that I wove baskets for a living. Oh, I can do sweetgrass or river-cane or white-oak or even pine-needle baskets, but my best work—and the ones that sell at craft shows and galleries—is honeysuckle vine. I learned how to do it from my father's sister. She spent time in a nuthouse down in Milledgeville.

Tapeworm led me into the examination room. Dr. Page kept a frightening poster up on one wall of dog eyeball scenarios, like glaucoma in various stages. I didn't like it. On another wall she kept a poster of a normal dog's alimentary canal, above a poster of dog mouths with tooth and gum diseases.

I said, "Tapeworm's fine in all ways except the shots needed."

I'd had dreams about Dr. Page, I have to admit. Who has dreams about his veterinarian? I wondered if my *dog* had veterinarian dreams. I know that we always see dogs paddling their paws and whining in their sleep, and we say, "Hey, the dog's dreaming about chasing rabbits." Maybe they're not. Maybe our dogs dream of running away from veterinarians.

I had dreams of Dr. Page wearing, you know, more of a traditional French maid's outfit than the blue pantsuit that she always wore. In one dream Dr. Page took out a special metal comb and ran it through my hair as I froze on the metal examination table. In another, Dr. Page announced, "Heartworm!" like that.

"What a day. Goddamn," she said to me while checking Tapeworm's coat.

I wondered how many veterinarians, percentage-wise, weren't Christians and used the Lord's name in vain, as I felt that they should seeing as too many people abused God's supposed creatures. I said, "It's okay, Tapeworm," and lifted her to the table. To the vet I said, "Is it really 'amputate' an eyeball?"

"That woman's insane, you know," Dr. Page said. "Did you have enough time to talk to her? Did you gather that she's crazy?"

I shrugged. I shook my head. "What?"

"Absolutely out of her mind. I'm scared of her, to be honest. If I could ever find a receptionist again who could be pleasant to people, I'd pay double just to have someone in here with me at all times."

What kind of segue did I have to offer? I said, "My aunt spent some time in a mental institution in Milledgeville, Georgia. Nowadays they'd say she was bi-polar, but back then she was known mostly as completely nuts by people in my family."

Dr. Page listened to Tapeworm's heart and lungs with a stethoscope. She checked her ears and said, "I bet your aunt wasn't convinced that government officials try to embed microchips into her."

I said, "No," not making a connection between Holly and microchips. I thought of my aunt. We used to go visit her in the hospital when I was a kid. She called my father—her brother—Elvis Presley. She tried to strangle my mother one time, screaming out, "I am not a vessel for your sticks and stones, I am not a vessel for your sticks and stones!" That might've been the last time we visited as a group. My mother called her sister-in-law a "basket case" over and over to anyone who'd listen.

I didn't get along very well with my mother—she forever contradicted Dad, and belittled him whenever possible, bringing up how no one in my father's family could be trusted, what with the crazy gene—and maybe that's what drove me toward basket weaving, out of meanness, shortly after I graduated college with a degree in journalism, and shortly after my father shoved a garden hose in his muffler and led the business end into the cracked open window of his Buick. I said to Dr. Page, "Are you kidding me?" and tried to make eye contact without imagining her in a French maid's outfit.

"That wasn't even her dog," Dr. Page said. "She goes around picking up strays, getting them shots, then dumps them back out. Or she offers to bring her neighbors' dogs in to get their toenails clipped, whatever. And then she gets in here and asks that I scan her body for computer chips she's convinced have been implanted by the FBI." She picked up her handheld scanner. "I scan the stray to make sure it's not a lost dog, and then I scan Holly."

I said, "Man." I couldn't think of anything else to say, and knew ahead of time what my next dream would involve with my veterinarian.

Dr. Page replaced the scanner and picked up a syringe. "This is for rabies and parvo, plus a new strain of canine polio that's going around." At least that's what I heard. It was something that I didn't believe really struck down dogs. Tapeworm didn't flinch, though I held her muzzle shut just in case. Dr. Page said, "How old is Tapeworm now?"

"Between twelve and twenty," I said.

"What a good dog," she said. Then, in that voice that's used by people who need to live where my father's sister spent most of her adult life, Dr. Page said, "Who's a good girl? Yes! Yes! Who's a good girl? That's right—you're a good girl."

I cradled my dog and pulled her down to the floor. I said, "Damn." I meant, "Damn—you just ruined my respect for you." I said, "You ever found a microchip on Holly?"

My vet laughed. "Sometimes I go *beep* when I'm scanning her, just for fun. No. From what I understand, back when you could just park in front of an airport and walk in even if you weren't flying anywhere, Holly used to walk through the metal detectors. She used to take off her jewelry, you know, and walk through in hopes of setting the thing off."

Dr. Page touched my chest. Well, no, she pushed me out of the examination room, in a way to let me know gently that her time with Tapeworm was over. I walked back to the waiting room with my dog. Dr. Page took a different turn, and ended up on the other side of the counter. She said, "Is Tapeworm on heartworm medication?"

I said, "She's inside the house, or with me. She never gets in a rabid animal situation. I have a privacy fence."

"Mosquitoes transmit heartworm, Edward. Mosquitoes can pretty much find ways to buzz over fences."

I felt like an idiot, of course. I said, "Oh. Well, then, I guess she's not."

"You need some protection, I promise. Especially now, what with the rain."

I said okay—she might've been flirting with me, what with that "You need some protection" comment—and Dr. Page turned to pick up a year's worth of Heartgard Plus tablets. She said, "Shots and check-up come to a hundred bucks. The heartworm protection's eighty." She typed on her computer. "Let's call it an even one eighty."

I hadn't spent a hundred and eighty dollars on my own health care in the previous decade. I said, "We need veterinary health care reform."

"Yeah, yeah, yeah," Dr. Page said. She said, "We need to make sure there's mental health coverage for that new girlfriend of yours, if you ask me. And for other people who've been in my life, I suppose."

I thought maybe she made reference to Dr. Leck's accidental overdose of horse tranquilizers. "You looking for a partner?" I meant, of course, "Are you looking to bring another vet in here to help you out?"

Dr. Page said, "I'm not a lesbian, Edward."

Back in my dreams! I thought. I said, "That's not what I meant," and handed over nine twenties. That's the thing about basket weavers. We have cash, always.

"Have fun with Holly. Hope to see you again one day."

I wanted to talk more, but the door opened and a man came in with a limping beautiful mutt. I knew the guy. I saw him sometimes talking to himself down at Laurinda's, or I saw him driving slowly with his face dangerously close to his windshield.

Dr. Page said, "Hey, Stet, what's up?"

He said, "Someone's setting traps around."

₹ ₹

WHAT SHOULD A divorced basket weaver do when tempted by a microchip-believing hippie woman intent on drinking before noon? I said to Tapeworm, "You want to go to a bar? Does Tapeworm want to go for a ride to the bar?" but I swear to fucking God I said it all in a normal voice, as if I might be talking to a friend from college, or my crazy aunt.

Tapeworm Johnson said nothing. Tapeworm Johnson sat upright on the truck's bench seat and looked straight out the windshield, as good found stray bird dogs are wont to do.

I drove down Scenic Highway 11 past my driveway, and past Looper's landscape rock operation, and past Laurinda's until, finally, I took a couple macadam roads and turned into Gus's Place. I tried not to go to this particular bar on the Saluda River very often. One time I showed up there and three men hid behind the counter, saying that someone had a gun. Another time I went in and a homeless drifter insisted that she was one of the premier book critics in the country. For the record, I would rather be in a bar with a possible gun toter on the loose than a drifter book critic. I remember telling Tapeworm that day, "Remind me to pay my tab immediately should someone next to me at the bar ever use the term 'postmodern.'"

I parked next to Holly's VW, the only car in the gravel parking spots. Inside, Gus stood behind the counter, mouth dropped open, staring at Holly. She'd leashed Loretta to one of the stools, which Loretta tipped over and dragged behind her in order to sniff my dog's butt.

"Haven't you ever ordered a scotch and Mr. Pibb?" Holly asked me.

Gus didn't close his mouth or move his mouth visibly, though his eyes shifted to me. I said, "I can't say that I've ever gotten to that point." To Gus I said, "I'll have whatever you have on draft that's not light."

"Sanity arrives," Gus said. "I don't even carry Mr. Pibb. Do they still make it?"

Holly scooted a stool a few inches my way and told me to sit down. She said, "No, but I have a stockpile, and I thought maybe you did, too. We've been to the vet's. We met at the vet's office. What a romantic story this'll be one day!"

"Tell your dog not to drag my stool around," Gus said. I got up, told my own dog to sit. She did, and I righted Loretta's stool and slid it over to the bar counter.

To Gus, Holly said, "Well, then, surprise me. But I can't drink beer. It has to be liquor, and it can't be straight."

Gus said, "You got it." He turned around and stared at his bottles, picked out the vodka, then turned around and stared at his mixers in a cold box.

No music played. The walls were bare, though squares and rectangles of a different shade proved that Gus, at one time, kept something nailed up which, I would bet, weren't Norman Rockwell reproductions. "All my dogs used to start barking at five o'clock every morning, wanting to go outside," Holly said. "Unless it was raining. If it rained, they all acted as if they didn't need to use the bathroom. So you know what I did? I bought one of those noise machines where you can click on to whales pinging, or ocean surf, birds of the Amazon, and *rain*. I put it on a timer in the kitchen, so it goes off at four o'clock every morning until seven. The dogs haven't figured it out yet. They sure don't whine and bark any-more until about five minutes after the machine clicks off. How about that? Pretty ingenious, huh?"

Gus placed a martini glass in front of Holly. He said, "Vodka and Jarritos. It's some kind of mango soda all the Guatemalans order. Cheers."

Holly said, "Cheers," and I thought about lifting my glass but I said, "That's not your dog," and pointed at Loretta.

Holly downed her poor man's screwdriver as if it were a shooter. She held her chin down to her throat and grimaced. Gus wiped his hands on what may have been the first bar towel ever made. It looked like a nicotine-stained tatter of cheesecloth. He said, "I normally wait until noon," and pulled a can of Schlitz out of the cooler.

Holly said, "Hooooo! That went straight through me. Can you watch my dog? I have to pee."

I nodded.

And then, of course, I went through her pocketbook that she left on the bar. I found a flask, a pack of that rolling tobacco, some papers, and two rolls of quarters. She had a skein of uncompromised two-dollar scratch-off tickets. Holly had some kind of Friend of the World Wildlife Fund membership card, and another from PETA.

Gus said, "Do you know her?" in a whisper.

I said, "Do you?"

"She's been here before. One time she brought in a snapping turtle, lodged in one of those cat litter boxes with a top that snaps on. Scared the shit out of my customers. That thing kept shooting its head out, like a foot-long pecker."

I said, "The vet says she's nuts."

I found no driver's license, social security card, credit card, or passport. Who doesn't have those things, outside of people on the lam, children under the age of fifteen, or illegal aliens who sit around drinking Jarritos mango soda in their spare time?

Gus cleared his throat. I understood it to be the international signal for "She's coming back out of the restroom."

I shuffled everything back into her purse, looked down at the dogs, said, "Hey, Loretta," and noticed that the dog didn't look up at me. *Her name's not Loretta*, I thought.

"Sure she's my dog," Holly said upon her return. "It's my dog. Did that bitch Janie Page say I brought in dogs that weren't mine? Why would I do that? She's hated me since I started going there. I'd go somewhere else, but the next vet's something like thirty miles away, you know. She's hated me! You wouldn't believe how many women hate me!"

My ex-wife used to say the same thing. That's what made me so surprised when she left for someone named Michele, before I learned that it was someone named *Michel*, a French-Canadian guy who'd come down south in order to write a book on folk artists.

Gus said, "You want another? If you drink them that fast, I can make you a triple and put it in a regular glass like his."

Tapeworm Johnson barked twice for some reason and began panting. She looked at Loretta, then chewed toward the base of her own tail.

Holly said, "Hell, man, if you have a tumbler I'll take a double-triple. I'm finished for the day. I've finished my work for the day. I've done my job, for the most part."

I couldn't tell if she wanted me to ask what she did for a living, or if I was supposed to comprehend that taking someone else's dog to a vet, getting ten of its toenails clipped, and having her own neck area scanned for microchips constituted a full day's activities. So I was happy when Gus asked, "What kind of work is it that you got, lets you be done before noon? I want that job, unless it's third shift."

I said, "Me, too," just to be one of the boys. I didn't even want the flexibility of being a basket weaver, to be honest. In another life I kind of wanted to be an astronaut, seeing as by then they'd have most of the kinks worked out.

"Oh, you know. I do what I do," Holly said. "I've been a couple things in corporate America, and then I got out before the bubble burst. Now I do what I do. Right now I'm helping some people raise money and awareness toward the plight of the Nepalese. I'm a fundraiser. If I feel like working in the middle of the night, I call potential donors in Japan. I have an altitude training tent that I sleep in and everything, just in case I get a call and need to fly to the Himalayas on short notice."

Gus said nothing. I stared at Holly way too long, trying to gather it all in. I said, "I've seen those things. It's like what a bubble boy lives in. Hey, what's your last name, anyway?"

Holly said, "I'm down to fifteen percent oxygen."

On my way to the men's room an hour later I thought about how Holly might've killed some brain cells. I had seen a documentary one time about some mountain bikers readying themselves for the Leadville 100 out in Colorado. They'd slept in an altitude training tent for three months. None of them could tie their shoes or figure out a zipper, much less sing the National Anthem or name two rivers east of the Mississippi. They could ride bikes up steep inclines, though. I thought, *Will it be immoral to have sex with a woman who's only using fifteen percent of her brain?* I thought, *As bad as corporate America's doing, I'm glad Holly isn't involved with it now, only using fifteen percent oxygen.*

I thought all kinds of things. I wondered how come I tuned Holly out with all her talk of Sherpas between my first and fifth beer, and obsessed with how Wanda would say, "I told you so, I told you so," like a mantra should she have entered the bar. I daydreamed about Dr. Page showing up not wearing scrubs, and telling me what a good, faithful friend I'd been for Tapeworm. I thought about how I couldn't get so drunk that I got talked into donating a series of honeysuckle vine baskets so the indigenous people of Nepal could carry them atop their heads like indigenous people. I read the graffiti in the men's room and wondered if whoever wrote, "The joke's in your hand, Stet," referred to the same man Dr. Pate greeted at her office as I left.

I came back to the bar proper to find Gus alone. Out the window I could see Holly's Volkswagen not parked next to my truck. Gus stood leaned over the drink box, wringing his hands with the bar towel. "Where the fuck's my dog?" I said. I walked straight out the door and ran to my truck. Gus followed. I yelled, "Which way did that woman go?"

Gus said, "She paid the tab."

I yelled out, "Tapeworm, Tapeworm, Tapeworm!" in the hope that she'd merely gone out the door, that she went looking for me.

"She took both dogs," Gus said. "She paid the tab and left me a big old tip, and then she said she needed to walk the dogs. I heard her car start up and the door close, but I wasn't thinking."

I didn't want to cry in front of Gus. I got in my truck, and drove way too fast and impaired away from the direction where I lived. Wanda leaving me was one thing, but losing Tapeworm would've sent me to Gus's Place daily. I rolled down the windows and yelled for my dog about every fifty yards.

When the road finally came to a four-way stop sign I pulled over and listened for the remnants of a puttering VW engine. When I called a 911 operator and explained the situation—unstable woman who steals dogs, thinks there's a microchip implanted between her shoulder blades, fundraiser for the impoverished goat herders of Nepal—the man on the other end informed me that it was a felony to misuse the 911 system, but I felt pretty sure that it was only a misdemeanor.

I made a U-turn, slowed down to see no one parked at the bar, and continued until I got to Dr. Page's vet clinic to see if she had this Holly woman's phone number and address. The lot was empty. I'm not too proud to say that I opened my glove compartment, found some old paper napkins from Captain Del Kell's Galley Bell, wiped my eyes and blew my nose.

Tapeworm sat in the waiting room alone, the handle of her leash looped around that doorknob attached to the counter.

I said, "Goddamn, I'm glad you're here," and bent down to hug my dog. Dr. Page came out of the back. Maybe I blurted out some blubbering sounds. I said, "That Holly woman stole my dog."

Dr. Page said, "What're you doing back here?" She reached down and scratched Tapeworm's jowl. "Did you forget something?"

I said, "I'm serious. That Holly woman stole Tapeworm when I went to take a leak."

My veterinarian shook her head. She looked at me as if I made everything up. Then she walked over to one of the end tables and said, "You really ought to reconsider getting a chip for Tapeworm, and some of this lost-pet medical insurance."

I untethered my dog. Later, I would blame my irrational thought processes either on too many beers in too short a time, or from just *thinking about* an oxygen deprivation tent. "I might only be a honeysuckle-vine basket weaver who supplies a number of arts and crafts galleries in the South, but I know a scam when I see one. You hire out Holly to pretend to be crazy, then she kidnaps dogs and you get some kind of kickback from the pet insurance and microchip companies. You can't fool me. You're not going to get this by on me."

Dr. Page didn't react one way or the other immediately. In future dreams, I would see her standing in my bedroom, wearing scrubs, acting nonplussed as a woven trivet. She would shake her head one way, her index finger working in tandem. I would feel guilty, as I did standing there with my dog's leash handle in one hand and a pamphlet for the lost-pet insurance in the other.

I could've walked out indignantly. I could've asked for Dr. Page to forget veterinarian-client privileges and give me Holly's address and phone number so I could run her down and seek justice. Instead, I stood there, frozen, my dog Tapeworm wagging her tail ready to go for another ride, and wondered if this type of situation finally caused my first vet to overdose.

"Maybe crazy Holly's like that Christo artist who covers things up, then unveils them anew. Maybe she wanted you to realize what you'd taken for granted in a pet," Dr. Page said.

I was stunned. How could a woman awash in Norman Rockwell prints understand the avant-garde work of Christo? I asked her if she'd like to meet somewhere, like Gus's bar, when she got off work. I couldn't think of anything else to say, and knew that no apology would work.

Dr. Page said it might be best if I leave.

I could not make eye contact. I felt empty, empty. When I asked my dog's veterinarian if she could sell me some horse tranquilizers, I tried to make it come off as a joke. I might've said, "Corporate America." I might've thought, *Choke collar.*

STAFF PICKS

ACCORDING TO THE RADIO STATION'S RULES, CONTES-
tants were permitted to place their hands anywhere on the RV
they felt comfortable. Staff Puckett chose the Winnebago's spare
tire, which was sheathed in vinyl emblazoned with the image of Mount
Rushmore. Staff had considered visiting the granite sculpture, off and
on, for twenty years, and now she vowed to herself that soon she'd make
her way northwest on mostly back roads, then stare down those four
faces whose stony expressions didn't look much different from her own.

But first she had to win the RV. She'd been one of the nineteen nine-
teenth callers during WCRS's nineteen-day "19th Nervous Breakdown"
marathon. Now she and the other eighteen contestants were gathered in
the parking lot of State Line RV World, near the border of Georgia and
South Carolina. The rules were simple: Contestants had to remain in
contact with the RV. The last one standing got the keys.

A man to Staff's left stuck his hand on the taillight, and a woman
with bleached hair reached up high onto the back window, which Staff
thought a questionable move. The other sixteen contestants—including a doughy, balding man whose shirt blazed with advertising logos—
chose the hood, windshield, door handles, random snatches of stripe.

"Good morning," the balding man said. While he waited in vain for
Staff's reply, he gave what seemed to be a sincere smile, and Staff auto-
matically believed that he wouldn't last long.

The bleached-hair woman said, "They say there's going to be good prizes for everyone who makes it toward the end, like camp stoves and whatnot. Like tents and sleeping bags." She said, "My name's Marguerite," but she didn't offer a handshake, knowing better than to take her palm off the window and get disqualified first, probably to receive only a pack of matches or a road atlas of the southeastern United States.

Marguerite wore too-tight blue jeans and a denim shirt she shouldn't've tucked in, Staff thought. Though this woman had youth on her side—she might've been twenty-eight at most—she'd fry in the sun. Staff wore an oversized linen dress from a company called Blue Fish that she'd not selected out of her closet in a decade. It was loose, with enough room to spread her legs should she need to urinate in between the every-four-hours-and-fifteen-minutes breaks for food and porta-potty.

Staff nodded. She didn't smile. She wished she'd brought along earplugs and chosen not to wear deodorant. She said, "Staff."

Staff's mother had named her after a dinner plate, though Staff liked to think she was named after an entire setting, or the factory over in England. Staffordshire Puckett. "She'll have enough problems with your last name, when kids start rhyming," Staff's mother said often to her father. "At least Staffordshire sounds regal." It was only a coincidence that, having been named for a plate, Staff soon developed a flat visage to match her moniker.

The condition wasn't exactly medical, but when she remained unsmiling—most of the time—her expression remained frozen in the countenance a mother rat snake might display while regarding her hatchlings. It didn't help that Staff's forehead appeared abnormally large, or that her neck was shorter than average. At the sight of her, ex-projectionists from movie theaters underwent flashbacks of blank screens when reels snapped apart. Art historians approached to ask if she was related to any of the wide-eyed, flat-faced girls portrayed in famous nineteenth-century portraits. They even had a term now for the look of her so-called resting face. Staff didn't like the term.

Fortunately for Staff, her body from the neck down did not look unlike those seen in 1960s auto-parts pin-up calendars. Staff's measurements came out—even at age thirty-nine—to 34C, 22, 36. Most heterosexual men soon forgot about her deadpan face. Gay men concentrated on her skin tone. All women distrusted her.

"Staph!" said Marguerite. "Like the infection? Steph, or Staph?"

"Yeah, like the infection," Staff said, hoping to cause the woman to release her hand prematurely. Staff sidled a half-step in Marguerite's direction. "My brother's named Mersa."

The man to Staff's left said, "I'm Cy, but they call me Cyclone. Y'all might as well let go of this RV now and go do some women's work. I already won a car this way back two years, and a Westinghouse washing machine for Lorene just six month ago." He wore khaki pants and a white T-shirt that read "I'M ¹⁄16TH EVIL."

Marguerite said, "I'm Marguerite! I guess we're in charge of the back end of this Winnebago here."

Staff looked over at Cyclone and wished she had a pistol in her pocket. He was exactly the kind of person she hoped to leave behind once she won this RV and hit the road for bigger and better places, a more worldly life. She said, "S-I-G-H, Sigh? Like that?"

Cy narrowed his eyes at her. "Are you okay?"

Staff said, "I'm killer."

She didn't say, "One time at a bus stop over in Atlanta somebody called 911 thinking I'd had a stroke."

She thought, *If I'd worn cut-off blue jeans and a red-checked blouse knotted midriff, all these men would be out of the competition by now.*

Disc jockeys from WCRS judged the contest. The station was doing a remote broadcast from State Line RV World, raising a giant antenna with a satellite dish in the middle of the parking lot. People had come from a four-county area to see their favorite deejays: Morning Woody, Crazy Ned-Ned the Pumpkinhead, One-Stroke, Cyclin' Mike, and Hellbent Heidi. On air, Hellbent Heidi came off as a vixen and claimed to have a skin condition that caused her to work naked, but here in the sun, she wore a traditional Eileen Fisher dress over her size 18 frame.

Marguerite said, "I feel like we've met before."

"I'm an archivist over at the Steepleburg Public Library," Staff said. "If you've ever been on the third floor where we keep historical documents, maybe you've seen me."

Marguerite said, "Say that word again? Ach-what?"

"You the one insisted on taking the Stars and Bars out of the History Room?" Cy asked. "I wrote a letter to the editor about that. I don't want my tax money helping out no library won't honor my ancestors."

Marguerite said, "Arch-ive-ist?" stressing the middle syllable.

"Archivist," Staff said, pronouncing it correctly. "Archivist." Her face didn't change. She didn't smile or frown. But she turned to Cy and stared so hard that he held his hands up in surrender.

Ned-Ned the Pumpkinhead roared, "We're down to eighteen!" Morning Woody cut short "Satisfaction" and segued into "19th Nervous Breakdown."

Marguerite said, "I can't say your job."

Cy looked at his hand like it had betrayed him.

Staff said, "Way to go, Cybernetics. Nice concentration. Maybe you come from a long line of ancestors who didn't concentrate when bullets came their way."

Hellbent Heidi stormed over, took Cy by the arm, and led him toward a tent set up with free bottled water for contestants. "I'm calling my lawyer!" Cy yelled. "That woman's evil!"

Marguerite fanned herself with her left hand. She said, "It's hot." She said, "I ain't asking for no sympathy, but I just got out of a relationship with a man who trafficked cocaine and heroin from Mexico. He said he worked for the Humane Society and that he rescued poor dogs and cats and goats from across the border down there in Juarez, but in reality he was shoving drug-filled rubbers down their throats, bringing them over, and then, you know, waiting for them to poop. I'm glad I got out of that! My mother warned me! But who wouldn't be attracted to a do-gooder Humane Society man? Anyway, he got caught, and I got questioned. The whole reason I want this RV is so I can do the Lord's work and travel around really helping animals in need."

Yeah, yeah, yeah, Staff thought. She'd braced herself for stories such as this. She'd done her research after hours in the library, reading up on scams, tricks, hoaxes, pity-me tales. A man up in Detroit lost his chance at winning a Cadillac because he believed another contestant's story about six kids and food stamps. A woman in Oregon didn't win a foreclosed house after being fooled by a man who claimed to have been on death row, falsely accused, for seventeen years.

Now Staff looked at Marguerite and considered what phobias her fellow contestant might possess. Dogs? Snakes? Tight spaces? Heights? But she needed something closer at hand. "It's supposed to get up to ninety this afternoon," Staff said, "and then the bees are coming out." As an archivist, she understood that five percent of the population suffered from bee-sting allergies, including, perhaps, one of her remaining competitors.

Marguerite said, "What?" and walked away from the Winnebago.

"And we're down to seventeen!" yelled out Morning Woody. He switched from the Allman Brothers Band into "19th Nervous Breakdown" again, blaring the song across the lot.

"I didn't want no RV anyway," Marguerite said as Hellbent Heidi escorted her to the contestants' tent. "Hey, can I get a four-pack of them WCRS koozies as part of my consolation prize?"

STAFF HAD ENTERED the contest soon after her fiancé, Leon—a math instructor turned semi-professional Texas Hold 'Em player—left her. He'd proposed after two months and then changed his mind, convinced that she made fun of him both at meals and in bed, because she kept a poker face at all times, something he could never do at the tables in Tunica, Shreveport, Vicksburg, Cherokee. After he was gone, she took the engagement ring to a jeweler in town called Sparkleworks, only to be told that the diamond was a zircon. The man at the counter, who sported a bow tie, would offer only fifty dollars for it, which Staff took.

Now, in an attempt to escape the relentless this-is-not-worth-it thoughts that accompanied boredom and fatigue, Staff cataloged Leon's annoying mantras: flush beats a straight; straight flush beats a full house; tapping fingers probably means a bluff; pair of kings beats a pair of queens; guy clears his throat twice when he's got a flush; pupils dilate when things look futile. Next she occupied her mind by recalling, chronologically, the displays, shows, and collections she'd conceived and produced at the library: The History and Importance of Pine in the County; The History and Importance of Peaches in the County; Confederate Money; Nineteenth-Century Garments; The History and Importance of Dairy Cattle in the County; The Sibling Outsider Artists Hilty and Duck Dodgen of Rock House Springs; Hairstyles of Our Congressmen; The History and Importance of Blackberries in the County; Cherokee Weapons and Implements. She went through it all. Staff recalled a one-month show about modern-day treasure hunters who had searched for the lost gold and silver of the Confederacy, which sparked townspeople to buy metal detectors and shovels to excavate the farmland and backyards of unsuspecting fellow citizens. Though the library's director scolded Staff for causing minor chaos, hardware stores on both sides of the river offered her discounts on any purchases.

Staff stared at the back end of the Winnebago, with its spare tire cover depicting the presidents' faces. She was still bored but undaunted. She thought about traveling to Mount Rushmore. She bet that, had she been born in a different time, and in South Dakota, she could have been a model for the sculptor, Gutzon Borglum. Staff daydreamed of sitting on a stool while Gutzon lovingly carved her in stone.

Next she daydreamed about Leon, seated for three-hour stretches, maybe in Biloxi, wondering if he could bluff a pair of ducks he held with a king-queen-jack showing on the river, knowing his opponents probably held face cards.

She ran down the list of famous archivists she'd learned about in graduate school. She wondered how her classmates—most of them plain, sincere librarians employed at colleges—felt about their career paths, if they'd grown as restless as she had. Staff thought about the periodic table, what she might plant in her summer garden, actors who might be attracted to her inscrutable stare.

By nightfall Staff had outlasted a woman on a Jazzy who'd tried to readjust her grip by scooting her machine to the front of the RV but braked too late, smashing into the grille and injuring herself. Staff then overtook a man with no arms—the crowd favorite—who had kept his forehead pressed against the end of the bumper until he fell asleep and slid right down to the pavement, disqualified. Within the hour she wished she'd brought along a sweater to go over her dress, but she stayed focused by thinking of warmer locales. She caught herself picturing El Paso. Another place she'd never visited.

One woman started crying uncontrollably when the radio station blasted "That Smell" by Lynyrd Skynyrd. She yelled, "That was our song!" ran to her 1988 Camaro, and peeled out of the lot, almost running over the woman on the Jazzy as she exited the first-aid tent.

"We're down to six contestants, folks!" Morning Woody said into the microphone. "And now it's almost time for our fifth break. Three... two...one...hands off! Let's see if Ms. Staffordshire Puckett might have to use the bathroom yet. We got bets going on whether or not she's wearing Depends."

Staff thought, *Have I been so focused that I haven't eaten? Have I not used my breaks to devour protein shakes and granola bars, like I promised myself?* She said aloud to no one, "Have I dehydrated myself unknowingly?" and then released her hand from the back of the Winnebago.

In the contestants' tent, Staff picked up a Gatorade, a bottle of water, and a blueberry muffin. She realized she'd stood there holding onto the RV in such a trance that she'd not comprehended the sun going down eight hours earlier, hadn't noticed the bats and nighthawks swirling around the giant antenna, attracted to State Line RV World's bright lights. She'd blocked the music WCRS blasted and replaced it with Shostakovich.

"You okay?" said one of the EMS workers, a stocky woman wearing cotton pants hitched past her navel. "We were worried about you. Thought you might've gone into a self-induced coma or something."

Staff nodded. She didn't smile.

"Your facial muscles don't seem to be working," said the EMS worker, shining a penlight into Staff's eyes.

Staff forced a tight smile. "Please don't do that."

The EMS worker backed off, and one of the remaining contestants sidled up. "I get drug-tested all the time," he said, "what with my being a professional athlete."

Staff turned to see the man with advertising logos all over his shirt. He wore polyester pants and had one of those unfortunate bald patterns with a small island of hair at the top of his forehead, surrounded by scalp. *When viewed from above,* Staff thought, *this guy's head might look like a period surrounded by parentheses.* Staff said, "What?"

"I'm Landry Harmon. I know that not a lot of people watch the pro bowlers' tour, but I'm in the PBA. I have two wins so far. I mean, I'm no Parker Bohn III, or Norm Duke, or Walter Ray Williams Jr., but I've done okay. I'm no Dick Ritger or Dick Weber, but my name ain't Dick. I'm no Earl Anthony or Pete Weber. But I've won. I've bowled a three hundred more than I can count. Well, about seventeen times, in tournaments."

Staff noted that her ex, Leon, looked exactly the opposite of Landry Harmon. How could a semi-pro poker player have a BMI of twenty while spending so much time on his rear end, staring at cards in a smoky arena? And how could a man like Landry Harmon—who probably lifted weights between matches—end up so soft, frumpy, and glisten-headed? Did he eat nothing but French fries while his opponents took their turns? Staff said, "Hello."

"Have you ever bowled?" Landry asked. "Your face reminds me of a bowling ball, and I mean that as a compliment."

Staff shook her head. No one ever complimented her face, and what Landry had said sounded more like an insult, but he pored over her features with what appeared to be genuine admiration.

"Daggum, woman," he continued, "you have the most beautiful skin of all time. And I admire how you stood up during breaks like Muhammad Ali used to do between rounds, to get inside his opponent's head."

Staff said only, "Huh," and turned away so Landry wouldn't see her cheeks flush.

AFTER THE BREAK, Landry Harmon followed Staff to the back end of the RV. He put his hand on the ladder. He said, "I should be holding onto the tow ball, make myself feel right at home, but it's so low I'm afraid my back will give out. I already got a questionable back. From bowling. On the Professional Bowlers Association tour."

Staff thought, *The whole time I was mentally cataloging displays from the Special Collections Room, Landry Harmon probably recited whatever statistics people who played bowling kept in their heads.*

She said, "You mentioned that."

"It's probably not a good idea for me to touch the spare tire, like you're doing. Get it? Spare. In my world, a spare's not a great thing, compared to a strike."

Later, she would wonder what kept her from attempting to irritate him. There was something about Landry Harmon's face—not blank and hard like hers, but soft and gentle. *If his face were an animal, it would be a koala*, Staff thought. If bedding, a down-filled pillow. She knew nothing of bowling and said, "What's your handicap?"

Landry Harmon's short-sleeved shirt was emblazoned with his sponsors: Brunswick, Vise, Dexter bowling shoes, Rogaine, Tanner's Natural Chamois, Newman's Own Dog Treats. He said, "Why you want to win this Winnebago? Please don't tell me you ain't got nowhere to live and get me feeling all sorry for you."

Staff shook her head. "Just want to travel, see some places out West, nothing more than that." Of course, there was a lot more. Leon breaking up with her had been a splash of cold water. If she won the Winnebago, she could sell her sad little house in this sad backwards town, quit her sad sleepy job, and start living her life for real, every day an adventure.

Landry turned and stared at the sun coming up. The deejay started playing a George Harrison song. Landry said, "I don't have no sob story neither. Being a pro bowler, I pretty much live on the road. Right now I drive a Ford Focus. Sure, it gets great mileage, but it doesn't have a bathroom, a dinette, or a private master bedroom with a flat-panel HDTV and solar-blackout roller shades."

Staff couldn't explain the attraction she felt.

She thought, *God put me here to meet this man Landry Harmon.* She said, "I read up about a man who tried to win a boat in one of these radio-station promos. It came down to him and a woman. The woman said she wanted the boat so she could give it to her father, who liked to fish. The man said he needed it because his wife had drowned somewhere off the Gulf Coast, and they'd quit looking for her after a week, and he wanted to go down there and keep searching for her body. The woman put her hands up to her face and lost." Landry and Staff kept eye contact even when two more contestants quit.

"My mother died," Landry said. "It wasn't sad, really. She died the way she wanted to. She had cancer and chose not to undergo chemo or radiation. She lasted almost three years."

"I'm not falling for it," Staff said. She didn't break into a smile, or laugh, or shake her head. She said, "Hg, mercury, 80. Tl, thallium, 81. Pb, lead, 82."

Landry placed his left hand over his right, one rung higher on the ladder. "Anyway, she got to see me win on TV. She saw me win Southeast Amateur when I was in college. She had no regrets. Died peacefully at hospice."

There were only three contestants left: Staff, Landry, and a man covered in tattoos holding onto one of the windshield wipers. Staff peeked around the corner of the Winnebago as best she could, to see if the tattooed man had fallen asleep, but instead she saw Hellbent Heidi passed out in her canvas folding chair. Crazy Ned-Ned squirted Reddi-wip onto her hand. One-Stroke started to tickle beneath Hellbent Heidi's nose, and Staff yelled out, "Stop that right now!" as she might at visiting schoolchildren wanting to touch a fragile document in the Special Collections Room. Hellbent Heidi raised her head, and everyone else involved went, "Awwwww."

"There's nothing sad about my mother's death," Landry said. Staff said, "Rn, radon, 86."

"Well, maybe one thing," Landry said. "She had a lot of jewelry, and I didn't know if it was worth anything. I ended up taking it to this place Sparkleworks, in downtown Steepleburg. It supposedly wasn't so much a pawn shop as a place that specialized in estate jewelry."

Staff stopped talking. She stared at Landry.

He said, "This man named Lou said two diamond rings and a locket and a bracelet weren't worth but three hundred dollars. I didn't know. It ain't like I've had time on the Professional Bowlers Association tour to take up night courses in gemology. So I sold it all for that amount. Maybe a month later, I looked on their website and saw one of my mother's rings going for $2,700 and the other for $4,260. The locket? Four hundred. That bracelet? Sixteen hundred bucks."

Staff said, "Stop." She said, "Who are you? Is this some kind of joke?" She thought of the ring she'd sold Sparkleworks for fifty dollars. She thought, *Leon, Landry, Lou.* She tried to remember if there existed an element with plain L for its symbol. She said, "Li, lithium, three." Landry looked through his armpit at Staff. "I have a feeling that estate-jeweler dude thought I was dumb as okra. Standing there so smug wearing his seersucker suit and a bow tie. Seersucker for a c-sucker, if you ask me. Excuse my language."

"It's a small world," Staff said. "I wouldn't want to caulk it. But that same pawn shop? I think that guy ripped me off, too."

Landry didn't waver from his eye contact. He said, "Know what I'd like to do? If I won this RV, I'd like to smash it right through the plate-glass window of that place. The front of the Winnebago's the same height and width as Sparkleworks' display window. That's one thing all pro bowlers are good at, being able to measure things out by sight. If I got caught, I could say I lost control of the wheel. If I didn't, I'd grab my mother's jewelry, and nothing else. After hours, of course."

Staff held up her free hand. She said, "Don't you think when they took inventory for the insurance claim, they might notice how everything stolen happened to be yours?"

"Huh," said Landry. "It might be fortuitous that I met a woman like you. Did I say that right? You're the smart one, I can tell."

"You said it right. Woman. That's the way to pronounce it."

Landry opened his mouth, then smiled. Staff noticed that one canine overlapped the next tooth, much like a bowling pin edging over to knock down its lane-partner.

"Can't use my own car to do it," he said. "It's one of those ad-wrapped cars you sometimes see around town. Somebody might go to the cops and say, 'Hey, I saw a little Ford Focus with Brunswick, Vise, Dexter, Rogaine, Tanner's Natural Chamois, Newman's Own Dog Treats, and PBA written all over the hood and sides.'"

Staff almost caught herself saying, "How come you and I never met about ten years ago?" Instead she said, "You're putting a lot of thought into a crazy idea. Are you getting delirious? Am I about to win this RV?"

The man with the tattoos evidently collapsed.

Ned-Ned the Pumpkinhead blurted out, "And we're down to two finalists!"

What Staff didn't say to Landry Harmon was, "I want to go with you."

IN THE HISTORY of hands-on competitions, Staff had learned while researching at the library, most winners suffered through at least forty hours. One man in Beijing withstood a challenger over four days and three nights just to win a rickshaw. A woman won a thoroughbred in Kentucky; a man won a champion bull in Texas; an eighteen-year-old college student with a fake ID put up five hundred dollars to participate in, and then win, a "Touch the Foreclosed Drive-Thru Liquor Store" contest in Shreveport, Louisiana, sponsored by a forward-thinking local bank, whose president later got charged for contributing to the delinquency of a minor.

Compared to those the Winnebago seemed easy.

The sun stood high in the State Line RV World parking lot. It had been forty-one hours.

"Just you and me now, I guess," Staff said to Landry.

He reached into his left back pocket, pulled out a handkerchief, and wiped his upper lip. Staff drew her fingers across her forehead. She couldn't tell if sweat trickled down her temple, or if a persistent fly kept landing on her. She untangled her toes back and forth, feeling nothing but moisture.

WCRS went into a long commercial after playing Steve Miller's "Going to Mexico," and then Hellbent Heidi showed up with her microphone. To Landry she said, "So. You thinking about going to Mexico if you win this nice Winnebago?"

Landry said, "No, I don't think so." To Staff she said, "What about you?"

Staff shook her head. She said, "Matters who gets elected president next. Probably not Mexico, but maybe Canada."

One-Stroke, the sound effects specialist, went, "Boi-yoi-yoi-yoi-yoi-yoing!" and then said—in the deep, sinister, stereotypical Hispanic accent he employed during a politically incorrect daily feature called What Would Hey-Zeus Do?—"It's time to spill the beans." Normally, callers in this segment had to admit some kind of immoral activity that involved spousal cheating or workplace theft in order to win two free tickets to a concert, or two free entrées at Wild Wings, or two free suet stations from State Line Bird Supply.

"Christ went forty days and forty nights," Hellbent Heidi said. "Y'all willing to go that far to win this fine Winnebago here at State Line RV?"

Both Landry and Staff said, "Yes," and then, "Go away," at the same time.

Heidi said, "Well, it seems like we've gone completely into Stage Irritable, folks." She said, "What we got up next, Ned-Ned?" Then she turned off her mic and said to Landry and Staff, "Don't y'all turn hateful. If so we'll find a way to disqualify you."

Landry apologized. Staff avoided eye contact, knowing her face might be taken as a challenge. She said, "What if we take our hands off at the very same time? Would we split the prize? Would one of us have to buy out the other? I mean, would we split the prize, and maybe have to promise to accompany one another to, say, professional bowling games all over the country? Plus Mount Rushmore?"

Heidi said, "That's a good question. Let me go ask our manager."

Staff turned to Landry. She said, "Just in case, you know." Landry said, "It's called a tournament. Professional bowling tournaments, not games."

Hellbent Heidi returned and said, "They decided that if y'all happen to take your hands off at the very same time—and they used the word 'indiscernible'—if y'all take off your hands in such a way that no one can say something like, 'He pulled his hand off one-hundredth of a second before she did,' or vice versa, then it would be up to y'all to decide how you'd share the RV. Hell, Bobby said he'd buy it back from you for thirty grand, and y'all could split the profit. There's property taxes and insurance to think about, too."

Staff and Landry shared a look, and Staff knew they were both thinking about the estate jeweler, and how they weren't about to let themselves get ripped off again.

Staff said, "This Winnebago's brand-new."

Landry said, "Blue Book has it going for right under a hundred grand."

Staff said, "Anyway, who's Bobby?"

"Bobby owns State Line RV," Hellbent Heidi said. "It's up to y'all. Easiest solution, if you ask me, is for one of y'all to quit before the other one so's we ain't got no quandary."

Morning Woody leaned into his microphone and said, "You might add that we'd appreciate one of them making a decision soon, Heidi. They saying a summertime thunderstorm's headed our way. I ain't too keen on getting electrocuted." And then, perhaps using the same techniques employed by the FBI during long-term standoffs, he began a loop of four excruciating songs by the heavy metal band Jackyl, one of which included a chainsaw solo.

Staff and Landry plugged onward. They held onto the RV through the night. During breaks, they used porta-potties. They opened Nutri-Grain granola bars for each other, and Landry laughed when Staff said she'd poured prune juice for him instead of Gatorade. Landry mentioned how he didn't have groupies like some of his pro bowling competitors. He said, "I used to be completely bald on top before using Rogaine."

Staff said, "I'm thinking about retiring early from the library. Somebody needs to do a study about the effects of breathing musty books eight hours a day for sixteen years. I bet it's on par with asbestos." Rain began to spatter. Lightning spasmed in the distance. Later on, Staff would tell Landry that this was the moment when she first imagined them driving the RV through the front glass at Sparkleworks.

On and on they talked. Landry pulled his shirttail out, and the deejays made a pact to stand up to their bosses should they ever want to hold another hands-on contest. At the forty-eight-hour mark, Landry said, "You ever seen that movie *48 Hrs.*? That's a good movie. It's on about all the time, one channel or another, on cable." He looked up at the clouds. At only eight o'clock a.m., the sky had turned dark.

Staff said, "I've never seen it." "When this is over," Landry said, "maybe we can rent it on the Netflix. That movie should've won some Oscars. You ever seen *Another 48 Hrs.*? It's not as good, but it still should've won some Oscars. I met Nick Nolte one time. He likes to bowl in between making movies. At least that's what he told me."

A long rumble of thunder rolled in from the west. Staff said, "I'm not playing around, but I don't know how much longer I can do this."

"No, no, no, no, no," Landry said. Later he would tell Staff, "What I was really thinking was, 'This is the best date I've ever been on.'"

The rain beat down, soaking their clothes and shoes. Landry tightened his grip on the ladder. He said, "No matter who wins, let's promise to see each other again."

Before Staff could say, "That would make me happy," a bolt of lightning zapped the WCRS radio antenna, sending an explosion of sparks across the parking lot, followed by a clap of thunder that roared harder than anything Jackyl could've captured on vinyl. Staff and Landry let go simultaneously—they agreed that they did so, and Hellbent Heidi later lied and said she'd seen it too, them releasing in such a way that even an Olympic stopwatch couldn't have detected an outright winner.

Staff and Landry ran to the tent, where they found the deejays huddled with Bobby. There was supposed to be an official ceremony for the winner of the RV, complete with a photographer, in Bobby's office, but the lightning had knocked WCRS off the air. Bobby said something about how rules change every day, and then asked which one of them would sign the title papers. When Landry and Staff shrugged, he pulled a quarter from his pocket. "If this don't work out," he said, "we'll do rock-paper-scissors-dynamite."

Landry won the coin toss and asked what Staff wanted to do. He said he had a feeling, and that he trusted her.

Staff stared at him. "We could both sign," she said.

Bobby said, "I don't give a good goddamn what y'all do. I already got my free advertising."

And so Staff and Landry signed their names to the RV's title as the storm continued to pelt the tent. Bobby handed over the registration and an owner's manual. The radio people scrambled to their cars, leaving the tent and the busted antenna behind. The wind still blew, and Staff and Landry stepped out into the rain. The cars they'd come in, a Jeep and an ad-wrapped Ford Focus, sat with two spaces between them, like a 7-10 split.

"Your cars will be safe," Bobby said. "You can pick them up later. We got an automatic fence around the place. And let me tell you, if someone wants to steal something, I don't think it's going to be one of y'all's junkers. Listen, it's been two and a half days. I'm out of here. Congratulations." Bobby headed straight for his car, got in, and drove off.

STAFF DIDN'T HAVE second thoughts until she and Landry were inside, alone, drying themselves off at the kitchenette with hand towels bearing the logo of State Line RV World. Maybe she shouldn't have had them both sign the title, she thought, or maybe it was the most prescient thing she'd ever done. All she knew for sure was that she wasn't ready to part ways with Landry Harmon.

"Well?" he said, rapping his knuckles on the faux-marble countertop. "Shall we take this baby for a spin?"

Staff nodded. Landry thought to take off the temporary tag. Staff rode shotgun. Landry guided the big RV onto I-85. He didn't seem to have a destination in mind, and Staff didn't care. Soon they were crossing the state line into South Carolina. Just beyond the first rest area, they listened to the mechanical voice of the emergency weather channel: People living in low-lying areas should seek higher ground in case of flooding. Yet, people should seek low-lying areas if tornadoes develop. They passed a highway patrol car attending to a fender-bender, then a white pickup truck angled sideways in a ditch, then two tractor-trailers that had pulled over to wait out the rain, their hazards flashing. The interstate was no place to be. Landry took the next exit, which happened to be Steepleburg. Staff hoped he wasn't planning to drop her off at home, but Landry just talked about taking the RV to Milwaukee, the site of his next tournament.

Staff thought, *If you talk about something too much, you might make it real.* She pointed out the library where she worked, saying, "That's where I've spent way too many hours." They passed an all-night pharmacy and a mall so vacant of anchor stores that older people called it "the track," because that's where they walked early mornings. Landry straddled the white lines as they passed a hamburger joint once featured on a cable show about out-of-the-way dives. A prop plane flew across their line of vision, wobbling its way toward the county airport. Two dogs briefly splashed along beside the RV, barking at the tires.

Staff thought about everything she had to lose, and it wasn't much. More lightning flashed, its prongs reaching the ground like an upturned vase of a half dozen dead roses, and then the rain went horizontal.

"If there are power failures downtown," she said, "there'll be no security cameras working, no burglar alarms. We'll know for certain if the traffic signals are out. If they are, we could drive right through that jeweler's window and no one would know."

Landry gave a low whistle. He looked at her. He said, "How serious are you?"

Staff gave her best impression of a concrete slab. She said, "How serious are you?"

By now they were coming into downtown Steepleburg.

Landry shook his head and then nodded. "If we were to do such a thing—and mind you, I'm not saying we should—we'd want to get in and out real quick-like. I'd only take my momma's stuff. But you could take whatever you wanted."

Staff didn't care about the ring from Leon. But wouldn't it be funny, she thought, if they sold china at Sparkleworks? Wouldn't it be funny if the headlights of the Winnebago shone on a nice set of Staffordshire?

"Maybe I'd get a little something so I could look fancy rooting you on at that tournament in Milwaukee," she said. "Earrings, or a bracelet. Something nice but not ostentatious."

Neither of them said a word as they passed under a darkened traffic light.

Then Staff put out her left hand, and Landry took it. Staff felt her face begin to soften and relax, and then she broke into a bright smile, showing perfect, straight, white teeth.

"Wow," Landry said. "What's wrong?"

Staff said, "Ha-ha." She gripped his hand tighter. Her heart pounded faster than the windshield wipers. Up ahead, through the crashing rain, a plate-glass window reflected their headlights like a beacon.

TRADITIONAL DEVELOPMENT

MAL MARDIS SPUN TWO SPENT ROLLS OF COLOR FILM on the bar, didn't look up at Gus, and realized that cutting basic cable alone wouldn't solve the problem. He'd also have to find a way for his wife to quit subscribing to the magazines. This morning's mission was no different than when Brenda renovated their bathroom, den, or what used to be a two-car garage. Mal was supposed to drop off the film at any of the one-hour developers twenty miles from their house, use that time to buy at least two dozen frames, go back to the developer—Eckerd, JackRabbit, Walmart, One-Hour Photo—select the nicest shots, and ask that the person behind the counter now blow them up into eight-by-tens. Then Mal, according to his wife, could use that hour to visit Gus, have two non-brown liquor drinks, return to get the enlargements, and come home. Soon thereafter, Brenda would nail up on available wall space twentyfour photographs of the old kitchen, all of which looked down on the new tiled countertops, the laminated flooring, the new cabinets that replaced a gigantic island that once took up so much space they had to move the table outside to rot. Mal didn't get it. Keeping pictures of old rooms on the wall pretty much, to him at least, kept the new room looking old.

"You don't see women getting face lifts then plastering pictures of their old selves all around the vanity," Mal said to Gus. He sat at the counter. At the far end sat a man known as Windshield, who claimed that he still had tiny fragments of glass imbedded in his face from when he took a hard exit out of a Ford truck. Gus's bar had a sign out front that only read "Gus," for back when he bought the place he couldn't remember if it should be "Gus's Place" or "Gus' Place." Neither looked correct. No one who ever came into Gus Place knew the grammatical rule or cared. One time some fraternity boys came by and painted an H on the end of his name. Another time somebody from the Latin Club came and changed it to read "Caesar Augustus," which Gus kept for a good month until Mal told him that it might be an omen that he was going to get stabbed by an everyday regular drinking customer.

Mal tried to think of another analogy about the new kitchen, something about a hip replacement.

"Missed you at Frankie Perkins's funeral Sunday," Windshield called over to Mal.

Mal spun a roll of film, then set it upright next to the other. He said, "I didn't know Frankie Perkins."

"Well he was asking about you," Windshield said in a voice that started off a baritone and ended up so high he could've done a Memorex commercial for breaking wine glasses.

Gus leaned over to Mal and said, "Don't mind him. He said the same to me. For some reason he thinks this dead guy used to frequent the bar. Anyway, Brenda called and said you weren't allowed bourbon. She said you can have two vodkas." He laughed. He poured a jigger and a half of bourbon, placed it in front of Mal, then reached down and got him a can of Pabst. "I'm just kidding. She ain't called this time. Yet."

"Those fuckers on TV. How many shows are on about renovating or redecorating or do-it-yourself-ing? There's got to be twenty of those shows on nonstop between channels 70 and 80. Who are these people? I'm surprised there are any contractors left out there doing real work."

Gus stood up straight and half-turned. "I been thinking about changing around the bar. I'm getting tired of y'all getting to stare down at the water. Some kind of flood or freak tidal wave shows up, I ought to be the first to know about it, not my customers."

Mal stood up from his stool and craned his neck to look at the Saluda River. He said, "Beavers still working hard down there. Maybe Brenda can come on by and help them out with the interior of their den. I guess she'd have to use some kind of underwater camera for the before-and-after shots."

"Lodge," Windshield bellowed out. He stood up and looked out of the plate-glass window, too. "Beavers live in something called a lodge. Moose don't, even though they call it the Moose Lodge. My daddy used to be a member. I didn't notice neither of y'all at his funeral neither."

Gus said, "Don't make me cut you off, Windshield. I'll cut you off. You know that."

Windshield grabbed his can of Budweiser and stood still.

Mal drank the bourbon in two gulps. "I wish to God I'd never won that money from the scratch ticket. Who wins money off a scratch ticket? Back in the old days renovating the kitchen meant getting a new toaster oven."

Gus poured Mal another bourbon. He said, "You should've quit your job. Then you'd be home more to take the distributor cap off Brenda's car so she couldn't go down to Lowe's or wherever."

"I should've. I could hide the mail when those magazines show up and I could monkey with the TV and say the cable's out."

"Where you work?" Windshield said. He sat back down. "Where you work, Frankie?"

Mal said, "Home Depot. I'm in charge of the garden center at Home Depot."

WHEN THE DOOR to Gus opened, Mal Mardis looked down at his two rolls of film. He should've at least taken them by One-Hour Photo and left them and then come up with some kind of excuse. He could've said that the digital camera boom finally caused the death of traditional development. Or Mal could've at least placed the rolls in his pocket so that when Brenda stormed into Gus he could say he'd been by the first place, that they were backed up, that they apologized for having to become Six-Hour Photo.

Mal tensed, waiting to hear his wife's voice. Instead, a man who sounded already drunk called out, "You mind if I bring me a video recording device in here on a tripod?"

Gus looked up. Windshield smiled, and Mal turned around to find a stranger. Was this some kind of joke? he wondered. Is somebody playing a trick on me? Gus said, "What?"

The man walked in. He wore cowboy boots. "Pat Taft," he said, as if everyone should recognize him. He stuck out his hand to shake with Gus. "Prison Tat Pat, they call me. I need to film myself everywhere I go. It's a long story that involves an ex-wife."

Mal said, "Okay. Funny. I don't get it yet, but I know that Brenda's behind this somehow."

Gus said, "Long's it don't end up on *COPS* or *America's Most Wanted*, you do what you want."

"It'll end up on one of the goddamn home decorating shows, believe me," Mal said. "Ha-ha-ha. I get it. Brenda's gone too far this time."

Prison Tat Pat seemed to have a thyroid problem, which made the regulars think that he kept a look of surprise on his face. He said, "I've been doing it between here and Nashville. Everywhere I go. I just set up the camera and prove that I act and react normal with people. My ex-wife says she left me 'cause I couldn't act and react properly in public. I'm going to send her the video, when the time's right." He screwed the camcorder onto a miniature tripod and placed it on the far end of the bar, opposite of Windshield. He got behind it and looked through the eyepiece, focused.

Windshield said, "This ain't ever happened here. You gone be famous, Gus."

Gus said, "Tell me again what this is all about? There's a six drink minimum for capturing our essence."

Mal looked at Gus and squinted. "'*Capturing our essence*'? What'd you do, go to perfume college?"

Pat Taft said, "Okay. Here we go. Mind if I sit down?" He sat two stools away from Mal and stuck the knuckles on his right hand out. "This is why they call me Prison Tat Pat."

Where most people have L-O-V-E or H-A-T-E tattooed in India Ink or cigarette ashes across their knuckles, Pat Taft had a crude G-O-L-D. Windshield got up from his seat to examine it. He said, "Cold."

"*Gold*," Pat Taft said. "It says '*Gold*.'"

"That's a good idea," Windshield said. "You could put HOT on the other hand, and then you'd always remember which handle on the sink meant what. Like if you got All-timer's you could remember what was hot and what was cold." He lost interest and returned to his seat.

Mal Mardis placed the film in his right-side pants pocket. He said, "It kind of does look like C-O-L-D."

"Well it's not. Anyway, I'm from Nashville. Just quit my job working as a stockbroker, you know. Been with Edward Jones for sixteen years. Company didn't like what I was doing, letting my clients get all rich and all. They said that the last thing a brokerage firm needs is people making so much money that they can afford to buy a computer and start trading online, you know. I wouldn't toe the company line. No sir. They'd tell me to push Putnam Voyager mutual funds, or DoubleClick, and to not let anyone buy a stock under four dollars a share. Let me just say that I got people into Amazon and Google when they went public going for nothing." Gus cleared his throat and didn't make eye contact with anyone.

Mal looked past Prison Tat Pat at the red light on his camcorder. He brushed hair out of his face. He said, "I work for Home Depot. I get stock options, but I don't trust the market."

"He won two hundred fifty thousand dollars playing one them scratch cards" Gus said. "Now he's got a house that's worth eighty grand on the outside, and about two hundred grand on the inside."

Prison Tat Pat didn't respond. He said, "So I lost my job—and I used to be the stockbroker for the likes of Sheb Wooley and Porter Wagoner and Boxcar Willie, you know—and Emma left me, and I decided that I was going to do what I've always wanted to do. I sold my house, bought an RV, and am on my way to Myrtle Beach. I tattooed myself on the right hand, but I can't decide on what I want to do with the left. Maybe I'll print out B-R-I-C-K. Or S-O-L-I-D. Or C-O-I-N. Not only am I going to prove that I can keep up a conversation with normal people, but I'm going to prove I have a dangerous side to me. Emma said she thought I was too safe, too absorbed. So here we are." He turned to Gus and said, "If you got moonshine, then I'd like to buy some moonshine. If you don't, then I guess I'll take a Miller Lite."

Windshield got up off his stool and looked down at the river. He said, "Is that your Winnebago nose down in the river? That ain't safe."

Prison Tat Pat hadn't used the parking brake. He said, "I would cuss, but I don't want it on camera."

Mal Mardis's cell phone began to ring in his left-side pants pocket. It came out James Taylor's "Fire and Rain." Brenda was always changing his ringer tone, as a joke. He spent a month showing people plants at work while his pants rang out "Parsley, Sage, Rosemary, and Thyme" before he figured out what his wife was doing.

Mal pulled his phone out and read "Brenda" on the readout. It kept ringing. He shrugged, looked at Gus, and answered. He said, "Man, you won't believe what happened down here. I went down to the One-Hour Photo place—they're closed because the UPS guy didn't bring the right chemicals or something—so I stopped by Gus's place to ask if he knew another photo shop, and this guy walked in saying he's the reason why Merle Haggard and George Jones have so much money, and the next thing you know his RV's in the river. You wouldn't believe it!"

Brenda listened. She said, "I just realized that I don't have enough grout. I need more grout. Now, sometimes they don't have it marked right, so I want you to go into Lowe's and open up the ten-pound bag of Keracolor Gray. It's supposed to be something called Gris Gray but I opened up some Gris Gray that ended up being red. Originally I thought about using red, but I looked at it and didn't like it. They got some kind of grout they call Rouge Red, but I don't want that. I want Gris Gray. I need one more ten-pound bag of Gris Gray."

Mal held the phone away from his head. Down on the riverbank, Prison Tat Pat and Windshield looked at the Winnebago. Brenda didn't seem upset that he was in the bar already. He said, "I'll get right on it. This might take some time. Gus says the next closest one-hour picture place is about thirty miles away."

"Have you got the frames yet?" Brenda asked.

"Yes. Yes, I got the frames. I went straight to the Kmart and got the frames. Noir Black, just like you said."

After he pressed the hang-up button he pushed it down hard so as to turn off the phone altogether. Gus said, "It ain't called 'gris gray,' you idiot. That just means French gray, English gray. It means gray-gray. Just like 'noir black' means black-black. French black, English black."

Gus lost his reputation. Mal said, "How do you know that?"

Gus turned around and said, "I should maybe call the law. I'm thinking this guy is in some trouble we don't need to know about. One thing we need to do is be careful about not blurting out how we got those plants upriver. Last thing we need is for some hammerhead we don't know to find out about the crop."

Mal said, "It's a good thing Windshield has no memory."

They didn't think about how the camcorder still ran.

Prison Tat Pat and Windshield returned. Pat said, "That's all right. I can pull that one out of the water and get it to a mechanic and lease me another one in the meantime." He sat down and said, "Miller Lite ain't doing it for me. Do you know how to make a perfect Manhattan? You got you any cherries back there?"

Windshield said to Prison Tat Pat, "Frankie Perkins once had a girlfriend they called Cherry. I went to his funeral on Sunday, but she didn't show up there. He asked about her, though."

Pat Taft said, "You kind of remind me of Frank Sinatra, my man. One time Frank and all his boys came to Nashville, back when I lived there. Well, let me tell you, they say that Nashville cats know how to party hard, but they ain't got nothing on the old Brat Pack." Gus said nothing about the misnomer. "They was wanting to smoke some dope? And I just happened to have some with me? The next thing you know—they got Sammy Davis Jr. to pop out his glass eye. Then old Frank took some screen and put it in the empty eye socket, you know. Then he pinched a good bowl down there. You had to hold Sammy's nose clamped and inhale from his mouth. It was the damnedest bong I ever hit in my life. Good old Sammy Davis Jr."

Mal sat up and looked at the Winnebago. He said, "You say your ex wants to know that you can act right in front of people? I haven't ever studied up on the etiquette books, but maybe you shouldn't be telling her about smoking the marijuana." Mal looked at Gus. He gave a look that let Gus know that this was Mal's way of changing the subject.

"She was there!" Prison Tat Pat said. "Hell, man, she was there! Well, I take that back. She might've been off showing Joey Bishop and Peter Lawford Tootsie's Orchard at that point, I forget."

Gus said, "You full of shit, man. I was going to hold off, but I call bullshit on all this. You ain't much more than forty years old. Joey Bishop and Peter Lawford were long gone from the Rat Pack by the time you could've been old enough."

The bar's telephone rang. Gus stared at Prison Tat Pat. Mal said, "If that's for me, I'm not here." It rang another twenty times before stopping. "It was for me."

Pat Taft placed his right palm up. He looked back at his camcorder and said to the lens, "Tell them, honey. Tell them it's true." He drank his Manhattan—which was really only bourbon and a splash of Cheerwine mixed together—and said, "You some kind of racist? If you're some kind of racist judging me because I pinched down Sammy Davis Jr.'s nose and intook weed from his face, then I don't want anything to do with you. It wasn't like I was kissing him."

Gus shook his head. "I'm not a racist. You might just be in the wrong place, buddy."

"Okay. As long as you ain't a racist. I handled both Charlie Pride and B. B. King at one time. Say, this is good," he said, drinking Gus's version of a Manhattan. Prison Tat Pat looked back at the camera. "Hey, I'm not slurring my speech or anything."

Mal Mardis thought, *I should call up Brenda and ask her to meet me here.* She could look at Prison Tat Pat and understand that living with a lottery card-scratching drunk isn't all that bad.

Pat Taft said to Gus, "You know anyone around here with a tow truck with a wench? You mind if when I pull out the RV I leave it here for a while till it dries out and I can sell it? I'll pay you rental space. I'll pay you whatever they charge at one of those RV storage places."

Gus said, "Beer's five dollars a can. The Manhattan's ten." They weren't, but they would've been in Nashville, he figured. Gus liked to memorize all the bar prices from around the nation, just in case a stranger walked in. People used to make fun of him for knowing what the going price was for a margarita in Los Angeles, a gin fizz in Detroit.

"You take credit cards?" Prison Tat Pat asked. "You got an ATM machine?"

"The answer's no to all of your questions, going all the way back to the tow truck."

Gus poured a bourbon and placed it in front of Mal. He said, "Three bourbons, two beers. Your tab's six fifty." Prison Tat Pat didn't flinch at obvious favoritism. He smiled at the bartender, then back to his camcorder.

Mal got up to go to the bathroom. Inside, he called his wife.

WINDSHIELD FINALLY CAUGHT up with the conversation and said, "You used my head for a bong, you might get a mouthful of glass. They say I still got little chunks of glass stuck in my face."

Mal came back from the bathroom and slid his bourbon toward Prison Tat Pat. He said, "You might need this more than I do. Hey, Gus, make me some kind of vodka drink and set it in front of my seat. Brenda's on her way over and y'all need to say I didn't drink any brown liquor. I need to run over to the closest place that sells frames so it looks like at least I got that far."

Gus said, "I tell you what. Stranger from Nashville, you drinking anymore Manhattans?"

Pat Taft said, "They call me Prison Tat Pat."

"I need me either some real cherries in a jar, or a couple more bottles of Cheerwine soda, Mal. Whichever you come across first."

Mal said okay and left. He got in his pickup and made sure to keep one foot hard on the brake before getting in reverse and popping the clutch. He looked down at the bottom side of the Winnebago and thought about how it resembled a lodged metal turtle of sorts. He thought, *That guy did it on purpose, so we'd all feel sorry for him.*

Mal drove his truck south on Saluda Dam Road not more than two miles before coming up on a Dollar General store he'd never noticed. He went inside, brought twelve frames they had on the shelf up to the check-out, and read the cashier's name tag. It seemed misspelled. "Hey, Maime, I got a lot of pictures I need behind glass. You think y'all got any more of these things in back?"

Maime looked at Mal hard. She chewed gum. She said, "You might want buy breath mints. Cop comes in here smells you, charge for public drunk."

Mal picked some Tic Tacs off the counter. He shoved them beside his stack of frames. He said, "I know, I know. I normally don't drink this early, believe me."

"I ain't judging you none," Maime said. She picked up one frame, studied it, and yelled toward the back of the store, "Hey, Rena! Rena! Go in back and see we got any more these big frames." To Mal she said, quieter, "How many you want?"

"I need another dozen."

Rena called from the back, "We got some. I know where they are."

"Fifteen more!" Maime yelled. "Not the little ones. The *noir black* ones."

Mal laughed out loud. Maime cocked her head as if to say, "I'll call the deputies on you, son." She said, "What?"

He shook his head. He stepped back and picked two sixteenounce bottles of Cheerwine out of the point-of-purchase soft drink cooler. He set them on the counter. Maime ran them across the electric eye and placed them in one yellow plastic Dollar General bag. Mal said, "Nothing. I'm just laughing at my own wife." He explained how she renovated rooms then put pictures up on the wall of the old room.

Maime said, "I'd like to meet her. Damn. That's a good one. Back when I lived in Rock Hill, I had me a second husband used to make a big production out of painting the bedroom about twice a year. Word was someone got shot in there before us, and Byron thought the blood still bled through. Anyways, he'd paint a different color every time he painted and always leave a little square down behind the bed to show what the last color looked like. It looked like a gotdang weird checkerboard by the time I finally had enough and moved out."

Mal tried to imagine what she talked about. Rena brought the fifteen extra frames, which he bought without correcting anyone. There would come a time, he knew, when he'd need to fill up the walk-in closet with photographs of the old walk-in closet. *I'll have a head start*, he thought. To Maime he said, "Where in the world is 'Raw Kill'?"

"Rock Hill's up by Charlotte. You ain't ever heard of Rock Hill?"

He shook his head. He paid in cash and said he didn't need a bag. "Raw Kill," he said on his way out of the store. "Raw Kill, Raw Kill, Raw Kill." He said, "Maim me. Maim me. Maim me. Raw Kill."

MAL WAS SURPRISED to not find his wife's car parked in front of Gus. He walked in to find Rodney Sheets sitting in front of what Mal assumed was his last bourbon ordered. Mal said, "You off not doing chores today, Rodney?"

"Pretty much. Is this your drink? I been here ten minutes. Where'd everybody go?"

From where he sat, on the other side of the camcorder, Rodney couldn't see the river. Mal pointed and said, "We had a little episode earlier. This guy let his RV slip on down into the river."

Rodney got up and looked. He said, "Gus won't mind if I just keep a tally," and reached across the bar for a plastic cup. Then he walked around the bar and grabbed a quart of bourbon. He said, "No, I don't have any chores today. Wife's gone off to spend some time with her old college roommate in Chattanooga." He grimaced to himself. Rodney didn't like to let on that his wife went to college or that he taught American literature to ESL students at one of the satellite campuses. As far as Mal or Gus knew, Rodney harvested marijuana on the banks of the Saluda in order to make ends meet, just like everyone else did.

"If you don't want strangers knowing your business," Mal said, "don't say anything in front of the camera. This old boy wants to make a film of himself for his run-off wife, or something. I might didn't catch everything he said."

Rodney walked back around the counter and turned off the camera. He said, "No problem." Then he changed barstools in order to look down at the Winnebago. Gus had his arms outstretched. Prison Tat Pat nodded. Then they both looked downstream before trekking uphill.

"I'm definitely going to need a tow," Pat Taft said back inside the bar. He looked at Rodney Sheets and said, "Prison Tat Pat," and stuck out his hand. "You can sit there, I guess. You won't be in the way." Pat Taft sat down to the right of Rodney. Mal thought, *There are a dozen barstools here and we're sitting three together like fools.*

Gus came in and said, "If it tears up my land, you're paying me some money." He handed over a cocktail napkin that he'd stolen from another bar. "Sign your name here at the bottom and I'm going to fill out an IOU if it costs me money in grass seed and whatnot," he said to Pat Taft.

"And you got it on film," Pat said, pointing his thumb to the camcorder. Mal and Rodney said nothing.

The door behind them opened, and again Mal inwardly cringed. But it was Maime. She said to Mal, "I figured you'd be here," and plopped down the two bottles of Cheerwine he'd forgotten to pick up off of the Lazy Susan plastic bag dispenser. "You forgot these. Well, I admit that I forgot them, too."

Prison Tat Pat said, "Now we're talking. Say, do you know the country superstar Jeannie C. Riley? I'm the one who talked her into changing over from bonds into goldmines. See here?" Pat showed off his knuckles.

"You off work?" Gus asked. "You want you one them rum drinks?"

Maime said, "I tell you what I want. I want me a new job. Me and Rena ain't exactly getting along so well. Me and Rena, and me and Cindy, and me and whoever the manager is today. I need me a job either waiting tables or bartending."

Mal thought, *Me need some attention*. Gus said, "Well I'll keep you in mind."

"What's with the camera?" Maime said. She shook hair out of her eyes and smiled at the lens. "It ain't on, you know."

Prison Tat Pat said, "Damn. What happened?"

Rodney Sheets said, "The lights flickered in here a few minutes ago. Maybe it turned it off." No one thought about how the camera wasn't running on electricity.

"What happened to Windshield?" Mal said. "Where's Windshield? His moped's still out front."

Maime said, "Turn it on."

"Do you know that 'Harper Valley PTA' song? I'll turn it on if you sing the 'Harper Valley PTA' song," Prison Tat Pat said.

"I know that one, and I know some more," Maime said.

Mal Mardis looked out the window. He watched as Windshield emerged wet from beneath the carriage of the RV. He had a rope in his hands, and Mal knew from experience that the other end held a grappling hook Gus kept nearby in case anyone ever needed to drag the river.

WHEN BRENDA SHOWED up, covered in grout, paint, caulk, sawdust, and glue, Maime stood in the center of Gus, her legs spread apart unnaturally, belting out "I Fall to Pieces" into Prison Tat Pat's camcorder. Mal sat at the bar smiling; he lifted his vodka tonic toward his wife. Rodney Sheets kept his back to the spectacle, and Gus looked up from behind the bar as if ready to pull out his pistol.

Windshield had looped the rope around one of the building's smooth, round pine pylons that served as supports for the back end of Gus's establishment. He tied the end to the back of his moped and revved the tiny engine, faced toward the non-submerged end of the Winnebago. Rodney Sheets said, "You might want to go downstairs and tell that old boy he's going to pull this bar off its foundation, if it works. And it *won't* work, by the way."

Gus turned around, cursed, and told Mal that he was in charge of the bar for a minute. Brenda arced around Maime and said, "I called up One-Hour Photo and the man said they haven't had problems with deliveries. He said they were open for business."

Mal got up from his barstool and went around to Gus's side. He said to his wife, "Let me fix you a little something." He raised his voice. Windshield's moped sounded like a chainsaw below.

"Okay. Fix me a triple scotch. Is that the most expensive drink there is?"

Maime finished up the song, extending the word "pieces" into a trill of about twenty syllables. She said, "I won karaoke one night doing that song."

Prison Tat Pat said, "I'mo tell you what. You stay in touch with me, and I'll get you a Nashville contract. Or at least one in Branson. I know everybody there is to know. Well, to be honest, there's one record producer we can't talk to seeing as I had him invest in a mutual fund called GUNK they specialized in Guyana, Uganda, Nigeria, and Kenya. That didn't quite work out like some people thought it would." Prison Tat Pat turned to Brenda and said, "Well hello there."

Brenda took her triple scotch from Mal and threw it in his face. She said, "That was good. I'll have another."

They all heard Windshield yell, "No!" and gathered at the counter, looked out the window. Either the rope broke or the knot untied, and Windshield rammed into the back of the halfsunken Winnebago at thirty miles an hour. Rodney Sheets said, "If this were a movie, the post would've come loose downstairs, and all of us would've fallen down to the ground. Rising action, climax, denouement. Traditional development. I guess things don't work out around this part of the South like they do in movies."

Mal poured his wife another scotch. He only poured two shots, though. "You need to pace yourself," he said, laughing. He shook booze out of his hair. Mal said, "Go ahead and throw it," but Brenda took a sip and placed the cup down. They all looked down at Windshield. He tested both arms, then felt his face. "When he comes back up here," Mal said, "let's all call him Bumper. Tailgate. I bet he won't even notice."

"Traditional development," Brenda said. "Where's the film rolls? Give me the film and I'll go get it done myself."

"I'll do it right now," Mal said. "I promise. Let me just finish this last drink and I'll do it myself." Brenda stuck out her hand. Mal fished in his pocket and handed her the rolls.

Prison Tat Pat said, "I need him here to help me get my RV out of the water."

Brenda got up. She looked at Maime and said, "You *should* go to Nashville. From what I hear, there's a lot more opportunities for karaokeists there."

Prison Tat Pat nodded. He said, "Let's all live dangerously and try to pull my RV out of the water. It'll be fun. I'll buy drinks for everyone if it works out right."

Brenda didn't respond. She walked out of the bar, got in her car, sat there a moment, then returned to Mal and his new comrades before they emerged from the bar to dislodge the Winnebago. Maime now sat at the bar next to Prison Tat Pat, the camera turned their way. Mal stood at the end of the counter, and Rodney used the bathroom. Brenda walked slowly so as not to spook her husband and said, "I might as well confess, even though I'm still mad at you for coming here."

Mal said, "What now? I'm just going to help these people, Brenda. That's it."

"Yeah, yeah, yeah. I was going to say, you didn't need to get the pictures developed anyway. I changed my mind. That gris gray grout would've stained too much. I'm going to—"

Was she going to tear up the tile and re-grout the entire project? Mal wondered. Brenda stopped in mid-sentence, for she overheard Prison Tat Pat's conversation. Pat was in the middle of saying, "I can't believe no herbiculturalist ain't thought of it before. But I know a man in Nashville who's right at the brink, and I'm investing all my money in him."

Brenda said, "Say all that again. Hey, man from Nashville, start your story over."

Prison Tat Pat said, "Pat Taft. They call me Prison Tat Pat." He spoke louder, obviously for the camera. "I got a good acquaintance who has developed bonsai grass. It'll grow two inches, and that's it. Never needs cutting, you know. You plant it, you water it, it gets two inches high, and you're done. It's going to revolutionize the lawn care business. Hell, once this spreads nationwide, it'll cause enormous unemployment for people who cut grass for a living. It'll knock out John Deere lawn mowers. Snapper. Husqvarna. Murray push mowers. There's already a bonsai grass out on the market, but it ain't as good as my friend's will be."

Mal Mardis sat down at the nearest barstool and dropped his head on the linoleum. He didn't bring up how he managed the Garden Center at Home Depot. Mal thought, *It'll knock out miniature golf courses seeing as everyone would have one on their front yard. Eventually, it'll cause my unemployment, and then I'll be stuck at home.*

Brenda kissed him on top of his head and spit gravel out of the parking lot, but not in an angry way, Mal understood. No, she left excited. Already he envisioned how her next project would involve taking up entire squares of sod and replacing them. He tried to imagine what his yard would look like with eight-by-ten photographs of the old lawn. Would Brenda nail them to the trees? Would she balance them right on the ground? Would she obtain and blow up one of those satellite photographs of the housetop and surrounding land as it is now, and maybe glue it to the front door, the driveway, the mailbox?

When Windshield returned muddy-kneed, wet, and bruised, Gus followed holding the grappling hook. Gus checked his bottles behind the bar and asked who'd gotten into the scotch. Mal thought, *This is how people end up making what strangers call a rash decision.* He thought, *If we get that RV out of the water, I'm getting in.*

He asked for water. He said, "I need to lay off the chemicals and sober up."

Two weeks later he'd think the same thing, once he figured out that Prison Tat Pat viewed his own videotape, heard what Gus and Mal had to say about their marijuana plot, then snuck back onto the property and down the river—maybe with Maime at his side—in order to harvest their entire crop. Mal would tell Gus that maybe it was for the best. That's the way things run around here. He'd point out that if he sold off the pot, then he'd have a bunch of money. Soon thereafter he'd spend that on scratch cards, and he'd win. Winning money, as he had learned, wasn't necessarily good fortune, at least not for people like him.

HEX KEYS

THE FOURTH WOMAN STOOD OUTSIDE HER TRAILER, wearing a smudged orange pantsuit, holding a dead three-foot-long rat snake by the tail, near the roadside ditch. The look on her face said something like, "This is nothing, comparatively speaking." She looked like she might bellow out, "This ain't as bad as dealing with smoke damage inside the bedroom." Later on, I couldn't imagine my father planning a better scenario. What did he expect when we pulled down that clay-rut road? I would've bet that he plainly wanted to drive by the single-wide, maybe see the woman out there sweeping her dirt driveway with a cheap rake missing prongs, if anything, then his getting back onto some valid blacktop as soon as possible. He would've said, "See?" or, "There you go," or, "What do you think you'd be doing inside that place, if she'd been your mother?"

"I almost took that woman to the prom," my father said. "We were dating, I asked her, and then her daddy said he didn't like me. Said I wasn't what his daughter deserved, or something like that. Anyway, she could've been your mother."

This occurred in June, Father's Day, 1972. I was twelve. My father had friends in Vietnam. I had a couple older cousins over there, too, plus neighbors with sons and relatives unlucky enough to serve. I'd bought my father a new set of Allen wrenches and had them wrapped up nicely on the kitchen table for when he got up and ate his everyday breakfast of Cream of Wheat with blackstrap molasses. We didn't eat breakfast on Father's Day, 1972, as it ended up. He woke me, had my pants and shirt laid out on a chair, and said, "Come on. Hurry up. We got some places to go today I want you to see."

Our first stop was a breakfast joint one town over called Mama's Nook. Somebody had spray-painted an "ie" after the name on the side of the cement-block building. This wasn't any kind of raised-letter sign, or neon. It wasn't a nice porcelain sign or even a cut-out piece of plywood attached to the cinderblock. It looked as if the owner hired out someone with a proper stencil set to flat-out paint right onto the exterior. I didn't know the term "nookie" yet. I knew "poontang" only because, right after my mother took a temporary hiatus from the family in order to "tend to more important tasks in the long run," my father took grease pencils and wrote P-O-O-N on the labels of Tang that he drank each morning with his Cream of Wheat.

I said, "I got you a Father's Day present."

My father turned into the narrow lot. He stared straight ahead and, without moving his lips much, said, "Mama's Nookie's the place to be."

At this point I didn't know that my father had an established plan for the day, and that he'd been saving it up. I'll give him this: He didn't seem to blame my mom for checking herself into some kind of clinic that treated chronic depression and pain. Me, I'd said some bad things about her to friends. When my buddy Clay called up to tell me how his mom made him wear ironed blue jeans, or told him to quit eating Milk Duds, I'd said, "At least your mother doesn't mind seeing you in the morning" and, "At least you have a mother who doesn't want you to ruin your teeth." To be honest, I didn't quite understand my mother's alleged predicament. She'd been gone two months, and I doubted that she would return ever.

We walked in and sat down at a booth. This was a Sunday, so everyone else inside, it seemed, wore church clothes. The men—all fathers—sported boutonnieres, and I felt a certain shame for not thinking to clip a rose from one of our bushes out front.

The waitress who came to our table wore a name tag. My father said, "Hello, Arlene."

"Well, well, well. I heard you might be back to alone. Wondered when you might come crawling over here." She wore a yellow dress with a stain along the right side. Her hair probably wasn't formed into tight pin curls naturally, nor platinum. Arlene's head reminded me of a vegetable scrubber we had under the sink.

She tossed down two laminated one-sheet menus, front only. She said, "We out of liver mush, so don't ask. We had a run on liver mush, and Mama ain't had time to go to the store."

My father said, "This is my son, Preston," and nodded his head once across the table, my way.

I said, "Hello."

Arlene smiled. She had all of her teeth, which kind of surprised me. She said, "Hey, Varlene, get on over here," without taking her eyes off me.

Varlene wasn't a twin, but the two women looked alike. They wore the same uniform and went to the same hairdresser, at least. Varlene showed up from behind the cash register and said, "Buck Hewitt. Hey, Buck. Is this Buck Jr.?"

She didn't look at me. My father said no and introduced me again. For some reason I thought it the perfect opportunity to set these two women straight. I said, "A lot of people call me Presto, like if you took the 'n' off my name. I do a lot of magic tricks." "A lot" was an exaggeration. I knew about four card tricks, and could make a quarter disappear about half the time.

Varlene said, "Magic. Like father, like son." Then she returned to the register without saying goodbye.

My father said, "I'll just have an egg sandwich." To me he said, "Hey, Preston, Arlene and Varlene have a sister. Guess what's her name."

On my second try I figured out "Darlene," and then I ordered a waffle.

"Waffle," Arlene said. "I could've guessed that one from a Hewitt." I figured out her allusion years later.

My father didn't move his lips much and spoke quietly. He said, "When I get the sandwich, I'm not going to eat it. You eat up your waffle just fine, but I'm going to plain sit here."

I leaned across the table. "Say that again?"

My father looked to his left, at all the people bowed in prayer before their breakfasts showed up. For the first time ever I noticed how his face resembled a half-melted back porch citronella candle. He said, "Never eat food served to you by someone you've hurt, Preston. If I can teach you anything, that's it. Well, it's one of the things." Then he went on, quietly, to tell me how he'd dated Arlene and broken up with her, dated Varlene and broken up with her—even took Darlene out to a movie once, but halfway through she stood up and made a scene. My father said that her two sisters paid her five dollars, which was huge money back in the early 1950s, to break up with him. "It's not like we were going together, you know. But it was kind of embarrassing in front of all those people watching Marlon Brando."

Our food came. Varlene brought it out. She set my waffle down lightly, and pretty much slung my father's plate down. It rattled and wobbled like a dropped dime on a cookie sheet. My father placed a five-dollar bill on the table. I said, "I got you a Father's Day present."

My father said, "You ain't got to give me nothing, Presto. Just coming out to meet women who could've been your mother is enough gift for me."

I'd decided on Allen wrenches—they'd been used, sure, but I'd gotten some three-in-one oil and sanded off the rust—because my father'd broken a couple of little ones while unsuccessfully trying to unstick gravel from the treads of his tires. My father called them "hex keys," and he needed them for the Fortuna automatic skivers and United Shoe Machinery splitters he worked on at the behest of independent textile supply companies and cotton mills that demanded his presence when their machines ran afoul. My grandfather started the business, and when he died my father dropped out of college— where he met my mom—and took over.

I said, "What I got you is better than this, I bet."

My father shook his head. He said, "We got a couple more places to go."

WE LEFT MAMA'S nook and took Highway 54 toward the town of Glenn Springs, where—according to my father—a special curative mineral water got bottled and shipped to high-ranking members of the Confederacy, and the entire operation dwindled once General Lee or someone accused an interloper of bottling a tainted tonic that induced dysentery in the troops before the First Battle of Kernstown or the Battle of Appomattox Station. Maybe it was Stonewall Jackson who blamed Glenn Springs water, or the white supremacist Lieutenant General Jubal Early. One of them. Glen Springs still featured a number of wooden two-story antebellum houses owned by the descendants of bottlers and shallow-water-spa attendants, but each house fell more and more into disrepair.

I didn't speak during this twenty-minute trip. Maybe I got all obsessed with how either Arlene or Varlene might've sprinkled rat poison in my waffle batter. I thought about how it wouldn't be all that hard to stir some kind of liquid poison in a syrup container. My father took a left turn and said, "It's around here somewhere." He hit his brakes, accelerated, hit his brakes, accelerated, and I rolled down the window of his truck in case I needed to get sick.

About ten o'clock we turned down a pea-gravel and pine-straw entrance to what ended up being one of those Sears Craftsman bungalows. My father pulled up to the house and opened his door. I slid out his side, for he parked way too close to a rock wall on the right. "I'm back here. Hey! I'm back here," a woman called out as my father approached the front door.

My father took me by the right shoulder and directed me around the house. He walked with a sudden and pronounced limp, it seemed, and leaned on me as we curved around.

"It's Buck and Preston," my father said when we reached an open chain-link fence. He and I both looked around eye level, swooping our heads this way and that like half-lighthouses, like indecisive street-crossers, like adamant naysayers. My father said to me, in a louder-than-normal conversational voice, "We're here to see Rayelle Purvis."

"I'm up here," Ms. Purvis said, and we looked up into the limbs of the kind of oak tree usually seen in movies that involve hangings. She stood on an eight-by-eight-foot platform of two-by-twelves, at least twenty feet in the air. No ladder stood nearby, and no low limbs protruded from the trunk. She said, "Buck Hewitt? What the hell are you doing here? I thought you were smart enough to know better."

My father said, "What're you doing up there?" He didn't introduce me. I craned my neck. I tried to figure out if this woman scrambled up the tree like some kind of squirrel, or trick pit bull.

Rayelle Purvis looked up at the sky, then back down to us. She said, whispering, "I hope you didn't go to the front door and wake up Floyd."

My father shook his head no. He whispered back, "I just wanted to see how you're doing."

"Floyd would kill you if you came to the door. If you woke him up or not. You know that." To me she said, "Hey, little fellow."

I waved but said nothing. My father said, "We're just out on a tour today seeing who's alive and who's not. Maybe I'm feeling middle-aged, you know."

A live brown field rat fell off Rayelle Purvis's platform, landed closer to me than my father, then skittered off slowly. I won't say that I didn't jump. I won't say that I didn't maybe let out a little squeal. She said, "Damn it to hell." Rayelle squatted down out of sight, then stood back up holding a silver industrial stapler. I guess she'd had her toe on the rat's tail up until this point.

"Do you want me to try and catch that thing?" my father said. He said, "I wanted Preston to hear about how you and Ginny used to be roommates. I wanted for you to tell him how his momma's smart and normal, I guess."

"Smart and normal" seemed an odd thing to push a stranger into admitting, I thought, even then. I looked off to where the rat ran— under a pile of what ended up being the past winter's butterfly bush clippings—then back up to Rayelle Purvis. She stared at me and said, "Your momma and I used to be roommates in college. We were KD sorority sisters. I introduced her to your daddy, and my lot in life got decided because of *Ginny's* drive."

My father said, "Well. That's not exactly how I remember things, but okay. Come on down from there, Rayelle."

For some reason I felt empowered enough, maybe because this woman said my mother's name in a way that almost sounded like a curse, to say, "Are you more comfortable with rats than with people?" I'd read some kind of *National Enquirer* thing my mother left behind about people who cared more for vermin than humans. There were human beings out there who held Cheerios in their mouths and let rats climb up their shirts.

Rayelle said, "It's a good thing you didn't go to the front door and wake up Floyd. He was up all night trying to catch an owl. I'm trying to catch a hawk. We got us a dream to travel around showing the school-children injured birds of prey."

My father said, "So you'll catch a normal bird, then injure it?"

"Hey, you shouldn't be so unaccustomed to such a thing, Buck," Rayelle Purvis said. "Am I right or am I right?" She pointed off in the distance and said, "We got another platform over there with roadkill possums and coons stacked up for turkey vultures. I got to keep an eye out for them, too."

I said, "Mom was in a sorority?"

My father said to Rayelle Purvis, "I wish you nothing but the best of luck. You should be proud. You and Floyd both should be proud."

I said, "Was she a cheerleader or something?"

My father waved upward, and took my right shoulder again, and led me to the truck. We got in. He said, "That woman's insane, you understand. I knew it would be bad, but I didn't know she would be that crazy."

He started the truck and turned his head to back out of the long driveway. He put his arm around the back of the bench seat, and I could smell Ivory on his skin. I said, "Is her husband mean or something?"

My father said, "Yes, he's mean and out of control. He's a loose cannon. I went to high school with him. Floyd got kicked off the football team for beating up a trumpet player in the pep band he thought blew off-tune. He could headbutt a Coke machine into spitting out bottles."

"What if he'd answered the door?" I asked. My father swung the steering wheel hard. He put the truck in first gear and peeled out on the asphalt.

"I was going to say we had the wrong house. That's what you do. I was going to say, 'I'm sorry. We're looking for the Snopeses.' Listen, Preston, in these kinds of situations, always say you're looking for the Snopeses. It's kind of a joke. It's a long-winded joke I'll tell you about sometime. I learned it in college. Floyd wouldn't remember me, for one, and he never read about the Snopeses, for two."

I said, "Let's go home. I want you to open up what I got you."

He didn't say, "Two more," didn't say, "Having you spend the day with me is Father's Day enough." I think I heard him mumble, "Still better than checking in voluntarily." He drove back toward town a couple miles, then took a left. He said, "Old Canaan Road. Old Grist Mill. Old Stone Station," to himself, like a mantra.

Between us he had a folded map of the entire county, which he didn't need, for he'd memorized his routes.

WE GOT HOME right before noon. My father pulled into the driveway. We lived in a normal middle-class subdivision, one of those places that emerged in the early 1960s filled with brick ranch-style houses, all sixteen hundred square feet, some with half-basements that always flooded. I wanted to hurry inside and see the look on my father's face when he unwrapped the hex keys. I foresaw his pulling those things out one by one and twirling them between his thumb and forefinger, maybe saying, "This little L-shaped wrench will work perfectly on a skiving machine." Maybe he'd say something like, "It's three inches long," and I could say, "That's 76.2 millimeters!" seeing as we'd been going over the metric system in math class right before summer started.

My father closed his door and said, "Let's take a little walk."

He held out his hand for me to grab. I did. I said, "Come on. Come inside so you can open up your Father's Day present." Maybe I stomped my foot like a big baby.

"Two more," my father said. He looked at his wristwatch. He said, "Your mother would want it."

When I say "normal middle-class subdivision," I should mention that it was only half a subdivision. It was a sub-subdivision, a circle divided by two streets. We lived on Great Smoky Circle. The two streets that intersected Great Smoky were Yosemite and Yellowstone. Everyone who lived on Yosemite pronounced it "Yoze-mite," two syllables. We walked down Great Smoky for a while, then continued on a path surrounded by kudzu on both sides. My father took me through a place where—years later—two children would be found dead. We walked down a path that, when the subdivision developers continued their project, would turn out a slave cemetery on either side.

We walked what must've been a half mile, until we reached what I learned later was an old unpainted heart-pine sharecropper house between two creeks, set in a four-acre expanse of bottomland. My father hunched low and whispered, "I should've brought the binoculars for this one. Be quiet."

A woman came out in denim overalls. She didn't wear a shirt beneath them. She had her head wrapped in a red bandanna. This might all have taken place about fifty yards away, not far. Two mixed-breed dogs trotted behind her, wagging their tails, their heads lifted in search of any scent, I imagined. Twenty chickens stood high on the gutters of the house. The woman held a silver two-gallon metal bucket that she swung by her side. A hawk went, "scree-scree-scree," overhead. I don't know if she hummed a tune, or if music merely followed in her path. If we'd gone to this woman's house first I might've said to my father, "Witch!"

Except I'd never seen a more beautiful woman in my life. My mother was pretty, but this woman held an exotic appeal that could've been recognized by Ray Charles and Helen Keller alike. I said, "This woman could've been my mother?" I felt ashamed for saying it. Betraying my depressed mother wasn't something I planned to do on Father's Day.

"Shhh," my father said. "No. No, never."

The woman stopped and turned our way. She looked perplexed for a second, then started laughing and said, "Is that you, Buck?"

My father eased up to his full height. I didn't. If anything, I crouched down farther. My father lifted his right hand and said, "Hey, Bess. I'll be damned. Is that you? Me and my boy here are looking for his dog. His dog ran off. And we're looking for it." My father ambled slowly toward this Bess woman. "You haven't seen a dog out this way, have you?" To me he said, "Come on, boy, don't be shy."

Understand that I'd never been shy in my life, but this woman's beauty apparently stunned my synapses to the point where no muscle knew how to function. My father walked back toward me, grabbed my collar, and stood me up. Bess said, "I ain't seen no strange dog out here since these showed up to live here. What kind?"

When we entered what might be considered her yard, my father said, "I don't know. What kind of dog would you say you got?"

If it weren't Father's Day I could've called him on all of this. But I said, "Oh, it's a mixed breed. Maybe part collie and part something else." I couldn't think of one breed besides collie. I'd seen *Lassie*, but never *Rin Tin Tin* or *Old Yeller*. To my father I said, "Maybe if he shows up here it would be good for her to know its name."

My father said, "Richard. The dog's name is Richard."

Richard? I thought. My father must've been thinking of the president or something.

Bess lifted her arm to wipe sweat from her brow. A rooster ran off under the house. I noticed about two inches of blond hair emerging from Bess's armpit. Off to the right a mule brayed, then kicked at nothing with both back legs. He stood in a corral of sorts, surrounded by a large garden of tomatoes, corn, and sweet peas. I said, "My name's Preston. The dog's name's Richard." Again, I cannot explain this woman's outright sublime nature. *Two inches of armpit hair*, I thought, *equals 50.8 millimeters*.

My father said, "Yeah, looking for the dog. You still growing your 'organic' vegetables?"

She nodded. She said, "You need to change your ways, Buck. The government's into killing off people with chemicals they spraying on. Oh, the government's telling people they depend on to not eat store vegetables, but everyone else don't know. They got secret ways of letting their rich backers know to buy from me, but they ain't telling no one else. You know why? Because of integration. Ever since the integration, the government's been happy to kill off every black and white-trash linthead who can't afford private schooling so's to start up a new race of people, just like Hitler wanted. You know who buys from me? I'll tell you. Both our senators, for one. Funny thing is, they send they slaves down here to pile up the backs of they Cadillacs full of peas, corn, tomatoes, beans, and sweet potatoes. I might look like I live in poverty, but I got a bank account you wouldn't believe." She said all this fast, like she had it memorized and wanted to get it out of her throat.

There on the outskirts of Bess's garden I said, "Dad."

He said, "Well, okay, Bess. I guess we better go look for Richard elsewhere."

She walked up and squatted down to me. She said, I think, "Go to a private school, if you can talk your daddy into it. You need to be around people only like you, always. They's going to be a race war in time. You and your dog need to know about it."

I thought, *How can my father have ever been interested in a racist woman?* What would have happened to me had this Bess ended up my mother? Would I have been driving around in a convertible, wearing a hood like all the Ku Klux Klan members I'd seen driving through our sub-subdivision? Would I forever make fun of people not like me?

We got back home, and my father turned on the TV. I kind of forgot about the hex keys, which still sat atop the kitchen table, next to an empty bowl.

Finally my father got out of his chair with a grunt and walked into the kitchen. I heard him tearing apart the wrapping paper. Then, I couldn't tell if he laughed or cried. He made noises. I never asked.

The next time we visited my mother, he brought the hex keys along to show her. He said, "They make me remember how adjustments need to take place daily." When my father knew his death loomed, three decades later, he gave those tools back to me. Over the years I've kept them in my pocket, and roll them between my thumb and index finger often, instead of saying to my own son, "She could've been, she could've been."

UNEMPLOYMENT

MY SECOND-GRADE TEACHER DIDN'T THINK AHEAD when she agreed to let us sing that "Name Game" song the last hour of Valentine's Day class. Because—as Miss Dupre even admitted—her homemade heart-shaped cookies turned out warped into looking more like bananas, it seemed almost necessary to sing. My friend Compton Lane had suggested everything, seeing as we no longer took music classes weekly; the chorus teacher had quit during Christmas break, saying she couldn't distinguish an on-key student in all of Forty-Five Elementary.

I didn't quite understand the implications of Compton's request, didn't realize what lyrics would occur in a class that, oddly, included two Chucks, a boy named Lucky, another named Tucker, and an unfortunate girl—unless later on in life she had gathered work in a Nevada brothel—whose parents tabbed her Bucky.

"Okay," Miss Dupre said. "We'll sing the song starting with Compton. Then, Comp, you point to whoever's next." She went on to say how we would hand out our cheap Valentine's cards to each other afterwards and eat her misbaked cookies that, once she realized hadn't come out heart-shaped, were iced yellow with HAPPY VALENTINE'S DAY painted in red.

As years went on, I remembered those cookies as reading only HAPPY V.D., but maybe my memory turns that way because twenty-three-year-old Miss Dupre had gotten fired soon after handing them out.

The class stood in a circle, surrounded by four corkboards that stressed personal hygiene, poisonous plants, things to do on rainy days, and how to crouch during both natural and unnatural disasters. Compton pointed at me when his name was done, only because we were best friends who both had crazy runaway mothers. We went, "Mendal, Mendal bo bendal banana fanna fo fendal," et cetera, and the whole while Comp jerked his head for me to call on Tucker. I pointed toward Tucker next, not knowing—this was second grade in a town where people gossiped when someone said *dam* or *heckfire* after falling from a roof—that our song would have a term I'd heard only once, when my father stepped on a nail.

Miss Dupre didn't even know the bad word, at least from the expression on her face. Later on I figured that she'd been trained thusly, in her education classes, in some course like Psychology of Pranksters or whatever.

Tucker pointed at one of the Chucks. Chuck pointed at the other, and then that Chuck chose Bucky, in succession.

From down the second-grade hallway I'm sure it sounded like a ship-load of merchant marines were holding a sing-a-long.

I know this because our principal, a stern, unamused man named Mr. Uldrick, happened to be taking a group of state legislators on a tour of Forty-Five Elementary at the time, hopeful that we'd get more funding to at least reroof the place so there wouldn't be doves nesting in every classroom's ceiling and attracting hunters during season, which subsequently made it difficult to comprehend Miss Dupre over the shotgun blasts.

Uldrick motioned for us to stop, then took our teacher outside the door. I made out, "See me in my office after school," and then Miss Dupre said, "My cookies came out funny. I didn't take any home ec classes in a South Carolina state-supported college."

Compton held his shoulders almost to his ears and his eyebrows toward the doves' nests. Glenn Flack said, "I heard my daddy say those bad words one time to my mom. He was talking about the Korean War."

Miss Dupre walked back in slower than she normally moved. Her red-and-white-polka-dot skirt didn't swish. "I think we're going to have to stop now, class. I think y'all did a wonderful job. But Mr. Uldrick says it's very important that we have no fun until three o'clock. It's officially quiet time. Y'all can pass out your cards to one another and come get two each of my cookies. But we can't make noise. I'm sorry."

I didn't know at the time that presently we would have a new teacher who'd start each day singing a hymn, that Miss Dupre would quit and never teach again. But I swear I studied her face and noticed the same thing I would later see on my own wife's face and on the faces of both men and women in a textile town gone bust during the Reagan and Bush administrations.

We tiptoed across our linoleum floor and handed out those BE MINE, I'M ALL YOURS, and YOU'RE SPECIAL nonfolding cards. Shirley Ebo, the only black girl stuck in an otherwise nonintegrated school, gave me a card that must've been a reject or a second. Instead of LET'S BE FRIENDS it read only, LET'S FEND. She hadn't signed it.

I said, "Thanks, Shirley Ebo."

She said, "Does your name stand for something else, Mendal? I mean, is it short for something?"

I said, "I don't know. Men-doll. I doubt it."

Comp came over and said, "My mother says my name means 'free,' but she didn't want to name me that." Comp was my best friend from birth onward. In college, he would tell women that his name was short for Complimentary, Compulsive, Compatible, and Complex.

Shirley said, "My last name means something in Africa. I'm a warrior."

I said, "Uh-huh," and took more cards from my classmates. Miss Dupre sat at her desk, opened the drawer, and stared down. I had completely forgotten to sign a card for her and had no other choice but to approach the desk and hand Miss Dupre what Shirley Ebo had given to me earlier. "'Let's Fend,'" my teacher said aloud. "That's funny, Mendal. Let's fend. I agree with that."

And then she stood up, walked around her desk, took my face in her young hands, and kissed me on the forehead. When she hugged me, the side of my face wedged directly into her cleavage. My classmates let out an "ooh" in a way none of us could perform in music class. I blushed, almost cried, and then the bell rang.

On my way out of school that day I passed Mr. Uldrick's office. My teacher sat across from him, her face turned away. I stood there and watched the principal wave his arms. Then he leaned back in his chair and spread his feet on the desk. Miss Dupre stood up, pointed at him, then looked at me standing by the door.

Years later I would say that she blew a kiss, mouthed, "Thank you," and waved to me in a manner that meant for me to get away and keep going.

HOW ARE WE GOING TO
LOSE THIS ONE?

ALEX MULL SAYS IT DOESN'T MATTER IF THE PHONE book's expired. What would it matter? It's not like costume shops go in and out of business. Alex has a plan—first the costume shops, then the taxidermists. Taxidermists don't go out of business, either. He doesn't have any facts on hand, but he imagines that most men who mount animals learned from their fathers, and so on. The bartender hands it over and says, "Costs a dollar to use the phone," because he's never seen Alex. In most cases the bartender only charges a quarter for strangers, but since Alex wears a suit—no one has ever worn a suit inside Doffers Paradise Lounge—it doesn't seem like too expensive a request.

Alex says, "I got my cell phone." He pats the inside of his coat pocket. He turns to the Yellow Pages and tries to think of other places besides costume shops and taxidermists.

Doffers Paradise Lounge is three streets over and down from where Poe Mill stood before it burned down from either arsonists or the homeless, like about every other ex-cotton mill not yet turned into condos in South Carolina. At one time every stool and booth filled with men and women off their shifts, pockets full of money, hair full of lint. Nowadays the place attracts only what few retirees remain in the mill village, or college kids out trying to gain some real-world experience beyond Starbucks, or daring men and women alike willing to ask the bartender if he knows where they can find some crack.

"Are you Doffer?" Alex asks. Then he says, "I guess I'll have a Bud," and points to a display of choices behind the bar. There are no light beers, only Budweiser, Pabst, and regular Miller, all in cans.

From where Alex sits, he can look at the mirror and see out the window behind him to a house where, a week earlier, a crudely tattooed black man not more than twenty years old adopted a medium-sized stray mutt from the Humane Society where Alex has worked for three years. Alex got out of college with his degree in sociology, went straight to graduate school for a master's in public relations, and—despite offers from advertising firms in Atlanta and Charlotte—settled down in Greenville. His parents tell him that he should've never taken an elective course in ethics and a seminar on Darwin. His parents tell him one person cannot make a difference when it comes to behavior, whether human or canine.

That's about the same thing his ex-fiancée Laurie said, and thus why she's getting married to another man tonight at seven o'clock. It's why Alex wears a suit, in case he gets the courage to show up at the wedding on the other side of town, unannounced and uninvited.

The bartender, who's wearing a work shirt with "Slick" above the left pocket, says, "Young man like you from not around here wouldn't know." He sets the beer can in front of Alex and says, "Two dollars."

"I live here," Alex says. "I'm from here. My name's Alex." He sticks out his hand.

Slick shakes it firmly. He says, "Doffer's a job. Not a spinner or weaver. Doffer." He doesn't offer up his name.

Alex looks through the Yellow Pages, places a finger on a costume shop's phone number, and pulls out his phone. When a woman answers he says, "Y'all got any bear suits?"

The door opens, and an older man steps in, leaning on a carved stick. He says, "Another day, another doldrum." Slick reaches into the cooler and extracts a PBR. The customer reaches into his pocket, pulls out four quarters, and stacks them beside the can. Slick slides them closer to his side of the counter.

Alex says, "Thank you anyway," and hangs up. He looks at the new man's stick and says, "Cool. Did you carve that yourself?"

The man sets it lengthwise on the counter. There are snakes and frogs carved into it mostly, but the handle's a dog's head. He says, "Yessir. That's about all I do now. Sell it to you for forty dollars."

Alex thinks, That would make a great wedding present. He says, "Let me think about it."

The man says, "Shupee."

Alex smiles. He thinks it might be some local way of saying, "Hurry up," or, "I'll be here until you decide."

"I sign every one of them, right down at the bottom." He points. "Shupee. That's my name right there."

"Among other things," says Slick. He laughs and looks at Alex. "You just come back from a funeral? I hope you ain't *going* to one with beer on your breath. That ain't right."

Soon enough, Alex thinks, he will explain, in detail, the entire situation about Laurie. And he'll admit that the man she's marrying is some kind of national mountain bike champion named Todd, that they're going on their honeymoon to a number of trails so he can keep up his regimen, so Laurie will learn to love the sport as much as he, so they can—this is Alex's theory—use the entire honeymoon as a tax write-off. Alex figures he will even ask the bartender and Shupee what they think about his plan: to dress up in a bear suit and try to scare the new groom on one of the trails they're going to ride up in the Blue Ridge.

They'll think that they're talking some sense into him.

Alex checks the mirror. He sees the black man come out on his porch, the mutt beside him on a leash.

ALEX HADN'T CONSIDERED the danger when he volunteered to track men who adopt probable pit-bull bait. He'd said to his boss, "If we can just get it in the breeders' heads that we're on to them, that'll slow things down somewhat. And we can also get some of them arrested."

His boss, rightly, said, "No."

But Alex made a decision. Until today, he hadn't realized that perhaps he profiled pit-bull breeders as young African American men with barely visible green tattoos on their biceps, and that more often than not he found himself following these men out into the country or back to the failing clapboard houses that surrounded mill villages. He took notes. Sometimes he came back at night and circled the prospective breeders' neighborhoods, looking for incriminating activity; in his mind he saw himself calling 911 while watching men, hundred-dollar bills waving above their heads, betting on dogfights in the front yard of one of these residences.

Laurie had warned him about this. She had said, "I bet if you got on the Internet and did some research, you'd find out that there are little old white women adopting pit bulls, or adopting stray dogs used in training pit bulls." Alex knew that she probably had a point. As a nod to her—even after she left him, met the guy who wore a helmet on his head more often than not just like some kind of shell-shock victim, and got engaged within a few months—Alex followed every tenth old white woman home. They all seemed to have whirligigs in their yards, he noticed. That had to mean something sociologically, he thought.

AFTER THREE BEERS Alex looks at his watch and reminds himself to set a pace. Four hours until the wedding. The black man with the stray mutt has gone back inside his house.

Shupee says, "No. Whatever you do—and Slick will agree with me on this one—don't go dress up in a bear suit and try to scare your old girlfriend and her husband. First off, you'll get caught somehow. And when you get caught, you'll come across as—what's the right word here?"

Slick says, "Idiot. Insane. Pathetic."

"Those are right about on target," Shupee says. "No, you need to do the opposite of all that. I ain't talking the opposite of a bear costume. What would be the opposite of a bear costume?"

They all think for a moment, and then Alex says, "Salmon."

"I ain't asking you to consider going up to the mountains wearing a salmon costume, I'm asking that you act as though she don't matter none to you anymore. Do the opposite of pining. You don't want to appear that you pine for her." Shupee picks up his stick and looks at it. "This is from a tulip poplar. It ain't pine. Maybe you need to carry this stick around with you all the time as a way to remember."

Alex smiles. He shoves the telephone directory back to Slick. He says, "I think you're probably right. How much did you say that stick costs?"

"Sixty dollars."

"Let me keep thinking about it. I might go fifty."

Slick pulls out an *Iwanna* newspaper from under the bar. He says, "I might get me a pop-up camper. I made the mistake of promising a pop-up camper for the grandkids. I might get me one and just park it in the back."

Alex thinks of this as a perfect opportunity to say, "I read the other day where people are keeping their pit bulls in pop-up campers so as to make them meaner. Something about the confined space, you know, and they get meaner."

Alex tries to read their faces. Slick turns the page of his newspaper. Shupee says, "That sounds pretty dumb, but I wouldn't know." He looks at his wristwatch. "Daggum it. Today is Friday, right? I got to go get Francine's baby. I keep forgetting that I promised to get Francine's baby. Hold my spot," he says. He takes his cane off the bar and leans it between his stool and the counter.

Alex waits until Shupee's gone. He says to Slick, "All that talk about pit bulls seems to have him a little antsy. Is it my imagination, or did he seem a little uncomfortable?"

Slick says, "What? No. Shupee just forgot about his wife's new boy. He keeps him on Fridays and Saturdays so Francine and her husband can have some alone time."

Alex nods. He thinks, You mean *grand*son. Who would keep his ex-wife's kid if it wasn't his?

He looks at the mirror behind Slick and notices the black man again, this time sitting without the dog. Alex turns around to look out the window. He says to Slick, "What's the story with that guy?"

Slick meanders around the bar counter and looks out the window. He goes to the door, opens it, and yells out, "Hey, Lawrence! Man in here wants to know your story."

Alex says, "Shhh. Shhh." He laughs. He reaches for Shupee's carved stick.

Lawrence waves and goes back inside his house. Alex turns around to

Slick and says, "Don't do that, man." He points for another beer, then presses down on Shupee's cane to test its rigidity.

THE DOOR OPENS, and Shupee walks back in with a baby in a car-seat carrier. He sets the thing atop the counter and says to Slick, "Some things don't change. I got yelled at for being a half hour late."

It's a boy. He doesn't cry.

Alex points Shupee's stick back his way and says, "That's your son, or grandson?"

Slick says, "There he is. You can ask him yourself," as Lawrence walks into Doffers Paradise Lounge. He wears a sleeveless T-shirt, and his blue jeans ride low. Shupee says, "What's up, Lawrence?"

Lawrence says, "Hey," and turns his head around to look at Alex. "I know you. I got my dog from you."

At first Alex thinks about denying it all, about saying something like, "I've never seen you in my life," or, "I have an identical twin." He says, "You wouldn't have a bear suit by any chance, would you?"

"Are we back on that?" Shupee says. He takes a beer from Slick. "I thought we had that all settled before I left. Goddamn. I can't leave for five minutes. Loosen your tie, son."

Lawrence sits down between Shupee and Alex. He says, "I know you from the Humane Society. I saw you four or five days ago, man. You were right there."

Shupee asks Slick to turn on the television. He says, "The Braves are playing an afternoon game. I want to see how we're going to lose this one. They're playing the Cubs. I want to see how either one of them's going to lose."

Alex nods his head at Lawrence and says, "That's right. I'll be damned. You got that old mutt."

Lawrence stares at Alex, then looks to the bartender. He says, "Hey, Slick, I'll have a Miller's and a Goody's Powder." To Alex he says, "That ain't no mutt. That dog I got from you has some of that dog-jump-off-the-ship-when-the-Spanish-Ramada-sank-offshore in him. You know what I'm talking about? Wheaten terrier. Those dogs jumped off and swam to shore."

Alex thinks, I don't think *Ramada*'s the right word. He thinks, That dog you got is not whatever you're thinking. If anything, it's a wirehaired pointing griffon. He says, "I've had too much to drink." Then he imagines his ex-girlfriend and her new husband checking into a Ramada Inn somewhere outside of Barcelona, ready to take on any mountain bike trails of the far-off Pyrenees.

"He's thinking about going to his ex-wife's wedding," says Shupee.

"No, man!" says Lawrence. "Big mistake."

"She was just a girlfriend. She wasn't my ex-wife. Shupee's exaggerating. She wasn't my wife ever."

Slick opens up the *Iwanna* again. He says, "I'm thinking I might get me a tiller. I need me a good tiller."

Shupee's wife's son raises his hand and groans. Shupee looks up at the television set and says, "They'll find a way to lose, believe me. They should be called the Atlanta Confederates, or the Atlanta Rebels. No offense, Lawrence."

Lawrence says, "I got you, Shupe."

"I know you're thinking this got to be my grandboy, but it ain't," Shupee says to Alex. "Let's just say that my wife and I split up, and she got remarried, and then this come out. Who'd've known? It ain't like we didn't have a child. We got us two children, both went to college as a matter of fact. And then she got remarried and had another at age fifty-two. It's not some kind of record. I mean, it might be some kind of record here on the mill hill, but it ain't no kind of *world* record. I checked up on that. I thought I might could get us all some money for that."

Shupee shakes the jar of pickled eggs on the bar so that they swirl around like a poor man's lava lamp. His ex-wife's son turns his head slowly and smiles. He lets out another groan. Shupee nods.

Lawrence says, "How they going to lose today?" and jerks his head at the screen. "You got your error, your blown save, your walk-off home run. Who wants to make a bet? I say walk-off homer."

Alex stares at the child. He looks normal. He's not cross-eyed, overly obese, or missing fingers. Alex glances back up to Shupee and says, "That baby looks a lot like you."

Shupee keeps his eyes on the television set. He says, "Change the subject."

≥ ≤

AT SIX O'CLOCK Alex loosens his tie. He's proud to have shut his mouth and listened since Lawrence came in. The dog that Lawrence retrieved from the Humane Society, as it ends up, will be a gift to Lawrence's grandmother, once the dog's house-trained. Finally, Alex says, "A wheaten terrier will never become house-trained, my friend. I mean, he won't pee or crap on the floor, but getting him to stop running in circles around the yard, or getting him to *obey sit* and *lie down* and *shut up*? Forget it. Those dogs are incorrigible. They're loveable as all get-out, but they're wild. Maybe that's why the Spanish Ramada sank. Maybe the captain was running around trying to catch his dog."

Lawrence says, "*Armada.* Yo. I hear that, my brother-man."

Shupee lifts his head up for Slick to pay attention. He mouths, "Coffee," for Alex, who is now slurring his speech. Shupee says, "One more hour and you won't have to worry about going to that funeral no more."

Lawrence looks up at the television and says, "This will be the answer. They're bringing in that guy from the bullpen. Anybody want to take some bets as to how many pitches before he gives up a home run?"

Alex orders another beer, but Slick acts as though he doesn't hear him. Alex says, "It's her wedding. Not a funeral, a wedding. And I have a confession to make." The left side of his face is an inch from the counter. He's eye level with the bottom of the baby carrier still set atop the bar. "When you said 'bet,' it reminded me."

Slick looks at Shupee and says, "That reminds *me*. Maybe that's why I said 'funeral.' I thought of something else you need to take with you in your coffin. A anvil. So's in case you go to heaven, somehow, and you don't like it. Maybe a anvil will bring you back down to earth, and then through it, and on down to hell."

Shupee laughs. He pulls a bent and smudged Mead memo book from his top pocket and flips through pages. He motions for Slick's pen, then writes down *anvil*. "I'm up to forty things. Might have to hire on some extra pallbearers, especially with an anvil in there."

Lawrence says to Alex, "What kind of confession?"

Alex holds up his finger and says to Shupee, "What're y'all talking about? What're you taking in the casket?"

Lawrence says, "I know what that confession's all about. You followed me to where I lived just to make sure Simone was getting a good home. You people were thinking that a nice wheaten terrier deserves the best house possible."

Alex shakes his head. "Not even close. I thought you got the dog in order to kill it by pit bulls. It's a long story that may or may not involve ethnic profiling, and I'm not proud of it. As a matter of fact, I'm ashamed. It wasn't my idea," he says, lying. To Slick he says, "Can I get a beer for myself, and two for Lawrence? I have some payback. I owe him. I feel guilty as all get-out."

Slick looks at Shupee. Shupee nods and says, "I got his keys already. Let him do what he wants."

Alex feels in his pocket, notices that he doesn't have his keys, but doesn't ask how anyone got them. Lawrence says, "Thanks, man. No problem. My people have been putting up with such since the beginning. I'm used to it. God will set it straight to you white people one day. You folks need to learn what people are, and be what people learn."

Shupee turns to Alex and says, "I bet you never thought you'd come in here today and learn so many things, did you? People we get who ain't from around here, they come in thinking they'll be surrounded by the lost and the losing. But we're some regular philosophers, when it all boils down."

"Explain it," Slick says. "I'm not taking any credit for this one. Most days I think it's outright stupid, but you never know."

"See," Shupee says, picking up his cane—the baby cries out three times, widens his eyes, and expels a spit bubble that won't pop on his lips—"I don't want to say that I believe in an afterlife, but I'm afraid that if there is one, I won't be happy with what they got to offer. I sure know that things ain't exactly worked my way in this life. So. What I've come up with is this: I want to be buried with a crowbar, in case you *can* take it with you, and in case I want to pry myself out of a situation. At least that's how it all started. Then I realized that maybe I should be buried with a fire extinguisher—you know, in case I need to cool off the flames. Slick here just added the anvil. I've also got some them cold packs they got stay frozen up to seventy-two hours, my two pistols, a battery-operated Sawzall, one them blowup sex dolls, a bullhorn in case

I go upwards and need to give some advice for the baby, and I'm hoping for a mostly-filled oxygen tank, in time. There are some other things. I keep forgetting to record them when they come to me." He flips through the pages.

Alex stares at Shupee for a moment, then says to Lawrence, "I'm all for restitution, if it matters any." Shupee shows everyone where he's carved an angel and a devil on both ends of his cane.

AT SEVEN ALEX starts humming the "Bridal Chorus" from *Lohengrin*. Everyone has a pickled egg in his possession, even the baby. Slick had run one under tap water for a couple minutes to lessen its heat. Alex thinks, Would I ever be able to take care of Laurie and Todd's child if she asked me? He thinks, I need to remember some of those accouterments, and he wonders when was the last time he used the word *accouterments*.

He says, "Todd," elongating the name.

There's been a long rain delay in the baseball game. The teams need to finish, since they won't meet again this season. TBS shows a rerun of *Gunsmoke* during the delay. "You need to quit singing that song," Slick says to Alex. To Shupee he says, "You need to change that baby before the crowd comes in."

Shupee says, "It's the pickled eggs that smells. It ain't this boy."

Alex says, "What crowd? Please tell me it's not karaoke night or something. Is it karaoke night? I hope it's karaoke night."

His cell phone begins to vibrate. He looks at the readout and sees that it's his old college roommate Paul Borick who, more than likely, is attending Laurie's wedding. Paul studied architecture, became an architect, and never questioned his decisions. Alex flips open the phone and presses the answer button. He says, "Where are you?"

Paul says nothing. Alex can just barely hear what must be the preacher asking Laurie and Todd to share their special, from-the-heart, spontaneous vows. Alex motions for Slick to turn down the volume to *Gunsmoke*. He looks at his new comrades and whispers, "On three, y'all yell out, '*Don't do it!*' like that. Loud as you can."

Alex figures Paul Borick must be sitting on the aisle, maybe only a couple of rows behind the bride's parents, holding the phone out and away from his body so Alex can hear this sacred moment—so, when Slick, Shupee, Lawrence, and Alex scream, "Don't do it, don't do it, don't do it," over and over, both Laurie and Todd must turn from the altar. Shupee's stepson lets out a wail that may be even more audible than the drunken Doffers Paradise crew yelling. The guests must be craning their necks. Paul's phone clicks off.

Alex says, "Hello? Hello?" He smiles toward Lawrence and says, "Hello?"

Slick turns the volume up on the TV, and Festus says, "Well, I suspect there's a time and there's a place for such mischief, Matthew."

The baby settles down. Shupee says, "I can't believe that's what's on the TV right after what we done. Walkie-talkie! I been meaning to write down walkie-talkie for something in the coffin. Or half of one. Talkie."

They sit silent until they all seem uncomfortable. Lawrence says, "I need to feed Simone. She starts eating the table legs if she don't get her food on time."

"Bring her in here," Slick says. "I don't mind. Hell, she's got to be more hygienic than a baby crapping his pants."

Lawrence leaves. Shupee says, "He's a good man. Lawrence's a good man. I'd trust my life with Lawrence."

Slick says, "Uh-huh."

When *Gunsmoke* cuts off just as the bad guy's pulled his pistol on a little kid who spooked him, and when there's nothing but dead air for five seconds before the baseball game resumes, Alex thinks about how he could've made a mistake, easily, by turning Lawrence in for fighting dogs. He thinks about how he could be standing at a church altar with Laurie at this moment, confused from the sound of four invisible men screaming about how it's all a mistake. Alex thinks, I have a mission in life—I'm here to make sure that dogs and cats live better lives than dogs and cats.

He bends his beer can in the middle with his thumb and middle finger. With his fist he squashes it straight down into the size of a puck. Slick says, "There *might* be a crowd. One night there might be a crowd. If I don't keep thinking that, I might as well quit."

It's the seventh inning when the game resumes. Lawrence returns with his ex-stray on a makeshift bungee-cord leash. Shupee puts his stepson down on the floor in his car seat. The dog licks the baby's face repeatedly. The baby waves his arms, then lets out a squeal. On the television, one of the announcers points out that no one has left the stadium during the long delay. The dog bounces up and down below the pickled-egg jar, then lunges at Alex playfully, tongue lolling. Alex closes his eyes and wonders what it would feel like should Simone change her terrier mind. He imagines the dog tearing into his calf, jerking her head back and forth, digging deep into muscle.

He opens his eyes. Simone sits at attention, her paw atop the baby's leg. Shupee tries to get the child to hold the dog's leash.

After the pitcher warms up, rain begins to fall again. The camera turns to the stands where a man in a bear suit—perhaps a locally known unofficial mascot—holds his gigantic furry head in his hands. Alex starts laughing, points to the screen, and says, "That's not me. I could've been that guy, but I'm not."

The baby doesn't seem interested in the dog or the leash. Shupee pulls out another round of pickled eggs for everyone.

PERFECT ATTENDANCE

MADISON KENT'S FATHER SAID THAT THEY COULD EAT anywhere, but Madison remembered this trick. The last time they saw each other—a month before the boy began high school—Charlie Kent offered the same boastful invitation. His son chose the Peddler Steakhouse, one of the pricier restaurants in town. Charlie Kent swung by a McDonald's on the way, and they ended up eating dollar-menu burgers and fries in the parking lot of the Peddler. So on this next occasion—the late afternoon of his high school graduation—Madison said, "I don't care," over the phone. "You pick. Maybe we can park beneath a tree."

Like the last time they spoke over the telephone, Madison heard traffic in the background—car horns, plaintive cries from people living in a neighborhood Madison couldn't picture. His father plunged change into a pay phone. Who used pay phones anymore? Madison wondered. Where were pay phones in the first place? Madison's only experience with a pay phone occurred back when his parents still lived together. They had abandoned a trip to Florida after the car blew an oil gasket and threw a rod. Charlie Kent sold the car for junk after two days of staying at a Motel 6 in Valdosta that had a swimming pool in back and a bar across the street. Madison's mother had walked across the street to get her husband, stopped at a pay phone mounted to the building's exterior, and called her sister collect. Later on, Madison's mother said she had to make decisions about her husband *and* her blood relatives.

"You think it'll be all right for me to be in the same audience as your momma? I don't want to get all settled down in my chair for your graduation and have your mother pull out a tape measure and decide I'm within however many feet I'm supposed to keep between us."

Madison said, "Are you still living in Myrtle Beach? Mom said for me not to expect you to really show up, especially if a bike rally is going on down there." Madison didn't say, "She said you'll just go off on a binge and forget," though she had. He wanted only for his biological father to forget Madison's given name.

"Living in Myrtle Beach, yes. Got me a job as a caretaker for a trailer park between South Myrtle and Murrells Inlet. I'm a glorified handyman. They give me a place to live free. And a golf cart to go from one problem to the next."

Madison didn't know that his father could fix anything. His mother told stories of having to tie her ex-husband's shoes. Before everything fell apart financially, physically, and in the porous bubble of matrimony, Charlie Kent had worked as an H&R Block tax preparer, which meant that he kept busy from January until mid-April. He told friends and strangers alike, "For four months out of the year I work on numbers. For eight months out of the year, numbers work on me." Then he'd extract a joint from his pocket, sock, wallet, or from behind his ear, as if to prove that he never exaggerated.

His son couldn't think of a proper segue. He said, "Are you going to drive all the way up here, then turn around?"

Charlie said, "I've already heard from your mother. She says you changed your name. She didn't say if you did it legal-wise or not, but that you changed it."

Madison said, "Yeah, you never know about Mom. Maybe you shouldn't come to the actual graduation ceremony. First off, you're right—she might have that restraining order still going on about not being within a hundred yards of her. On top of that, I'm just walking across the stage with four hundred other losers. I'm not the valedictorian."

"You like seafood?" Charlie Kent asked. "I eat nothing but the freshest seafood down here every day. Flounder. Scallops. Catfish. Crawdads. I know this sounds weird, but I miss fish that *ain't* so fresh. Y'all still got that Cap'n Del Kell's up there? Cap'n Del Kell's Galley Bell, is that what it's called?"

"Yes sir." He didn't bring up how catfish and crayfish weren't seafood.

"Let's you and me meet there. Your graduation's at two, so let's meet about four. That should be enough time, don't you think? Hey, you got a girlfriend? You can bring her along."

Charlie Kent's son *did* have a girlfriend, Laney. They would both be attending Reed College in the fall—either nine or eleven states away from South Carolina, depending on the route taken—on full scholarships. Laney, in fact, would be giving the valedictory speech. Her boyfriend, Madison, third in his class, would receive special recognition for never missing a day of school, from kindergarten onward. He would get booed, laughed at, and taunted by his classmates, and he didn't want his father to witness such a spectacle, especially after driving two hundred fifty miles.

"I didn't change my name. I just don't go by Chip anymore," Madison said to his father. A computerized voice asked Charlie to put in ninety-five cents more. "I'm using my middle name."

"You don't go by Chip anymore?" his father bellowed. "Damn, son. That was our whole thing—Charles and Chip. Charles Chip. Like those potato chips that come in a big can. Home delivery and everything. Your middle name? That's your momma's maiden name, right?"

"I don't think those potato chips come that way anymore," Madison said. "Yeah, we can't go around doing that anymore. I'm not even sure I've seen any Charles Chips lately."

"They still make them," his father said.

Madison thought, *Maybe they're available at all fine pay phones everywhere.* He said, "I go by Madison. It's not a big deal."

"Madison sounds like a lawyer's name. Or a fancy hotel," his father said. Then the line went dead.

AFTER THE CEREMONY, Madison drove to Cap'n Del Kell's Galley Bell alone. He left his friends—all of whom would come running back home one day after their college degree, he felt sure—at the entrance to the gymnasium, and said that he'd meet them later in the Walmart Superstore parking lot. One of last year's graduates now ran a cash register, and promised to fake-check fake IDs. Madison kissed Laney, said, "Great speech," and left to see his father. His mother came up to him in the parking lot and said, "Call me when you order, call me when you're done. Do not let him talk you into lending him your graduation money."

In the history of seafood restaurants, Cap'n Del Kell's fell somewhere between Long John Silver's and Red Lobster. Cap'n Del strode around asking how everything was, and sometimes he drank too much and tried to wear a wooden leg. The waitresses wore bandannas on their heads, said "matey" more often than needed, and always approached a table with, "What can we hook you up with?" They prided themselves on hush puppies.

Madison Kent said, "Lemonade," when the woman asked what she could "hook him up with." He thought at first, *You can hook me up with a grammar textbook, and I'll show you how come you're not supposed to end questions with prepositions*, but he decided against it. Laney might've done so, seeing as she graduated first in the class.

"I'm waiting for someone," Madison said. He looked at his wristwatch. "Maybe I'm late, though. Has anyone come in here saying he was waiting for a Chip?"

The waitress pointed at her name tag, which was the shape of a curled smiling shrimp. She said, "I remember you. You graduate today? I'm from last year. I'm just doing this until I get into dental hygiene over at Tri-County Tech. I ain't doing this the rest of my life. Like I see it, though, I get to take notes on people's teeth while they chewing, you know. I ain't got all the technical terminology down right, but from what I can see firsthand, most people dining at Cap'n Del Kell's either got gum disease or a variety of problems with their canines, all the way through their molars. Anyway," she said, still pointing at the flat plastic shrimp below her collarbone, "I'm Karla."

Madison thought, *I remember her being a cheerleader.* He said, "Yeah, Karla. I know you."

"I'll bring the lemonade. You going to be waiting long? I'll bring over some fish nuts while you're waiting."

Madison didn't have time to ask what they were. He yelled out, "Okay," but Karla had gone in the kitchen.

"Hey there, Chip," his father said from behind Madison's booth. "I know the back of a Kent head from a mile away."

Madison didn't know whether to say, "Hey" or, "Hey, Dad," or, "Hey, Mr. Kent." He giggled nervously, and blurted out, "Our waitress used to be a cheerleader." Charles Kent sat down across from his son. His broad, pink face beamed. Madison hadn't seen his father in four years; he remembered less hair and more Vitalis or Brylcreem.

"Does this place serve beer?" his father asked. "I don't drink anymore. I mean, I don't drink *every day* like the old days, but I'll have a beer or two on special occasions. You know what I mean? You and me—let's have a beer, and order some fried oysters."

He looks like that actor who's always having a mugshot aired on TV, Madison thought. He said, "I have to be twenty-one."

"Screw that, son. Are you kidding me? They don't teach law in high school anymore?" Charlie Kent said, his voice high. He rubbed both his sunburned arms down toward the table top, and his son couldn't tell if sand or dead skin landed. "You with a parent, you can drink all you want. Hey, cheerleader. We need some service over here."

Madison almost said, "Dad." He said, "Come on, she'll be here. Shhh."

"Can I help you?" Karla asked. She held a squirt bottle of tartar sauce in one hand and her order pad in the other. "Y'all ready?"

Charlie Kent said, "I'm Charles. This is my boy Chip. Charles, Chip. Charles Chip."

She said, "Uh-huh."

Madison said, "She already knows me as Madison. Back in high school I went by Madison."

Charlie Kent lifted his scaly eyebrows. He said, "Okay. Not a problem. I bet you were scared how I'd react, taking your momma's maiden name and all. Fuck. Madison's better than another million names. It's a president's name, by God. It's a president's name, and it's better than Adams, or Jefferson, or Roosevelt for a first name."

Madison remembered his mother's stories: His father swore off drinking one time, but within a week came back from the grocery store loaded down with three dozen jars of Vita brand pickled herring in wine sauce.

The next morning Madison's mother found the jars sucked dry, the fillets standing on edge in their containers. She told a story of his father one time scraping his knuckles on purpose so he could apply isopropyl to the abrasions, in order to lick the alcohol. Madison could remember others.

Karla said, "I know you ain't twenty-one."

Charlie Kent said, "Damn. A psychic! We can't get past her. Maybe you should get a job down at the carnival." He tousled his own hair, making it stand up in unnatural ways. "What do you want, son."

"Lemonade."

"He ordered lemonade already," Karla said.

"Y'all got any vodka? Y'all ain't got no vodka, I know," Charlie said, craning his neck around in search of a proper bar. "Okay. One lemonade, and let me get two beers so you don't have to keep returning to us every five minutes. Two draft beers. I don't care what y'all even have, as long as they're not light. Y'all got regular, regular draft on tap? I want two of those. And his lemonade."

Madison looked at his father. Karla didn't question Charlie's order. She returned with beer, lemonade, and straws. She said, "Your teeth are in good shape."

CAP'N DEL KELL kept a cheap gold-plated bell by the door, with a sign beside it that read IF ALL WENT WELL, RING CAP'N DEL KELL'S BELL. Various knotted ropes hung on the walls. The booth backs had been painted to resemble the sterns of Key West and Cape Cod yachts. Charlie Kent raised his mug. "Perfect attendance, huh? Damn. I'm proud of you, son. I don't think I ever went a month without missing a day of school. Back then, though, I had to help out on your granddad's farm."

Madison didn't process this last statement. He didn't mention how his father's father sold insurance, lived in a subdivision, and never seemed to dress in anything outside of a short-sleeved white shirt and slacks bought from the back page of a Sunday magazine. Madison said, "How'd you know about that? Were you at graduation?"

"Saw it on the news. It was on CNN, a big thing on how only a few kids nationwide never missed a day of school." Charlie drank half of his beer. He said, "Beer tastes about the same here as down in Myrtle Beach."

Madison sat forward. "Are you kidding me? Did you record it? We don't have cable TV anymore. I didn't see it."

Charlie Kent smiled. He rose his hand to Karla. When she approached he said, "We're both going to get the fried shrimp and oyster extravaganza. Y'all use real mayonnaise in your coleslaw?"

She said, "Fried shrimp's my favorite."

"If the coleslaw's made with no-fat mayo, or whatever it's called, you can keep it. And listen. I know this'll sound strange. But Chip and I have this old family tradition where we eat our shrimps and oysters using fancy toothpicks. You know what I'm talking about? You got any of those toothpicks back there with the cellophane twirled on the other side of the business end?"

Karla said, "A toothpick can be a valuable tool in the prevention of gum disease and tooth decay." She said, "We use them on the BLTs. I'll bring you a handful."

"I don't remember that particular tradition," Madison said. He remembered his mother locking his father out of the house when he showed up drunk at two in the morning. He remembered his father, drunk, throwing his own socks, underwear, and ties into the fireplace on Christmas morning, and his father borrowing the neighbor's dog whenever he drove to the liquor store drunk, for he believed that no police officer would arrest a drunk man driving his dog around town. Although Madison tried to block certain memories, he saw himself leaving the house for school and hearing plates crashing into walls behind him—that particular tradition.

"You weren't on CNN, Chip. I mean, you weren't on CNN, Madison. Goddamn. Are you sure you're ready for college? Maybe you should've played hooky a time or two and watched some kind of documentary on how gullible people can't make it in the real world."

Madison's cell phone vibrated in his pocket, then rang. He said, "I bet it's Mom."

"I bet it is, too. You better talk to her. Settle her nerves. Let her know that I didn't kidnap you back to having some fun."

Madison flipped open his phone after his mother had hung up already. He said, "Hello?" and paused. "That's so nice. Thank you, Mr. President."

"The *president's* calling you?" Charlie Kent said.

Madison shoved his phone back in his pocket. He shook his head, smiled, and pulled the other mug of beer his way. "I think that makes us even. Dad."

KARLA SAID SHE piled three or four extra shrimp on each platter. "My graduation present to you," she said to Madison. "What did you get him, Dad?" she asked.

"I haven't given it to him yet," Charlie Kent said. "I still got it in the car." Karla dropped a couple dozen toothpicks down on their folded paper napkins, then left for a table of two other graduates that Madison knew, with their parents. "I meant to wrap it up, but I was running late," Charlie said to Madison.

"You don't have to give me anything," Madison said. He pushed his father's beer back across the table. "That stuff's nasty. I don't like beer."

Charlie Kent took the paper sleeve off of one straw. He looked around, then sat up to check on Karla's whereabouts. "Watch this," he said. He stuck a fancy, frilled blue cellophane toothpick in the mouth end of his straw, leaned his head back, and blew hard. The toothpick stuck in a textured ceiling tile above their booth. "You ever done anything like that?"

Madison said, "Please don't do that. We'll get kicked out of here."

"It's like horseshoes. It's like that bowling game the French people play all the time. In a perfect world toothpicks are blue, red, and yellow. Or green. Now, you blow one and see how close you can come to that first one. The first one's like a stake." Charlie Kent picked through the remaining toothpicks and said, "I'll continue being blue. You're red. We'll just remember the original stake up there."

"No." Madison ate one fried shrimp and set the tail down on the side of his plate.

"You might go off to that fancy college in Oregon and end up studying anthropology and need to know how indigenous people shoot blow guns," Charlie Kent said in a singsong voice.

Madison envisioned shooting a toothpick across the booth perfectly and landing it in his father's forehead, or eyeball. He said, "I'm serious. How'd you know about that award I got?"

Karla brought two more mugs of beer. Madison wondered if he'd missed his father making some kind of secret sign, or if Cap'n Del Kell instructed his waitresses to keep them coming no matter what. Karla said, "Everything okay?" She didn't look up.

"Great!" Charlie Kent said. "You're the best." He smiled in an unnaturally large way, Madison thought, then said, "No."

"Eat up," Karla said.

Someone rang the bell, and exited.

"No matter what she says, your mother still loves me," Charlie said. "I ain't bragging. And I know that I wasn't exactly husband material. I'm a good father. I could *be* a good father, if your mother would let me. Please understand that when I talk to your momma—and I do way more often than you'd know—I always ask that she let you come down and live with me. I've got a fold-out couch, after all. And we have a high school you could've gotten to without missing a day."

Madison tore the end from his straw and blew the wrapper toward his father. It dive-bombed into tartar sauce. "I'm not going to study anthropology," he said. "I don't know what I'll end up doing, but I'd bet that I'm going to major in mathematics, or astronomy. I would also be willing to bet that Mom told you that, too."

Charlie Kent blew two toothpicks at once. One veered off like a haywire missile and stuck in the ceiling three feet from the original one. The other actually hit the first toothpick and fell back down onto their table. He said, "So tell me about this young woman Laney. Would I approve of her?"

When he daydreamed about the future, Madison saw Laney and him graduating from college, then going off to graduate school, then joining the Peace Corps. He saw himself trying to convince tribe members that they could count beyond, "One, two, many." Madison said, "She's really smart."

"That don't cut it," Charlie Kent said. "Smart cuts it only in France. Does she have a nice set? Does she give it up?" He picked up a homestyle fry and shook it at his son.

"Laney's perfect," Madison said. "Don't worry about it."

"Your mother was perfect," Charlie said. "I bet you can't shoot a toothpick and land it anywhere between those two up there."

Madison said, "Some people now call me Mad. Or Madman." He stuck a red-ended toothpick into his straw and blew it hard at his biological father. It, too, landed in the tartar sauce.

"You're a terrible shot," his father said. "Listen. I want you to do something for me. I want you to talk to your mother. I *know* she still has a little fire in her for me. She never got remarried, did she? Did she ever even date anyone? You know, and this is neither here or there, but I didn't have to help her out once you turned eighteen. I kept on sending in child support, though. I sent in what I could send in. I've been working kind of part-time, doing people's taxes at the trailer park, you know. I use that money to help you."

"I don't care what y'all do after I go to college. Y'all can get remarried for all I care." Madison picked the breading off of his oysters and set it aside. Laney's mother had had a gall bladder attack twice.

"I don't think that's going to happen," Charlie said. "Maybe we could live together, at best. I could quit all my bad habits for ten years and your mother would find a way to bring them up once a day. Person like her drives people into drinking and doing drugs. If you're going to be guilty all the time in someone's eyes, you might as well have fun."

Karla came up to the table, took a french fry off Madison's plate, and ate half of it. She said through clenched teeth, "I'm looking the other way best I can. Hurry up with that beer before Cap'n Del shows up. He always shows up around six." She placed the other half of her fry on top of Madison's discarded breading, and skipped to another table.

"She likes you, Chip," Charlie said. "She's flirting with you. Hotdamn to be young again."

"No, she's not. She's a cheerleader. Cheerleaders don't go for guys who make straight A's, except in American history." But Madison wasn't thinking about what he said. No, he thought of Laney, and how she brought up daily how he couldn't get his grade point average up to second in the class. *Every day* she found ways to bring up, "I'm first and he's only third," into the conversation. They could never watch a baseball game together, Madison knew, or she'd bring it up every half inning.

Charlie Kent reached over and picked up an oyster from his boy's plate. He said, "Anyway, your mom and I aren't getting back together. The company that owns my trailer park's starting up another development way up in some place called Pleasant Unity, Pennsylvania. I might be asked to move up there and get things started. I might do it. That's one thing. I also have this buddy who's a bagrunner, needs some help."

Madison said, "Running drugs?" He reached over and drank more of his father's beer. It wasn't as bad as the first had been.

"No. Idiot. Driving lost luggage out to hotels and such." Charlie Kent laughed. "What's your mother been saying about me? I don't do drugs anymore. Too expensive, for one. Anyway, my buddy's a bagrunner, and he says that the airline industry—especially Delta/Northwest—is so fucked up that you might as well forget seeing your suitcase arrive when you do. I ain't even talking about making a connection in Atlanta or Charlotte. I'm talking you get on a plane for New York nonstop, and they send your Samsonite to Nova Scotia. Luggage could write a travel book, man."

Madison blew a toothpick into the ceiling. He and his father tried to high-five each other and knocked over a full mug of beer.

"I GUESS I'M supposed to give you some fatherly advice," Charlie Kent said. "One, don't take any wooden nickels. Two, don't ever work for H&R Block, and probably not for Delta or Northwest airlines. Three, make sure your wife has a sense of humor, and some patience. Well, don't ever get married and you can strike off that little problem right away. Four—do you have a checking account?—write a bad check so you don't go around worrying about having bad credit all the time." He drank from his mug. "Five. Goddamn. I practiced this whole speech on the way up there. I had six things."

Madison said, "I don't care if you call me Chip." He craned over to the beer with his straw and sipped hard. "You can call me Chip."

Karla brought two more mugs. She said, "Cap'n Del called in sick. Do you know what this means? He never calls in sick. They say he ain't missed a day since his wife died two or three years ago."

"Thanks, Karla," Madison said. "I tell you what, when you become a dental hygienist I'm going to start going to a dentist every month. You know what would be cool? If you could clean teeth, and do a split at the same time."

"Five!" Charlie Kent yelled out. To Karla he said, "Well, we're sorry that we're going to miss Cap'n Del. Give him our regards." He gathered empty mugs and slid them toward the table's edge. Turning back to his son Charlie said, "Five. Your first day of college? Miss all your classes. Listen. Every day you show up for school, or a job, or a marriage—it's like winding up the rubber band on one of those balsa wood airplanes with the plastic propeller. Sooner or later the rubber's going to crack up and break, you know what I mean?"

Madison looked at his wristwatch. He thought, *I need to call Mom.* He said, "I have to pee," and got up. In the men's room, which had only a toilet, he locked the door. He punched his home number, it rang four times, and the answering machine picked up. He said, "I'm still here. Everything's fine. Dad might get a part-time job as a bagrunner, which isn't the same thing as a drug runner, according to him. Anyway. I'm still here. Cap'n Del called in sick, though."

He hung up, then peed in the sink.

WHEN MADISON RETURNED to the booth, he found his father sitting there with his plate pushed aside. In front of Charlie Kent sat a folded map of the Southeastern United States, an auto-parts calendar, and a car jack. "Happy graduation," he said. "Like I said, I'm sorry that I didn't have time to wrap them up. Six—I remembered the sixth piece of advice—always have a dog with you, no matter what. And get a stray. Don't go buying some kind of fancy pedigree. I meant to get you a dog for your graduation, but I figured it'd be best if you picked one out yourself. Plus it might be frowned upon by your roommate."

Madison sat down. He said, "Dad."

"Anyway, these are all things you might need in the future. Fold-up map? You need to find a way back home, correct-o? The jack's so you can either change a tire, or mess with your roommate's bed in college. One day I'll tell you what I did to my roommate in college. The story takes too long. It involves a fold-out from one of those magazines, a bunk bed, and his girlfriend. Your mother knows all about it. She was there! Your mother knows all about it, but she wouldn't want me telling it yet. The calendar's so you'll know, you know, the date. So you'll know that it might be the day not to be such a goddamn drone. Worker bee. Ant, you know?"

Madison thought to say, *So I'll be totally irresponsible, like you?* but didn't. He thought to say, *Go put this shit back in your car,* but didn't. *From what stock do I hail?* he thought. He said, "Thank you."

"There you go," his father said. Charlie Kent pushed against the table, but it didn't move. "So," he said, "what did your mother get you?"

Madison's mother had saved her spare change from his birth onward, and put the money in a savings account. She'd handed over a certified check for ten thousand-plus dollars. Madison said, "A microwave oven."

Charlie Kent blew another toothpick into the ceiling tile. Madison looked up and noticed that he'd blown others while Madison was absent from the table. Charlie said, "That's practical. That's good."

Karla placed the bill down. She said, "I ain't rushing y'all none." A man rang the bell and walked out. She yelled, "Thanks, Mr. Looper." Back to Madison and Charlie she said, "He might be crazy. They say his wife took off for somewhere, and he might be crazy."

"Well," Charlie said. "Huh."

When Madison pulled out money from his wallet, Charlie Kent didn't stop him. Madison understood that, in the future, he'd be paying his father's bills, more than likely. He envisioned his being a professor somewhere, teaching freshmen and sophomores the importance of pi, or how come some rocks in southern Utah exist only there and on Mars, and then meeting up with his biological father at a fast food restaurant, in South Carolina, or Pennsylvania, or the Pacific Northwest. He imagined Charlie Kent waving his right hand, saying he didn't need help. Madison foresaw his being there always, should his father need help.

Madison didn't have a wife in any of these scenarios.

"You got something to do?" Charlie asked.

"I'm supposed to meet some friends at a party," Madison said.

Charlie looked out the plate-glass windows of Cap'n Del Kell's Galley Bell. He said, "It's almost dark." He pointed outside and said how he would have clear weather on his drive back. He said that he needed to get back home so he could look at someone's trailer axle. Charlie said, "You know what? Let me borrow that jack of yours, and the map, too. I'll bring it back next time. I'd hate to have trouble going home."

Madison said, "I agree."

"You keep the calendar, though. I can get back home fine without a calendar." Then he pointed to the array of toothpicks stuck to the ceiling and said, "Look, the Big Dipper. It's always there, somehow. Every time I do this, the Big Dipper always comes out."

On his way out of the restaurant, Madison asked Karla if they needed any help. He said he wanted only a summer job, nothing permanent. She told him to come back the next day at six o'clock to meet the captain, and be on time. She told him to lie, though, and say he planned on working there forever.

THE OPPOSITE OF ZERO

I T TOOK UNTIL SEVENTH GRADE BEFORE I HAD—WHAT I thought of initially as—an idiotic teacher call my name wrong on the roll at the first of the year. She got through Adams, Bobo, Davis, Dill, Farley—the easy ones: there were only easy last names in Gruel, no foreign names like Abdelnabi, Gutierrez, Haughey, Narasimhamurdhy, Napolitano, Nguyen, Papadopoulos, Xu, Yablonsky, Yamashita, Zhang, Zheng, Zhong—Goforth, James, Knox, LaRue, before she came upon my last name. Me, I came from a long line of utopians who pronounced our last name like the opposite of silence. Noyes, like *noise*. My great-great-great-great something was John Humphrey Noyes, leader of the Oneida community, a man who believed that God spoke to him, et cetera. Mrs. Latham went through her junior high class roll and when she came to me she said, "Gary No Yes?"

I said, "Maybe."

Of course I'd been in school with my classmates from kindergarten on, and they all yelled out, "No, Yes!" like that.

"No, Yes!

"No, Yes!" They had never noticed the possible mispronunciation, but then again I hadn't either.

"Gary No Yes?" Mrs. Latham said. "Well. I bet you'll do quite well on true-false tests."

And that was it for me. No one ever called me Gary Noyes again. I took shit from that point on until my comrades started having sex, started telling me about how their dates kind of yelled out part of my name during intercourse—either, "No, no, no, no," or, "Yes, yes, yes, yes." Some of them— debutantes-to-be—went ahead and said my name in full, over and over.

It didn't matter that all of my other teachers pronounced my last name correctly from eighth grade onward, that even some of my philosophy, religion, and literature professors in college up in Chapel Hill had studied up on, and written about, my great-great-great-great whatever. Every one of my classmates called me Gary No Yes for the remainder of my time in Gruel. In French class they called me Non Oui. I changed over to Spanish and became No Si. Gruel Normal didn't teach Greek or Latin or German. These days I blame my lack of globe-trotting on the fact that I only took two first-year introductory courses in separate foreign languages.

Right after the original incident I came home and said to my mother, "There's a new teacher at Gruel Normal and she may or may not be stupid, Mom. She can't say our last name. She calls me No Yes. She thinks my name's Gary No Yes."

My mother's maiden name was Godshell, but that's another story.

"You must take farts and turn them into rafts to float away on, Gary," my mother said. "Your father will tell you the same thing. He once told me that your great-great-great-grandfather—or maybe your aunt—underwent a similar problem because of his ancestry. It makes us all stronger people. You must take s*hit* and turn it into *hit(s)*."

My mother never said anything about turning lemons into lemonade, oddly. I could count on her to stay away from the clichés, and always wanted her to turn dirty words into aphorisms. After I became No Yes I would come home sometimes and say, "Patty Goforth said to me, 'Eat me now,'" only so I could see my mother drop her vacuum cleaner and rewire her brain to figure out what *Eat me now* could turn into.

"Meant woe!" she would yell. "Patty Goforth is in some pain, Gary. What she's saying is, she's hurting. Probably from her home life. You need to be a lot nicer to her, what with the situation she's in."

My father said, more often than not, "I wish someone had called me

No Yes when I was a kid. That's all right. No Yes. Ha! I think you're lucky to have Mrs. Latham for a teacher." Then he made us hold hands at the dinner table while he prayed for something like eighty minutes. My father had trickled down from being an Oneida plate maker into a man who sold specialized Venetian blinds to people living in mobile homes. My mother—a Godshell—hailed from people in eastern Kentucky who thought anyone without a toolbox might as well be standing next to Satan.

Should anyone come up to me now and ask—let's reach way out and pretend, a psychologist—"Do you think you come from a fine, fine, hardworking and moral family?" I'd say, without thinking twice, "No, Yes."

Mrs. Latham confused me daily. She claimed to use the Socratic method of teaching—which none of us figured out, seeing as she never explained anything about Socrates—and later on I realized that she kind of misrepresented, or stretched, pedagogical terms. Maybe my memory's off, but I remember her saying more than once a week, "If Sparky walked ten miles north at five miles an hour, and Rufus walked five miles south at ten miles an hour, would they meet halfway in between?"

Lookit: My name might've been No Yes, but I fucking knew that it mattered where they started. Let's say if little Sparky began his wayward and unlikely hike in the Yukon Territory, and Rufus started in Pensacola, then Sparky'd be frozen and Rufus would drown. *Who were Sparky and Rufus, anyway?* I thought. Was this the beginning of some kind of off-color, racist joke? Sometimes my father came home from a highly productive day of selling six-inch-wide Venetian blinds and tell my sister and me a joke about little Johnny ingesting BBs and later shooting the pet dog. "No? Yes?" Mrs. Latham would prompt.

I wouldn't even raise my hand, thinking she called on me. I said, "Maybe," every time, without divulging my keen geographic knowledge.

"Miz Latham, I have a dog named Sparky," Alan Farley always said. "He's fast. He can go a lot faster than ten miles an hour, I know. He can chase a car all the way down to Old Greenville Road. My daddy dropped him off in Forty-Five one time and he found his way home in less than an hour. Forty-Five's something like twenty miles away."

"No? Yes?"

Becky Herndon said, "I have an uncle named Rufus but he keeps saying he's going to change his name so no one doesn't think he's black."

I thought each day, *You idiot, Becky.* I said, finally, "Sparky and Rufus need to find other ways to entertain themselves, ma'am. As many times as they walk north and south, they'll hit foreheads too many times."

"Exactly! Pretty soon they'll learn to walk east to west, right?"

I didn't get it. I wanted out. Every time Mrs. Latham asked us about Sparky and Rufus—and she was supposed to be teaching us English and U.S. history, not math—I came home and told my mother. I said, "Mom, Mrs. Latham keeps asking us about two guys walking toward each other. In the real world do people walk toward each other at different speeds every day? Is this something I need to know about? Yes or no."

My mom always put down her dust mop, or can of Pledge, or Lysol, or prescription bottle of "special pills," or spatula, or can of Raid, or feather duster, or putty knife, or bottle of vodka "your father doesn't need to know about," or box of jigsaw puzzle pieces, and said, "There are many, many words that you can come up with for *Yes or No*, son. As in, *Rosy One.* You can figure out the others. Right? Can't you?" Then, usually, she'd say, "Here comes your dad. Hey, don't say anything about the bottle of rubbing alcohol."

I would nod, then find my way to the push mower, even at dusk, even in winter. Usually I'd find my sister somewhere out in the backyard, either gnawing bark off a sweet gum tree or burning insects with a magnifying glass. Judith was in the fifth grade, in my old elementary school wing at Gruel Normal, when I sat in Mrs. Latham's class. Judith had a destructive streak no one in our family could trace back in the gene pool, seeing as we came from those utopians.

MRS. LATHAM MUST'VE really enjoyed her wood-burning kit at home. Each year she made little personalized signs to go on her students' desks, kind of like nameplates used by CEOs, or professors who needed to remind colleagues that there was a Ph.D. at the end of their family names. Mrs. Latham handed these nameplates out on the last day before Christmas vacation—Mr. Adams, Miss Bobo, Misters

Davis, Dill, and Farley, Miss Goforth, Miss James, Mr. Knox, Miss LaRue, Mr. Pendarvis, Mr. Pinson, Miss Seymour, and so on. They were perfect, on thin oak, and slid into specialized metal stand-up frames balanced at the front of our desks. Everyone else's was perfect— she didn't write out in cursive *Pin son* or *Go forth*—except for mine. There, in quarter-inch-deep brown letters, stood my name as she pronounced it.

When the three o'clock bell rang Mrs. Latham said, "Gary, I need to speak to you for a moment before you go." Everyone else ran out the door with their empty book bags, half of them thinking it was the end of the school year.

I said, "What did I do? I didn't do anything," which wasn't quite true. Earlier that day I intentionally wrote down every wrong answer on a true-false test because I knew that John B. Dill—that's what he insisted on being called—copied from my paper. At the bottom of my test I wrote "Opposites" so Mrs. Latham would get it. Because it was Christmas Mrs. Latham lobbed up some softballs, too: "Antarctica is the most populated continent," "The capital of the United States is Gruel," "Abraham Lincoln is best known for his tales of the Mississippi River."

"You let me know who's cheating on tests, and I want to thank you for it," Mrs. Latham said. "When you get your paper back after the break, I'll put a big fat zero at the top in case John B. Dill looks over your shoulder at it, but write 'Opposite' above it. That's not what I want to talk to you about, though, Mr. No Yes."

Already I knew it was a trick. I tried to think of the opposite of zero. Was it one? Was it a hundred? Was it infinity? I said, "I need to get home pretty soon because my mom wants to go shopping up in Greenville," which wasn't true, either.

Mrs. Latham sat down behind her desk. She shoved aside the gifts our parents had bought, wrapped, and handed over for us to give. Ten kids out of our class moaned, at eight thirty that morning, when the first present happened to be a pencil holder. Mrs. Latham got so many wooden-block pencil holders she could've built a cabin, as it ended up. John B. Dill's parents gave her a tie, for some reason. My father—bless his heart—gave her a gift certificate for specialized mini-blinds, should she ever move out of her regular house into a trailer.

"The opposite of zero is Yes, by the way—I can tell by the look on your face that you're trying to figure it all out. But that's not what I want to talk to you about, specifically, either. I want to talk to you about the two most powerful words in the English language. You might go to church and hear that those words are Good and Evil, or Love and God, or—around here—Cotton and Gun. But the real answer happens to be Yes and No. More has happened in the history of our land because of someone answering Yes or No than any other two words, Gary. That's why I like to call you Mr. No Yes. I don't like to advertise it here in Gruel, but I took a bunch of philosophy courses in college—a load of courses about the existentialists. Yes and No were major themes in all of their treatises, which you—I hope and feel sure—will come to understand later on in life. Do you understand what I'm talking about?"

Another trick, l thought. Was I supposed to offer up one of the two most powerful words in the English language? I had no choice but to nod. I didn't want to let Mrs. Latham down, here in the holiday season, by saying, "Maybe."

"I would also like to tell you that sometimes in March or April the farmers have put their gardens in. They've planted tomatoes, beans, okra, squash, watermelon, and cucumbers to take over to the Forty-Five Farmers Market. And out of nowhere a giant frost comes in for just one night. A lot of people think that it'll kill the plants, but a good gardener knows better. His plants become what is called 'frost-hardened' and they somehow become stronger. No one knows why, but frost-hardened plants can later withstand bugs and drought and too much rain. Even hail."

I said, "Yes ma'am," like I knew where this was going. I didn't.

"And that's what I'm doing for you, Gary No Yes. I'm frost-hardening you. After you get out of my classroom, you're going to be so strong you'll be able to withstand anything that comes your way. I made a promise to someone years ago to act thusly. Do you understand what I'm talking about?"

I didn't nod this time. I said, slightly, "Yesnomaybe, uhhuh."

Mrs. Latham said, "Good." She said, "All right," and clapped her hands together. *She wore a sweater with a Christmas tree on it, with two ornaments right about where her nipples would be,* I thought. I tried not to look. I tried not to think about how I hadn't noticed this earlier in the day, maybe when we had to stand up and do jumping jacks beside our desks. "Now. For more important things: What's Santa Claus going to bring you? Your ma tells you all about Satan Claus, doesn't she? Oh— that's called a Freudian slip. I mean Santa Claus."

I stood up to go. "Well. I don't know. We don't make a big thing out of Christmas. Dad says we should celebrate the birth of Jesus more and the birth of Sears, Roebuck less. I'd kind of like to get a new globe, a telescope, and maybe a set of encyclopedias." *Where did that come from?* I even thought right then.

In my eyes Mrs. Latham's Christmas ornaments shook up and down, though she didn't appear to laugh. She said, "I want to give you an extra credit question for your test. Yes or No: Mrs. Latham is stupid to believe in Santa Claus."

I looked behind her at the clock. *Could it be that only ten minutes had passed, or had I been there for twenty-four hours and ten minutes?* I thought. I imagined my friends already playing basketball down on the square— or our version of basketball, which meant hitting Colonel Dill's statue straight on the nose for two points—and my mother circling the den with a drink in one hand and a box of rat poison in the other, worrying that I had run away from home. I said, "Please don't do this to me. I can't take it anymore. I don't mean to be disrespectful, ma'am."

Mrs. Latham got up from behind her desk and clicked her way toward me standing there. Her hair stood up on end in a way that spaghetti might look infused with static electricity. She put her right hand on the crown of my head. I might be wrong here—maybe she told me to scoot on off and have a wonderful holiday—but what I heard came out, "Wait till we get to Easter, No Yes."

I ran home without looking back, scared that a life-threatening disease had happened upon me. This was seventh grade, but it was the early 1970s, understand, and I had no prior reason to ever get an erection in Gruel, South Carolina.

My father wanted to invite my seventh-grade teacher over for day-after-Christmas leftovers. He said, "We can straighten all of this out." He said, "We'll invite Mr. and Mrs. Latham over, and we can have turkey hash. We should've invited them over four months ago, as a matter of fact. Town like Gruel, we invite newcomers over. Did we bring them a pie or cake when they moved in? Hey, if there's one thing that I can understand from my ancestor John Humphrey Noyes, it's that forgiveness is next to godliness."

My mother, tilting in the den, said, "My dictionary has some words in between, which start with f or end with *damn*. But that's just me. That's just my personal dictionary. Listen. Like I said before, you can turn *Latham* into *halt Ma*. That's all I have to say. I can't believe that it didn't hit my brain earlier. That's all I need to say! That woman is damaging our son, I can tell. When have I been wrong?"

This occurred on Christmas Eve. My sister Judith huddled in the bathroom with a watercolor kit, as usual. Mom had encouraged her artwork, though only on the shower curtain where it would come off four times a day. Because I always woke up earliest, I discovered such dictums as "We shall never repent from our immoral ways!" or "It's a straight line between boredom and death!" or "May the Prince of Darkness teach us forever!" or "Roses are red / violets are blue / I've got a secret: / may the Prince of Darkness come out of nowhere in the middle of the day and select you for one of his minions." Judith wasn't right in the head, I figured out early on. This was before any of those scary movies, too. She'd get straightened out two years later, I thought, when Mrs. Latham called her Judith No Yes.

"Maybe you were wrong when we got married," I almost heard my father say. He looked up at my mother's secret cabinet above the refrigerator. I do know that he said, "You thought I'd only be selling Venetian blinds to convicts, ex-cons, runaways, and ne'er-do-wells. Look how that ended up. I seem to be putting food on the table. I don't hear you wanting for want."

My mother stomped around a bit, between running into various pieces of furniture in our den, living room, and kitchen. She asked me for a syllabus, kind of—she said, "Hey, Gary No Yes, get me that long sheet of paper that has y'all's day-to-day activities typed up on it mimeographed with the goddamn teacher's name and address on the top of it"—and found Mrs. Latham's home phone number.

And she called. Only later in life did I find it sad that Mrs. Latham answered the phone, considering. Here it was, Christmas Eve, and she should've been either visiting her folks or her in-laws, like every other American with any sense of duty. I hung out by the stolen Christmas tree my father bought from a man on the side of Highway 25, and I pretended to be enamored with a couple gifts wrapped for Judith and me that were obviously either socks or underwear. My mother said, "Hello, Mrs. Latham?"

I assumed that my teacher said something other than, "Get lost, it's Christmas Eve."

"Hey, this is Gary No Yes's mother, and I would like to invite you and Mr. Latham over for some day-after-Christmas turkey hash. I have this recipe I got from my mother's mother, and she got it from my husband's father's father's father's mother." I looked beneath the tree and saw a box that might've actually been a set of encyclopedias. "Yes, that is odd how my family could know my husband's family, but that's the way it goes. Anyway, we want you and Mr. Latham to come over on December 26. It's so much trouble for people to take care of everything the day after Christmas, we understand."

I picked up a package and shook it. The card said "From Mom/To Gary." This is no lie: *glug, glug, glug* emanated beneath the box. *Booze*, I thought. It wasn't hard to figure out how my mother made it sound that she would bear the brunt of taking on all day-after-Christmas eaters. I listened to my mother listen to Mrs. Latham.

My mother said, "Uh-huh. Uh-huh. Okay. Uh-huh. Well that would be great, then," like that.

To me she said, "Well that's settled. She seems to love you, Gary No Yes." Back in the bedroom later I heard her tell my father, "She has no right to call herself Mrs. Latham. Halt Ma! She's not even married. What kind of a woman would pretend to have a husband? Most sane women walk around town with their husbands, but pretend like they're strangers who happen to walk in the same direction at the same pace."

The next thing I knew, my father got me out of bed, told me to put on some tennis shoes but stay in my pajamas, and we were off in his Dodge to place surprise Christmas gifts on the miniature porches of house trailers. He gave out extra-thin feather dusters, made especially for the Galloway micro-mini-blind. Somewhere halfway to Forty-Five he said to me, "Gary No Yes, it's important to make people feel like their homes are first-rate. Remember that. Even if the homeowners aren't clean, it's important for them to feel that their trailers are first-rate. Am I clear on this?"

I thought, *We must turn* first-rate *into* rat strife. *We must turn* first-rate *into* tar fister. I said, "Yes," got out of the car, wove my way through about twenty curs, and propped micro-mini-blind dusters against aluminum doors. I imagined my sister inside the bathroom, painting a picture of Satan Claus with horns and fangs.

THE *GLUG-GLUG-GLUG* gift ended up being a quart of aftershave, something I would use in about five years. Judith got a new shower curtain, some more watercolors, a white leather Bible, and a slew of knee socks. Me, I got underwear, some knee socks that were probably meant for Judith and mispackaged, and one of those miniature black Magic 8 Balls that you shook to get a Yes or No answer. I'm ashamed to admit it now, but when my father said, "Ask it a question and see what comes up," I secretly asked myself, "What does the future hold for me, in regards to Gruel?"

I hadn't quite gotten the hang of how to ask it questions, obviously. The answer came up, "It's in your future." I kind of thought how maybe Mrs. Latham came from the family that manufactured these things.

So we sat around the table for a few hours seeing as my father needed to pull off a two-hour grace, he couldn't carve the turkey right, and my mother kept throwing away entire cans of congealed cranberry sauce when they didn't slide out unmarred. "It's bad luck to have dented cranberry sauce," she said. "We must turn *dented* into *tended*."

Fa la la la la, la la, la la.

My mother shaved, honed, scraped, and pulled what turkey carcass scraps she found soon thereafter, chopped the meat into dust mote-sized bits, set them in a pot of boiling turkey broth she'd saved, added enough jalapeños to cure the world of head colds. The next day she got up earlier than usual, took the lid off her turkey hash, sampled a wooden spoonful, and declared, "One day I might open up a diner here in Gruel. What this town needs is a good diner."

I waited for my mother to turn one of her words into another, but she didn't. No, she seemed happy and confident and optimistic.

When Mrs. Latham came over at noon, my mother took off her apron, answered the door, and performed a perfect sweeping arm gesture for my seventh-grade teacher to follow into the den. Mrs. Latham said, "Merry belated Christmas, Mr. Noyes," to either my father or me, I couldn't tell. She didn't use the normal No Yes form of salutation.

"Judith, come on in here and meet Gary No Yes's teacher," my mother yelled out, though. I prayed that Mrs. Latham wouldn't have to go to the bathroom during her visit. Sure enough, Judith had taken her new water-colors and painted a nice representation of Grant Wood's *American Gothic*, but instead of a pitchfork the farmer only held up his middle finger, and the farmer's wife had blood running down both sides of her mouth.

Judith came out all smudged and said, "I guess you'll be my teacher in two years, if I don't fail on purpose. My last name's Noyes, not No Yes, by the way. You have from now until then to memorize it."

I said, "Ha-ha-ha-ha-ha-ha-ha. Judith got a new Bible for Christmas."

Mrs. Latham said, "If I'm here in two years you can go ahead and shoot me in the brain, Judith," as my father pulled the dining room chair out for her. "Did Santa bring you that set of encyclopedias you wanted, Gary No Yes?"

My mother pulled out her own chair and sat down. "How come you insist on people calling you *Mrs.* Latham when you don't even have a husband?"

My father said, "Dorothy Marie." I never knew my mother's middle name up to this point.

Judith said, "Marie? Marie?" and ran back into the bathroom to paint something else.

I said, "We are humbled by your presence here, Mrs. Latham," because I'd seen it in a movie.

My teacher scooted up. She looked at my mother and didn't blink. "My husband was in Special Forces. He was killed in 1968, somewhere in a Vietnamese jungle. I don't know about you, but where I come from we keep our deceased husband's name. We'd met in college up in Chapel Hill, and I asked him not to volunteer, but he was too patri-otic. His father and two uncles all died in France and Pearl Harbor. My husband had straight A's right up until he left college his junior year.

He studied philosophy and religion, and minored in literature. He had hopes of one day teaching elementary school either in an inner city or way out in the country—kind of like here in Gruel—so kids could have some kind of future. My husband didn't so much believe in the war in Vietnam, though, let me make it clear. He thought that he'd studied enough Buddhism to talk the enemy into giving up altogether. He's buried down in Florence, at the national cemetery there, should y'all wish to ever visit and place a small American flag on his grave. The one I placed yesterday should be faded by the end of January or thereabouts."

My father stuck out his palms to hold Mrs. Latham's hand and mine before he said grace. I looked at my mother and noticed how I could've taken every available linen napkin, wadded them up, and still not filled the space her open mouth created. My father only said, "Let us remember our heroes and victims. Amen."

Judith shouted from the bathroom, "Amen."

My mother let the canned cranberry sauce fall out at will, on a silver-plated stick-butter plate. She served the turkey hash atop cheese grits, with homemade bread to the side. Mrs. Latham finally said, "My husband had straight A's, just like Gary does. That's maybe why I'm a little hard on your son."

My parents said nothing. Even Judith knew not to say anything about how she wanted to be a tattoo artist later on in life. We ate, Mrs. Latham left, and my father and I spent the next week visiting his micro-mini-blind customers to see if they'd tried out their surprise feather dusters. When I went back to school for the second semester, Mrs. Latham took me aside on the first day right before we filed off for a lunch of cling peaches, black-eyed peas, corn bread, steamed cabbage, and sloppy joes. She said, "Yes or No—that story I told your parents could've gotten me a movie award."

I looked into my teacher's eyes and realized that I would be getting such questions for the entirety of my life. I wore my sister's knee socks that day, though no one could tell seeing as we didn't have a P.E. class at Gruel Normal. But I felt the smile coming on, and let it go before laughing out loud. I said, "Christmas." Mrs. Latham put her hand on the top of my head and walked with me toward the cafeteria. She said, "Every day."

EMBARRASSMENT

EVERY COUNTRY BOY ON OUR LITTLE LEAGUE TEAM could hit that knuckleball during practice. We had no choice. Coach D. R. Pope and both of his assistants had worked in the cotton mill, and all three of them had undergone tragic digit loss due to spinning frames, looms, and/or pneumatic presses of one sort or the other. D. R. pitched batting practice most of the time with his right hand, which had only a thumb and a little finger. So the baseball always lolled toward the plate without as much as one rotation between his grasp and the Louisville Slugger. Our own pitcher during games—a farm boy named Yancey Allison—must've thought that the knuckleball was some kind of Forty-Five, South Carolina, miracle, for he'd perfected it, too. Yancey let his nails grow out an inch beyond his fingertips, he dug them into the ball's seams, and even with the arm movement of a catapult, the ball crossed the plate at maybe twenty miles an hour. Our foes regularly hit Yancey's pitches a good hundred feet past the outfield fences. Meanwhile, all the rest of us stood stock-still when the opponents' pitchers threw fastballs, sliders, changeups, and curves in our direction. I wasn't the only player to take a mighty swing after the ball reached the catcher's mitt and he threw back to his pitcher. One time I actually got two strikes called on me by the umpire because I stood there and watched for strike one, then fouled off a ball as the catcher threw back and I finally swung.

Let me make it clear that the grounds on which we played needed regular tending before each game, for hunters would steal onto the field at night, regardless of legal hunting season, and deposit salt blocks and mounds of sweet corn to attract deer. If anyone decided to sleep in the bleachers overnight, like my friend Compton Lane and I did once, he'd be awoken an hour before dawn by camouflaged men sporting anything from .410 shotguns to thirty-aught-sixes. D. R. and his assistant coaches sent us out like boys with metal detectors to scour the rye grass between the infield and the cheap outfield signs advertising 45 OFFICE, 45 EXTERMINATION, 45 FLORISTS, 45 LUMBER, 45 GRAVEL and, 45 MEN'S WEAR, 45 DEBS AND BRIDES, 45 JEANS, THE FORTY-FIVE PLATTER NEWSPAPER, 45 TRASH PICK-UP, 45 RECORDS, 45 MODERN BARBERS (who sponsored our Little League team, the Flattops), SUNKEN GARDENS LOUNGE (which used to sponsor our team before Mr. Red Edwards decided he couldn't afford a losing team's destruction of his reputation), and RUFUS PRICE'S GOAT WAGON store. We took wheelbarrows out with us while the opposing team got to stretch, run wind sprints, take infield practice, and get ready to raise their collective batting averages.

"Just do the best you can, Mendal," my father always said as we pulled into the parking lot of the Forty-Five rec center. "I'll talk to D. R. and see if we can't get you playing first base, or left field." More than once he'd said something about how Bennie Frewer didn't really have head lice, and that it was okay for us to touch the baseball after Bennie threw it in from right field on those odd occasions when somebody from the other team didn't hit the ball over the fence and Bennie would gather it up and throw it to first or second base.

"I don't like being catcher," I said to my dad. "I'm a faster runner than anyone else. Why's D. R. have me be Yancey's catcher? A slow fat guy usually plays catcher. I've seen it on TV." Me, I crouched every game, waiting for Yancey to throw one of his knuckleballs. I waved my arm back and forth like a windshield wiper in hopes of only touching the ball coming my way. A blind boy could've caught for Yancey just as well.

My father never answered. Years later, I would think that for some reason he knew it would be best for me to hear what went on in the stands, right behind me, as I crouched, eyes closed, while the slow projectiles came my way.

"Hey, Mendal, you might want to get two catcher's masks," Coach D. R. Pope said more than once. "Find a way to fashion one over your privates."

"Yessir," I always squeaked out. D. R. held up his right hand with that thumb and little finger poked out like the biggest peace sign ever, like a big-time Texas Longhorns fan, like a deaf man saying he loved me, like—I would learn later—a man trying to approximate the length of his pecker. "We don't want to set no records as to the worst team in Little League baseball, Mendal. You a smart boy. Can't you not figure out nothing to say back there to avert the batter none?"

I'd think, This is some kind of double- or triple- or quadruple-negative trick on me. And then I'd crouch, and close my eyes, and smile with glee about every tenth time, when I'd actually catch a ball thrown by Yancey that didn't either get thrown in the dirt or smacked straight over the "45 FEED AND SEED COMPANY" sign in center field.

I sat in front of the umpire two days a week for an entire summer and listened to him bark, "Ball!" unless our opponent's batter blasted a pitch out of the park. A lot of times I missed catching it completely, of course, and the umpire's shin stopped the ball. He said often, "Goddamn you, Dawes, I'mo send your daddy my doctor's bill for bruises."

And I always said, "A man with his leg stuck hard on the ground isn't going to go far in life," like my father told me to say, which wasn't the smartest thing, of course. Or I thought, *A man with his leg stuck hard on the ground will never learn how to fly no matter how hard he flaps his arms.* Invariably the umpire was one who'd worked at the cotton mill at one time or another and was missing digits, too.

Coach D. R. Pope wouldn't get his wish in regard to the team not setting a losing-streak record. Our team had lost all of its games for the three years before I could play and went on to lose until D. R. quit the mill and moved down to Myrtle Beach less than a year later. He got a job, I found out, as the maitre d' at a fancy shellfish restaurant in Murrells Inlet. He had always talked about his dreams and goals and ambitions after we lost games by enormous margins, but I thought he talked big like that so that we would play harder the next game, maybe win, and not chance losing him for a coach who popped his players' hamstrings after every strikeout or error.

"My wife's cousin Sandy married into a rich family down there at the beach. They made they money paving driveways with seashells, you know. And then they thought, Hey, why don't we open up a big old restaurant, and we can get our clam and oyster and scallop shells for free every night? So that's what they done. And Sandy's husband, Claude—he's no-account, and the family just flat-out give him his place to manage called Sandy Claude's—he said I'd be perfect for greeting eaters, when the time was right."

D. R. Pope told me his little story after everyone else left the players' bench, while I tried to stuff my mask, glove, shin guards, and chest protector into an old duffel bag.

"You know what's keeping him from going down to that restaurant today?" my father asked me as we drove home maybe midway through the 1968 season. This was a time before some touchy-feely psychologist figured out that losing kids would feel better about themselves if a game plain ended when one team was behind by ten runs at the end of the third inning or whenever. We'd lost this particular massacre 49-0. I remember only because their coach kept yelling at D. R., "Hey, we done scored seven touchdowns and every extra point after!"

To my father I said, "Coach doesn't want to go on to Myrtle Beach until we finally win a game, I guess."

My father honked the horn at nothing and laughed. "He'd never get to go to Myrtle Beach if he waited for that." He laughed and laughed. "That's a good one, Mendal!"

I said, "I ain't trying to be funny and you know it. Why's he waiting, then?"

My father pulled into the Dixie Drive-In so we could get milkshakes. "The mill pays those boys a thousand dollars for every missing digit. It's something like five thousand dollars for an arm from the elbow down. Times get tough, a man like D. R. Pope just grits his teeth and sticks his arm in a machine. I'm thinking that his cousin-in-law wants D. R. to go ahead and lose the matching fingers on his left hand so he'll look more like a lobster. Or crab. Or any of those other things with pincers. Like a scorpion. And I bet D. R. needs three more thousand dollars in order to make the move, you know. If he puts his other three grand in a bank account, that's a pretty nice little jump start."

I ordered a plain vanilla when the carhop woman showed up. I always got plain vanilla. My father ordered weird things, like strawberry with a glob of peanut butter whisked through it, but I think he just did this in order to shock people. "He doesn't put his hand in any of those spinning frames," I said. "Anybody that crazy doesn't care about coaching baseball."

My father turned the radio dial to some man singing opera. "Anybody that crazy doesn't want to hang out around kids who can't hit a baseball. Ask him. Or ask those other two coaches helping out. You make a buck-sixty an hour after a number of years and feel your lungs turning inside out, you'll about do anything to move away. If you're smart. D. R. Pope's a smart man, son. His daddy was a smart man. Why you think he's named D. R.? It's so when he got a checking account it looked like 'Dr. Pope.' People treat him with respect when he writes out a check. Dr. Pope. You can't be a surgeon with all those missing fingers, of course. But you can be a dermatologist. Or an English professor."

My father went on to list a number of doctors, from allergists to zoologists. He didn't say, "Gynecologist." The carhop returned with our extra-large milkshakes and said, "I ain't never heard no one order a strawberry peanut butter milkshake. What's it taste like?"

My father pulled out his straw, turned it toward the woman, and said, "Stick this in your mouth and give me your opinion." I didn't pay much attention to what was going on over on that side of the Buick. I sucked.

"Hey, did you ever work over at Forty-Five Cotton?" my father asked the carhop. She wore a paper hat.

"Both my parents do. I made a pact with myself, though. I said I wanted to get out of high school and do better for myself. My momma and daddy never got a tip on their jobs."

My father nodded. He said, "What's your name?"

"Emmie Gunnells." She pointed at a nametag half hidden beneath her collar.

"Emmie Gunnells, I want you to help my boy and me with a little argument we're having. Did your folks ever have any tough times financially? I'm talking, like, back when gasoline prices went up to thirty-five cents a gallon?"

Emmie leaned down and looked at me closer. She said, "Y'all ain't union organizers are you? We've already had the union organizers over to the house."

I shook my head. My face felt like an hourglass, that's how thick the vanilla milkshake was. My father said, "Hell no, we ain't no organizers. I'm only trying to prove a point with Mendal here."

"I don't know," Emmie Gunnells said.

My father said, "How many fingers has your father lost at this point in time?"

Emmie Gunnells slapped her hip with the tray she was holding. "Law!" she said. "How'd you know?" She stooped back down to look at me. "Y'all are from the fair, I bet. Y'all are those people who can guess ages and weights and family trees."

My father said, "How many?"

Emmie Gunnells said, "He's got six left. It's enough for him to drive his Cadillac."

SEEING AS THERE was little else to do in Forty-Five, everyone came out to the games. If a mastermind thief ever traveled through, he could've broken into about every house in the entire town on early-dusk nights. And he might've gotten gold watches and pearl earrings from those doffers and weavers who'd jammed their hands into machines. Here's what I heard from behind the plate every game: "Y'all are an embarrassment to Forty-Five;" "Hey, Bennie Frewer, see if you can get knocked in the head with the ball so no one will touch it and you can run around the diamond;" "Nice reflexes, boy. Remind me not to let you in on my driver's ed class in six years;" "You boys must all think you're famous, standing there like statues;" "I thought y'all'ses were the Flattops, not the Heart Stops."

I couldn't *not* listen to what went on. I mean, I was prepared to hear, "Ball!" four times in a row from the umpire, or, "Hotdamn, I hope NASA ain't sent up a mission—that ball might hit one them astronauts up there," when Yancey Allison offered up a slow melon with no movement on it.

But I never was prepared to hear Compton Lane's father say something like, "This is going to be a long game. Do y'all have anything back there that's got arsenic in it?" from the concession stand. Midway through the season I heard my own father's voice. He tried to whisper, but I could tell that he had sat down next to Emmie Gunnells. "I thought me up another concoction," he said. "Banana and liver pudding. You know what liver pudding does for a man, don't you? And, hey, I thought of another concoction. You and me."

The concession stand was owned and operated by Danny Clement's father, and for some reason it occurred to me that he must've been in cahoots with D. R. Pope. Games lasted sometimes five hours, and probably each sad, sunburned, tired spectator averaged a Coke an hour, a couple hot dogs, maybe some potato chips. These were brown-bagging days, too, so every player's father might've put away two Cokes an hour to go with his Old Crow or Rebel Yell or Southern Comfort. Forgetful mothers loaded up on zinc oxide. Bored little kids inevitably started a game of tag or hide-and-go-seek or kick-the-can in the gravel parking lot, fell down, and required Band-Aids sold by Mr. Clement.

During one particular game against Calhoun Falls—a town that later got mostly submerged by shallow and algae-ridden Strom Thurmond Lake—the Calhoun Falls team batted around three times in one inning. I heard the parents of our shortstop, Bev Lagroon, get in such a fight that they vowed to end the marriage. Then they went off to the concession stand separately—she ordered chili tater tots, a Dr Pepper, and some Juicy Fruit gum; he, two Cokes to go with his Jim Beam, a corn dog, and pork rinds—before finally settling back down just before a six-foot-two-inch fourth grader from Calhoun Falls hit a ball that went through the 45 DRUGS sign in left field right where it read COSMETICS! The umpire said to me, "We better call the fire department and make sure that ball's not smoldering back there on Leonard Self's dry land."

Mr. Lagroon said to his wife, "I didn't mean nothing by all that. Let's you and me go down to Myrtle Beach and renew our vows."

I called time out and walked to the pitcher's mound. The bases were empty and there were no outs. I called the infield in and kept my back to D. R. Pope. Bev Lagroon came in pounding his fist to his glove. I said, "Okay. We're getting smeared. But not all's bad. Bev's parents are going to Myrtle Beach next week for some kind of second honeymoon. I'll steal some of my father's beer, and, Yancey, you steal some of your father's peach-bounce moonshine, and we'll all meet at Bev's. That okay with you, Bev?"

He faced the stands. "Shirley Ebo's waving at us up there."

Comp said, "Hey. When this games over, let's all beat these boys up. Let's get in a big fight and kick them in the nuts instead of shaking hands."

I turned around and looked at their bench. I said, "No. No way. The only thing we got going for us is knowing that the best thing those boys got going for them is moving to Forty-Five, getting jobs at the mill, and losing their fingers on purpose. Let's just let them beat us silly."

It's what I said. My father had given me a pep talk of his own before this particular game. He said that the funny thing about Emmie Gunnells thinking he was a union organizer was that he really was one, in his own way. My father had said, "Down here, if they was called rebel organizers we'd have a lot better chance. All them mill workers would have the same chance in life as D. R. Pope's lucky marriage into a crab joint-owning family. But let us learn to live the way we live, and do the best that we can. Let us be strong and proud and forward-looking."

I said, "Amen."

He whapped me a little too hard upside the head. "Amen? What the hell are you talking about, boy? I thought I taught you better than that." Luckily I was wearing my catcher's mask already.

I said, "I wasn't thinking. I'm sorry."

My father opened the car door for me. I threw my duffel bag on the backseat. He said, "You're not sorry. Your team is sorry, but you're not sorry, son. You're the best goddamn thing that's ever happened to Forty-Five. What you need to do is get out of here and tell everyone about it."

I said, "I'm not doing so great in English."

He said something about how stand-up comedians don't need to write things for print. He said that archaeologists and anthropologists didn't either, what with the advent of the television documentary.

THE SEASON DRAGGED on, and I continued listening to all the conversations that went on behind the backstop. I caught wind of people making plans, breaking promises, speculating who'd be the first dead Forty-Fiver sent back from Vietnam. People made bets as to who would be the first player on my team to foul a ball off, actually get a hit, or knock himself out plowing into one of the outfield signs. They made bets as to what time the seventh-inning stretch would take place, when the game would end, and who would be the first batter to throw his bat toward the opposing team's bench. Coach D. R. Pope smiled throughout our long, long losing season. He clapped his hands to make puttering muffler sounds. Grover Henderson, the local dermatologist, salivated in the bleachers, for he knew that skin cancer was growing on the nine of us in the field and the couple hundred local spectators.

"We gone be leaving Forty-Five within the next year for Myrtle Beach," I heard D. R. Pope's wife say one extended first inning. Mrs. Pope sat with Danny Clement's mother. "I know I give him a little bit of Hades, but he'd do about anything for me. He's promising another three thousand dollars before September. Then we ready. I'm thinking I might could get a job down at that hammock factory, what with my skill before a loom. D. R.'s got a fancy job lined up, due to my family connections."

This was the first inning of the last game against the team from Graywood. Yancey Allison threw a knuckleball that came closer to our third baseman than it did the plate. I tried to point my ears in another direction. I tried to listen to Shirley Ebo and her daddy talking about how they might invest in some horses, seeing as horsehide got so worn out at our Little League games, et cetera. But I couldn't get it out of my mind, my coach sticking his hand in a spinning frame just so he could wear a shiny suit at the entrance of a place that probably prided itself on its homemade cocktail sauce. I heard Mrs. Pope say, "If I don't get a job at the hammock place, then I might see if D. R. can bring some oyster shells home. I had a dream one time about putting those little plastic wiggle-eyes on shells and selling them as ashtrays."

"Time out, please," I said to the umpire.

I walked to the mound and motioned for the infield. Yancey said, "That last pitch slipped from my hand." He showed me his index finger. "I broke off half the nail trying to pry off some old nasty bathroom tile my daddy said had hidden treasure behind. It didn't."

I said, "Coach D. R.'s planning on cutting more fingers off."

One of the assistant coaches yelled out, "Watch the runner at first," even though there was no one on base, seeing as their lead-off batter was still standing there with a 3-0 count.

"There's got to be a better way to spend the summer," I said. My father had started me reading Kierkegaard.

I looked out at Bennie Frewer in right field and it came to me as if God had tapped me on the forehead to think harder. Without even looking back to our coach, I yelled out so that the opposing team on its bench could hear—and everyone on our team and the people in the stands—"Bennie's got head lice real bad! Let's have him pitch!" I motioned for Bennie to come in. He pointed at his own chest just like in a sitcom, like in a cartoon, and I sent Yancey out to right field. "Head Lice is going to pitch!" I yelled. "Come on down here, Head Lice."

Bennie could throw in a straight line, I knew that much. He didn't have much range or velocity, but that didn't matter. Coach D. R. came out to the mound at the same time as the umpire to get things going. The umpire said, "Y'all know that these games already last longer than a Pentecostal Sunday. Come on. I got things to do tonight. I promised my wife we'd play Yahtzee later."

D. R. Pope said, "Yancey's our pitcher, Mendal. You kind of stepping on my authority." He held his deformed hand out like a manta ray.

I might've been four foot six back then, but I said, "We'd kind of like to make a showing, once."

My father yelled from the stands, "I told you reading that Danish fellow would get you thinking right!"

The coach went back to the bench. I sent the infield back out to their positions. Yancey started crying until I said that I had a feeling that the Graywood team's left-handers might start hitting the ball toward right field, and only Yancey could run a ball down and catch it. I said to Bennie Frewer—a boy who looked as if he'd been whipped every day since he'd starred in an educational television-produced documentary about the myths and realities of head lice—"You can lob up pitches softball-style for all I care. Just leave it to me. I'll talk to the batters."

Like I said, Graywood's lead-off batter had a 3-0 count. I crouched back behind the plate and said, "This old boy Bennie Frewer's got lice so bad I'm afraid if he scratches his scalp and touches the ball, it might look like sparks coming off our way."

Bennie threw his first pitch overhand, but it came up in a loop the likes of a top-heavy bottle rocket. The umpire hesitated before saying, "Strike one?" The batter practically ran back toward the on-deck circle.

Danny Clement's father understood what was going on. He yelled from his concession stand, "Somebody get me another pot to boil dogs in, boys!"

The Graywood players jumped back from each pitch as if it was soaked in toxic waste. They regularly struck out watching, as if they played for Forty-Five. And our players—me included—did about the same at bat, seeing as we couldn't hit a pitch whatsoever. This continued. Somewhere between the twelfth and thirteenth inning Coach D. R. Pope came up to me in the dugout, gripped my neck like a C-clamp, and said, "You a different kind of boy living down here. How come you didn't figure this out about game number two?" I shrugged. "This game might last ten days. They's got to be some kind of record for the longest Little League game ever in the history of boyhood."

"Maybe you won't have to cut off the rest of your fingers and go down there to the beach," I said. "Maybe you can get on television."

The umpire yelled out, "Play ball!" again, the score tied nothing to nothing. Bennie Frewer, our hero, came to the plate. Evidently Graywood's team had a boy with something like my ability to figure out ways to win. Their pitcher hit Bennie right in the head with a fastball that must've clocked in at seventy miles an hour. Bennie went down. The Graywood catcher ran away from the batter's box.

It didn't take a second for me to figure out what to do next, I swear. I'm not sure if it was reading Kierkegaard, or if my father was beaming ESP into my brain from his vantage point behind the backstop. I said to the coach, "If we use a pinch runner for Bennie, he can't go back in. Let's just set him down on first. The next two batters are going to strike out anyway."

Coach D. R. Pope gave me a thumbs-up. He gave me a pinkie-up, too, of course. Glenn Flack and little Johnny Scott came up next, and stood there to watch their three balls zip straight over the plate. Bennie sat on first base with his head turned backwards, probably trying to regain his senses. Coach Pope said, "What're we going to do now, smarty-pants?"

Smarty-pants! I envisioned him working at Sandy Claude's and saying, "Where do you want to sit, smarty-pants?" or, "Would you like a menu or the buffet, smarty-pants?" I was that way—looking into the future—even back then. I said, "I'll pitch. Bennie Frewer will play second base, but really let him just stand there by me on the mound. Go get...I don't know," I looked down the bench for who might be able to play catcher. I looked up to the stands at Shirley Ebo, who shook her head no. I said, "It doesn't matter. You pick someone."

Coach Pope gave a death-ray point toward Blink Harvel—a little fat kid with the IQ of a doorknob—and said, "You catching, boy." Harvel spent most games finding a way to sneak off the bench to scour beneath the bleachers and retrieve the outside paper wrappers of Doublemint, Juicy Fruit, and Fruit Stripe gum he used to make chains and necklaces.

Blink Harvel said, "Okay, Coach," and dropped his paper chain. He would've said the same thing if the coach asked him to pull off his pants and run down the third-base line.

When we got to the field I motioned for Blink to approach me at the mound. I said, "This won't be hard. I'm going to throw the ball to you just like playing catch. You don't worry any."

Blink said, "How'm I supposed to know if it's a ball or a strike? I've never called balls and strikes." Blink went on to get a doctorate in administrative studies, and got a job with the Department of Education as a grief-therapy expert. He got interviewed on the local news whenever a tornado hit some trailer park where children lived, or a fourth grader shot another fourth grader, or when Clemson lost a football game and no little redneck kid felt like living anymore.

I explained to him that it was the umpire's job. I said, "Just catch the ball and throw it back to me. That's it."

Blink Harvel nodded his head around, wearing my catcher's mask.

I jerked my head to Bennie Frewer, who lolled around near second base. He wandered my way and said, for no apparent reason, "This itches, y'all."

I said, "Uh-huh." Oh, he'd have trouble in his later years—maybe rob a couple of banks or whatever—and try to say to both judge and jury that his damaged frontal lobe had caused it all. I said, "Take off your hat and just stand beside me. Right here."

Graywood's first batter came up and held the bat like Carl Yastrzemski. I held the ball in my mitt, rubbed my hand on Bennie Frewer's head as if his head were a lucky piece, then threw toward home. Yastrzemski stepped back twice, and the umpire yelled, "Strike one!" Blink Harvel handed the ball to the umpire, who acted like he didn't want to touch it, then told Blink, "Throw it on back to the pitcher, son."

And so it went. I rubbed Bennie's head, the Graywood batters thought head lice was still coming their way, I struck out three batters in a row each time, and we—the Forty-Five Flattops, sponsored by 45 Modern Barbers—came in at the bottom of the inning to act likewise.

We didn't win. But we didn't lose, either. It was the end of the season, and there was no way to make up the game later. About an hour after dark, it seemed, the umpire motioned both managers to the field and explained how he had to call the game. I was glad, because my palm was burning from rubbing Bennie Frewer's head so much. It was the twenty-sixth inning. Probably a record, everyone said. For the first time in my life I knew what it was like to be Bennie Frewer, for when both teams lined up to shake hands, no one would touch me. No one touched Blink Harvel, and no one shook hands with Bennie.

On the drive home my father said, "This worked out exactly as I wanted it to work out, son. Did you learn anything about life today?" He laughed and looked at his watch. "I mean, today and tonight?"

I nodded. To be honest, I didn't get it.

We went to the Dixie Drive-In and barely got there before it closed. A new woman took our orders. My father asked about Emmie Gunnells. The new carhop said that Emmie had quit, that she left without notice, but word was she had hitchhiked down to Myrtle Beach and gotten a job as a third-shift desk clerk at the Anchored Sloop hotel. My father said, "I'll be damned," and I heard the sadness of loss in his voice.

We didn't talk after we got our milkshakes. He rubbed my head a couple times in the same way I had rubbed Bennie Frewer's. My father and I both came down with head lice within the week, maybe from Blink's borrowing my catcher's mask. But we didn't tremble around the house. My father and I scrubbed our scalps, washed our bedsheets. We furrowed our hair with those special nit combs. My father promised a weekend of camping out in the Forty-Five rec center bleachers, where we could point a flashlight and look for what deer were staring back, either mesmerized or transformed, not knowing whether to jump the fence or not.

WHICH ROCKS WE CHOOSE

L
UCKILY FOR EVERYONE IN THE FAMILY ON DOWN, THE
mule spoke English to my grandfather. Up until this seminal point
in the development of what became Carolina Rocks, a few generations of Loopers had tried to farm worthless land that sloped from
mountainside down to all branches and tributaries of the Saluda River.
From what I understood, my great-great-grandfather and then his son
barely grew enough corn to feed their families, much less take to market.
Our land stood so desolate back then that no Looper joined the troops
in the 1860s; no Looper even understood that the country underwent
some type of a conflict. What I'm saying is, our stretch of sterile soil
kept Loopers from needing slaves, which pretty much caused locals to
label them everything from uppity to unpatriotic, from hex-ridden to
slow-witted. Until the mule spoke English to my grandfather, our family crest might've portrayed a chipped plow blade, wilted sprigs, a man
with a giant question mark above his head.

"Don't drown the rocks," the harnessed mule said, according to legend. It turned its head around to my teenaged grandfather, looked him
in the eye just like any of the famous solid-hoofed talking equines of
Hollywood. "Do not throw rocks in the river. Keep them in a pile. They
shall be bought in time by those concerned with decorative landscaping,
for walls and paths and flower beds."

That's what my grandfather came back from the field to tell everybody. Maybe they grew enough corn for moonshine, I don't know. My own father told me this story when I complained mightily from the age of seven on for having to work for Carolina Rocks, whether lugging, sorting, piling, or using the backhoe later. The mule's name wasn't Sisyphus, I doubt, but that's what I came to call it when I thought it necessary to explain the situation to my common-law wife, Abby. I said, "If it weren't for Sisyphus, you and I would still be trying to find a crop that likes plenty of rain but no real soil to take root. We'd be experimenting every year with tobacco, rice, coffee, and cranberry farming."

Abby stared at me a good minute. She said, "What? I wasn't listening. Did you say we can't have children?"

I said, "A good mule told my grandfather to quit trying to farm, and to sell off both river rocks and field stone. That's how come we do what we do. Or at least what my grandfather and dad did what they did." This little speech occurred on the day I turned thirty-three, the day I became the same age as Jesus, the day I finally decided to go back to college. Up until this point Abby and I had lived in the Looper family house. My dad had been dead eleven years, my mom twenty. I said, "Anyway, I think the Caterpillar down on the banks is rusted up enough now for both of us to admit we're not going to continue with the business once we sell off the remaining stock."

When I took over Carolina Rocks we already had about two hundred tons of beautiful black one- to three-inch skippers dug out of the river stockpiled. I probably scooped out another few hundred tons over the next eight years. But with land developers razing both sides of the border for gated mountain golf course communities, in need of something other than mulch, there was no way I could keep up. A ton of rocks isn't the size of half a French car. Sooner or later, too, I predicted, the geniuses at the EPA would figure out that haphazardly digging out riverbeds and shorelines wouldn't be beneficial downstream. Off in other corners of our land we had giant piles of round rocks, pebbles, chunks, flagstones, and chips used for walkways, driveways, walls, and artificial spring houses. Until my thirty-third birthday, when I would make that final decision to enroll in a low-residency master's program in Southern culture studies, I would sell off what rocks we had quarried, graded, and according to my mood either divided into color, shape, or size.

I never really felt that the Loopers' ways of going about the river rock and field stone business incorporated what our competitors might've known in regards to supply and demand, or using time wisely.

"Can we go back to trying our chosen field?" Abby asked. She wore a pair of gray sweatpants and a MoonPie T-shirt. Both of us wore paper birthday cones on our heads. "Please say that we can send out our resumes to TV stations around the country. Hell, I'd give the news in Mississippi if it got my foot in the door."

She pronounced it "Mishishippi." She wasn't drunk. One of our professors should've taken her aside right about Journalism 101 and told her to find a new field of study, or concentrate in print media. I didn't have it in me to tell Abby that my grandfather's mule enunciated better than she did. When she wasn't helping out with the Carolina Rocks bookkeeping chores, she drove down to Greenville and led aerobics classes. I never saw her conducting a class in person, but I imagined her saying "Shtep, shtep, shtep," over and over.

"It's funny that you should mention Mississippi," I said. I thought of the term *segue*, from when I underwent communications studies classes as an undergraduate, usually seated right next to Abby. "I'm going to go ahead and enroll in that Southern studies program. It'll all be done by email and telephone, pretty much, and then I have to go to Mississippi for ten days in the summer and winter. Then, in a couple years, maybe I can go teach college somewhere. We can sell off this land and move to an actual city. It'll be easier for you to maybe find a job that you're interested in."

I loved my wife more than I loved finding and digging up a truckload of schist. Abby got up from the table, smiled, walked into the den and picked up a gift-wrapped box. She said, "You cannot believe how afraid I was you'd change your mind. Open it up."

I kind of hoped it was a big bottle of bourbon so we could celebrate there at the kitchen table as the sun rose. I shook it. I said, "It's as heavy as a prize-winning geode," for I compared everything to rocks. When it hailed, those ice crystals hitting the ground were either pea gravel or riprap, never golf balls like the meteorologists said.

"I'm hoping this will help you in the future. In our future." Abby leaned back and put her palms on the floor like some kind of contortionist. "I don't mind teaching aerobics, but I can't do that when I'm sixty. I can still report the news when I'm sixty."

"*Sixschtee.*"

I opened the box to uncover volumes one, two, and three of *The South: What Happened, How, When, and Why.* Abby said, "I don't know what else you're going to learn in a graduate course that's not already in here, but maybe it'll give you ideas."

I might've actually felt tears well up. I opened the first chapter of the third volume to find the heading "BBQ, Ticks, Cottonmouths, and Moonshine." I said, "You might be right. What's left to learn?"

I'M NOT SURE how other low-residency programs in Southern culture studies work, but immediately after I sent off the online application—which only included names of references, not actual letters of recommendation—I got accepted. An hour later I paid for the first half year with a credit card. I emailed the "registrar" asking if I needed to send copies of my undergraduate transcripts and she said that they were a trusting lot at the University of Mississippi-Taylor. She wrote back that she and the professors all believed in a person's word being his bond, and so on, and that the program probably wouldn't work out for me if I was the sort who needed everything in writing.

I called the phone number at the bottom of the pseudo letterhead but hung up when someone answered with, "Taylor Grocery and Catfish." I had only wanted to say that I too ran my river rock and field stone business on promised payments, that my father and grandfather operated thusly even though the mule warned to trust nothing on two legs. And I didn't want to admit to myself or Abby that, perhaps, my low-residency degree would be on par with something like that art institute that accepts boys and girls who can draw fake pirates and cartoon deer.

A day later I received my first assignment from my lead mentor, one Dr. Theron Crowther. He asked that I buy one of his books, read the chapter on "Revising History," then set about finding people who might've remembered things differently as opposed to how the media reported the incident. He said to stick to Southern themes: the assassination of Dr. Martin Luther King, for example; the sit-in at Woolworth's in Greensboro; unsuccessful and fatal attempts of unionizing cotton mills; Ole Miss's upset of Alabama. I said to Abby, "I might should stick to pulling rocks out of the river and selling them to people who like to make puzzles out of their yard. I have no clue what this guy means for me to do."

Abby looked over the email. I was to write a ten-page paper and send it back within two weeks. "First off, read that chapter. It should give you some clues. That's what happened to me when I wasn't sure about a paper I wrote once on *How to Interview the Criminally Insane* back in college. You remember that paper? You wussed out and wrote one on *How to Interview the Deaf.*"

I'd gotten an A on that one: I merely wrote, "To interview a deaf person, find a sign language interpreter." That was it.

Abby said, "There's this scrapbooking place next door to Feline Fitness. Come on in to work with me and I'll take you over there. Those people will have some stories to tell, I bet. Every time I go past it, these women sit around talking."

We sat on our front porch, overlooking the last three tons of river rock I'd scooped out, piled neatly as washer-dryer combos, if it matters. Below the rocks, the river surged onward, rising from thunderstorms up near Asheville. I said, "What are you talking?" I'd not heard of the new sport of scrapbooking.

"These people get together just like a quilting club, I guess. They go in the store and buy new scrapbooks, then sit there and shove pictures and mementos between the plastic pages. And they brag, from what I understand. The reason I know so much about it is, I got a couple women in my noon aerobics class who showed up early one day and went over to check out the scrapbook place. They came back saying there was a Junior Leaguer ex-Miss South Carolina in there with flipbooks of her child growing up, you know. She took a picture of her kid two or three times a day, so you can flip the pictures and see the girl grow up in about five minutes."

I got up, walked off the porch, crawled beneath the house a few feet, and pulled out a bottle of bourbon I kept there hidden away for times when I needed to think—which wasn't often in the river rock business.

When I rejoined my wife she'd already gotten two jelly jars out of the cupboard. "There's a whole damn business in scrapbooks? Who thought that up? America," I said. "Forget the South being fucked up. America."

"You can buy cloth-covered ones, and puffy-covered ones, and ones with your favorite team's mascot on the cover. There are black ones for funeral pictures, and white ones for weddings. There are ones that are shaped like Santa Claus, the Easter bunny, dogs, cats, cars, and Jesus. They've even got scented scrapbooks." Abby slugged down a good shot of Jim Beam and tilted her glass my way for more. "Not that I've been in Scraphappy! very often, but they've got one that looks like skin with tattoos and everything, shaped like an hourglass, little tiny blond hairs coming off of it. It's for guys to put their bachelor party pictures inside."

I didn't ask her if it smelled like anything. I said, "I wonder if they have any bullet-riddled gray flannel scrapbooks for pictures of dead Confederate relatives." I tried to imagine other scrapbooks, but couldn't think of any. "When's your next class?"

WE DROVE DOWN the mountain on the next morning, a Wednesday, so Abby could lead a beginner aerobics class. Wednesdays might as well be called "little Sunday" on a Southern calendar, for small-town banks and businesses close at noon in order for employees to ready themselves for Wednesday-night church services. Sunday, Monday, Tuesday, little Sunday, Thursday, Friday, Saturday—like that. My common-law wife took me into Scraphappy!, looked at a wall of stickers, then said, "I'll be back a little after noon, unless someone needs personal training." She didn't kiss me on the cheek. She looked over at six women sitting in a circle, all of whom I estimated to be in their mid- to late thirties.

"Could I help you with anything?" the owner asked me. She wore a nametag that read Knox—the last name of one of the richer families in the area. In kind of a patronizing voice she said, "Did you forget to pack up your snapshots this morning?"

The other women kept turning cellophane-covered pages. One of them said, "Pretty soon I'll have to get a scrapbook dedicated to every room in the house. What a complete freak-up."

I had kind of turned my head toward the stickers displayed on the wall—blue smiling babies, pink smiling babies, a slew of elephants, Raggedy Anns and Andys, mobiles, choo-choo trains, ponies, teddy bears, prom dresses, the president's face staring vacantly—but jerked my neck back around at hearing "freak-up." I thought to myself, *Remember that you're here to gather revisionist history. You want to impress your professor at Ole Miss–Taylor.*

But then I started daydreaming about Frances Bavier, the actress who played Aunt Bee on *The Andy Griffith Show*. I said, "Oh. Oh, I didn't come here to play scrapbook. My name's Stet Looper and I'm enrolled in a Southern studies graduate program, and I came here to see if y'all wouldn't mind answering some questions about historical events that happened around here. Or around anywhere." I cleared my throat. The women in the circle looked at me as if I walked in wearing a seersucker suit after Labor Day.

Knox the woman said, "Southern studies? My husband has this ne'er-do-well cousin who has a daughter going to one of those all-girls schools up north. Hollins, I believe. She's majoring in women's studies." In a lower voice she said, "She appears not to like men, if you know what I mean—she snubbed us all by not coming out this last season at the Poinsett Club. Anyway, she's studying for that degree with an emphasis in women's economics, and I told her daddy that it usually didn't take four years learning how to make a proper grocery list."

I was glad I didn't say that. I'd've been shot for saying that, I figured. The same woman who almost-cursed earlier held up a photograph to her colleagues and said, "Look at that one. He said he knew how to paint the baseboard."

I said, "Anyway, I have a deadline, and I was wondering if I could ask if y'all could tell me about an event that occurred during your lifetime, something that made you view the world differently than how you had understood it before. Kind of like the Cuban Missile Crisis, but more local, you know."

"Hey, Knox, could you hand me one them calligraphy stickers says, I TOLD YOU SO? I guess I need to find me a stamp that says LOSER," one of the women said. To me she said, "My husband always accuses me of being a germophobe." She held up her opened scrapbook for me to see. It looked as though she'd wiped her butt on the pages. "This is my collection of used moist towelettes. I put them in here to remember the nice restaurants we've gone to, and sometimes if the waitress gave me extras I put the new one in there, too. But even better, he and I one time went on a camping trip that I didn't want to go on, and as it ended up we got lost. Luckily for Wells, we only had to follow my trail of Wet-Naps back to the parking lot. I don't mind bragging that that trip was all it took for him to buy us a vacation home down on Pawleys Island."

I wished that I'd've thought to bring a tape recorder. I said, "That's a great story," even though I didn't ever see it as being a chapter in some kind of Southern culture textbook. I said, "Okay. Do any of y'all do aerobics? My wife's next door teaching aerobics, if y'all are interested. From what I understand, she's tough, but not too tough." Inside my head I heard my inner voice going, "Okay none of these women are interested in aerobics classes so shut up and get out of here before you say something more stupid and somehow get yourself in trouble."

I stood there like a fool for a few seconds. The woman who complained about her baseboard started flipping through pages, saying, "Look at them. Every one of them." Then she went on to explain to a woman who must not've been a regular, "I keep a scrapbook of every time my husband messes up. This scrapbook's the bad home repair one—he tries to fix something, then it costs us double to get a professional in to do the job. I got another book filled with bad checks got sent back, and newspaper clippings for when he got arrested and published in the police blotter. I even got ahold of some his mugshots."

It was like standing next to a whipping post. I said, "Okay, I'm sorry to take up any of your time." *The place should've been called* Straphappy, I thought.

As I opened the door, though, I heard a different voice, a woman who'd only concentrated on her own book of humiliation up until this point. She said, "Do you mean like if you know somebody got lynched, but it all got hush-hushed even though everyone around knew the truth?"

Everyone went quiet. You could've heard an opened ink pad evaporate.

I pulled up one of those half-stepladder/half-stool things. I said, "Say that all again, slower."

Her name was Gayle Ann Gunter. Her daddy owned a car lot, and her grandfather owned it before him, and the great-grandfather started the entire operation back when selling horseshoes and tack still made up half of his business. She worked on a scrapbook that involved one-by-two-inch school pictures that grade schoolers hand over to one another, and she had them under headings like "Uglier than Me," "Poorer than Me," "Dumber than Me," as God is my witness. She said, "We're having our twentieth high school reunion in a few months and I want to make sure I have the names right. It's important in this world to greet old acquaintances properly."

I said, "I'm no genius, but it should be 'Dumber than I.' It's a long, convoluted grammar lesson I learned back in college the first time."

The other women laughed. They said, "Ha-ha-ha-ha-ha," in unison, and in a weird, seemingly practiced, cadence. Knox said, "One of the things that keeps me in business is people messing up their scrapbooks and having to start over. I had one woman who misspelled her new daughter-in-law throughout, the first time. She got it right when her son got a divorce, though."

"This was up in Travelers Rest," Gayle Ann said. She kept her scrapbook atop her lap and spoke as if addressing the airconditioning vent. "I couldn't have been more than eight, nine years old. These two black brothers went missing, but no one made a federal case out of it, you know. This was about 1970. They hadn't integrated the schools just yet, I don't believe. I don't even know if it made the paper, and I haven't ever seen the episode on one of those shows about long-since missing people. Willie and Archie Lagroon. No one thought about it much because, first off, a lot of teenage boys ran away back then. Maybe 'cause of Vietnam, I guess. And then again, they wasn't white."

I took notes in a professional-looking memo pad. I didn't even look up, and I didn't offer another grammar lesson involving subjects and verbs. For some reason one of the women in the circle said, "My name's Shaw Haynesworth. Gayle Ann, I thought you were born in 1970. My name's Shaw Haynesworth, if you need to have footnotes and a bibliogeography!"

I wrote that down, too. Gayle Ann Gunter didn't respond. She said, "I haven't thought about this in years. It's sad. About four years after those boys went missing, a hunter found a bunch of bones right there about twenty feet off of Old Dacusville Road. My daddy told me all about it. They found all these rib bones kind of strewn around, and more than likely it was those two boys. This was all before DNA, of course. The coroner—or someone working for the state—finally said that they were beef and pork ribs people had thrown out their car windows. They said that people went to the Dacusville Smokehouse and couldn't make it all the way back home before tearing into a rack of ribs, and that they threw them out the window, and somehow all those ribs landed in one big pile over the years." She made a motorboat noise with her mouth. "I'm no expert when it comes to probability or beyond a reasonable doubt, but looking back on it now, I smell lynching. Is that the kind of story you're looking for?"

Abby walked in sweating, hair pulled back, wearing an outfit that made her look like she just finished the Tour de France. She said, "Hey, Stet, I might be another hour. Phyllis wants me to fill in for her. Are you okay?"

The women scrapbookers looked up at my wife as if she zoomed in from cable television. I said, "We have a winner!" for some reason.

"You can come over and sit in the lobby if you finish up early."

To the women she said, "We're having a special next door if y'all want to join an aerobics class. Twenty dollars a month." I turned to see the women all look down at their scrapbooks.

Knox said, "I believe I can say for sure that we burn up enough calories running around all day for our kids. Speaking of which, I brought some doughnuts in!"

I looked at Abby. I nodded. She kind of made a what're-you-up-to? face and backed out. I said, "Okay. Yes, Gayle Ann, that's exactly the kind of story I'm looking for—about something that happened, but people saw it differently. How sure are you that those bones were the skeletal remains of the two boys?"

A woman working on a giant scrapbook of her two Pomeranians said, "They do have good barbecue at Dacusville Smokehouse. I know I've not been able to make it home without breaking into the Styrofoam boxes. Hey, do any of y'all know why it's not good to give a dog pork bones? Is that an old wives' tale, or what? I keep forgetting to ask my vet."

And then they were off talking about everything else. I felt it necessary to purchase something from Knox, so I picked out a rubber stamp that read, "Unbelievable!"

I'm not ashamed to admit that, while walking between Scraphappy! and Feline Fitness, I envisioned not only a big A on my first Southern studies low-residency graduate-level class at Ole Miss-Taylor, but a consultant's fee when this rib-bone story got picked up by one of those TV programs specializing in wrongdoing mysteries, cold cases, and voices from the dead.

SINCE I WOULDN'T meet Dr. Theron Crowther until the entire graduate class got together for ten days in December, I didn't know if he was a liar or prankster. I'd dealt with both types before, of course, in the river rock business. Pranksters came back and said that my stones crumbled up during winter's first freeze, and liars sent checks for half tons, saying I used cheating scales. After talking to the women of Scraphappy!, I sent Dr. Crowther an email detailing the revisionist history I'd gathered. He wrote back to me, "You fool! Have you ever encountered a little something called 'rural legend?' Let me say right now that you will not make it in the mean world of Southern culture studies if you fall for every made-up tale that rumbles down the trace. Now go out there and show me how regular people view things differently than how they probably really happened."

First off, I thought that I'd done that. I was never the kind of student who whined and complained when a professor didn't cotton to my way of thinking. Back when I was forced to undergo a required course called Broadcast Station Management I wrote a comparison-contrast paper about the management styles of WKRP in Cincinnati and WJM in Minneapolis. The professor said that it wasn't a good idea to write about fictitious radio- and television-based situation comedies. Personally, I figured the management philosophies must've been spectacular, seeing as both programs consistently won Nielsen battles, then went on into syndication. The professor—who ended up, from what I understand, having to resign his position after getting caught filming himself having sex with a freshman boy on the made-up set for an elective course in Local Morning Shows, using a fake potted plant and microphone as props—said I needed to forget about television programs when dealing with television programs, which made no sense to me at the time. I never understood what he meant until, after graduation, running my family's business ineffectively and on a reading jag, I sat down by the river and read *The Art of War* by Sun Tzu and *Being and Nothingness* by Sartre.

I said to Abby, "My mentor at Ole Miss-Taylor says that's a made-up story about black kids and rib bones. He says it's like those vacation photos down in Jamaica with the toothbrush, or the big dog that chases a ball out the window of a high-rise in New York."

Abby came out from beneath our front porch, the half bottle of bourbon in her grasp. She said, "Of course he says that. Now he's going to come down here and interview about a thousand people so he can publish the book himself. That's what those guys do, Stet. Hey, I got an idea—why don't you write about how you fell off a turnip truck. How you got some kind of medical problem that makes you wet behind the ears always."

I stared down at the river and tried to imagine how rocks still languished there below the roiling surface. "I guess I can run over to that barbecue shack and ask them what they know about it."

"I guess you can invest in carbon paper and slide rulers in case this computer technology phase proves to be a fad."

ALL GOOD BARBECUE stands only open on the weekend, Thursday through Saturday at most.

I got out a regional telephone directory, found the address, got directions off the Internet, then drove around uselessly for a few hours, circling, until I happened to see a white plume of smoke different than most of the black ones caused by people burning tires in front of their trailers. I walked in—this time with one of the handheld tape recorders the bank was giving away for opening a CD, I guess so people can record their last words before committing suicide, something like, "One half of one fucking percent interest?"—and dealt with all the locals turning around, staring, wondering aloud who my kin might be. I said, loudly, "Hey—how y'all doing this fine evening?" like I owned the place.

Everyone turned back to their piled paper plates of minced pork and coleslaw.

At the counter a short man with pointy sideburns and a curled-up felt cowboy hat said, "We out of sweet potato casserole." A fly buzzed around his cash register.

"I'll take two," I looked up at the menu board behind him, "Hog-o-Mighty sandwiches."

"Here or to go?"

"And a sweet tea. You don't serve beer by any chance, do you?"

"No sir. Family-orientated," he said. He wore an apron that read "Cook."

I said, "I understand. I'm Stet Looper, up from around north of here."

An eavesdropper behind me said, "I tode you."

"By north of here I mean just near the state line. I'll eat them here. Anyway, my wife introduced me to a woman who told me a wild story about two young boys being missing some thirty-odd years back, and a pile of bones the state investigators said came from here. Do you know this story?" I mentioned Abby because any single male strangers are, in the sloppy dialect of the locals, "quiz."

"My name's Cook," the cook said. "Raymus Cook. Y'all hear that? Fellow wants to know if I heard about them missing boys back then. Can you believe that?" To me he said, "You the second person today to ask. Some fellow from down Mississippi called earlier asking if it was some kind of made-up story."

I thought, *Goddamn parasite Theron Crowther.* "I'll be doggone," I said. "What'd you tell him?"

"That'll be five and a quarter, counting tax." Raymus Cook handed over two sandwiches on a paper plate and took my money. "I told him my daddy'd be the one to talk to, but Daddy's been dead eight years. I told him what I believed—that somebody paid somebody, and that those boys' families will never rest in peace."

People from two tables got up from the seats, shot Raymus Cook mean looks, and left the premises. One of them said, "We been through this enough. I'mo take my bidness to Ola's now on." Raymus Cook held his head back somewhat and called out, "This ain't the world it used to be. You just can't go decide to secede every other minute things don't turn out like you want them." At this precise moment I knew that, later in life, I would regale friends and colleagues alike about how I "stumbled upon" something. Raymus Cook turned his head halfway to the open kitchen and said, "Ain't that right, Ms. Hattie?"

A black woman stuck her face my way and said, "Datboutright, huh-huh," just like that, fast, as if she waited to say her lines all night long.

"You can't cook barbecue correct without the touch of a black woman's hands," Raymus said to me in not much more than a whisper. "All these chains got white people smoking out back. Won't work, I'll be the first to admit."

I thought, *Fuck, this is going to turn out to be just another one of those stories that've bloated the South for a hundred fifty years.* I didn't want that to happen. I said, "I'm starting a master's degree on Southern culture, and I need to write a paper on something that happened a while back that maybe ain't right. You got any stories you could help me out with?"

I sat down at the first table and unwrapped a sandwich. I got up and poured my own tea. Raymus Cook smiled. He picked up a flyswatter and nailed his prey. "Southern culture?" He laughed. "I don't know that much about Southern culture, even though I got raised right here." To a family off in the corner he yelled, "Y'all want any sweet potato casserole?" Back to me he said, "That's one big piece of flypaper hanging, Southern culture. It might be best to accidentally graze a wing to it every once in a while, but mostly buzz around."

I said, of course, "Man, that's a nice analogy." I tried to think up one to match him, something about river rocks. I couldn't.

"Wait a minute," Raymus Cook said. "I might be thinking about Southern literature. Like Faulkner. Is that what you're talking about?"

I thought, *This guy's going to help me get through my thesis one day.* "Hey, can I get a large rack of ribs to go? I'll get a large rack and a small rack." I looked up at the menu board. I said, "Can I get a 'Willie' and an 'Archie?'"

It took me a minute to remember those two poor black kids' names. I thought, *This isn't funny,* and took off out of there as soon as Raymus Cook turned around to tell Miss Hattie what he needed. I remembered that I forgot to turn on the tape recorder.

On my drive back home I wondered if there were any low-residency writing programs where I could learn how to finish a detective novel.

I TOLD MY sort-of wife the entire event and handed her half a Hog-o-Mighty sandwich. She didn't gape her mouth or shake her head. "You want to get into Southern studies, you better prepare yourself for such. There are going to be worse stories."

"*Wershtoreesh.*" I said, "I don't want to collect war stories."

"You know what I said. And I don't know why you don't ask me. Here's a true story about a true story gone false: This woman in my advanced cardio class—this involves spinning, Pilates, steps, and treadmill inside a sauna—once weighed two hundred twenty pounds. She's five two. Now she weighs a hundred, maybe one-o-five at the most. She's twenty-eight years old and just started college at one of the tech schools. She wants to be a dental hygienist."

We sat on the porch, looking down at the river. Our bottle was empty. On the railing I had *The South: What Happened, How, When, and Why* opened to a chapter on a sect of people in eastern Tennessee called "Slopeheads," which might've been politically incorrect. I said, "She should be a dietician. They got culinary courses there now. She should become an elementary school chef, you know, to teach kids how to quit eating pizza and pimento cheese burgers."

"Listen. Do you know what happened to her? Do you know how and why and when she lost all that weight?"

I said, "She saw one of those Before-and-After programs on afternoon TV. She sat there with a bowl of potato chips on her belly watching Oprah, and God spoke to her." I said, "Anorexia and bulimia, which come before and after *arson* in some books."

"Her daddy died." Abby got up and closed my textbook for no apparent reason. "Figure it out, Stet. Her daddy died. She *said* she got so depressed that she quit eating. But in reality, she had made herself obese so he'd quit creeping into her bedroom ages of twelve and twenty-two. Her mother had left the household long before, and there she was. So she fattened up, and slept on her stomach. When her father died she didn't tell anyone what had been going on. But when all the neighbors met after the funeral to eat, she didn't touch one dish. Not even the macaroni and cheese."

I said, "I don't want to know about these kinds of things." I got up and walked down toward the river. Abby followed behind me. "Those my-daddy-loved-me stories are the ones I'm trying to stay away from. It's what people expect out of this area."

When we got to the backhoe she climbed up and reached beneath the seat. She pulled out an unopened bottle of rum I had either forgotten or didn't know about. "There were pirates in the South. You could write about pirates and their influences on the South. How pirates stole things that weren't theirs."

I picked up a nice skipper and flung it out toward an unnatural sand-bar. Then I walked up to my knees into the water, reached down, and pulled two more out. An hour later, I had enough rocks piled up to cover a grave.

EVEN CURS HATE FRUITCAKE

WHENEVER I RETREAT TO WONDERMENT AT HOW MY life turned to one of hoardment and obsession, I stop at the memory of a muggy June night. I found myself inside a smoke- and curse-filled beer joint on Highway 301 near the Fruitcake Capital of the World. I bent over to pick up a fallen blue cube of Silver Cup cue-stick chalk, reached over to set it on one of two pool tables, then became startled by an overall-wearing mountain man—his gray beard as wind-blown as John Brown's—who yelled at me, pointed toward my hand, and asked if I got Stonewall Jackson or John the Baptist. That particular night, not two weeks after I'd graduated from high school, I ran through every reason to make my answer one man of history or the other.

"Don't rub it up, goddamn. *Look* at it. Whichen is it?" the man said. He leaned on a house cue stick so warped it could've been used as a bow. I saw a knife blade *spack* glare from his other hand.

I said, "I don't know." I looked down to see a perfectly carved visage on one side of the chalk. "Yeah, it's one or the other. But I'm not so sure I'd know Stonewall Jackson or John the Baptist if they both walked in the door."

This old man jerked his head once and held out the hand with his knife in it. I handed over the chalk. Two men from a fruitcake company— they wore work shirts with various candied ingredients sewn above their pockets—started a game of eight ball. The one who broke barely made the rack move, as if he was challenging Newton's action and reaction theory.

"It's one or the other, I believe, but I can't remember. And I carved the son-bitch," the man said. "Goddamn it to hell, I'mo have to get my book out again and see who this looks like. I got a book I keep at home. It's got famous people's pictures in it. Everything I carve ends up looking like somebody, somewhere." He handed the miniature near-bust back. "You figure it out and let me know."

Then he walked out. When he got to the door, without turning around, he yelled out, "If Stonewall Jackson and John the Baptist came in this bar alive and you couldn't tell the difference, I feel sorry for you, boy. One would be a-rolling and one would be a-strolling."

I had my back to the two pool players. One of them said, "I bet Brother Macon's on his way to the schoolhouse. They already told him he couldn't steal they chalk no more."

I went over to the four-stool bar and ordered a beer from a woman who wore the expression of a Rose of Sharon bud about to blossom. "You a buyer?" she asked me.

I said, "No ma'am. My last name's Dawes."

"Huh," she said. "That's not what I ast you, but that's aw-ight."

MY NEW BOSS, Marcel Parsell, suggested that I start in Claxton, move my way north to Tallulah Falls, Georgia, then drive east to Chimney Rock, North Carolina, south to Denmark, South Carolina, then back west. He said I could then go inward, always traveling clockwise in a smaller and smaller circle. This was my first real, not-gotten-by-my-father job. I was working for a disgruntled ex-editor of Fodor's travel guides who wanted to put out a book about places in the United States to avoid completely. From what I had gathered, from this year onward he would hire fifty or sixty new high school graduates every June to write sarcastic thousand-words-or-less articles about towns that offered no real cultural, artistic, or dining experiences. It was supposed to look like we'd gotten a scholarship, I guess. "A book like this will make everyone in bigger cities feel better about themselves and their lives. Plus, this idea has trade paperback bestseller written all over it, from here on out." I had answered an ad that read, "Like to travel for money?" Imagine that. How come my high school counselor never veered me toward a class in economics or ethics or logic, or ever took one herself?

I said to the bartendress, "I'm here because I'm writing a book on little-known places you might want to visit." I didn't want to end up being lynched for making fun of whatever slight populace inhabited places like Claxton, Georgia. And, since I hadn't taken that ethics course at Forty-Five High, I felt no remorse about lying outright.

Marcel Parsell—who had studied both geography and culinary arts—told my new colleagues and me that, just as it was okay to exaggerate how wonderful a city might appear, it was all right to exaggerate its limitations. "A local roadside diner that brags on its pork-flavored ice cream isn't a bad thing for our purposes," he said. I took notes.

"That man gave you piece chalk ain't like our regular people around here," the barmaid said. "Don't judge Claxton or its peoples from crazy Brother Macon. He says God told him to carve what he could into people God blessed before. He chose chalk 'cause it's made down in Macon. He seen a reason and connection."

I said, "I won't judge y'all by one man's vision."

"Hey!" she yelled. "This boy here's writing a book about us!"

At first I thought I'd've been better off only skimming the outskirts of all my tiny prearranged towns, that I should've been objective while detailing odd Catfish or Bucktooth festivals. Marcel Parsell handed all of us a ten-point dos-and-don'ts bulletin that included not falling in love with a local and not believing mayors.

I got paid fifty dollars for every article that made it into a book that ended up being called *Wish You Weren't Here*. I got paid five bucks for the towns Marcel Parsell decided against. This was 1976. I had no clue about money and saw myself getting about three grand over a two-month period, then moving on to work for the South American, European, and Australian versions of the same book, working college summers. It didn't occur to me that if fifty travel writers each got fifty thousand-word essays published, the book might be a little on the thick side. I didn't realize that staying in twelve-dollar-a-night motels went way beyond extravagant, that maybe I should've considered KOA camp grounds or the backseat of my old Jeep at roadside rest areas.

I never got the chance. What I learned immediately in Claxton—the Fruitcake Capital of the World—was that there were citizens who would pay decent money to have their place sound utopian, and just as many people who would offer favors to keep strangers away.

"Oh, I'll tell you all you fucking want to know about a place people elsewhere think we make fruitcakes for door stops," one of the pool players said.

"No, no," said his opponent. "This is a good place to raise children. Come talk to me about here."

Not that this has anything to do with my story, but over the years I've learned that any human who brags about his or her town being a good place to raise kids only says so because that particular town has no art museum that kids might beg their parents to visit. There's no theater without the word LITTLE on the sign. The horrendous school system doesn't offer after-school field trips and activities outside of dollar-admission sporting events. Nothing dangerous exists that might cause parents to *think* and *act* in these places. I was brought up in the town of Forty-Five, South Carolina, by God—the Raise Children Here Capital of the World.

Maybe my future background in anthropology jaded me, though.

I stood in the Rack Me roadhouse bar and fingered my carved cube of chalk. I didn't mention how I wasn't really writing a book solely on the Fruitcake Capital but tried to emit an air that, at any moment, I might change my mind and load up the Jeep, find some people to talk to in the Pecan Roll Capital of the World.

The barmaid opened a drawer beneath the cash register and handed me a dozen carved blue pieces of Brother Macon's chalk. The best one looked like Mount Rushmore on all sides and the bottom. The worst might've been one of those famous pirates, or a Cyclops, or James Joyce.

LOOKIT: THE AD went, "Do you want to make money and travel?" Then there was a non-1-800 number to call for a preliminary interview. For all I know, everyone who called made it through the first hurdle. I was asked to send a biographical essay, a descriptive essay about my hometown, an argumentative essay concerning my views on cats versus dogs, and a comparison-contrast essay about any two fast food chains. I almost told the truth about myself, Forty-Five, and dogs because I got kind of tired of the whole process. My final essay went, "I only know diners and home-cooked meals built over a fire out back. I'm from a town called Forty-Five, named after a piece of vinyl that revolves second-fastest." The stuff about my place of training wasn't all true, of course, but I feel certain now that it got me the job.

I didn't tell Marcel Parsell any of the other theories, of course, dealing with community theaters and art museums or the lack thereof. He called me, went over the payment situation, and said I could start immediately. He sent his ten dos and don'ts—my favorite, rule number nine, went, "Never let them see you spit out food"—and I drove to Claxton with a suitcase, some Mead composition notebooks, a cheap handheld tape recorder, and a camera.

I returned from Rack Me to my motel outside Claxton, a little L-shaped place called the Fall Inn. It advertised free TV, radio, and telephone. The dozen doors to the place were each painted a different pastel shade, which I learned later was symbolic of the different colored candies in a five-pound fruitcake.

I wasn't in the room five minutes on my first night when the phone rang. I expected my dad, or my imaginary girlfriend checking up on me, or Marcel Parsell wanting to offer congratulations on my first day at *Wish You Weren't Here*. I cleared my throat and said, "Mendal Dawes," all professional, like I had seen Frank Sinatra do in a 1950s movie that showed up at the Forty-Five Drive-In Theatre in 1972 or thereabouts.

It was the desk clerk. She said, "I'm calling to see if there's anything you need, hon."

When I checked in, she'd not spoken at all, just taken my cash money and handed me a crude flyer explaining check-out time and how I shouldn't leave lights or the TV on unnecessarily. The woman looked to be my age, and held her face in a way that told me she didn't hold fruitcake-working people in the highest regard. I said, "I'm fine."

"This is Cammie at the front desk."

I said, "Yeah."

"You sure you don't need anything? It's free. Soap, towels, a big old bucket of ice." She paused and lowered her voice. "You know. Anything you want."

It's hard to be a man and admit that I didn't recognize nuance at the age of eighteen. I said, "I wouldn't mind a beer, I guess, but y'all don't sell them in the Coke machine and the only store I've seen out this way won't open until morning." I took all of Brother Macon's carved cue chalks out of my pants pockets and lined them up around the rotary telephone. One of them looked exactly like Cammie—at least how I remembered her, all slack-jawed and blank-faced at check-in time. *It might not have been carved at all,* I thought. Or maybe Brother Macon had carved a *Night of the Living Dead* character, I don't know.

Cammie said in a drawl that could come only out of a southern, southern woman with a mouth full of honey, "Beer. Well, at least that's a start," and hung up.

The television received two channels. One showed the local news. Before I finished watching a piece with Claxton's mayor explaining why the jail needed two more cells added on, Cammie let herself in with a passkey. She carried two quart bottles of Schlitz under one arm, and held an ice bucket. I said, "Okay. All right. Come on in. Make yourself at home and tell me all about your lovely hometown."

She set everything down on a chair. "So word is you're the famous man come down here to write about all us. Call me patriotic, but I want you to know what a friendly place we got." She took out a church key and opened one bottle. "Don't think we're only fruitcakes here. They's much more to offer for fun."

I got off the bed and found two wax-paper-wrapped drinking glasses from the bathroom. I called out, "Oh, I know that. I'm only supposed to find places like this that're misunderstood."

I don't want to come across as crude or insensitive—and I need to make a point that I didn't instigate what occurred soon thereafter. The only other thing I remember Cammie telling me was, "We have field days all the time down at the rec center. It's a great place to raise children. I won the sack race one time. Back then I still went by my given name, Camellia. My momma let me change it when I turned old enough."

I'm pretty sure that's what she announced. I wanted to call up my father and tell him what I went through on my first real job. I wanted to say a bunch of things concerning the life of an artiste.

I focused on the television, though. The local weather man said it would be another hot and humid day.

MAYBE 1976 CLAXTON ran similarly to those backwards southern TV-sitcom towns where everyone eavesdrops on party lines, I don't know. But on my second day of full-time work I drove into town and hadn't gotten even close to the chamber of commerce office before I was stopped by people from all walks of life eager to exaggerate their hometown's worth and/or drawbacks. I couldn't figure it out, unless when Cammie left my motel room by midnight she'd called her best friend or mother and had her information stolen by half of the population. A woman at the drugstore, where I went to buy batteries for the tape recorder and headache powders for my hangover, said, "I can tell you that we have the clearest water between the Mississippi River and Richmond, Virginia, at least."

Out on the sidewalk, a Lion's Club member selling straw brooms said, "I've lived all over the place: Savannah, Atlanta, Chattanooga, Talladega. Not one of my neighbors in any of those cities ever asked me and the wife over for a barbecue supper. Here in Claxton, it happens almost every night. You got any children, son?"

I smiled and shook hands with complete strangers and nodded. A woman from Claxton Flowers ran out of her shop and gave me a boutonniere. A man from Claxton Gulf went out of his way to offer a free oil change and tire rotation. A cop came out of nowhere and handed me two complimentary tickets to the Claxton Policeman's Ball, which turned out to be a square dance held at the VFW. I got stopped by a man and woman in front of what appeared to be a vacant theater of sorts. Both of them wore Bobby Jones alpaca golf sweaters, and they shifted their weights from leg to leg. I slowed down. "We want you to know that people have come out of here and done good for themselves," the woman said.

"Grainger Koon's in the movies. He's got a list of credits longer than our telephone directory. He played Crazy Customer in one movie," the woman said. "He's played Man at Bar, Man on Bench, Man without Glasses, and Man with Goat—all in the same year. I forget what movies, though. What were some of the titles, LaFoy?"

"I don't recall, either," LaFoy said to me. "But you'd know him if you saw him. He's got a good face. He played Man Who Falls Off Dock in one of those teen movies. Me and Peggy here, we both taught him singing and dancing lessons. At the rec center. Grainger was in a *Munsters* episode, too."

"It's a good place to raise children," Peggy said.

"That's what I understand," I said, but didn't go into my theory about people who make such claims.

I walked and waved like a returning hero, or at least like a celebrity who had returned home after appearing as Scary Man in Park. I picked litter off of the sidewalk and carried it down Main Street until I found a receptacle. The hardware-store man came outside and handed me two complimentary yardsticks, and a beautician offered me a haircut. I could only wonder what these people would do should a rock star or visiting dignitary happen by. I kind of stood in front of the local bank, waiting for a teller to come out with a bag of unmarked currency.

And it was in front of the bank that a woman pulled her 1976 Pinto into a parking space and wiggled her finger for me to heed. I leaned down to the closed passenger window and heard her say, "Get in."

I did, what the hell.

Her name was Lulinda. She worked at the fruitcake factory, but her husband drove an eighteen-wheeler coast-to-coast. "I heard that you were in town, and I thought you might want to know what most people down here won't offer up."

I said, "Okay. I appreciate that." What could I say? She wore a polka-dotted cotton dress, the hem of which might've come down to her knees had she not hiked it up past mid-thigh.

She introduced herself and drove in the direction of my motel room. That's where I figured we were going. I kind of wished that I had more than one old high school friend to tell all of these stories about Claxton women.

"We won't keep you long, but we wanted to make sure you knew why no one should visit here, among other things." I caught the *we*. I tried to remember if, in the movies, hostages opened a moving vehicle's passenger door and tried to run, or if they covered their heads and rolled like crazy. I said, "I can't be gone too long. The mayor's expecting me. And the police chief," which wasn't true. I wondered what I should do with the yardsticks I had leaned against my right side. I glanced over at Lulinda's panties more than once.

We passed the Fall Inn and ended up at Rack Me. The parking lot was full. Lulinda said, "They ain't nothing to worry about. You ain't gone get hurt none," and smiled. She parked a distance from any of the pickup trucks and said, "I don't want anyone backing up into my car and exploding it." I carried the yardsticks inside but left the boutonniere on Lulinda's cracked dashboard. I went over kung-fu moves in my mind, how to deflect pool cues with my own two weapons. At the door of Rack Me the only thing I thought about was how difficult it would be to keep my Claxton, Georgia—Fruitcake Capital of the World—essay down to a thousand words.

Brother Macon stood at the bar, across from the barmaid I'd met the night before. The same two pool players were there, too, along with a group of a half dozen men wearing blue jean jackets. Brother Macon tossed me a cue-stick chalk and said, "This is for you, son. It's Marco Polo. He traveled around writing about places, too."

"It ain't too early for you to join us in a beer, is it?" one man said. He reached over the counter and pulled a can of PBR from the cooler. "My name's Gerald. Just like our president."

I said, "No sir."

Lulinda went back to the door and locked it. I could feel my knees shaking, just like any other normal cartoon character. My palms sweat so badly I went ahead and leaned the yardsticks against a barstool.

"You can't write no story about us, saying how Claxton would be a perfect place to bring the family on summertime vacations," another man said. He took the can of beer, opened the pop-top, and handed it to me. "We'd rather not go into detail, so let's just leave it at that."

Lulinda said, "It has to do with things changing, and things staying the same, and things changing. And then staying the same."

I put Marco Polo in my shirt pocket. Brother Macon said, "To be honest, I want people showing up to buy my carved works of God. But these old boys talked me into it, too. I got to go with the flow, you know. It's a democracy."

"Here." Gerald reached back into the cooler and pulled out a grocery bag. "You take this as a gift from *us*, and go off to somewhere else and forget that you ever come here." Gerald's hair stood up two perfect inches. One of his eyes seemed misplaced.

"Oh, you'll forget," someone said, and everyone started laughing.

I opened the top of the bag to find a good four or five pounds of thick buds I'd only seen on the national news. Brother Macon, already carving another piece of blue chalk, said, "They's certain parks and public properties we don't need people discovering, or trampling all over, you know what I mean. The way things are now, we ain't got nobody bothering us. Everybody thinks we just simple fruitcake-baking peoples. And they can keep that thought."

"It's not easy paying bills on what the fruitcake company pays out. All of us had to find other measures," Gerald said. "Now, if you'd prefer not to drive around with an illegal substance in your Jeep, Lulinda here has permission from her husband to buy it all back. We normally get thirty dollars an ounce for this stuff. Shit, it's so good we got people down in Mexico and South America buying from us."

I'd never heard of marijuana going for more than five dollars a nickel bag. This was a time before sinsemilla, or whatever cross-pollinations got developed out in northern California. I said, "Well. Hmm. Is there any way I could maybe keep a couple ounces, you know, and sell some of this back to y'all?"

The barmaid—wearing a bowling shirt this morning, but I doubted that her name was Cecil—said, "Let me tell him about the fingers, let me tell him about the fingers."

Gerald said, "I'm figuring there's two grand in that bag. You keep you a handful, and we'll still give you two grand. And then you leave us alone. Leave us out of the book. We'll run you down and find you, otherwise." He got off his barstool, pulled out his thick wallet, and extracted twenty hundred-dollar bills.

"Hey," Cecil yelled from her spot behind the bar. "Somewhere in America they's fruitcakes on the shelf with human fingers stuck inside from when LeRoy McDowell had his accident."

"There's worse than fingers," someone else said. "Don't forget about when Lulinda's brother's sister-in-law took that knife to her sleeping husband. Oh, she went into work that next morning and they never did find that old boy's manhood."

The jukebox came on without anyone that I saw putting in a quarter. Merle Haggard sang. I yelled out the only thing that seemed proper at the time, namely, "Drinks on me!" like a pardoned fool.

To be honest, I don't remember my return to the Fall Inn. I awoke in darkness, though, because Cammie banged on my door. I looked through the peephole to see her sporting a tiara and sash that read Little Miss Fruitcake 1972. She was holding a baton.

I opened the door and said, "Hey," wondering if she could smell what pot still hung in my clothes.

"It's your lucky day!" she singsonged out in a drawl. "You're officially our only lodger left. Are you hungry?"

I stepped back to let her in. "It looks like I won't be staying here much longer, either. I might be leaving in the morning." Cammie didn't enter. She looked to the side, waved her arm, and the same woman who had offered me a free haircut pushed a hand truck of boxed fruitcakes my way. "Mendal's cool," Cammie said.

The beautician said, "I still owe you the haircut if you want one and got the time. Or a full-body massage."

I had put my hush money in every single page of Revelation in the Gideon Bible. I remembered that much. Cammie said, "Open up your fruitcakes, open up your fruitcakes. My talent's baton twirling, but I can't do much with a low ceiling."

I said, "Oh, your talent might be something else," all wink-wink, as if the beautician weren't present.

"I'm Frankie," said the other woman. "Like in the song."

"Hey, Frankie," I said. "I remember you."

"Open the fruitcake like Cammie said." Cammie walked toward the sink and shimmied up on it. "It's from the Small Business Owners Association. I'm part of them."

I had no option but to believe in a God who looked down upon and cared about me. I pulled open the first box to find a fifty-dollar bill sitting atop the fruitcake. Subsequent boxes held twenties, tens, more fifties, and a roll of silver dollars. "What're you people doing?" I asked. This was a half-town of people willing to bribe me to leave them alone and another half-town bribing me to exaggerate their wonderful environs.

"You the money man," Frankie said. "The Christmas dessert and money man." She walked past me and stretched out on the bed. "I wish they was a good movie on tonight. Anyway, the association only asks that you let the world know how great Claxton is. Then people will indeed come visit. And it'll be nothing but an economic boom for the community as a whole."

All told, I got forty-eight free fruitcakes and another thousand-plus dollars. "Well y'all might win Friendliest Town in the South," I said. I foresaw a fine life of driving from one small forgotten place to the next garnering illicit payoffs, each town's populace evenly divided between hopeful do-gooders and ne'er-do-well outlaws. I said, "Do y'all want any of this money from the shopkeepers? I mean, did y'all come here to trade off some work, or what?"

Cammie said, "I got to get back to the front desk."

Frankie got up off the bed, looked at herself in the mirror, and fingered her hair upwards. She squeegeed her teeth and popped gum I'd not noticed before. "I hope you're not talking about what I think you're talking about, as cool as you are or not. Anyway. If the mayor or anybody comes by and asks tomorrow, don't forget to tell them we brought over the gifts."

That night I didn't call Marcel Parsell to tell him I'd be mailing Claxton in presently before moving on to Egypt, or Canoochee, or Kibbee, or Emmalane. I didn't call my father to say how I'd succeeded in finding a satisfying job, regardless of what I might go on to study. I thought about calling Shirley Ebo, my imaginary black girlfriend who worked the summer as a counselor at a camp for children with missing extremities. Shirley taught knitting, somehow.

I didn't telephone my lost and wayward mother in St. Louis, Nashville, New Orleans, or Las Vegas. Compton Lane—my best friend since birth—didn't get a call.

I had three thousand dollars in my room, in a town of a thousand people, during an economic recession.

I took my leftover marijuana and pressed it in the Bible, like an autumn leaf. Don't think I left money in there stupidly so the chambermaid could change her station in life. Then I called Rack Me. When Cecil answered I announced myself and asked if anyone was playing pool, then told her I'd come bring tip money in the morning if she would direct the receiver toward the pool table. I said something about how I'd unexpectedly needed to hear the crack of one sphere hitting the other, that I needed to prove to myself that at least one law of physics was working somewhere. She covered the mouthpiece, but I heard her laugh right before she hung up altogether.

I packed and made a point to fold my sparse collection of clean clothes neatly. It seemed important to place my money everywhere possible—in my shoes, in the glove compartment, between two opened fruitcakes shoved together. It would take another twenty years for me to understand what little value all of these bribes had, and how fortunate I was to—even if it was only a joke at the time—stick a carved cue chalk of either Henry Ford or William Tecumseh Sherman on my dashboard as I left for another hopeless group of citizens two hours away. My remaining collection of Brother Macon miniatures vibrated atop the passenger seat in an awkward and mysterious historical orgy, the participants of which would one day attract both friends and strangers to my door. Everyone in my later life would remark how great it was that I could line up these chalk busts and offer little lectures at tiny libraries to kids wishing for a place worthy of their rearing.

RICHARD PETTY ACCEPTS
NATIONAL BOOK AWARD

L ET ME SAY RIGHT NOW THAT THIS COULDN'T'VE BEEN done without the support of all the good Hewlett-Packard people. The Intel Pentium III, 550 megahertz with 128 megabytes of RAM done us right. There for a while we thought a 20-gigabyte hard drive wouldn't be enough for what we had to say, but hot almighty model 8575 chugged along and took the curves. I'm happy to say that we moved over from the 40x/CDRW CD-ROM to the CDRW/DVD CD-ROM—not that we couldn't've wrote what we wrote without it, but hey, we never felt like we was either too tight or too loose in the curves, or like we didn't flat-out have plenty of get-go when we felt pressure from all the other fine writers who published books this year. It's no secret that modem speeds in actual use may vary, but I got to hand it to the HP people for the way they kept me constant. There weren't no surprises, is what I'm saying.

I'd also like to thank the people at LaserJet Laser Paper for the strong, smooth, twenty-four-pound white paper that won't curl up and wilt, even at Darlington. We done some high-speed copying, and the ink and toner stayed consistent throughout. The extra weight and brightness always assured crisp text, which is important for resumes, brochures, report covers, newsletters, press releases, and the Great American Novel. Ninety-six brightness can't be beat when it comes to LaserJet 4050 Series printers, which gave us the ability to go seventeen pages a minute. We liked the 1200 by 1200-DPI resolution, and the fifteen-second start-up time probably kept us in business the same way my pit crew did down in Daytona Beach all those years—fast, fast.

Oh, I know I'mo forget somebody.

I can't say enough about the people at Martin Computer Office Grouping. Our credenza, hutch, two-drawer lateral file, deluxe executive computer desk with return, and print tower made it easy as coming down pit row at forty-five miles per hour every day when we set ourselves down to type and write each morning. We'd just pull our deluxe ergonomic manager's chair with pneumatic and independently adjustable seat height right up to the desk without even having to think about lumbar support, knee tilt, or durable fabric upholstery. Weavetek 100-percent Olefin put us in a good Dusty Rose 541 pattern that suited what we needed to say about the human condition, plus left us comfortable and dry during those humid summer afternoons of conflict between protagonist and antagonist.

Listen, the Great American Novel don't come all at once, and we'd like to thank the Greencycle Recycled Steno Book people for their high-quality six-by-nine-inch green-tinted Gregg ruled pads, where we took notes and drew charts up about conflict and plot. Let me say to all the aspiring writers out there that I wrecked a good twenty pads before finding the groove on the outside of the home office, I tell you what.

Now I know a lot of the rest of the field went with UniBall Roller Grip pens because the steel point added strength and resistance to smears, but I got to tell you—toward the end there we just decided to take a chance on Paper Mate stick pens in black medium. The durable ballpoint tip withstood everyday office use there down the stretch. I can't say for sure I'd've made it another couple chapters, but the team made a decision and stuck to it. For those of y'all not acquainted with the nuances of composition, it's a lot like taking on two tires at the end of the Coca-Cola 600 instead of opting for four new Goodyears.

I ain't too proud to admit that I partook of the *Webster's New World Dictionary* put out by Simon & Schuster. I ain't too proud to admit that on those cold winter nights when we couldn't even think of a good character's name I got some support from Jim Beam and Jack Daniel's and George Dickel, not necessarily in that order.

Listen, sometimes it takes a wreck to understand a work of art. That time I rolled the wall—and y'all seen the clips on ESPN—the whole time I only thought, *Well, the main character has to grow some by the end of the story.*

We can't forget the Xerox remanufactured cartridge people. I don't know how many nights I called them people up and said, "Hey, I need a remanufactured laser-printer cartridge pronto up here in North Carolina." They'd work all night long so I wouldn't have to start next day at the back of the pack, which ain't easy. Ask any driver in Rockingham, Richmond, or Pocono.

I remember one time at Bristol when I couldn't keep up with what went on. Back then I could've used a printing calculator with twelve-digit fluorescent display and markup/mark-down function. We couldn't've kept up our pace without the AC-powered Canon MP25D, just to let us know where we were in the novel, what with chapters, and scenes, and pages, and sentences. And words. Finally on the hardware front I got to tip my hat to the people at Acco for their smooth, nonskid regular and jumbo paper clips.

And the people at Brown Kraft recycled clasp envelopes, whose envelopes I used to send my first chapters off to the agent.

Now I know y'all in attendance might think writing the Great American Novel don't take much more than one idea and a support team like I done mentioned. Somebody famous said oncet, "Clothes make the man." Well, it's true. I don't know if I coulda finished up my pivotal climactic scene without the support of the people at Wrangler jeans. Combed cotton is the way to go having to sit on your butt six hours a day. Same goes for our people at authentic Dickies work shirts—another 100-percent cotton product made o'vair in Bangladesh. We couldn't finish a minor scene—much less a chapter—without the good work of the people down at Stetson. And Dingo boots. And Ray-Ban sunglasses, naturally.

And, more than anyone else, we want to thank Mrs. Louise Gowers, who taught us how to type back in high school. F-R-F-R-F-R. J-U-J-U-J-U. Don't look down at the keys. Ruler on knuckles. A lot of people think it only takes "Once upon a time" or "It was a dark and stormy night" or "Call me" whatever that guy's name was on the boat, but I'm here to tell you that it all starts with a ruler on knuckles.

WHAT COULD'VE BEEN?

T AKE A LEFT OUT OF THE DRIVEWAY. TAKE A LEFT AT the stop sign. Drive to the first convenience store—which used to be a 7-Eleven, or Pantry, or Quick-Way, but now offers scratch cards and Fuel Perks—and take another left-hand turn. Get in the slow lane.

Drive past the elementary school that looks nothing like the one you attended. A row of brick ranch-style houses. Maybe a set of clapboard mill village houses. At the light—there will be a McDonald's here—take a right. Pass the Dollar General, or the Dollar Tree, or the Dollar Store. Look to the left and see how the pawn shop sells guns and buys gold, as always. Pass the grocery store that used to house a different chain, that used to house a different chain, that used to house a different chain—Publix, Bi-Lo, Food Lion, Ingles, Winn-Dixie, Community Cash, IGA, Piggly Wiggly. You'll try to remember the succession.

The same will occur at the Bank of America. NationsBank, First Union, C&S, that other longtime local savings-and-loan where you started a checking account in high school.

Drive past a barrage of fast food restaurants that includes a Burger King, Hardee's, Dairy Queen, Sonic, Chick-fil-A, Zaxby's, Pizza Inn, Pizza Hut, Papa John's, Little Caesar's, KFC, Bojangles', Captain D's, et cetera. Outback, Chili's, Ruby Tuesday, Applebee's, Moe's

Southwestern, TGIF. Subway, another McDonald's, Firehouse Subs, Taco Bell, another Bojangles', Ryan's, Red Lobster, IHOP, and so on. Huddle House, Waffle House, Cracker Barrel, Shoney's. This will take about two miles. In between there will be a Walmart, a vacant Kmart, Lowe's, Home Depot, and Big Lots. Exxon, Texaco, BP, Citgo, Shell, Kangaroo, Sunoco—none of which have full service, or mechanics available who can fix a flat or check transmission fluid.

Take another right onto the four-lane road that used to be a two-lane country road forty years earlier, where you and your friends drove around smoking cigarettes, drank Miller Ponies, pulled over with the overhead light on into rusty-gated pasture entrances so someone could fumble with Zig Zag rolling papers. Drive past the dilapidated wooden building that housed the little store where your father bought Nehi grape sodas, or NuGrape—it's the place where the owner got murdered and the police never caught a killer. Or it's the place that the owner's children didn't want to operate, seeing as their father sent them off to college. Or it's the place where the owner had diabetes so advanced that the doctor said a leg needed amputation, and the owner felt as if he had no better choice—what with all the grocery stores nearby—than to put a shotgun in his mouth behind the ancient tree behind the property. One of your friends used to claim that a man got hanged from the lowest branch of that tree. One of your friends carved his initials, plus the initials of, say, Ann Guy, in that tree. Years later—twenty years later—you figured out that the "A. G." really stood for a boy who didn't smoke cigarettes, roll joints, or drink from tiny beer bottles: Alan Gray, or Alvin Gillespie, or Aaron Giles. He was the boy who got accepted to a college where no one from your hometown went, and he made a mark on the world before dying in a tragic manner, not much different from the owner of the store where your father bought bygone classic sodas, which made him smile.

Pass a junk shop that holds as much merchandise outside as inside the cement block building. There's a sale on drive-in speakers.

You're not that far away. Pass a subdivision of lookalike houses wherein all the roads are named for British monarchy. Pass a subdivision of lookalike houses wherein all the roads are named for famous golf courses of the world. Pass a subdivision of lookalike houses wherein all the roads are named for Ivy League colleges. Pass a subdivision of lookalike houses wherein all the roads are named for Native American accouterments.

You will reach the land where the drive-in movie theater once stood. The screen's structure remains, though the front of it peels away. Metal posts stand without their speakers, like the headless parking meters at the beginning of *Cool Hand Luke*, which you probably saw here. You should park your vehicle and walk these grounds—already scoured by men and women with metal detectors, already used for a makeshift flea market that somehow failed, already surveyed for a three cul-de-sac subdivision called Hollywood Hills that will offer nothing but drainage problems for the houses built closest to the screen.

Go to the back row—or at least where you think the back row might've been. Forget about the snack bar/projection booth. Weave through high weeds to the back row and think about how the windows fogged up. Think about how you never, through all of the pre-planning, imagined what difficulties a steering wheel might offer, or how the seats might nearly concuss both of you after pulling the levers, or how you tried to maneuver into the backseat as if you'd had experience as a rock climber and high hurdler. Think about the difficulties both of you encountered, brought about by a triple row of brassiere metal eye hooks there on your first real date, or at least the first date remembered. Think about the bad acting, the car chase, the unreal setting, the chainsaw, the shark, the blob, the giant insect, the monster, the seemingly normal neighbor with the unruly, untoward, and despicable urges. Think about tires on gravel and how you hoped the driver continued on, that it wasn't anybody you knew, that it wasn't your parents.

Were there swing sets down by the screen, where children played before the movie? Did you think to yourself, *Those poor idiot parents, bringing their children to a place like this on a Saturday night?* Was there some kind of Coming Attractions? Did you say to the person next to you, "I got your 'coming attractions,'" and think it was the wittiest thing ever said?

Stand on that spot.

Stand where you think your Opal, Datsun, Ford, Chevy, Buick, Toyota, MG Midget, or parents' Lincoln or Cadillac might've stood.

Look at the compromised screen. Go ahead and say, "Fuckin' A—how did I make it this far?" Say, "Jesus Christ, all that bad living. All those close calls. What could've been? What could've been? What could've been?"

Then there's the mother or father standing there, thirty minutes after curfew, and the story you have memorized. You have twenty lies, all of which you'll recycle for the rest of your life, though you didn't know it then, in the driveway, looking at your hand on the gear shift, thinking about putting it in reverse.

NOTES

"Outlaw Head and Tail," "Caulk," and "I Could've Told You If You Hadn't Asked," from *These People Are Us* by George Singleton © 2001 by George Singleton. Reprinted by Permission of River City Publishing. All Rights Reserved.

"Show and Tell," "This Itches, Y'all," "When Children Count," "The Half-Mammals of Dixie," "Richard Petty Accepts National Book Award," and "How to Collect Fishing Lures" from *The Half-Mammals of Dixie* by George Singleton © 2002 by George Singleton. Reprinted by Permission of Algonquin Books of Chapel Hill. All Rights Reserved.

"Embarrassment," "Unemployment," and "Even Curs Hate Fruitcake," from *Why Dogs Chase Cars* by George Singleton © 2004 by George Singleton. Reprinted by Permission of Algonquin Books of Chapel Hill. All Rights Reserved.

"The Novels of Raymond Carver," "John Cheever, Rest in Peace," "Lickers," and "The Opposite of Zero" from *Drowning in Gruel* by George Singleton. Copyright ©2006 by George Singleton. Used by permission of Houghton Mifflin Harcourt. All rights reserved.

"Perfect Attendance," "How Are We Going to Lose This One?" and "A Man With My Number," from *Stray Decorum* by George Singleton © 2012 by George Singleton. Reprinted by Permission of Dzanc Books. All Rights Reserved.

"Which Rocks We Choose," "Traditional Development," and "Columbarium" from *Between Wrecks* by George Singleton © 2014 by George Singleton. Reprinted by Permission of Dzanc Books. All Rights Reserved.

"Fresh Meat on Wheels" and "What Could've Been?" from *Calloustown* by George Singleton © 2015 by George Singleton. Reprinted by Permission of Dzanc Books. All Rights Reserved.

"Staff Picks," "Hex Keys," "Four-Way Stop," and "Probate" from *Staff Picks* by George Singleton © 2019 by George Singleton. Reprinted by Permission of LSU Press. All Rights Reserved.

"Director's Cut" appeared in *the Atlantic Monthly* "Summer Fiction" issue, 2005, by George Singleton © 2005 by George Singleton. Reprinted by Permission of *the Atlantic Monthly*. All Rights Reserved.

The Author is grateful to the following journals, magazines, and anthologies where these stories first appeared: *the Atlantic Monthly, Playboy, Harper's, One Story, Georgia Review, Book, Southern Review, Kenyon Review, Agni, Cincinnati Review, Carolina Quarterly, New Delta Review, Oxford American, Appalachian Heritage, The Raleigh News and Observer, Shenandoah, Ninth Letter, A Dixie Christmas, New Stories from the South—the Year's Best—*(1994, 1999, 2002, 2006, 2007, 2010), *The Pushcart Prize XL: Best of the Small Presses.*

Everyone I acknowledged in the previous books. So there. I want to thank great writer Mr. Tommy Franklin, and these fine, smart, talented, patient humans at Hub City Press: Meg Reid, Kate McMullen, and Betsy Teter.

The COLD MOUNTAIN *Fund*
S E R I E S

NATIONAL BOOK AWARD WINNER Charles Frazier generously supports publication of a series of Hub City Press books through the Cold Mountain Fund at the Community Foundation of Western North Carolina. Beginning in 2019, the Cold Mountain Series spotlights works of fiction by new and extraordinary writers from the American South.

The Prettiest Star • Carter Sickels

Watershed • Mark Barr

The Magnetic Girl • Jessica Handler

PUBLISHING
New & Extraordinary
VOICES FROM THE
AMERICAN SOUTH

HUB CITY PRESS is the leading independent publisher of Southern literature. Focused on finding and spotlighting new and extraordinary voices from the American South, the press has published over eighty high-caliber literary works. Hub City is interested in books with a strong sense of place and is committed to introducing a diverse roster of lesser-heard voices. We are funded by the National Endowment for the Arts, Amazon Literary Partnership, the South Carolina Arts Commission and hundreds of donors across the Carolinas.

RECENT HUB CITY PRESS TITLES

Sleepovers • Ashleigh Bryant Phillips

A Wild Eden • Scott Sharpe

Let Me Out Here • Emily W. Pease

What Luck, This Life • Kathryn Schwille